FREE

An American Novel

Bird Collier

Dedication

To the Love of My Life, King Collier. You never let me give up. You are the good soil that our life has bloomed in.

Table of Contents

Free's Prologue

For a story to be deemed worth telling and retelling… worth reading, the world demands tragedy, trauma, and pain. There can be glimmers of hope and joy. Moments of laughter and resolve. But unfathomable conditions with dire consequences are the cost of admission for an instant classic. That is the price. The run-of-the-mill discomforts of everyday living are never enough. Standard inconveniences, unrequited love, missed opportunities, and financial struggles are discarded as inadequate. Plebian. The mundanity of a comfortable and charmed life is only compelling for thirty-minute sitcoms, not for great life stories that become epics. I knew this to be true, because by my high school senior year, I'd taken every honors English reading and language arts course available in my small Jolivette school district, and then traveled into the big, endless expanse of Houston every summer for invite-only Rice University writing camps. And collectively, the required and recommended reading was all drenched in sheaves of suffering.

Beginning with Greek mythology, plodding through The Jungle, The Old Man and the Sea, and The Gift of the Magi. The Montagues and Capulets and all of

Shakespeare's tragedies provided just that, tragedy. The books my grandmother plied me with to ensure that my literary education remained balanced with authors of color supplied no quarter. The Color Purple, The Bluest Eye, Things Fall Apart. Their Eyes Were Watching God, Nickel Boys, Fences, and The complete works of James Baldwin - all heartwrenching and heavy. I delved into the work from the pens on the continent where life began in search of modern classics that were not compelled to fit into American tragedy core. But they held the same trauma. The Kite Runner broke me, and Homegoing haunted me for months. I felt my dream of becoming a notable writer, by writing about everyday life, slipping away as reality set in.

I didn't want to write about trauma and tragedy. I didn't want to become known for bleeding my own angst and longings onto the page. I especially didn't want to live any more trauma and tragedy than what I had already been gifted by being abandoned at birth.

What I wanted was an opportunity to chart my own path in a new place where my history could not hawk me down and cast long shadows over my place in the world. A life where my every accomplishment was not placed in juxtaposition to my heritage, my dubious parentage, or my skin color, and subsequently discounted by measure for all of the aforementioned reasons. I wanted to write bright, clear, witty prose that made readers laugh and felt undeniably, universally relatable. For both myself and my characters, I wanted a kind of pleasant obscurity that I now know would never be respected or rewarded by literary critics with declarations of greatness. And the very fact that I longed for both, to be numbered among the greats and to remain in veritable obscurity presented as a paradox that held no resolution. But even as I contemplated the impracticality of this future, the universe had already set into motion the plan to rip both obscurity and opportunity from me in a single ill-fated evening. - Freedom Walker

Chapter 1

May 15th Free

The complete absence of sound. That is what Free remembered most about the night of May 15th. The deafening silence suspended in time that threatened to swallow her. The world, devoid of sound, was actually eerily peaceful, she noted as she waited for her hearing to return. She also remembered feeling sleepy. Later, they would say what she was experiencing was shock, but at the time, she just felt exhausted and anchored like the night sky, thick with rain, had become a weighted blanket. She imagined that if there weren't so many lights, she could just close her eyes and everything would cease to exist. But there were so many lights. Penetrating the inky night with their violent strobing. Even when she closed her eyes to block them out, they flashed in a disjointed pulsing rhythm against her eyelids. They were unending, stretching on forever, casting garish shadows and stripes over the road.

Relentless, gaudy, and unnatural, the blue, white, and red lights screamed into the night sky, making it completely impossible for any living thing to close its eyes. Illuminated by the wash of red, then blue, then red again, Freedom Walker sat perfectly still on the edge of the driver's side floor of her grandmother's burgundy late model Suburban. Her legs were pulled tight to her chest, the toes of her Keds balanced against the running board. She was just a slip of a girl, a petite 120lbs, her hair a never-ending maze of caramel curls, and her skin a toasted golden complexion that her grandmother liked to call yellow, even though it was clearly brown.

When she was younger, her grandpop called her tawny, and it was a long while before she realized that tawny was a color, not just a nickname. Everyone else she knew called her Free. As she sat curled into the silence that was now transforming into a muted buzzing, the thought occurred to her that the sound may not return - and she could actually be deaf. She watched the people bustling around her, stopping to confer with one another, all in various uniforms. The uniforms she had tagged and cleaned and watched swish around in their protective plastic at the cleaning service her grandparents had owned and required her to work in since she was old enough to place a shirt on a hanger. But the uniforms had taken on a new life now. No longer inanimate laundry - they now felt ominous and official; puffed out by bulletproof vests, accompanied by shiny black boots, and partially obscured by dark blue rain slickers. They were everywhere.

One such uniform approached her, and she could see the man's mouth moving and feel his eyes searching hers, but she still couldn't hear him and instead found herself staring at the droplets of water collecting and pooling on the plastic casing he'd secured over his impressive hat. State Trooper, she thought. He's a State trooper. That uniform was withdrawn and was quickly replaced with another crisp uniform. An EMT, her mind registered as a light, shone into her eyes, and blue-gloved hands wrapped her in a scratchy blanket. Her unfocused gaze was drawn to the snake-wrapped staff embroidered onto the star of life on the man's front pocket. She always dreaded EMT uniform drop-offs because of the mystery stains. She had tried more than once to convince her grandmother that mystery stains were biohazards that they should decline to service. But Mama Jean insisted that impossible stains and heavy starch were the only reasons they were still in business.

From the corner of her eye, Free saw a jarringly bright camera flash that pulled her back to the present. She turned to look as the flash of the bulb exploded again and again. Her eyes slowly cleared and focused on the subject of all the flashing. On the soaked asphalt, twisted and slumped across the dotted yellow lines of the road was the broken shape of a male body. A tiny seed of panic in her stomach exploded and radiated outward until her entire body was both hot and shivering cold. She could taste the terror in her throat. She lurched forward, and the EMT who was still hovering jumped back to avoid the splash of vomit. And then, according to later news reports, she fainted.

Chapter 2

May 15th Andrew

The evening, Andrew Tucker got the call that his son was dead. He hadn't spoken directly to most of his own family in nearly two years. They all showed up at the same events and kept up appearances because the Tucker clan was a powerful political animal, known for big shows of solidarity and controlling perception. As it stood, he was the current figurehead of that power as the sitting mayor of Jolivette. But Drew hadn't picked up a phone to call any of them, invited them to his home, nor tagged along on a hunting trip or extended family vacation since the day his father died. He'd declined every invitation from his mother to the sprawling family ranch and excused himself from every holiday gathering with mumbled explanations about work. He had an extremely busy social calendar, so his excuses were generally plausible. His position kept him exactly as busy as he needed to be to avoid dealing with his family, and for that, he was grateful.

When the call came in, Drew had opened his sleep-dried eyes with some difficulty and glanced at his brother's name on the screen and then the glowing digits of his alarm clock nearing midnight. He pressed the phone to his face, his hand tightening around the slim device until his knuckles went white, but said nothing.

"Andrew?!" His brother's voice broke through the fog, but it still sounded far away to Drew, as though he were underwater.

He tried to process the words his brother was saying, but kept imagining that they were in a different language - their meaning not computing. He wanted to hang up; he wanted to have never picked up in the first place. His brother, who had always been as much of a foe to him as a friend, sounded genuinely hurt, grief lacing his words.

Finally, unable to process any more, Andrew released his grip on the phone and let it drop to the bed beside him as the room began to spin around him, first one way, then the other. He tried but failed to clamp a hand over his own mouth before an involuntary sob escaped. He heard his wife rustle awake beside him at the noise, and his heart squeezed tightly in his chest, some unseen vice twisting and compressing the blood from it. The thought occurred to him as acid began to burn in the back of his throat that he had not thrown up in over a decade—not since he was a college student drinking his way through the weekends. He concentrated on choking down the rising sickness.

Beside him, Rebecca clicked on her bedside lamp, then placed a hand on his shoulder. He returned his cell phone to the nightstand and turned slowly to face her, dread filling his body as he searched for a way to repeat what had just been told.

"Becca...our... he..."

Andrew choked on the first few words and made an effort to begin again. Rebecca's face was colorless, pale, and fragile in the moonlight.

"Who was that?" she asked, trepidation causing a tremor in her voice.

He watched her eyes widen with fear, as though she already knew.

"Becca..." he began again, but his voice broke. He cleared his throat and started a third time. "That was John. Something...s- something's happened to Eric."

Andrew watched his wife of twenty years fly out of the covers as though an invisible cord had yanked her into the air.

"Where is he?" she screamed. "What happened?"

Andrew grabbed her wrist as she rushed by him towards the closet and swung her back into his arms.

"He's gone, Becc," he whispered into her hair.

Her body began quaking immediately. Her mouth was open in a scream, but no sound escaped. Just when Drew thought she might not be breathing, the roar came, all at once. The sound she released cut through his chest like a heated blade, and he tightened his grip around her as she began to collapse toward the floor.

Chapter 3

May 15th Carlos

"For all those who exalt themselves will be humbled, and those who humble themselves will be exalted" Luke 14:11

"How can it be $12.50 when the menu clearly says $2.50?"

Carlos caught his voice amplifying in incredulity and quickly adjusted to keep the already agitated waitress from calling for reinforcements. He tried to tamp down his frustration. He'd driven for hours on end, watching the tall buildings and busy highway of Houston slowly become bustling shopping centers of swanky suburban cities, and then nothing but miles of nondescript brush and fields. He was momentarily awed at how clear the rural sky was as dusk turned to evening, and he could see constellations of stars he wouldn't have gotten a peek at through the city lights and petrochemical haze of Houston. But the beauty was outweighed by the hypervigilance that always took hold of him when he was in rural Texas.

He registered the growing sense of dread as the miles between houses stretched ever longer, and the billboards subtly changed from slick adverts to law enforcement campaigns and faded Trump 2024 MAGA ads. By the time he passed two back the blue signs, interrupted only by a reminder that he'd passed the only Buc-ee's in the area 20 miles ago, he was entirely uncomfortable. His shoulders had risen almost to his ears with the mounting tension of being black and alone in deep red country, and he blew a couple of deep breaths to force them back down. He tried to forcefully focus on the road and his playlist of 90s R&B hits. The trees out here grew close to the ground, more horizontal than vertical, to remain close to their water supply.

He recognized the iconic mesquite branches, casting weird night shadows fit for any horror film. The rest of the dry, indistinguishable brush was intermittently interrupted by large, seemingly endless fields that he knew in the daylight would reveal wheat, cotton, corn, or livestock—some burgeoning with new growth, others barren rows of neatly tilled land awaiting their next seeding. Eventually, he was forced to leave the highway and begin traveling the poorly lit Farm-to-Market roads, winding through unincorporated ranch land and pockets of humble homes sitting on enviable acreage. His body unconsciously tensed again as he lost the advantage of highway lighting. The picturesque landscape that would have been described as a lovely pastoral scene in any work of literature, was instead reminding him of what he knew to be the eerie backdrop to every terrifying Klan story he'd learned about rural Texas.

The places where a black man could very quickly find himself tied to the back of a truck. The places where, nearly 70 years after Emmit Till's open casket testimony to the brutality of racism, black mothers still warned their sons not to stop for gas or anything else in case they were in a sundown town.

Every time he was sent outside of Houston proper to cover another "small-town-football" story, he wondered whether it was worth it to travel back in time this way; to suspend the freedoms and ease he took for granted all day in the multicultural diversity of Houston, and catapult himself into the land of Jim Crow's quieter, more insidious cousin, James.

He usually filled his tank and packed as many snacks as he could shove in his cooler to avoid stopping anywhere after dark. But this time, he'd left straight from the office and found himself exhausted and hungry, still 40 miles from his destination, a moderately sized rural city called Jolivette. He had already tried rolling down the windows and blasting his music to stay alert, but his eyelids betrayed him by getting heavier and threatening to close. He knew he needed to stop for coffee somewhere well-lit, so the suddenly appearing lights of a roadside diner advertising the best burgers in Texas called to him like a siren. He should have stopped at the Buccees when he had the chance, he thought to himself with frustration. But instead, he had pushed it, and now this diner was all he had as a caffeine lifeline.

The waitress shifted her scrawny bit of weight to her other foot and slapped a bony hand on her imaginary hip. Carlos noticed the small pocked scars dotting her face and her brown, streaked teeth. This woman might be clean and sober now, but she had definitely been in a prolonged relationship with some recreational "etamine" at some point - meth, ket, or a close cousin. She looked every bit of 50, but probably wasn't a day over 30. *Drugs will do that to you*, he thought. He memorized her name from the peeling name tag pinned haphazardly to her stained shirt for future reference or in case he had to file a report. Bethany. She seemed to sense that he was making mental calculations, and her face took on a sour expression.

"Look, boy," she snarled at Carlos, "$2.50 is the local price for a slice of pie. And you ain't local. So the price is $12.50 plus tax. Now, settle up on this bill and head on back to wherever you are from, or I'll have someone put your ass in cuffs before you can hit the parking lot."

Carlos felt his anger levels rising quickly. He tried to talk himself down in his head. *It's only a little money,* his inner survivalist coached him. *You are a black man in a country ass, Texas diner full of white faces, and this slice of pie is not the hill you want to die on.*

Carlos did a quick sweep of the half-empty restaurant. Two gray heads right by the door; one hefty man at the bar with a confederate flag stretched across the enormous breadth of his t-shirt-clad back; one grease-drenched cook feigning disinterest while observing the confrontation through the pass-through window; one lone diner in the far corner with…

"Shit," he muttered under his breath as he registered the sharp creases and pleats on the back of the brown shirt as some sort of law enforcement uniform.

Everyone in the place was listening without listening. All conversation had stopped, other than the one between Carlos and Methany, and the tension in the room was suffocating.

"You know what," he drawled to the waitress in his best impression of her southern twang. "You're right. I'll pay what I owe, twelve fifty plus tax." He dragged it out as she had, so it sounded like "twelve feefty pluhhs tayucks."

Carlos plunked fourteen dollars down on the peeling vinyl of the table.

"Keep the change."

The waitress raised one brow and then lowered her eyes to slits, irritated by the fake accent Carlos had taken on. Carlos took the opportunity to gather his camera and messenger bag quickly. From the corner of his eye, he noticed the uniformed officer had rotated his body just enough to watch their interaction without having to turn his head.

Move slowly, Carlos silently coached himself. *If you want to make it to the car, you will move slowly and get the hell out of here.*

Carlos made sure to keep both of his hands visible on the straps of his bags as he rose from the table and took great care to avoid making physical contact with the waitress, who was still crowded menacingly close to his booth. He reluctantly turned his back on the room to head towards the exit.

As soon as he was through the first set of doors, he heard a howl of laughter go up from behind him. His ears began burning fiercely with embarrassment, but he pushed through the second set of doors and out into the night, making a beeline for his car. It took all of the restraint left in him not to peel out of the parking lot in a shower of flying gravel and screeching tires, but he maintained composure long enough to make a safe turn onto the feeder and then back onto the onramp for US Highway 59. He slammed his hand against the wheel over and over as he picked up speed.

"Dammit. Dammit, dammit, dammit!" he yelled into the windshield.

They had turned him into a joke. He was pissed with himself because he hadn't been able to resist being sarcastic when he knew the sarcasm could have gotten him killed. He was pissed that he had been afraid. He was pissed that he knew he was right to be scared. He was pissed that they had laughed at him when he left. He was even more pissed because underneath it all, he was relieved that he was alive and able to be pissed instead of dead or headed to lock up.

He blew out a deep breath of air, suddenly feeling his anger turn to sadness. These scenarios were supposed to be distant historical memories. The constant danger of being black was supposed to only appear in novels and documentaries about the civil rights movement. But here he was, walking the same treacherous paths as his father and grandfather before him, all these years later. With any luck, if he were killed or maimed these days, he could at least wind up as a viral hashtag, or his mom could win a windfall civil settlement, and in some sick way, he knew he ought to be grateful for that. For the fact that progress meant knowing that people would say his name. But it saddened him even more.

The idea that being remembered after a hate crime was a sign of progress felt hollow and hopeless.

His own grandmother had told him when he was younger, "Growing up back in South Carolina, if those white boys got you, you were gone. There wasn't anybody going down to the police station with a protest sign. Naw back then your mama would be lucky if she got your body back so that she could put you in the ground, proper. Most times, they wouldn't even bother to write a report."

Carlos never understood how people had lived their lives and raised families in a place where safety was a luxury that no one with darkened skin could ever afford. He gripped the wheel tighter, trying to squeeze the discomfort of his frustrations away and release the tension.

"God dammit! I hate these country ass towns," he yelled out loud to no one at all.

Chapter 4

May 15th Angel

"Many are the plans in a person's heart, but it is the Lord's purpose that prevails" Prov 19:21

Angel stretched her long, lean body across the chaise lounge until her toes pointed hard and strong like a prima ballerina, her arms extending over her head. Her back rose and arched up from the velvety cushions, and she realized that she had captured the full attention of her latest paramour, a professional basketball player. He spent more time on the bench than on the hardwood, but he was a marked improvement over the alcoholic singer she'd recently kicked to the curb, who had not had a song on the radio since the 90s, plus he was very easy on the eyes.

She let the stretch go on a few moments longer than needed, then turned lithely to face him. His eyebrows were slightly raised, and his mouth curled into a suggestive smile. Angel checked herself when she realized she was about to roll her eyes and returned the sweetness to her face as she began her tried and true goodbye sequence.

"I have an early call time for an audition today," she said with her mouth turned down in a cute pout.

He groaned and reached for her. "No, baby, don't go. You don't even need to work. You are too pretty to be working anyway."

Angel cocked one eyebrow up in surprise. He misread her confusion as excitement at the idea of not having to work, but she was actually trying to figure out why he thought she would leave for an audition and allow him to linger around in her condo. They had only been dating for two months. She'd known her housekeeper, Consuela, for nearly a year before she trusted her enough to give her the lock code to clean the condo unattended.

She stood up slowly and padded over to the dresser to grab her robe. He followed her every movement with his eyes, a sly grin on his face. She almost rolled her eyes again, but remembered that he could see her reflection in the mirror on the dresser. She silently chided herself for being so thin on patience, but honestly, she was tired. Bone tired. Soul tired. She had come to L.A. to be famous. Rich and famous. To see her name in lights and walk red carpets. Instead, she had done one commercial series for menstrual cramp relief pills, waited tables at a few Michelin Star restaurants, and let a bunch of D-List celebrities pay her living expenses.

She could act. She knew she could act. She'd studied improv, method—you name it. And she was beautiful; drop-dead gorgeous if this latest ball player's constant declarations of love were to be believed. But her beauty—this nearly forty-year-old beauty—wasn't quite keeping up with all of the twenty-something, injected, plumped, slimmed, and smoothed beauty that leapt off of social media feeds and onto the sets of full-length feature films.

Despite her best efforts, she was now simply doing her best to keep her life afloat, which meant surviving off 20-year-old royalties and men with short, unguaranteed contracts in the NFL and the NBA.

She chuffed at herself in the mirror, disgusted. What had she done with her life, really? Then she shook her head to banish the self-loathing that was quickly filling every crack in her polished veneer and return herself to the present. She spun around in her robe and gracefully arranged herself across Mr. Basketball's lap where he had perched on the edge of the bed.

"Don't worry, babe," she cooed. "I will call you as soon as I get out to tell you how I did. And then you can swing by and pick me up after practice tomorrow. A girl has got to have a dream," she whispered while nuzzling his ear. "And acting is still mine."

He shivered, his arms tightening around her frame, curvy and strong like a Broadway dancer. He groaned, then scooped her up and tossed her back onto the bed. She was caught off guard by the swift move and actually laughed a real laugh from down deep, not one of her practiced tinkling laughs.

He leaned over her, his eyes sparkling. "You are incredible."

Her laugh faded some then and became a faltering smile. In that moment, he'd reminded her of someone she didn't feel like remembering. The memories had been rushing back more and more frequently these days as she was forced to take stock of her life. A first love that had consumed her and then spit her out. A second love she had abandoned in a fit of fear and panic. The two ghosts had begun escaping from her night terrors and emerging as daylight haunts, invading every quiet moment. They were calling to her like sailors' sirens, reminding her of every moment she had tried to lock in the vault of her mind. She felt the threat of tears welling in her eyes and snapped herself out of it.

"Okay," she said louder than intended as she sat up suddenly, pushing her paramour aside. "Out you go! I have to shower and run my lines."

"I can help!" he protested. "With both activities."

She slapped his hands away and gave him her practiced disarming laugh again. "Shoo!" she said, and then grabbed her phone and disappeared into the bathroom, shutting the door behind her. She turned on the shower, then leaned against the door to listen as he gathered his keys and bag then left. When she was sure that he had gone, she hit the front door locks from the app on her phone and stepped into the steaming shower and let the tears fall. She had given up so much to come to this place, and gotten very little in return. She buried her head in her hands and stood under the rain head fixture, hoping that the water would wash away the guilt that was threatening to swallow her whole.

Chapter 5

May 16th Andrew - Burying the Lead

When his breath departs, he returns to the earth; on that very day, his plans perish. Ps. 146:4

Andrew sat across from the coroner and tried to make sense of the information being communicated. His brother, John, had arrived just moments after him, supposedly for moral support, but was instead throwing his weight around in a typical display of bravado and brashness. His brother-in-law, Grant, who was also the county sheriff, was leaning so far across the coroner's desk that his belt buckle had toppled the coroner's neatly stacked files as he demanded answers. John was pacing the room, creating a frenetic energy that was beginning to wear down what little mental stability Andrew still had intact.

"That's enough," Andrew said softly. Then louder, "THAT'S ENOUGH! Both of you, out!"

The men looked at him red-eyed and angry, but left the room without challenging him once they saw the resolve in his red-rimmed eyes.

Drew couldn't even remember driving to the coroner's office; he must have gone on autopilot. But he did remember identifying his son's body or what was left of it. It was seared into his mind now and continuing to play on a never-ending loop, drowning out everything happening around him. He kept having to shove the image down and ask the coroner to repeat himself. He gathered himself with a deep breath, inhaling the antiseptic smell of the tidy office.

Silence had quickly filled the room in the wake of his brother's departure, and Andrew was struck, not for the first time in the last several hours, by the idea that he could just be having a nightmare and his alarm might jar him awake at any moment. He waited for a beat to see if the sound of an alarm was coming, but it didn't, so he rubbed his eyes and tried to shake himself back into reality. The coroner, the picture of patience, waited also. There was a kindness in the coroner's posture, his manner.

Despite having just endured the complete jackass treatment from John's ill-tempered antics and Grant's booming demands, the coroner's face remained filled with the calm patience that Andrew imagined must come with many years of delivering horrible news as a matter of routine. His deep bronze skin and halo of tightly curled white hair made for an interesting contrast, like a black

Santa Clause. Even more remarkably, the coroner didn't seem tired, despite it being nearly four o'clock in the morning, an ungodly time for anyone to be summoned into work.

"Can we back up a bit?" Drew asked, " I missed some of it with my brothers squawking." The coroner nodded in calm agreement and carefully began explaining again.

"We need to issue an official cause of death before we can release the body and let you make burial or other arrangements. Because of the incredible amount of damage to his body from the impact of the 18-wheeled transport truck, we are inclined to believe that the truck was indeed the ultimate cause of his death. However, we did find several bullet fragments from what appears to be hunting-caliber shotgun ammunition in his left shoulder. It might have shattered the shoulder, but then again, so might have the impact with the truck. We may have additional forensic reports, including ballistics, as the week unfolds. Still, it does appear from the injuries that he was struck by the vehicle and was then dragged several feet, causing hematoma, extensive lacerations, fractures, and burns before his body was detached from the undercarriage - at which time his body then sustained additional injury from the rear wheels."

No longer able to fight it back, Andrew grabbed for the small dustbin by the coroner's desk and heaved the contents of his stomach into it until he was certain there was nothing left to bring up. Even then, he remained curved around the small waste basket, the sour taste of bile and disbelief lingering. As he breathed over the can now in his lap, the coroner added another kindness.

"Mayor Tucker, I can assure you that your son died on impact and did not suffer those later atrocities. We cannot, at this time, definitively say when or how the shot entered his body because of how incredibly severe the other injuries he sustained were. The bullet wound was fresh and had to have happened around the time of the accident based on the state of the tissues and bone where the fragments were found. A forensic and expert ballistics team could probably tell you the exact distance the shot was fired from, but we can't determine that level of information from our examination."

The coroner motioned towards Drew's still-damp shirt. "As you know, it rained heavily throughout the night, and it is still pouring pretty good. At that, he motioned his hand generally above his head, where the noise of rain pelting the aluminum awnings of the flat tar-roofed building was creating a cacophony of sound. The rain has added difficulty…er..complexity to discovering many clues that we might typically expect to have remained on the exterior of the body and its immediate surroundings."

Grant must have stepped back into the room because Drew heard his gravelly voice chime in on the conversation.

"He's right." Grant gestured to the coroner. "I talked to the local guys that responded, and they didn't even find any shell casings. They swabbed the girl's hands, who was on the scene, and did a few pulls on her clothing for gunpowder residue, but honestly, they are not expecting that to pan out. The vehicles, the road, and even the girl were drenched, and there were no weapons recovered."

Grant's voice faded out when he realized that he wasn't really contributing anything helpful to the conversation. The coroner tapped his pen on the drawing where red circles marked the area of the body where the shot fragments were recovered.

"Your son was indeed shot, Mr. Tucker. But he would have survived those injuries. It's the truck that got him. We gave the police what we could recover. Everything has been sent out to the police department's forensic lab to analyze and identify further. I don't have any more answers for you. We will release the cause of death as blunt force trauma and catastrophic head, neck, and thoracoabdominal injury resulting in internal bleeding and organ failure."

Drew tried to get a coherent sentence to leave his throat, but he was struggling.

"Just to be clear," he croaked, You think that someone was trying to kill him, on purpose?"

His hands tightened their grip on the trash bin in his lap. The coroner raised his hands in front of himself as if physically separating himself from the question.

"I am not a judge or a jury. All I can say is that he was shot. But it doesn't look like the shot would have killed him. It was nowhere near his vital organs. The truck and road did all the real damage before he was released from the undercarriage."

Drew looked back to his brother-in-law for something more solid to grab onto than a mystery truck, missing weapon, and an unknown shooter.

Grant shook his head. "To be honest Drew, if he was already down from the shotgun blast, the truck driver may not even realize they hit a person. Those long-haul guys run through deer, armadillos, stray dogs, and everything else across that stretch at night. With the weather conditions as they were…this is the worst-case scenario we could be in right now."

Drew looked back at the coroner, watery-eyed and spent. He wanted the coroner or someone to say more, to make things make sense.

"I understand that you want answers, Mr. Mayor, but any more answers that come from this will inevitably come from law enforcement."

The coroner's gaze moved over Drew's slumped posture, grief pressing him into the chair.

"Your brother-in-law will know more than anyone in that regard. There are serious limits as to what information we can determine within this office. The medical cause of death, time of death, and basic manner of death—that's what we do here. Like I said, we will need to finalize the death certificate before the body can be released to you from the morgue. At that point, your chosen funeral home can cremate or try to reconstruct your son for a casket funeral."

Andrew felt bowed and broken by the last 24 hours of his life. Was this even his life? What was he supposed to do next? He did not want his son reconstructed like some arts and crafts project just to lay in a casket. What would Rebecca want? He cleared his throat as another question formed.

"He will have to stay in that...that freezer...until you can issue an official cause of death?"

The coroner nodded solemnly.

"Okay," Drew resigned himself to the obvious decision. "Please release the cause of death as...the...the trauma you described, and we will begin making arrangements with Brothers Funeral Home."

"Now, wait a minute!" John yelled.

He had come back into the room undetected. Hearing John's voice grated against the already raw emotions that Drew was trying to keep in check.

"We need to get to the bottom of this before we issue a cause of death." John bellowed, "You heard the coroner! Somebody shot Eric! This is a murder case! Right?" John looked to Grant for backup.

Drew leaped from the chair, slamming the wastebasket to the floor, and rounded on his brother as his sadness was quickly eclipsed by anger. Grant moved to step between them, but Drew gave him an icy look, so he stepped back out of the way.

"Listen to me," Drew whispered fiercely, now just inches away from John's face. "This is my life blown apart! MINE! Not yours. That is the son that I raised lying in there, mangled and broken! I left MY wife at home in tears, trying to deal with the hardest moments she will ever face in her life! My wife, my life, my son - not yours!"

Drew saw a shadow of something dangerous pass over his brother's face, and he knew he was pushing the exact buttons that would hurt him, but he stayed the course. He didn't have the energy to play the nice guy, big brother role with John tonight. He'd been doing it for far too long. In fact, Drew had spent most of his life trying to go easy on John because his father had been so hard on him. Their father was a self-proclaimed winner. He'd staked his name and reputation on being a man of unrivaled stock, steeped in intelligence and physical prowess. He'd reveled in opportunities, real or imagined, to triumph over others in battles of wits or will. And as soon as Drew and then John came squalling into the world, their father demanded that same level of spectacle-worthy performance from them both.

Drew, naturally gifted, athletic, and driven, had delivered on his father's demands consistently. He was tall, strong, and bright. He led his class with the highest SAT scores, and the football and baseball teams to State Championships - setting school records that had not been challenged since. But not John.

John was smaller, less studious, and struggled. There was no way to hide it. His father repaid that struggle by directing more of his drunk rage to John than to anyone else. John had tried for a while to dig himself out of the bucket reserved for disappointments, but had never been able to rise to a level their father deemed worthy. Instead, he began to exist perpetually in Drew's shadow. He tried his hand at baseball, and he was competent but unremarkable. He spent long nights trying to advance his ranking in academics but maintained an immovable B and C average. Their father wasted no time drawing a wedge of comparisons between the two that he drove deeper every chance he got.

Drew tried to get John to shake it off, and went out of his way to shield John from the worst of it. But it wasn't enough, and the relationship between the brothers began to fracture and fray. By the time they were teenagers, John could barely stand to be around Drew or their father. But as tables always do, they turned.

Drew had fallen in love, and their father had not approved of the girl. Drew continued to see her anyway in open defiance of their father, and   John finally saw his opening to move up in favor, and he took it. Any time their father started in with the slurs and curses, dragging the girl's name like so much dirty laundry, John would jump right in with him, in lockstep - throwing in his own colorful epithets with flair.

Their father, more caustic and consistently drunk than ever before by then, loved the commiseration and lapped it right up. John would find ways to take verbal jabs at the girl or embarrass her, then come home and tell his dad about it over beers, watching him double over in laughter until he was red in the face and slapping John on the back. Anything their father rewarded him for, John would do - And above all, their father rewarded cruelty. Drew had made a few efforts over the years to strike a peace with John-mend the rift, but there came a point where the efforts were futile.

Drew knew that John hadn't deserved the grinding down that their father had subjected him to, but he also didn't know how to stop it. And now here they were - locked in a battle of wills over how to handle Eric's death. Drew would have given almost anything to be able to lean on his brother right now; to be the two little boys who would run from their drunk and angry father, hiding in the barn together, telling far-fetched stories and planning adventures. But the look in John's bloodshot eyes as the coroner and Grant looked on with apprehension, made it clear that he would sooner shoot Drew than help him end this quietly. Drew sighed and tried again to reason with his brother.

"John please. Rebecca is barely holding it together. If I go home and tell her that she can't bury her son, or worse, give her time to come down here and see Eric like this, it is going to kill her." Drew said again. He was sure now. He knew he was doing the right thing. "No. We are not going to drag this out. She has to be able to bury him. We must spare her this additional pain. We will shoulder it for her. Do you understand?"

John's face was red but unreadable. He stood perfectly still, his hands clenched tightly in fists at his sides. He said nothing.

"Please, John. This information would kill her," Drew said, then turned to the sheriff. "Have your people bury that part of the report."

Grant nodded reluctantly and swallowed whatever else he might have said, but John was still visibly fuming, his face a mask of hatred, and Andrew knew John wouldn't stay quiet for long. He never could.

Chapter 6

May 16th Free - Tell Us What Happened

"Music was my refuge. I could crawl into the space between the notes and curl my back to loneliness." - Maya Angelou

When Freedom awoke, the soft light in the window was grainy as if it were forcing itself through the cloud cover like a sieve. She couldn't tell whether it was dusk or dawn. From the flickering lights on the wall outside her door, she could assume that her grandmother was in the living room watching the TV, and since the television never came on before 5 pm, that answered the question of time—it must be evening. Free was shocked by the realization that she must have lost an entire day to sleep.

Mama Jean rose at four am every day without fail. She said prayers for an hour, made breakfast, then Tuesday through Saturday, headed out to open Walker's Cleaning and Alterations. For decades, she'd worked tirelessly and through long days of pressing, hemming, embroidering, and alterations, pausing only to pick at her lunch of leftovers, which she never bothered to warm. In the last few years, she had hired help: younger women with supple fingers that could whip through twice as many alterations in a day as her 70-year-old hands could keep up with.

She was a woman of habit and unshakeable values. Mama Jean was faithfully married to her routine, and every bit as loyal to it as she had been to her husband of 42 years before he passed. In the evenings, she paid her small group of employees, ran through the ledgers, and closed the shop.

On Wednesdays, she would head over to the church to lead women's bible study. But every other weeknight, she would head home to turn on the six o'clock news. She'd spend the entire news hour sucking her teeth, shaking her head disapprovingly, and praying under her breath at the state of affairs in the world. She liked to run through the entire selection from CNN to Fox News and back, pointing out inconsistencies, signs of the end times, and hypocrisy.

"How can they just get in front of God and man and tell lies like that!" Mama Jean constantly remarked when politicians were caught in overt falsehoods or husbands reported spouses missing, only to be later charged with their murders.

As long as she watched the news, Mama Jean never ran short on information to be disappointed with. "Whole world going to hell!" was her favorite news-hour phrase. When she reached peak disgust, she would make an elaborate scene of turning the TV off and tossing the remote down before throwing up her hands, flipping the TV back on for an episode of Wheel of Fortune, and then finally heading to her room for evening prayers and bed. She brought the same level of exasperation and general disapproval for the news cycle to Wednesday night bible study, which may explain why attendance had been dwindling.

Freedom craned to hear the sounds of the TV but instead heard Mama Jean's gravelly voice just above a whisper. Her eyes narrowed in concentration as she tried to make out a few other voices that were not coming from the TV set. Who was here? She began to feel a distant sense of panic creeping into her chest. A familiar sense of dread.

If her cousin Trent were still alive, he would say, "Something has changed in the matrix."

It was an annoying habit he'd picked up, saying the summer they'd all gone to see The Matrix at the dollar movies. Trent had been her best friend, her only friend really. But Trent's dad, like so many of the real dreamers from Jolivette, had been too big for the town. After two years of the city council denying him the permit to build an apartment complex or open a Chik-fil-A franchise, followed immediately by the Tuckers breaking ground on a senior living facility on the same location and opening their own Chik-Fil-A, he'd seen the writing on the wall, taken a new job in Oregon, and moved his entire family out of Jolivette. Free and Trent had tried to keep in touch, but he was older than her and had his own stuff going on. Last time she'd spoken to him, he had joined the Air Force and was being stationed in Japan.

Freedom shook her head fiercely to shake off the sense of sadness, then slipped out of bed, threw on an oversized sweatshirt, and padded softly into the hallway. She positioned herself just out of range of the large hall mirror so that she could not be seen, but she could see the living room reflected in the glass. She caught the gleam of Mama Jean's salt and pepper hair peeking over the top of her recliner and the profile of two men on the love seat. One had close-cropped graying hair, and the other seemed younger, at least based on the hair and partial profile she could see, but they were both wearing sport jackets.

On the far club chair, she could make out the full pudgy face of Pastor Simmons. His brows were furrowed in concern, and his glasses were sliding down his nose as was their usual custom.

There were many Sundays when Freedom had to fight the urge to walk up into the pulpit and push his glasses back up where they belonged on his face. The longer he preached, the lower they would slide until he was practically holding them up with his upper lip. She could never understand how the pastor benefitted from his glasses prescription when he only ever looked over the top of them. But she liked Pastor Simmons, notwithstanding his resemblance to a puffer fish and foolish misuse of spectacles.

Freedom stood leaning against the wall, straining to hear their hushed conversation and trying to put what she was seeing into context. The pastor was at her house. Why? And who were the other two men on the sofa? Why were they dressed so formally? Something about the suit jackets and the haircuts registered police, and she suddenly remembered a snatch of the evening before with all of the police cruisers and their strobing lights.

Her head began an intense throbbing, and the hall suddenly felt like it was tilted. She turned quickly to get back to her room, but her foot caught on the hall rug. She threw a hand out to steady herself, which slammed into the wall but didn't grip, and she landed sprawled in an awkward position, arms akimbo on the same threadbare rug that had just tripped her. She heard the living room go silent in the wake of her noisy fall. *Please don't let them hear me, please don't let them hear me*, she prayed silently while puffing air through her nose and hearing her heart thud in her chest. She tried her best to slow her breathing. *Maybe they didn't hear me?* she thought. But it was wishful thinking. She let out a groan as Mama Jean's sensible Naturalizer shoes appeared in the hallway.

"Freedom, I'm not sure why you are on this floor, but there are some people here to speak with you about the accident."

Mama Jean's voice sounded steady, but even as a woman with few tells, her tightly laced fingers were a telltale sign to Free that she was stressed or worried or both. Freedom dragged herself up from the floor and headed into the living room.

"I'll see you later, Jean," Pastor Simmons called as he headed out to the front porch. "We will keep you all in prayer."

Mama Jean closed the door behind him and motioned for the men and Free to head into the kitchen.

Free sat at the table, running her hands back and forth across the rough rattan placemats and staring at the Daily Bread. It was just a miniature plastic bread loaf, faded by time and sunlight. The middle was hollowed out and jam-packed with bible verses typed onto little strips of cardboard that resembled stiff sticks of gum. The thing had to be older than Mama Jean. The edges of the strips were dog-eared and splitting apart as the glue succumbed to the effects of time. There was a solid chance that Freedom could quote every single verse included in the little tchotchke. For years growing up, they could not eat dinner until she, Mama Jean, and Pop Pop had pulled a verse and read it aloud. She couldn't remember when or why they stopped doing that. Maybe it reminded Mama Jean too much of Pop Pop after he passed. Freedom instinctively reached and pulled one out, but she didn't read it. Instead, she just flipped it over and over in her hands as the man with the graying hair cleared his throat.

"Ms. Walker, I'm Detective Cooper, and this is Detective Johanson," he motioned his hand towards the younger man. "I understand that you may still be in a bit of shock, but I'm here to speak to you about what happened yesterday evening," he said, sliding a small tape recorder towards the center of the table. "Do you mind if I record?"

Mama Jean reached one weather worn hand out and clicked the recorder off, sliding it back towards the detectives.

"Yes, we mind."

Her voice was pleasant, but her eyes, despite turning up into a smile, held a warning.

The detective cleared his throat and returned the recorder, wordlessly, to his bag. Freedom continued to flip the small card in her hands as she watched the exchange. The second detective spoke up.

"We came to speak with you earlier, but you were asleep, and your grandmother thought it was best that you get your rest."

Freedom stole a look at Mama Jean, who had raised one eyebrow at her and stopped flipping the card.

"What did you want to know?" she asked as the Detective's eyes shifted from Mama Jean back to her.

"Well, about the accident out on County Road 35," he said, leveling his gaze. "What can you tell me about what happened? We haven't been able to track down the vehicle that hit him yet."

Freedom's brow furrowed in confusion.

"I don't understand," she said slowly. "Is this...I mean, am I...am I in trouble?"

Freedom's eyes darted back to her grandmother, whose face had returned to its familiar stoicism. Her grandmother's expression calmed her, and she pushed the panic back down into her chest.

"What do you want to know?" Freedom asked again. "I told the police everything that night."

The two detectives shared a look, and then Detective Cooper turned back to Freedom.

"Yes, of course. But we have some new information about that night, and so we have to walk through it again."

"New information?" Freedom asked, her face puzzled, brows furrowed.

"Yes, your classmate, Eric Tucker, was killed, but we don't think it was an accident. The coroner found injuries consistent with large-caliber hunting ammunition in his body. There is no way a truck did that," Officer Cooper said, a sarcastic smile on his face. "But maybe you saw who did."

The detective's gaze remained trained on Freedom, and her hand flew to her mouth to stifle the panicked yelp that was forming. Freedom could suddenly feel Mama Jean's eyes on her as well, hot with concentration.

Freedom's heart felt like it was skipping time in her chest, constricted like a vice. She had to remind herself to breathe.

"I don't understand," she sobbed around, her hand still clasped over her mouth and nose. "Shot?!" she exclaimed, her entire body shaking.

Cooper scribbled down some illegible notes in his notepad. The detectives gave her a moment to try to gather herself, then continued.

"You gave the police a statement." Detective Cooper looked down at a small notebook. "You stated that you saw the truck, but it was moving so fast that it was gone by the time you realized it had made an impact with Eric Tucker. Do you remember hearing a shot? Gunfire of any kind?"

Freedom knew that they were looking to her to make this new information make sense. She knew they expected her to have the information, and she was beginning to feel caged and claustrophobic.

"Did you get a look at the truck at all?" he asked, changing tack. I mean, we understand it was going fast, but if you noticed the color, writing on it, or anything unique about it, it could really help. Maybe start earlier in the day and walk us through to the moment Eric was killed. That sometimes helps."

The detectives were alternating questions despite her not having answered any yet. Freedom turned to her grandmother for help as the older detective threw an exasperated look at his partner.

"Just do your best to remember anything," Mama Jean said softly, meeting Freedom's pleading eyes with the steady look of assurance that was the Hallmark of Mama Jean. The old lady was unflappable.

"Take your time," she said and covered Freedom's hand with her own.

Freedom squeezed her eyes closed, signaling that she was trying to remember yesterday.

"Okay...Saturday," Free mumbled, steadying her mind.

She began recounting the day aloud for the detectives. She remembered breakfast, she said, because Mama Jean made pancakes, which she rarely does anymore. She'd washed her hair and then done two loads of laundry while she waited for her wash and go to dry. Her thick spiraled coils required product detangling and diffusing, which always slowed down the go part of wash and go. She'd also had lunch with Mama Jean, who clucked and tsked through the whole meal about Freedom refusing to straighten her hair, but she left all of that out of her retelling and stuck to the big events for the officers. That evening, around 4 pm, she'd driven over to the library to work on her speech for graduation.

"What kind of speech?" the younger detective asked, his voice full of cynicism.

"My valedictorian speech." Free deadpanned, anticipating the incredulity that she had become accustomed to from people learning that a valedictorian in Jolivette would look like her.

The detective balked, but before he could respond, his partner cut in.

"Who was there with you? At the library."

Freedom pictured the faces she'd seen as she searched for a quiet space to work. There was only a small group of usual suspects that would do schoolwork over the weekend. She said their names as their faces flashed across her memory: Jessica Lynch, Kathy Sorrels, Renita Jeffers, Marcos Guzman, and Kathleen Cao—all top 10 percent of the class students who couldn't let up on their academic pursuits even with graduation looming and college admissions secured.

"Did you see Eric Tucker at the library?"

The officer flipped a new page in his small notebook. Freedom started to experience a sinking feeling, but she pushed through. She couldn't afford to seem hesitant, so she continued talking through the day.

"I did see Eric come into the library," she said, "but he didn't stay long."

The detective raised both brows in a look of surprise.

"Oh!" He remarked. "So you know when he came and when he left? Did you know him, personally?" The detective's questions were beginning to feel less like questions and more like a trap.

"I...I mean...everyone knows Eric," Freedom offered, measuring her words carefully.

The detectives shared another look.

"What I mean to say–" she offered, "Is that he is pretty popular. We were never really in the same classes or activities, but people notice when he is in a room and when he leaves. He is.—I mean, he was—a pretty big deal at our school."

Tears pricked behind her eyes as she corrected her tense, aware that Eric was really dead and she was really sitting here talking to detectives about it. She tried to blink them back, but one or two escaped anyway, and she brushed them away hastily.

"And what about you?" the detective pressed on. "When did you leave the library?"

"The library was closing," she thought aloud - "So it had to be right around 7 pm. I remember it was getting dark, and I don't really like to drive on the roads in the dark. I've only had my license for a year."

Freedom gripped the sides of the chair she sat in, fighting the urge to run away from this conversation and inwardly praying they were nearing the end of their questions.

"Okay, so what happened to your tires?" Cooper pushed.

Trying in vain to fight the rising panic, Free's eyes darted up towards where Mama Jean had been sitting for support, and she realized that the chair was empty and Mama Jean had crossed the divide of the table and was now standing beside her.

"It's ok, honey. It's okay." Mama Jean whispered.

Mama Jean was not a big woman. Strong, petite, and wiry, she didn't physically take up much space, but her presence next to Free was powerful. And her hand on Free's shoulder felt like an anchor, the only thing keeping Free from drifting over the edge of the universe. Freedom steadied her breathing, buoyed by Mama Jean's quiet confidence.

"On my way home from the library, it started raining, and the car began making noise. At first, I wasn't sure, but then I realized that I had a flat tire. Two flat tires," Freedom continued, her voice thready now.

"That's unusual," Cooper interrupted her retelling. "Have you ever had two tires blow out on your car before?"

"Well, actually, I've never had a flat tire at all. I wasn't even sure that was what was happening at first. Like I said, the car was making a lot of noise, and then the whole thing started pulling hard to the left. I couldn't hold it straight. The Suburban is pretty big and heavy - it was scary. I tried to pull over to the side as far as I could, but those roads don't have much of a shoulder. When I got out, I could see right away that the front driver's side tire was all but gone. But then I realized the back one on that side was damaged too. They were both totally flat."

"Okay, and did you try to change one of the tires?"

"I thought about it, but the suburban tires are too big, and it would have been too hard for me to get the lug nuts off. So I tried to call my grandmother to ask her to come get me, but before I could even tell her where I was, Eric just kind of - showed up. He pulled his truck over behind me and said he could help, so I hung up the phone and showed him where the spare tire and donut were."

Detective Cooper pulled out photographs from the night of the accident.

"We've looked at the vehicle and the photos from that night over and over again. There are some…irregularities that are rather striking."

Free's brows furrowed with confusion, and he continued.

"First off, the tires weren't just flat; they had been sliced. Slashed. Intentional cuts. Why would that be the case?"

He fixed his eyes on Free's awaiting an answer.

"I..I don't know, "Free" stuttered. "I didn't know that. It was dark. I just knew they were flat."

"Well, that's the other odd thing," the detective interjected. "You said that Eric stopped to help. We didn't see a car jack, a lug wrench... anything at all removed from either of your vehicles that could be used to change a tire. Why is that?"

"Well, he never had a chance to help with the tire." Freedom's voice was shaky now, husky with the effort of holding back tears. "Everything happened so fast. It was raining hard and I - I. I don't know how the truck clipped him. One minute he was standing there by my door and then…"

Freedom buried her face in her hands, her body heaving with the release of pent up emotions. The detectives shared a look with one another. Mama Jean placed another hand on Freedom's shoulder and addressed the detectives directly.

"We are going to have to continue this another day. This is too much for her."

The detectives shared a look.

"Just one more question, Miss Walker," Cooper asked.

"No," Mama Jean stated firmly. "No more questions."

Chapter 7

The Family Tucker

"But as for me, my feet were almost gone; my steps had well nigh slipped. For I was envious of the arrogant, when I saw the prosperity of the wicked." Ps. 73:2-4

For better or worse, Jolivette, Texas, belonged to the Tuckers. The sitting mayor, Andrew Tucker the Fifth, was the fourth consecutive Andrew Tucker to serve as Mayor, and the Mayoral has come to him the same way as his predecessors- when the previous Tucker was dead, dying, or suffering from dementia.

Individually, Andrew "Drew" Tucker, fifth of his name, was widely viewed as a just and honest man, but the Tuckers, more generally, had always been a mixed bag. There were good Tuckers, bad Tuckers, and Tuckers that you couldn't quite put your finger on. As with most families, the ones with questionable character were the loudest, most visible, and tended to control the family narrative, while the rest were left to run damage control and patch up goodwill with offended parties.

As far back as history remembers, the original Andrew Tucker had made an early fortune in the 1800s as a slave trader who ran a breeding enterprise. He was particularly good at breaking the spirit of willful men and women until they were a far more docile commodity—ugly and vicious work by all accounts. Over time, and with the changing sensibilities that followed the Civil War, having a family history of human trafficking had gradually lost its charm in more gentile social circles, so Andrew the First was rebranded in the Tucker family retellings as a goods and supplies trader. But rebranded or not, he is remembered, even within the family lore, as terrifying and devoid of moral compass, endlessly ambitious and enterprising.

Rather unfortunately, this first Andrew the Terrible was the architect of his family's early fortune and managed to pass many of his more monstrous traits down through the generations like a nightmarish inheritance, hopscotching over some then embedding deeply in others like the American, personality disordered version of the Hapsburg chin.

By pure luck, the sitting Jolivette Mayor appeared to have won in the game of genetic roulette on several fronts. For one, he was objectively, strikingly, and classically handsome. The symmetry and chisel of his features and musculature were the stuff of Greek mythology. He stood at an intimidating six-foot-five inches, and his piercing green eyes tended to flash gray when he was speaking passionately about a subject. Beyond his looks, he was notably prone to kindness, and fairhandedness in his political approach. There is no single explanation for why the fifth Andrew Tucker, who insisted on being called Drew, took such a noticeable departure from the cut-throat personalities of many of his predecessors, but his father went to his grave furious about it.

"I should have never let you go to school on the west coast with those tree-hugging, bleeding heart, pansy-ass, liberal professors," his father would growl as he verbally accosted his son for one thing or another that invariably included being too forgiving, not wielding his sizeable political power in the right way, or keeping company with quote, colored folk—a term that was so outdated and out of place that every time his father said it, Drew had the strange sensation that he was in a time warp and had quantum leaped back into the 1960s. Drew, for his part, knew exactly what his family's legacy was. He had seen the Klan memorabilia in the family library and heard his father fondly retelling stories of his childhood that were supposed to be humorous but smacked of brutality, violence and oppression. A generous helping of references to fa*s, ni**ers, injuns, and wetbacks was always sprinkled throughout his father's unsolicited advice, which became increasingly more angry and nonsensical as he struggled with dementia and cirrhosis at the end of his life. Drew recalled standing at his father's funeral and feeling overcome by a wave of incredible, bone-deep relief, followed by a pang of choking guilt when he recognized how unequivocally glad he was that his own father was dead.

Drew had instinctively buried his face in his hands, a sign the other mourners took as grief, but in truth covered his own horror. He was afraid of himself at that moment; appalled at his callous inner-celebration for the demise of a man who had quite literally given him everything. Drew's inner conflict sprang from an unshakeable belief that his father had wanted good things for him and that his father had actually loved him, but had been emotionally incapable of love in any healthy sense of the concept and had somehow conflated the concept of hazing with parenting.

When he was away at Stanford, the liberal college his father came to loathe, Drew had thrown himself into several psychology courses to try to understand his childhood and family dynamics. Eventually, he had the jarring realization that under every theory of psychology, his father and several of the Tuckers before him would have been classified by professionals as dangerous sociopaths. Yet in their time, they were feared and revered as shrewd businessmen, a trait for which they were rewarded with ever more land, wealth, and power. Drew spent so much time and effort trying to understand how his father came to be who he was that he graduated as a double major, earning both Political Science and Psychology degrees. He'd interviewed every living family member and documented as much as he could for his senior thesis, only to discover the truths that his thesis laid bare were too nightmarish for public consumption; so he'd decided at the last minute to refuse publication - instead simply taking the course grade without the academic publishing credit.

According to the history he'd gleaned, Andrew the First married a girl of just 15 years old when he was 30. She bore him five sons and three daughters before she was found swinging by her neck from their bedroom ceiling, still in her twenties. Instead of grieving properly, Andrew the Terrible refused to bury his wife. Outraged by her actions, he'd shipped her body back to her parents with a letter to advise them that their daughter's death was an indicator of her weakness of mind and admonishing them for the part they'd played in raising her in such a manner. He never remarried but was rumored to have taken many liberties with the souls he was responsible for breaking and selling, producing a menagerie of additional offspring of "dusky coloring and features" that he kept on the estate as a strange parallel lineage of domestics alongside his wife's children.

The next several Andrews and their siblings managed to echo this tradition of both detesting and desiring the women they owned, resulting in an expansive extension of the parallel lineage that trailed the family down the Eastern seaboard into the deep south and then into Texas once they relocated. These unclaimed Tucker children went without legal acknowledgment but shared so many of the Tucker features that one did not even have to squint to pick them out in the grainy black-and-white photos that filled the library at Drew's grandmother's estate.

When the prohibition on slavery drove Andrew the Terrible and his progeny from the Eastern seaboard to the rebellious, seceding arms of Texas, there was land to be had and an unspoken agreement to carry on as though the war was more unresolved than unsuccessful. The Tuckers then leveraged their significant fortunes and their domestic help to acquire and harvest timber from hundreds of acres of land along the Brazos River, eighty-nine miles southwest of what is now Houston, Texas, and raise livestock.

As it would happen, much of that land was already owned and occupied by freedmen, vaqueros, and a smattering of indigenous tribes when the Tuckers arrived. Undaunted by these trivialities, the Tucker men traded on their well-honed mastery of intimidation, brute force, and financial sway to chase families from their land, homes, fields, crops, and cattle. They needed the surface of the land for commerce, but even moreso, they quickly discovered that they needed the oil rights to what lay beneath to secure their futures in perpetuity.

For what it is historically worth as a sobering fact, the Tucker force du jour did not spare poor whites in their personal manifest destiny scheme either. If they ran across a property owned by Eastern European immigrants who had settled before them, they would manipulate the sale to themselves at absurdly low prices by poisoning the wells on the target's property or burning their crops under cover of night with a promise to return and do the house next. These were some of the more merciful acquisition methods. From everyone else, the Tuckers had simply taken, even if that required eliminating the rightful landowners altogether. As the Tucker family acquired the full collection of lands and properties that they most desired, their overt terrorism began to subside. Running every last soul off would have left them without labor or customers or constituents, and the Tuckers, ever the strategists, understood when to pull back for their own benefit. They founded the town of Jolivette in 1908 and set about creating a city government that could run to their benefit with impunity.

For some of the present-day Tuckers, this garish history was an eternal source of guilt and discomfort, and it was hard for Drew to extract accurate information or keep them talking while researching his thesis. For others, however, the stories were still told with a grandiose sense of pride and a lofty spin toward Manifest Destiny. With each new generation, this family dichotomy of ideology created larger rifts and wounds that ran so deep that several Jolivette Tucker descendants married early just for the ability to change their last names and leave the area.

As the oldest of his father's children, Drew had been slow to learn the history and therefore enjoyed many years as his father's favorite -, the golden son. But once he was willing to look closely and examine the impacts of his family's legacy and his father's continuation of it, their relationship soured quickly. Drew had tried to convince the family to make things right with the community they had taken so much from to build their fortune. To say that his efforts went poorly would have been an understatement, so instead, he fell back into the family tradition of political aspiration.

Once he was elected mayor, he knew they couldn't stop him from trying to fix things, and he began creating minority business incentive programs right away. Those in his family that had enjoyed the spoils of the Tucker monopoly in their respective business ventures quickly graduated from disbelief to unchecked anger, forcing Drew to the fringes of the family where he gladly contented himself to remain on the outs, occupying only the superficial edges of Tucker-family life and tradition while quickly and quietly diversifying access to successful enterprise and upward mobility in Jolivette.

Despite the ire it raised within the Tucker ranks, Drew carried the Tucker name and pedigree, and he had a son, an heir - so they would never turn him out of the family altogether. Or at least he'd had an heir up until last night. Now he wasn't sure what he had left.

Chapter 8

May 16th - Carlos - The Plot Thickens

At exactly 8:00 am on Monday, on the dot, Carlos walked into Jolivet High School. He'd had a poor night's sleep, unable to keep his mind from replaying his run-in at the diner, and was glad for a chance to think solely about work instead.

He'd checked his assignment notes for today's interview on the rising high school football star and plugged the address into the map app on his phone. The city wasn't big enough to get lost in, but he wasn't risking accidentally winding up on private property via a wrong turn and having to duck and dodge any castle doctrine enthusiasts. The directions to the town's only high school seemed simple enough, and he spent a few extra moments lining up his beard and selecting a cologne before heading out the door.

"I'm here to see Coach Bromstock." Carlos flipped his press badge photo up and slid it towards the overweight woman sitting at the front desk.

"No more press. Sorry," snapped the heavily made-up bleached blond without even looking up.

Carlos heaved a sigh of frustration.

"Look, Miss…" He scanned quickly for a name tag or plate and came up with nothing. "What's your name?"

He did his best to conceal his frustration. The apparent clerk slid his press pass back towards him, ignoring his inquiry and posing a question of her own instead.

"Carl, is it?" She'd glanced down at his name on the credentials and still said it wrong anyway.

He didn't bother to correct her mispronunciation of his name on a hunch that she'd said it wrong intentionally.

The clerk met his bemused expression with a steely look of her own.

"My name is Shelly Winters," she continued with one eyebrow now raised. "I am the desk clerk for Jolivet High School as well as the office coordinator, and I have been given strict instructions to refuse any media personnel from this campus in order to protect the grieving students, so you will need to leave now, or I can arrange to have someone escort you out."

Carlos took a step back to avoid intimidating the woman.

"Ma'am, today I have a scheduled interview with Coach Bromstock and his star quarterback, Eric Tucker. It has been on the schedule for weeks now, and I have gotten all the proper clearances for this meeting. My camera crew is in the lot now, and we have driven a great distance to be here today."

Carlos made a quick mental note to revisit later why he had just lied and referred to his sole cameraman, Ralph, as a "crew."

Shelly's face softened a bit, and her hand flew to her face.

"My word? You don't know, do you? How can you be a reporter and not know?"

Carlos shook his head and stepped back in towards the clerk.

"What don't I know?" he asked.

"Eric is dead," she whispered at stage volume. "He was hit by a truck on Saturday."

Carlos immediately felt like he had been hit by a truck also. His mind spun in a million different directions.

"The family is making arrangements," Shelly continued, "as soon as they release the body..."

She lowered her voice, took on a more conspiratorial tone, and leaned in closer. "...or maybe he'll just be ashes because from what I heard, the body is so bad that there isn't a funeral home in business that can get him casket-ready. But as soon as they release him to his family, there will be services."

Shelly looked Carlos up and down as though she were making some additional assessment of his trustworthiness. Carlos set aside his shock and leaned toward the small opening in the plexiglass from which she reigned supreme from behind and served her with his million-dollar smile, complete with both dimples to encourage her to side with him.

"You know everything that goes on around here, don't you?" he asked.

Her face betrayed her, and he realized that she found him attractive. Jackpot! he silently cheered for himself. Shelly smirked to indicate that yes, she DID indeed know everything that went on around there.

She whispered on. "THOSE boys just took this small town team all the way to a state championship, and then they lost the quarterback just like that." She snapped her fingers for emphasis. "It's unbelievable. Some of them kids had no prospects, but once they made it to the big show, well they were suddenly fielding calls from all the big name schools, and the Tucker boy could take his pick of colleges after the season he had! They may not have won the big game, but they put this city back on the map for Texas football. Yes, indeed. "

Shelly barely took a breath before she shifted into second gear with her gossip.

"Now the big scuttlebutt going around is that the boy got hit trying to help another student with car trouble. People are saying it was a little Black girl and even saying that the two of them had something going on...you know, like INVOLVED. ROMANTICALLY!"

She stressed as though Carlos was slow on the uptake.

"I know his daddy is just sick over the rumors. Can you imagine? A Tucker blueblood with a...nig–"

The clerk went wide-eyed, and her hand flew up to cover her mouth when she realized what she'd been about to let slip.

"Oh, mercy! I didn't mean any offense by that, Carlos! That's just how folks talk around here. Truly. I believe we are all God's children. Shucks, I dated a couple of Black guys myself when I was younger," she rushed to smooth over her near-slur.

Carlos held his palms up and smiled, noting that she did, in fact, know how to pronounce his name when she felt like it.

"No offense taken, Shelly."

He rolled up the dress sleeves on his shirt so Shelly could see more of his rippling forearms and a bit of the biceps that tended to work magic on his female interviewees. Shelly was visibly distracted by this, but continued letting words tumble from her mouth.

"Uhh…no, really, I was just mentioning she was Black because it seems like, you know, maybe he died as kind of a hero. Oh!" Her hand flew to her mouth again. "I'm not saying because he helped a Black person that makes him a hero. Or uh African American, I don't know what they call ya'll these days, but honestly you know, he didn't REALLY have to stop, with his family being so wealthy and important and all, but he still was out in the rain, helping her. That's what I heard."

She threw her hands up as though she was doing the best she could with sketchy sources.

Shelly reached through the plexiglass opening, placed her hand over Carlos's hand, and squeezed. "You know what I'm trying to say, right?"

Much skilled in the art of teasing out information by refusing to fill awkward silences, Carlos let Shelly continue to forge ahead with her barrage of now-flustered information delivery, oiled by the slippery lubricant of the guilt she had for saying something accidentally racist every few sentences.

"The Sunday paper said that he was out in the rain on that road, trying to help that girl, and he was hit by an 18-wheeler that didn't even stop! That's all the news here has said. But those are just dry facts, Carlos! They didn't mention that little Black girl in the paper at all! All they wrote was *Jolivette's Son: 'Rising Football Star Mowed Down in Hit and Run.'* I've got the article here somewhere," she said, fishing through the papers stacked on her small desk. And I bet they left it at that because that boy's daddy owns everything around here, including the papers, and heads would ROLL if more than that was reported!

"But ain't no point trying to keep secrets because these high school kids have ways of getting all kinds of information, and the halls are buzzing today. And you know what, I think it just ought to be said that not everyone around here would stop to help a girl with car trouble. No, siree. People aren't kind like that anymore. And in the rain, too. I don't mean you, of course." She fixed her eyes back on

Carlos. "You look young and handsome and strong, so I'm sure YOU would help any lady in distress."

Carlos registered the lowered lashes and shift in tone and processed that Shelly was switching to a new agenda, so he began executing his exit strategy as she dropped then raised her heavily mascaraed lashes to meet his gaze. He pulled his phone out and frowned at it as though reading an important message. Oblivious, Shelly forged ahead.

"You look like you work out a lot. What are you about 6 feet tall?"

"Six foot-two," Carlos said as he slid his other hand out from under the Clerk's damp palm while scrolling through his phone with the other hand.

"My boss is trying to reach me, Shelly. I've got to take this," he said hurriedly.

"Well, don't be a stranger," she drawled, her lips pushing out into an awkward pout.

Thanking her profusely for getting him up to speed and being so lovely, Carlos side-stepped towards the door. Internally, he was both amused and annoyed by her obvious advances, and casual racism, but he couldn't afford to burn a bridge in this small town, especially one that was so chatty.

"I'm sure I'll see you again," he told her, pointing to his card, which he'd left on the counter, and offering her a half smile showcasing only one of his dimples this time.

"You call me, ok?" He made her promise.

She flushed to a deep pink, and Carlos turned on his heel and raced back out to the car to call the station.

He could hardly control his excitement. For two years, he had been humping it for his station without a good story. The first year, he hadn't graduated yet, so he was technically an unpaid intern. But once hired, he was filling in for reporters on vacation. Then came the puff pieces like political power weddings, local conventions, and feel-good charity coverage. While the stories did keep him around a bevy of interested and often infatuated young Houston socialites, he'd quickly concluded that most of them were just the same woman over and over, wearing the same designer labels and carrying the same shallow points of view. He wanted more than groupie-perks. He wanted a serious career. He'd been begging for a real story for months and was both furious and crestfallen when he left the last assignment meeting with yet another high school football player piece.

He understood that in Texas, where football is king, there were no shortages of games to cover. Even pee-wee football got a little press during the season. Carlos had spent the better half of last year slapping at mosquitoes and interviewing hopeful, padded, and cleated kids on the sidelines or in cafetoriums that always smelled faintly of vomit and chicken. Meanwhile, the senior correspondents and a number of Carlos' colleagues were covering police brutality, huge political corruption, and campus shootings. Gun control was being defended or attacked by every elected official in the state. They'd thrown him a small bone by insinuating that he was going to cover LGBTQ civil liberty issues once, but when the smoke cleared, it was just another assignment covering high-profile weddings; the only difference being that this time he was being hit on by men and women instead of just women at the receptions.

He knew he hadn't paid enough dues to be asked to cover elections or a major exposé, but high school football and expensive weddings were not going to propel him onto a major news network. He didn't care how many of these kids would become professional athletes or how many gay spouses would now be fighting it out in divorce court with the rest of the population. He believed in a lot of things, but marriage was not one of them, so he was sick of the wedding beat. He'd tried to spin his last high school football story into an editorial piece about the long-term effects of multiple concussions in young adults. The data was there, and the scientific evidence was jarring. But when he pitched it, the station wouldn't go for it. They all but bum rushed him out of the pitch room.

When he joined KVH2 Houston right out of undergrad, he was excited. It seemed like the station was leading the charge against corruption and fraud. Their reporting had serious impacts on the government and policy. They were the station that still reported the news instead of just cycling current events. But Carlos wasn't getting any of the action.

The manager kept telling him, "You've got to pay your dues like everyone else."

This weird development—the Jolivette football star story—felt like a sign that his luck was turning ever so slightly around. Yeah, sure, Jolivette was a small city, but Shelly's racially charged overshare seemed to indicate that this little story was taking on some complexity now, however morbid, and he was going to find a way to scoop it. His mind was off and racing! A story about a local rich-kid football star cut down in his prime while saving a poor Black classmate—and then throw in a big trucker hit-and-run twist? This story smelled of racial undertones, polarizing interests, big business liability, and a tragically derailed Cinderella story.

Judging from the silence of his phone all weekend, no one in Houston had gotten wind of it, so he still had a chance to pitch breaking news. His mind was spinning as he dialed the station manager. Maybe he wasn't totally sure of what he had, but he knew what he didn't have, and that was time to waste.

Chapter 9

The Family Walker

Freedom, born Freedom Grace Walker, was an anomaly in every way for Jolivette, Texas. Nothing about her was expected or accepted. For one, she was not born under the glare of sterile hospital lights. Instead, she was born in the clawfoot tub of the bathroom just off the main living area of her grandmother's house during the hottest summer in Jolivette history. The midwife who delivered her was a family friend who had driven two and a half hours through the night the moment Mama Walker called her. Mama Walker hadn't expected the baby to come for another couple of weeks, so by the time the midwife arrived, Freedom was already out of her mother to the neck, and the midwife had only to ease her shoulders out, help deliver the placenta, and then clean her up.

Because Freedom's grandfather, Pop Walker, had built their home with his own hands, their house on 201 Friendship Drive maintained some design peculiarities that set it apart from the more modern and prefabricated homes in the area. For one, the bathroom floors, like every other floor in the house, were composed of original hardwood planks. All of the other homes in the area had tile, or linoleum, or some other water safe material, but not the Walkers.

Additionally, there was no clouded or patterned glass block window to allow natural light into the main bathroom while maintaining modesty. Instead, a full-length traditional double paned window that could be cranked open on an angle or fully opened by lifting it up, took up a large part of the exterior bathroom wall.

Freedom had remarked on more than one occasion as a little girl that they were the only people on earth with curtains hanging in the bathroom, and complained that she thought it weird and creepy. But when the home was first built, before central air was installed, a breeze through that window on a hot summer night could turn a bath into a vacation. When the separate standing shower was added years later, the window, cranked open, allowed the shower steam to escape, saving the wooden floors from taking on unnecessary moisture that could lead to ruin. On the night that Freedom was born, the window had been lifted just enough to allow the summer breeze, however infrequent, to whisper across the room and soothe her mother, Monica, as she labored in the tub. A second station had been set up down the hall in Pop Walker and Mama Jeans en suite to wash the baby and take all of the necessary measurements while the tub was drained and cleaned, and Monica was allowed to towel off and put on clean clothes.

Once Free was born, just as planned, Mama Jean hustled to the kitchen to prepare a soothing tea for Monica, and the midwife began her work on the baby with speed and efficiency. However swift they thought themselves, neither the midwife nor Mama Jean were as fast as Monica. By the time baby Free had been bathed, wrapped, and weighed, Monica had dressed and slipped out of the house undetected with no plans of returning.

She didn't leave much behind in the way of explanation other than a handwritten note that said, "Please name her Freedom. I have nothing else to give her. I'm so sorry."

No one had expected that. Mama Jean had fretted for the first couple of weeks that Monica would turn up in the obituary Jane Doe section. "She could be bleeding out on the side of the road somewhere," she would whisper to her husband late at night. "She must be in pain." But Pop Walker was more than just a pastor; he was a man of unshakeable faith, and he would insist that God had Monica in His hands as he held his worried wife each night until she fell into a fitful sleep.

When she was younger, Free would constantly ask her grandparents to retell her birth story until they bristled or distracted her with something else. She would ask Mama Jean why her mother left, where she was now, and if she was ever coming back.

Mama Jean always had the same response. "Life is not about worrying over the folk that left, baby. Life is best spent loving the ones who stayed."

As Free became old enough to really understand what her mother had done, the story lost its shine and became a truth she wanted to avoid. But by then, she could not. The story played on a loop in Freedom's mind any time she found herself sitting in the quiet or standing in what was now her own bathroom, gazing through the anomalous bathroom window that had served as an unexpected path of escape from motherhood...from her. She began trying to drown out the sharp pain of the reminders by filling the quiet spaces with music, studying, or poetry. Anything but the silence. She stopped asking to hear the story, but by then, she didn't really need to hear it anymore anyway because she could feel it. It had become a part of her skin, her consciousness, and her identity. She clung to the bits of the story that made her feel strong, like a survivor. And she locked the rest of it in a place in her heart that was increasingly shuttered and cold, save for the letters that she wrote to her phantom mother.

The letters, first scrawled in a spiral notebook and later continued in two bound leather journals that she'd saved two months of allowance to buy, were to a mother that she had conjured for herself. They were the conversations she imagined she would share with the type of mother who would have stayed, rather than the one who had done a runner before her firstborn had reached room temperature. Each handwritten missive began with Dear Mom, and poured out whatever emotion or issue of the day was of concern. At times, the letters were lighthearted and witty. At others, the paper wound up warped and the ink blurred from her tears as they chased her pen across the page. But they always asked the pivotal question, why did you leave? By the time she reached her seventeenth year, the journals were swollen and softened from her frequent reading and rereading of each, trying to envisage the reaction she could have expected from the phantom mother she had invented.

Still, there was a small part of her birth story that Free didn't mind remembering. A single positive sign that she clung to in an otherwise ignominious story. Mama Jean always emphasized that Freedom did not cry when she was born. Mama Jean noted that she and the midwife had stared down at baby Free, covered in vernix and blood, waiting for the reassuring noise of a cry or bleat, the reassuring squall that generally accompanied new life - but it never came. Instead, Free's entrance to the world was marked by total silence. Monica, exhausted from the birthing, had let her head roll back against the cool edge of the tub, eyes shut and breathing shallow, barely aware of the eerie silence. Mama Jean, however, was fully dialed in and felt the first seeds of rising panic begin to form as a bead of sweat escaped down her back. She turned silently to the midwife, hoping not to alarm Monica.

The midwife, whose hands were busied with the task of clearing Free's mouth and nose of mucous with the bulb syringe, locked eyes with Mama Jean and shrugged. "She is breathing," she whispered in a hallowed tone. "She just isn't crying."

As Mama Jean framed it, Freedom must have known that there would be plenty of reasons to cry in this life, and decided that being born wasn't one of them.

Aside from not crying, Mama Jean's second favorite part of the birth story to tell was how everyone who saw little Freedom could not look away from her eyes. Her eyes were striking and unexpected, an ethereal honey gold base that appeared even more translucent in direct light. Flecks of blue and green would pop up as she turned her face this way and that under a summer sky. The midwife had trouble documenting the color and advised Mama Jean that the color may well change in the coming days, as babies' eyes sometimes do. For the time being, she marked them down on the birth form as hazel, but they were something more rare, more special than hazel. Either way, once Mama Jean began to take Free out on errands, those eyes captivated the attention of much of town and raised a lot of questions. Nosy country folk, as nosy country folk tend to do, wanted to know what the daddy's people looked like, which is just a roundabout way of asking who the daddy was without asking.

Mama Jean, whose serious reputation and distaste for gossip preceded her, never fielded such requests for information, so the answer remained unknowable and unverified. Never content to let a secret lay unexamined, there was plenty of gossip from the church congregation and neighbors trying to suss out an answer. A few of the local boys known to have been enamored with Monica had to endure months of accusatory whispers and glares as the possible culprits. But with Monica having spent the previous year at UCLA, miles away from their little corner of Texas, the local chatter eventually died down, and people settled into assuming that some college boy had gotten Monica pregnant and then sent her home to have the baby by herself.

With time, even those whispers faded into the background as more shocking and relevant mini-dramas took center stage and played out in the closely-knit black population of Jolivette. Church rivalries, cheating deacons, shady landlords—there was no shortage of distracting intel for those who liked to be in the know. Eventually, for the folk on their side of the tracks, Mama Jean and the blue green golden-eyed baby were just one more thread in the Jolivette tapestry. A tea that had gone too cold to serve.

Unfortunately for Freedom, kids, unlike adults, do not move on nor do they avoid questions that are rude or inappropriate, so Freedom didn't get the same reprieve that Mama Jean did. Her elementary classmates teased her relentlessly for being both motherless and fatherless. Though they became colder and more distant as she erected her own fiery wall of defense against her classmates, her eyes under her sweeping lashes, paired with her full lips, and regal bone structure continued to draw attention—some good, some not. Kind strangers would sometimes stop to tell her she was pretty. The not-so-kind ones would leer suggestively and make lewd overtures. Freedom met both types of interactions with the same measured reserve she was known for. True to her birth story, she was still not a crier. Her teachers described her as precocious or mature for her age on her report cards. But in truth, many of them found her confident aloofness to be unnerving.

She rarely averted her eyes or backed away from conversations with authority figures, a habit that tended to antagonize teachers and classmates alike. Instead, she would nod and show understanding of what was being said, her face registering obvious, unmistakable disdain, but she never responded in the tone that her face belied. Instead, she carefully chose words that left the listener unsure of whether they had been acknowledged or dismissed. When being redressed, she would never look away with fear or embarrassment. She would just let the words wash over her, her countenance unflinching and unrepentant until the speaker had concluded their thoughts. Then she would deploy her signature nod, curt and formal, and go on about her affairs.

A number of Mama Jean's friends and a few teachers over the years counted the habit as disrespect and let Mama Jean know that the girl was too grown and uppity for her own good. Mama Jean, a stalwart supporter of respect for elders, inexplicably found a tremendous amount of leeway with which to fiercely defend her granddaughter to others. But in private, she chided Free to soften her way and be more approachable. To her credit, Free tried to adjust, but she complained about the futility of the effort to Mama Jean.

"Why should I respond to their barbed comments if they haven't asked me a question worth responding to?" she'd complain. "People talk to me because they enjoy the sound of their voice, want me to stay in my place. That does not warrant a response from me. And why do they not want to meet my eyes as they try to humble me? What should I do- stare at my shoes?" she'd ask her grandmother in frustration.

Mama Jean would shake her head and laugh. "Well, that's why they don't want you looking at them," she'd replied, "Because they know that they aren't speaking truth, and don't want you to look at the lie."

Chapter 10

May 17th Carlos - The Coroner's Tea

Carlos crushed his half-smoked cigarette underfoot and hustled toward the rear door of the Jolivette Morgue. He'd picked up and quit smoking during his university years, but had suddenly felt compelled to grab a pack while gassing up the car before heading here. He silently reminded himself that he would have to quit again once this was all over. He signaled to his cameraman, who was parked just around the side of the building, that he was going in as he slipped through the entrance, which was rather fortuitously propped open while what appeared to be the groundkeeper sat in his truck eating lunch and listening to Tejano music at a deafening volume. It didn't take him long to hustle down the antiseptic-looking corridors and locate the office with the nameplate that read "Aaron Fletcher, Coronor, M.D., FOP." The door was closed, but he could see movement beyond the frosted glass, so he went ahead and knocked.

"It's open!" came the terse reply, and just that quickly, Carlos stepped into the conversation that changed his life.

Doctor Aaron Fletcher was not a young man. He looked to be teetering somewhere between 65 and 70 with a deep sorrel complexion and a beard that had gone all silver and white. His hair, apparently more determined than his beard to remain youthful, was more salt and pepper. He was dressed simply in a starched white shirt, black tie, and lab coat over pressed slacks, but he had the presence and grooming of a gentleman from some other, more dapper era in time. In fact, Carlos would not have been a bit surprised if Dr. Fletcher had pulled out a pocket watch to check the time. But he didn't. He wore wire-rimmed glasses that could have just as easily belonged to Benjamin Franklin and greeted Carlos with a stoic expression that gave Carlos the impression that the Dr. was not inclined toward humor. Carlos instantly registered that he was interrupting something important and therefore wasted no time on his usual attempts at charm.

Carlos introduced himself as a reporter from Houston who was covering the death of the rising Jolivette football star and stated that he understood the body had been brought here to Dr. Fletcher. He admitted that he did not know if there was any actual investigation going on, but was wondering if Dr. Fletcher had already completed his report and, if so, if he would be permitted to take a peek at it. Dr. Fletcher listened to his entire speech without expression.

After Carlos had exhausted his elevator pitch of purpose to ingratiate himself, Dr. Fletcher removed a small silver ball of tea leaves from the fine china cup on his desk and placed it on the equally ornate saucer. He stirred the steaming liquid with a tiny silver spoon and then placed it on the opposite side of the saucer. Carlos felt impatience crawling up the back of his neck as the Coroner took the slowest sip known to man and then replaced the cup to the saucer; but he held the silence, somehow innately aware that patience was the only thing that would be rewarded in this moment.

Apparently satisfied with the brew and temperature, Dr. Fletcher folded his hands on the desk and turned his attention back to Carlos. "How did you get in here?" he began.

Carlos mentioned the back door being propped open and saw a shadow of annoyance cross the doctor's face.

"And how old are you, son?"

This second question caught him off guard a little, but Carlos decided to consider the fact that he was being questioned rather than escorted out as a good sign and willingly answered it and the barrage of personal questions that followed.

"I'm 22, sir. Yes, I'm a television journalist, but I did an internship at the Chronicle and tried my hand at the newsies. No, I haven't won any awards...yet. No, my parents are not still together. My parents emigrated in their twenties, and my father returned to Jamaica when I was seven, but we stayed in touch. No, I'm not married. No, I don't have any children. My degree is from the University of Houston. Where is this going, sir?"

The coroner held eye contact but let Carlos' return question go unanswered so that the pause in conversation dragged into a long, awkward silence. Then, astoundingly, he smiled. Or at least Carlos thought he saw a nearly imperceptible smile of approval flit across Dr. Fletcher's face.

"I'll tell you what, Mr. Jackson," Fletcher said, joining his hands in a diamond just under his chin. "I don't like many people, and I don't particularly like you, but I don't DISLIKE you either. Maybe that's because you remind me a bit of myself. When I open these bodies, I am replacing speculation with fact, and I reckon that's what you aspire to do as well. I wanted to be a reporter way back when I was in knee pants, but when I was coming up, Black boys from around here weren't encouraged to have soft-edged dreams like that. You learned a hard science, or you picked up a trade. I chose science. And even then, I had to wait many years to be able to move back to my hometown and get this job because the good old boy system still reigns supreme in Jolivette, Texas."

"I say all that to say that I fought to get here, but I had a little help from some unexpected places. In the spirit of paying that forward, I am going to tell you something that can help you, but what you do with the information is far more important than the information itself, so you think about it real good before you make a move. And if it pans out for you, come back and see me. If it doesn't, I don't ever want to see you again. Do we have a deal?"

Carlos felt a sharp tingle of excitement ripple down his back and fought hard against the urge to yell out, "What is it!?"

He knew there was a warning embedded in Fletcher's chosen delivery, but his interest was now piqued to its bursting point.

"You've got a deal," he replied, extending his hand.

"Before you get too excited," Fletcher ignored Carlos' extended hand and started in like he was no hurry to get to the point, "My report is already with the police chief now and has likely been leveraged for a press release so you won't have much of a head-start on anyone else there, but there is something interesting in my original report that did not make it to the final version. If this gets out, a lot of folks are going to seem surprised. But I have lived in this place for a long time, and you should know that not everyone who acts surprised really is."

As Dr. Fletcher finished his disclaimers, he slid a small stack of papers towards Carlos, but never removed his hand from the pages. Carlos's eyes flitted across the top page, trying to make sense of what he was seeing and put it into context. There were markings on a human form outline and a host of medical terms. His mind zeroed in on the words "entry and exit," perhaps because of their simplicity, perhaps because they felt familiar.

Fletcher, having run out of either patience or time, filled in the rather large blank that Carlos was struggling to fill with the words in his line of vision.

"As you probably know, Eric was hit by a large commercial truck, and that is listed in the findings as what ultimately killed him. But before that truck ever got to him, he was hit with a whole mess of buckshot, which shattered his entire shoulder."

Fletcher tapped on the places that had been circled in red. Then, he pulled the papers back to his side of the desk.

"Does that help your story?"

Carlos fell back in his chair. He rubbed his hands over his face. He wanted to yell out; he wanted to dance; he wanted to cry. He knew there was something morbid and morally offensive about how excited he was to have just heard about a potential murder, but that didn't stop the feeling of euphoria from spreading out from his chest and radiating down his arms until his fingers tingled. He had a real story. No subtleties or innuendo—a legitimate, murder mystery, whodunit with a rich, white star quarterback and Black girl from the opposite side of the tracks at the center of it. He reached for the report, but the doctor pulled it back just out of his reach.

Carlos curled his fingers into his palm reluctantly, nodded his understanding, and then rose from his chair to half-walk, half-sprint back to his car. Maybe his feet never touched the ground. He couldn't remember. There was nothing whirring in his brain other than calculations on how long it would take him to get to city hall and break this story before some other plucky reporter convinced Dr. Fletcher to share information. He was not going to chance it.

***

Carlos stood on the steps of the local police station, which was rather conveniently sharing a parking lot with City Hall. He was taken aback by how quiet and unaffected the building appeared. Compared to the throngs of protesters, reporters, and general public that turned up in and around Houston PD following high-profile deaths, this town, its press, and its law enforcement appeared to be sleepwalking. He reminded himself that most of the town was just waiting for the name of a trucking company toward which to direct their rage over this senseless accident, so perhaps there wasn't much to get riled up about for them, but he was planning to upset that apple cart.

The little local newspaper coverage had focused on the family's importance to the city and called for swift justice while discussing the danger of over-tired, long-haul truck drivers. The entire ordeal had been painted as a tragic hit-and-run. No mention of a girl or a gun. The writer had asked that consideration for the Tucker family be shown in their state of immense grief.

In the 97 minutes Carlos had to kill waiting on his station to send the all-clear to run the live coverage segment, Carlos managed to Google and record-search his way a bit deeper into the Tucker name and reach out to his favorite chatterbox by phone, Shelly. She'd helped fill in the pieces that connected the dots on an image of an entire city ecosystem built and operating under the thumb of a single family. The town Mayor was and has always been a Tucker. The immaculate field that the high school football teams both in Jolivette and surrounding cities played on was named Tucker Stadium. Jolivette Gazzette, the local newspaper, was Tucker-owned. The high school principal was a Tucker cousin by marriage. The school district superintendent was a Tucker by birth, and there were acres and acres of Tucker land stretching from the edge of town and across the county, all yielding both crops and cattle. On a gut feeling, he'd looked up the local sheriff, assuming he'd find the Tucker name. Instead, he found Grant Oltorf. Not a bloodline Tucker, but married to one who was a former Miss Texas and happened to be the sitting mayor's sister.

Carlos also spent a considerable amount of time and charm getting Shelly to help identify the mystery girl with the flat tire she'd mentioned, who was allegedly the only witness to the accident. Shelly, insisting she couldn't afford to be caught providing a minor's name or identity to a reporter, gave Carlos the name of the girl's next of kin instead and told him he should be smart enough to figure it out from there. Getting the information had cost him a great deal of dignity and almost five minutes of something very close to dirty talk, but Shelly had delivered, and Carlos was filled with gratitude for not writing her off after his first encounter with her.

Carlos hung up with his station manager and signaled with a curt nod to his cameraman, Ralph, that they were cleared to go live in 20 seconds. He blew out a deep breath, shifted his jaw back and forth, and did his best to still his racing heart. He pulled a series of ridiculous faces, each escalating in absurdity until he was fairly certain he'd worked the tension and stiffness from his face that could lead to stuttering and stumbling over the copy he'd written and already committed to memory.

As he stepped out of Ralph's van, the air smelled muggy as the morning's earlier rainstorm evaporated and steamed upward under the Texas sun. The steps to the police station were all but deserted, save a few folk speaking tersely in the parking lot as they secured children in car seats, undoubtedly doing mandatory custody exchanges of divorce-casualty kids, a childhood hell that he was all too familiar with. Yup, no more parking lot kid swaps for him. Ralph waved a hand to get his attention and started the five-second countdown to go live. Carlos cleared his throat at four, popped his knuckles, shook his hands out by two, and was the epitome of collected confidence by one, listening to the desk anchor in his ear toss the show to him.

"Good afternoon, and thank you, Steven. I am live in Jolivette, Texas, a quaint town known for its rich history of successful cattle ranching and often celebrated for launching high school athletes onto a road of professional success. But today, a day that should be marked by happy preparation for graduations, college commitments, and pep rallies to herald the graduating members of Jolivette's star athletes who recently made an excellent showing at state championships, the town is instead somber and quiet-marked by mourning."

Carlos gestured widely to note the inactivity outside the police station, but from the corner of his eye, he could see that he was drawing a small patch of onlookers who'd noticed the recognizable station letters on Ralph's camera.

"Nearly two days ago," he continued, "Eric Tucker, high school football star and son of the sitting mayor, Andrew Tucker, was tragically killed on a small county road just south of here when he stopped to help a female classmate in car trouble."

Carlos felt a familiar electricity buzz through him as he leaned into the camera to deliver the big finish.

"But while the city mourns his death, the police seem to be asleep at the wheel. Even as the papers continue to report that Eric was hit by an 18-wheeler, our sources reveal that the Jolivette police are in possession of a detailed autopsy report clearly indicating that Eric was murdered, shot at close range, and left to die on that dark stretch of highway."

Carlos heard a series of incredulous gasps and murmurings begin in his small police-step audience. He stared into the camera, imagining himself in living rooms all over Houston.

"Why haven't the police disclosed this murder? What are they hiding here in Jolivette, Texas?" Carlos finished with flourish, not aware that he had drawn the attention of more than just bystanders.

The uniformed officer was on him before he'd even realized someone was approaching, and Carlos's microphone was slammed to the ground. Carlos threw up his hands, but the fury in the officer's eyes did not fade in the slightest as he leaned his body into Carlos, forcing him to stumble backward and lose his footing.

"You are not authorized to be here. Get the hell out of here boy! You are on municipal property!" the officer roared as he shoved his weight against Carlos again.

At 6 foot 2 inches and 200 pounds, Carlos was not a small guy, but in dress shoes and having never regained his initial footing, the officer's shove was enough to send him to the ground. As he went down, he craned his neck to see if Ralph was still getting the footage, but Ralph was locked in a dangerous game of tug-of-war with another officer over his camera. Carlos could hear the anchor in his earpiece asking him if he was okay, so he knew he was still on air. He scrambled to grab his microphone and took the opportunity to loudly narrate the abrupt turn of events while struggling to get to his feet.

"Several officers have come storming out of the precinct and are physically assaulting us. We have done nothing wrong. This is public property. We were not previously asked to leave and were therefore not trespassing. Please do not break our equipment, sir!"

Carlos grabbed again for the microphone that the officer had just snatched from his grip. Thankful for his years of college football training, Carlos rolled right, breaking the officer's grasp while snatching his equipment back, and leaped down the stairs, four at a time. Carlos scanned the scene as he ran and saw that Ralph was headed for the van at full speed with the camera returned to its place on the gimbal anchored to his waist, so he'd no doubt come out triumphant in the tug-of-war.

Carlos faked left to avoid another approaching officer, then scrambled right through the parked cars and across the lot. He jumped on the van's running board and yanked the door open just as Ralph was hitting the gas, threw himself into the seat, and yanked the door shut behind him. He heaved in the air to catch his breath and caught Ralph's eye as they cleared the parking lot and slowed to a regular speed. They shared a look, eyes glimmering and adrenaline pumping. A slow smile spread across Ralph's face, and Carlos knew that he was reading his mind. They had a story. They'd just become breaking news. They had a scoop. He could almost smell the accolades. Visions of award season danced in his head. This was happening for him. Maybe he'd taken a few small liberties in retelling the details of the autopsy report. But he'd worry about that later. Right now, he had momentum.

Chapter 11

May 18th Andrew - The Last Thread

Andrew sunk deeper into the leather seat of his car. He had pushed the button that cut the engine nearly 40 minutes ago, and yet here he remained. He could hear the soft rain pattering onto the garage roof and streaming in rivulets along the gutters. With the car off and the air not blowing, the temperature in the garage had quickly become too stuffy. Yet, he could not bring himself to exit the car and re-enter the world. Here in the car, time did not exist. Here, responsibilities and arrangements, funerals, and slowly lowering coffins did not exist.

He couldn't really recall much of the funeral anyway. Everything seemed to have rushed by in a blur. He had shaken all of the hands and nodded solemnly to the endless parade of well-wishing faces. He had wrapped his arms around his wife and walked, or slightly dragged, her back towards her seat when she wailed and laid across the closed casket. Eric wasn't even in the casket. His body had been cremated. Andrew felt the squeezing sensation in his chest as the memories of identifying Eric at the coroner's office slashed into his consciousness again.

The worst part of it all was the swarming buzz of the hungry media. From the moment he'd left the coroner's office, he had been meticulous about shielding Becca from any information that would exacerbate her grief. He had taken her phone for the first day, disconnected the internet, and removed the TV from their bedroom. He probably hadn't needed to do any of that since she'd barely gotten out of bed other than to shuffle to the restroom for three days. Her already slender frame looked gaunt now, despite his insistence that she eat something…anything.

They'd entered the funeral through the rear doors of Jolivette First Episcopal church without harassment, but as they exited through the main doors, following the casket, things had gone downhill quickly. An unexpected horde of reporters rocked both him and Rebecca back on their heels. Rebecca, already partially shielded behind large sunglasses, covered the rest of her face with the black scarf she'd had wrapped around her shoulders, and Andrew instinctively shielded her with his body, but there was nothing he could do to silence the crude questions shouted indiscriminately by the throng.

"Mayor Tucker! There are rumors online that Eric's death was not an accident and that he had been shot!"

"Who do you think shot him?"

"Was he into drugs?"

"Do you know the girl he was with? Were they romantically involved?"

Drew had felt Becca's body go stiff as steel in his arms, and she wrestled free from his hold to face the reporters.

"WHAT DID YOU SAY?" she screeched.

Andrew pulled her back to him, trying unsuccessfully to shield her face with his jacket as her scarf slipped away.

"Get out of here! You jackals!" he yelled, trying to move his wife forward to the waiting car.

"You didn't know he'd been shot?" yelled another reporter, shoving a microphone towards his wife.

Andrew felt himself filling with rage. It would be so easy to just start swinging into the crowd, but that was exactly what had caused his family's grief to morph into a viral sensation for public consumption in the first place—his idiot brother-in-law shoving that loud-mouthed reporter on live TV had started a firestorm he was having trouble keeping a lid on. No one had proof that Eric had been shot, but that hadn't stopped the story from spreading.

Andrew scowled into the sea of faces. Their jackets and microphones were emblazoned with random frequency letters and locations: KVI3Houston, WZG2Dallas, Austin, San Antonio, El Paso, and destinations farther like Tampa, Florida, Oklahoma City, and Arkansas.

He could barely believe it. Andrew knew that this was his fault somehow. He was the one who had arranged a media interview for Eric to get him wider exposure to college football programs, and the very kid who was sent to Jolivette to do the interview had broken the story about the autopsy report instead. He couldn't prove it yet, but Andrew was sure that his brother had something to do with the leak. John never could be trusted to keep his trap shut. Andrew's cellphone had been ringing nonstop since the story aired. He'd turned it off along with Rebecca's. He had told himself it was to protect Becca, but now he realized he was protecting himself too. He knew that when she discovered that he had withheld information, the last thread in their threadbare relationship would snap.

He'd always known that he couldn't keep the truth from Becca forever, but he thought he would have a little more time. How could the press possibly believe a funeral was an acceptable place to accost the family with questions? The very idea was monstrous, and yet here they were. They were nothing more than vultures circling a story.

Drew had managed to hustle Becca into the limousine and was shutting the door behind her when she looked up at him.

"You aren't coming?" she asked, her voice barely above a raspy whisper.

"I can't," he replied, never meeting her gaze.

She had paused with her hand on the door and asked, "Is what they are saying true?"

Andrew shifted uncomfortably, looking for the right words. She didn't wait for him to find them. She pulled the door shut and left him standing on the curb, reporters at his back, his heart full of regret. That's all he ever seemed to have anymore. Regret. Maybe he should have told her everything from the start, but he was so sure he was protecting her. God, how had everything backfired so completely?

After the funeral, Drew had just driven around wasting time, avoiding the hurricane he knew was brewing at home. But even once he arrived, he couldn't go in. He'd pulled the small flask from his pocket, still unable to will himself from the car. By now, his wife would be home from the repass, and with all of the Tuckers in one place like that, whatever anger she'd felt towards him at the church was probably magnified by now.

What do I have left? Andrew thought as he felt the warm liquid from the flask burn and then warm him all the way down to his center. He wasn't sure whether he had thought the question or asked it aloud, but he formed the question again and held it just behind his closed eyes as he took another long pull from the flask.

What do I have left? He had always prided himself on being rational, logical, and methodical. He loved to take inventory of things, situations, and circumstances and walk through the benefits, challenges, and options.

*What do I have...*he thought again. He asked himself this question often when he felt trapped, discontent, and ready to bolt from the pressures of his work and family.

He could remember vividly the day he sat in his father's office, listening to him provide an inventory of what he had and what he stood to lose. At the time, Andrew was 19 and in love. He had strode into that office, resolved to argue passionately for his cause but instead sat under the intimidating gaze of his father and all of the big game animals, stuffed, mounted, and staring down from the office walls, slowly losing his nerve altogether. He'd wanted to get married, strike out on his own, and start something new. Basking in the electrifying glow of his first, great love, he thought the possibilities were endless. But his father asked him, "Would you give up all that you have—all that we have sacrificed for you, to run after some impossible dream of a love that will vanish as quickly as you imagine it to have appeared?"

Andrew had opened his mouth to argue, but his father had walked him through the inventory of what was on the line: a guaranteed lucrative career waiting for him, the family business, and a good life with plenty of beautiful children that could follow in his footsteps. His father then switched to all of the people Andrew would alienate by deviating from the plan they had all invested in for his life.

"Son, you can always have whatever little piece of tail you fancy on the side. Plenty of Tuckers have enjoyed their romps on the dark side. But you have a duty to marry well and continue this family's legacy here."

He had listened to his father as the list ran on and on, disgusted by the realization that his father had so cavalierly thrown out the phrase "The dark side." His father continued drilling into the flaws in Andrew's plan to build a life with his high school sweetheart and how naïve and unaware of the world he was. And without so much as a raised voice, Andrew had folded. He had walked away from that great big love, convinced by his father, a man married at that time for 40 years, that love was not enough to sustain a relationship. That tradition and family loyalty are the only true foundations of a lasting marriage.

Yet, despite what his father had assured him, nothing and no one had been able to replace that big love for him, not even Becca, God bless her. And what had he gained from that devil's trade? Had he really needed that Ivy League degree just to come home and run the town that his family already owned most of? Had he really needed his father's money to buy a piece of land that no one in the town would have denied him?

His mother loved to brag that he was the youngest mayor in the history of Jolivette, but he could have run and won the seat with just his name. No one cared or doubted his plans or policy. They assumed every step he took would be in lockstep with every decision that had preceded him. He was a Tucker, a Jolivette Tucker. And the Tuckers had an unrivaled formula for success. Who would have seriously challenged a Tucker son? And then there was Becca herself.

She was widely thought to be the prettiest girl in town all through high school, and she had waited for him. She'd been glad to bask in his attention the few times he visited home from college, and then she'd married him and moved to the west coast to keep up his apartment and cook his meals as he waded through graduate school. She'd never complained once. She'd given him a son and then endured countless miscarriages while trying to build their family. And for what? Now he sat with her, in near silence, at almost every dinner because the effort at straining for conversation that could hold both of their attention was too great. Maybe it was all the loss, baby after baby, that began to drive the silence between them like a wedge. But they still had Eric. At least up until this tragedy, they'd had Eric to hold them together, a shared commitment and purpose.

So now what? Eric was gone, and his Becca had transformed from distant to a haunted shadow of herself in a matter of days. Drew was suddenly and painfully aware that he had made a bad trade. He stared blindly at the steering wheel, fighting back the pain threatening to overtake him. Finally, he shoved the flask into the glove compartment and headed into the house. He could not afford to cry, not in front of Becca. The lights on the first floor were all off, and as he walked up the stairs, he knew. It wasn't just one thing but rather the totality of all the things he did not feel or hear or smell as he rounded the hallway to their master bedroom that made him realize she was gone.

Chapter 12

May 18th Angel - End of an Era

It was uncharacteristically hot in LA for May, Angel and her friend Yami had sought a reprieve sitting in a gorgeously appointed velvet and leather booth in one of the city's newest swanky sports bistros. The gleaming mahogany bar with gold railings and plush velvet and leather accents gave off a high-end lounge feeling, but the endless and enormous televisions angled down from the joints where the high walls met the even higher ceilings made it clear that the space was curated for high rollers who had parlays in the sports betting world.

"The key to seeing and being seen in a town like this is to have access to the places that no one knows about yet," Angel was explaining to Yami.

"That way, you ensure that the place is not yet overrun with the Instagram girls, fresh off the BBL table. The who's who will show up while it's new, relatively assured that the paparazzi aren't onto the spot yet. They will have been invited because they know the chef, the restaurant financiers, or the realty firm that leased the space. We get a table and keep them laughing and drinking, and the house will cut us in. Got it?" Angel was explaining the deal she had with La Rev's owner to drive traffic to his grand opening.

Today's pop-up at La Rev was purely a reconnaissance mission. The goal was to have lunch, be gorgeous, and see what type of old money or new long money walked through the doors. Then, when they returned, it would be as dates of men with money to blow on sports bets and bottles.

Angel looked around at the large flat screens, each playing a different sporting event or news station. *Interesting*, she thought. *Definitely didn't expect news, but perhaps they want to draw in some thinkers too.* Then she turned her attention to food.

"What are you thinking about ordering?" she mused as she began to scan the menu. "Did you hear me? Yami?" she asked, looking up to see why her friend had gone quiet.

Yami was watching the television intently with her eyes furrowed. Angel turned to see what was on the screen that Yami was glued to, but whatever story they were teasing had gone to commercial.

"What is it?"

Yami kissed her teeth in disapproval before responding. "Well, you know every summer as soon as the kids are outside, all of the "accidental" police killings of Black boys and flocks of Karens start showing up..."

"Oh, sure," Angel said, turning back to her menu.

Angel had been outrunning the trauma of folk killing, stealing, and destroying Black lives with impunity her entire life. She was not even remotely interested in watching reminders of it on her off day.

"Well, I thought things seemed to be getting a little better or at least quieter," Yami went on.

Angel let out a sarcastic "PPPFft" at the unspoken reminder that Yami had an intense enthusiasm for and optimism about social justice that she only ever flexed during high-brow, left-wing parties or when she had roped Angel into watching CNN in an endless loop while eating Chinese and trying out new hydrating face masks. Angel could never relate to Yami's silver lining; things are looking up Disney outlook.

Angel knew Yami was too pie in the sky when she had gotten the covid-flu-strep throat combo last year, and instead of sinking into the misery of the situation, had instead celebrated hitting her goal weight due to what was basically involuntary starvation.

"It will never slow down. And it will never stop," Angel said flatly, unwilling to embrace Yami's toxic positivity. "Because white people will NEVER get tired of grinding Black people under their heels. It is more than just a sport for them. It is a way of life. Black people will always be the backs that the rest of society stands on to get a better view."

Yami's brows shot up, and she turned to look directly at her friend, surprised by this rare display of emotion and even more shocked at the dark, heated cynicism that coated her words. Angel had always been a realist, but that last comment felt like something personal and tinged by hopeless resolve. Yami considered her words carefully before responding. She knew this conversation was new territory for their friendship.

"Well, I won't tell you what to believe," she started. "But you know that I have always maintained that there are good, enlightened white folk in the fight for justice also. And it felt like we were making collective progress these last few months. There is a real solidarity emerging. People are tired of the hate. They are starting to see through the orchestrated infighting that only benefits the uber rich."

Angel rolled her eyes and kept perusing the menu.

"Anyway," Yami went on, "I was just going to point out that whatever positive coalition-building momentum we are seeing won't last very long if rich white boys start turning up dead this summer."

"What do you mean?" Angel said, her hackles rising. "Are you telling me that if a white boy is killed, you think it will be open season on Black lives? Is that what you were watching? Because I can tell you now, that the folk who don't like us don't need an excuse. They can invent one. A little private school suburban Dennis the Menace looking kid could die from an asthma attack, and they wouldn't even do an investigation - they'd just pin it on whatever Black kid was walking by when he hit the ground. Never mind that most people are killed by someone who looks like them in their own personal circle. Logic goes right out the window when there's a Black scapegoat that's more convenient. And I see you looking at me like I'm crazy, but I was born into that reality. I don't know how life was for you in Panama before you came to LA, but in the U.S. of A. nothing is getting better." Angel was gesticulating wildly, her hands punctuating every word she said. "Who on this earth is more singularly dangerous than a white person who knows they can lay the blame for all of their wrongdoings at the feet of any conveniently unprotected Black person?"

Yami's brows shot up again as she processed what she was hearing. She and Angel had been running around the L.A. scene for nearly a decade, and their typical night out included charming men—and sometimes women—of all races, creeds, and colors to secure high tips and access to exclusive events. Not once had she seen Angel recoil or even hesitate at the idea of a night in the company of a good old-fashioned, run-of-the-mill, white guy, young or old. Was it possible that this latent hostility had always been there, simmering just below the surface of Angel's perfectly calm façade? Plenty of the guys they crossed paths with had been cocky narcissists, fetishizing Angel's dark, glowing skin and big face-framing coils. Angel would have had plenty of opportunities to lash out if she wanted to.

In fact, most men were drawn to Angel as though she were a tall exotic rarity, with her deep, brown skin, smooth and unmarked; thick, perfect cupid bow lips, curving hips, gravity-defying bottom, and dancer's slim waist. Her hair always entered the room before she did, big and wide and long, textured strands sweeping the middle of her back.

She wore it curly or blown out, but never, ever silk pressed or bone straight. Angel was the black woman that non-black men went looking for when they decided that they wanted to date a black woman. She was also the black woman that other women saved photos of to take to their surgeons. Yet, she had always let every loaded statement, open stare, jealous dig, and objectifying comment slide right by as if she hadn't even heard it. So to Yami, this pissed and fuming Angel before her, railing against racism and white folk in general, felt like a complete stranger. She considered dropping the subject, but instead tried once again to make her point.

"I hear you, Angel," Yami said cautiously. "And you may be right about how seriously the cops will or won't investigate, but I've seen people in these rural, backwards places overreact in the most terrifying ways when they think a white child has died at the hands of a minority. And from the way that reporter was just describing it, Jolivette, Texas could be this summer's powder keg."

Yami turned back to the screen where the newscast had returned from break, and in doing so, missed Angel's expression change from sour to shocked. Angel twisted quickly around in the booth so she could see the newscast, just as the entire screen filled with the photo image of a handsome young man. His hair was a tussle of youthful golden curls, and although he couldn't have been more than 18 years old, he was built like an athlete. His neck and shoulders were so broad, that even beneath the material of the football jersey he was wearing, you could almost guess his life story of two-a-day practices, multiple sports, and year-round lifting.

Angel's jaw dropped open, and her hand involuntarily rose to press against her chest to halt the rising unease in her body. The family features were unmistakable. The captions continued to play across the screen. Young son of City Mayor...Tucker...allegedly gunned down then run over...unnamed witness at the scene...anyone with information asked to come forward...

The photo on the screen then changed to a late model burgundy SUV, sitting abandoned on the side of a road, surrounded by crime tape. The camera angle zoomed in to show a small cross made of dried palm leaves swinging in the front windshield. Memories of making the exact same small ornaments on Palm Sunday in her father's church flew across Angel's consciousness, and then she noticed the bible sitting on the dashboard of the vehicle and Angel froze.

"Angel...Angel...Angel!" Yami's voice finally broke through the fog, although Angel was not sure how long Yami had been calling her name.

She pulled her eyes from the screen and tried to focus on breathing in and out.

"Angel, are you okay?" Yami said, touching her arm. "You look like you've seen a ghost!"

Angel's fingers fumbled for her clutch that had slid over to the corner of the booth.

"I have to go," she said, pulling her arm away from Yami and standing up.

"What's wrong?" Yami asked, looking panicked.

"It's nothing...it's...I don't feel well," Angel stuttered out, trying to recover.

"Okay, wait a second!" Yami rose to her feet as well. "I drove you! Let me just get the check first for the drinks."

Angel nodded, but when Yami turned to flag down the waiter, Angel headed for the door instead while hailing a ride on her Uber app. It was downtown L.A., so the car had pulled up before she reached the end of the block, and just like that, Angel was headed home.

Chapter 13

May 19th Free - Trapped

Free moved silently about the room, selecting her favorite clothing and essentials. She knew it was all over. Her life was over. She and everyone else in the developed world had seen the newscasts that were now popping up everywhere, so anonymity would soon be off the table with the college acceptance and scholarship funds right behind it.

In the days after Eric's death, things had been so quiet that she'd allowed herself to believe that the entire ordeal might just be chalked up to an accident. She'd started to imagine a reality where life just returned to something normal, a normal she now realized that she had very much taken for granted. In all of her anger and angst about living in Jolivette, surrounded by expectations and social hierarchies that should have been buried with the last generation of grand dragons, it had never dawned on her, even once, that there were things she would miss about her life. That being overlooked and ignored, while demoralizing, was also an advantage in a world that likes to dissect and then destroy the objects of its attention.

At this moment in time, she should have been finalizing her valedictorian speech and preparing for her move to the east coast over the summer, where she'd already accepted a full ride scholarship to Columbia University. If Eric's death had been simply noted as a tragic accident, she'd have been prepared to let the dust settle and then return to school sometime the following week. But it was now apparent that this wasn't going to blow over as an accident. Someone knew that Eric had been shot, and now everyone knew. When she finally caved to her own curiosity and logged into her burner social account, she was horrified to discover that not only was it being discussed as though murder was a foregone conclusion - there was a growing social media sleuth community mobilizing around the quest for answers and accountability.

She continued folding and packing only the most necessary items from her room as her mind raced a hundred directions, chasing down every worst case scenario it could muster. She paused at the pretty cardboard boxes stacked neatly beneath her desk, decorated in a print of poppies and peonies, with reinforced silver metallic corners. The box held journal after journal of letters, short stories, and poems she had been writing since she could hold a pencil. For a moment, she considered moving past them, but couldn't resist the urge to sit and open at least one. She flipped through a journal, some written in her early childish script, others scrawled in her angry, hyper loopy middle school style, and stopped on a page that caught her eye.

Hi Mom,

I hope you are okay. I have so many questions for you and about you. Did you get any of my cards? I make a card for you every year on your birthday, and Mama Jean mails them to you for me. I thought that maybe you would write back, or call to say you got them. I would like to talk to you. Do you ever think about me? I am afraid to ask you, so I will just write it all down here.

Love, Free age 7

Dear Mom,

Things are really hard here. Pop Pop died. The house feels strange and empty now. Mama Jean is very quiet all of the time. She prays under her breath all day and all night. I can't make out what she is saying, but sometimes she starts singing PopPop's favorite hymns, and the tears come. Sometimes she can't finish because of the tears, so I sing the song for her. Do you know this song, Mom?

Precious Lord, take my hand
Lead me on, help me stand
I am tired, I'm weak, I am worn
Through the storm, through the night
Lead me on to the light
Take my ha-and, precious Lor-ord
Lead me home

When I sing it for Mama Jean, she sits with her eyes closed until I finish, and I know that we are missing Pop Pop together. She says it's just us now, but that's not true. It's not just us. Somewhere out there, we have you too. Don't you want to come home? Mama Jean said you are chasing dreams, but can't you come and visit at least? How long does it take to catch a dream? Maybe I can come with you and help. Maybe there is room in your dream for me.

Love, Free Age 10

Free slid the book back into the box and grabbed another slender journal. She flipped quickly towards the back, letting her eyes roam over the entries in the slanted writing that always accompanied her anger.

Monica,

I'm writing you this letter knowing that you will never see it. But if I don't write the words, they build up in my chest and begin to ache. I can't even bring myself to call you mom anymore. When have you ever been a mother? I used to wish and pray that you would come home, but now I hope you never do. You don't deserve to come home. Pop Pop wished and waited for you to come home until he died, and for what? He left this world with a broken heart because you just couldn't come and check on him. Your own father. So I suppose I shouldn't be surprised that you don't ever check on me either. Do you know what my life is like? I'm a joke to everyone. A sad, rejected kid. Is that the life you thought I deserved? Well, guess what… I don't need you. All of these years, I thought I did, but today I realized that if you don't need me, then I don't need you either.

> *Free, Age 14*

> *Hello Monica,*
>
> *Today, Gramma talked about you a bit, something that she almost never does. I know it was only because I upset her. I didn't mean to, but I hate this place. This town, these people, the way that the whole place feels like it is frozen in time. Jolivette feels like every civil rights movie and book I have ever read, but without any of the heroes. I don't fit in anywhere. I am one of the smartest kids in my class, but some of these kids will still call me a stupid n*gger any chance they get. Why? What have I done? Who have I*

offended by just being alive? There are only a few other Black kids at the school, and I haven't made big fans of them either. Mama Jean says this is because I am standoffish. I don't have the heart to tell her that standoffish is not a word. But there is a reason I keep to myself. The topics that my classmates want to talk about don't mean anything to me. They discuss things like who kissed who under the bleachers…who cares? The bleachers are still in Jolivette, which means that I am trying to put them and everyone under them in my rearview mirror. I've been studying the history of Jolivette for my AP history course, and it's really just one family taking over everything. The truth of this city and my place in it made me so upset that I told Mama Jean today that I cannot wait to leave this horrible town. She did not take it well. Her face looked like it turned to stone. She said I was just like you, always running away. She said that from the time you were twelve until you graduated high school, all you ever wanted to do, all you ever talked about was leaving Jolivette - leaving her. She said that life is hard everywhere and only dreamers think that changing locations is better than growing where you are planted. For the first time in my life, I almost felt like I understood you…understood why you left. I think I know why you couldn't stay in this town; a town that slowly suffocates the life out of anything special or worthy if it's not a Tucker. Still, while I understand the feeling, I will never understand why you couldn't take me with you. Why would you leave me here in a place that was bad enough for you to want to escape? You cursed me with the exact life that wasn't good enough for you, and took any chance of me having a mother or father with you. I will never forgive you for that.

>   *Free, Age 15*

>   *Monica,*

>   *Mothers are supposed to protect, a job you decided was beneath you. You left me to fend for myself against an evil that is so concentrated and complete that no one can stop it. Eric Tucker has been basically stalking me, and he is pure evil. It vibrates from inside him and radiates from his skin. He is terrifying and determined, and he has set his sights on me. He is rich, and his family is powerful. His family is the police and the school administrators. No one can touch him. And what am I? Motherless, fatherless, cast onto my grandmother's pile of burdens with no defenders in sight. I can't escape him. Everyone notices Eric, but he seems to only notice me. His smile is the scariest thing I have ever seen. It never reaches his eyes, and even his laughter is cruel. He sucks all of the air from the room when he walks in, and he always gets what he wants. What he wants right now is to break me. That's what you left me here to fight. Alone. That is your legacy to me, Monica. You named me*

Free, then left me in a cage with the lions. I hope you never know joy.

> *Free, Age 16*

> *Monica,*
>
> *I want you to know that I am going to survive this place. I am going to be worth everything you didn't believe I was worth. And then I am going to find you. And when I do, you will understand what my name really means.*

Free read the last two entries, fear and anger pricking the backs of her eyes and building a lump in her throat. Then she tore the pages from the journal and began shredding them into thin ribbons with her hands.

Chapter 14

May 19 Carlos - Chasing the Lead

Carlos sat at the cheap hotel room desk, drumming his ballpoint pen against the peeling laminate as he ran back through his notes. He finally had the station's attention, and although they were sending additional resources, rather than feeling elated, he only felt the mounting pressure to deliver. He'd already had two prime time spots since he broke the Jolivette story and was being referred to as the chief correspondent on location. Other stations that were late to the party had to quote his report in order to update their viewers; but now the town was full of news vans, and the sharks were swarming. He would have to work harder to continue to scoop the other stations, and so far, his only consistent weapon was front desk Shelly. He ran back through the rough timeline and potential headlines he had pieced together.

· High School Football Player's Rising Star is Shot Down (Eric) o Mayor's Son/Well connected/Elite

       Varsity rising highschool junior

· Hometown Hero Run Down By 18-wheeler ~~accident~~ (foul play suspected)

    · Who shot Eric Tucker?

       o Local police (some related to the victim's father) are intentionally not reporting on the shooting

    · Who could have done it (No suspects announced)

       o Lead from Shelly - One high school girl on the scene at the time of death (Walker is the last name on county records for address)

Carlos had already located at least 75 Walkers in the Jolivette population of 100,000. The list was too long, so he had moved on to googling local news articles about the high school, hoping that the girl was some sort of standout UIL competitor or athlete. He needed a photo, but because she was a minor and hadn't been named yet in the media, her name was the only piece of information he had left that nobody else had. He had two options at his disposal to find the girl. One was to return to the information well of Spill the Tea Shelly. Alternatively, he could tap into the endless source of incriminating oversharing that was minors with smartphones. He decided on option two and spent most of the morning taking on the persona of a bored and sarcastic teenager on Snapchat, Twitter, and Instagram. His account handle, @RunThisTown, had already friended and been friended by nearly 300 accounts as he rapid-fire posted messages and images he'd shot locally on his phone with #RIPEricTucker and #JolivetteStrong tags. There was no shortage of images to use as makeshift memorials popped up at the accident site, the high school, and some of the local teen hangouts.

Nationally, the chatter was exactly what you would expect from the crime-cast junkies and polarized corners of the nation. Conjecture, allegations that this was the start of a war on white people, chased by allegations that this was a frame job to create political unrest. The hot takes and conspiracy drivel was so constant and poorly constructed on social media that Carlos felt himself yawning as his eyes skimmed through the vitriol. It was nearly noon before he'd finally gotten deep enough into the algorithm to discover the real, local Jolivette post' matrix and find the type of post he was hoping for. #WhokilledEricTucker was now trending, and users with Jolivette High School in their profiles were weighing in. In Carlos's opinion, there was no place more ripe with solid leads than unsupervised teens on the internet. The problem was that there was also a great deal of lies, dead ends, and falsehoods in that crowd too. But if you were willing to sift through the garbage, there were diamonds, and he finally stumbled onto one.

Topic: Justice for Eric

@WhoShotETucker	This is crazy, guys! The news is saying that Eric was not just hit by a truck. He was shot! Who would kill Eric Tucker? #justiceforEric
@Ilovetaylorswift	No way! Like SHOT shot? It was a murder? I thought it was a hit-and-run.
@weedislife	Yo! We've got a real-life murder mystery in JTown. Legit.
@FootballGod27	Probably a rival team bro! We were about to take it all

	at the State Championship next year. #justiceforEric
@CatsnKittens	Are you ***** serious blockhead? No one cares that much about high school football. A kid is dead, and you are thinking about a game? Who would want to kill Eric?
@GetOut	The real question is who WOULDN'T want to kill Eric Tucker? He was a douche.
@FootballGod27	OMG! Somebody block this troll. Not cool bro.
@GetOut	LOL! Block me then. You know I'm right. Was there a worse human on earth than that guy? Sociopath in

	the making.
@CatsnKittens	So not cool. You shouldn't talk **** about the dead.
@WeedisLife	Ah **** this is getting good now. BRB. Need to grab a snack for this.
@GetOut	What? Y'all want to pretend he is a hero now? He wouldn't piss on a single one of you if you were on fire, but now we have to say nice things. Hard pass.
@FootballGod27	Whatever keyboard warrior. Easy to talk sh** with no profile pic and a fake name. I bet you wouldn't be saying all that to his friends' faces. Maybe

	you did it!
@GetOut	Of course you would cape for him, Trevor. You were just as bad as he was. What happened on Tracy Jackson's birthday, hunh? Why did she transfer out of JHS her senior year? I heard you were in the room. Since you are a big Eric fan, why don't you tell us.
@GetOut	Oh, now you're all quiet.
@GetOut	Where'd you go @FootballGod27? I thought you wanted to talk.
@GetOut	No response. I guess he's busy now. Coward.

Carlos could smell dirt. He sent a direct message:

@RunThisTown	Hey @GetOut whatever DID happen to Tracey? I never knew why she left.
@GetOut	Yea well the school did a pretty good job of covering it up. But anyone at that party knows what really happened and that it wasn't the first time.
@RunThisTown	I guess I wasn't cool enough to get invited.
@GetOut	Count yourself lucky. Eric was good at a lot of things with the #1 thing being taking what he wanted and using family money to cover his tracks.

@RunThisTown	Hell yea. That Tucker money is long.
@GetOut	Yea long and dirty. SMH
@RunThisTown	Yo I looked up their family history and that whole family tree seems shady AF!
@GetOut	Shady is not even the half of it. They are thieves. Land, money, and bodies. If they want it, they can buy it. If you won't sell it, they will take it. They take #culturevulture to a whole other level.

@RunThisTown	If they are so powerful then why haven't they done anything about this murder? Do you think it was the girl with the flat tire?
@GetOut	Who Free? I doubt it. She doesn't do anything but go to church and study in the library. She is mad antisocial. Real smart, but she doesn't run in any of the circles Eric did.
@RunThisTown	Yeah but you would think they would have more answers or made some kind of power move by now. They've got city hall and the sheriff's office in the

	family. They can touch anybody.
@GetOut	Oh they will. It's coming. If the rest of the family is anything like Eric, they will bring the pain. They probably aren't naming the person who did it, so they can take justice into their own hands. And What's up with your screen name? @runthistown You a Jay-Z Fan or what?

Carlos realized he'd have to throw this teen off his trail in case she was as tech-savvy and smart as she seemed. He only hesitated a moment before he decided that while online he would need to be a girl.

| @RunThisTown | Nah! Jay Z is a little too much misogyny for me but I love Rihanna. She's my spirit animal. |
| @GetOut | Yessss! Me too. #rihannanavy |

Carlos logged off and did a quick celebratory whoop and fist pump into the air. Free! He had a whole name now. He opened the senior yearbook he'd found in the library and flipped back to the juniors. That's where she would have been last year when this was printed. It took forever because she was on the very last page of juniors, but there she was with the W's: Freedom Walker. Thanks to Shelly, he had the address and now, thanks to social media, he had the name. Visions of a pulitzer commenced dancing in his head all over again.

Chapter 15

May 19th Andrew - Remembering the Invisible

A ndrew stood under the pulsing jets of the oversized shower. When his wife had shown him the design plans for this shower, he had teased her for weeks, insisting that she would drown under the four water jets coming from each direction and the dual rain showers mounted in the ceiling.

"For someone who doesn't like to swim, this seems like an awful lot of water," he'd said.

But for all his relentless teasing, the shower had turned out to be his favorite place in the house. A long, deep bench ran across the back wall, and a simple click of a button could fill the entire space with steam. Rebecca had a true gift for beautiful, functional design, which was second only to her unparalleled skill at spending money. She had designed every single aspect of their sprawling 6,000-square-foot home set half a mile back from the road down a winding tree-lined drive. The estate was a marvel of glass, and stone, with a double-decked infinity pool, surrounded by a curious combination of soaring cypress and sprawling live oak trees that provided both shade and privacy. The project's grandeur, expanse, and expense were to be expected of the former favorite son of Jolivette's first family. The property was perfect, the stretch of trees a direct nod to the timber that had been one of the first rungs in the Texas ladder of the Tucker fortune, after real estate and before cattle.

Much like the shower, the house had been a perfect metaphor for their marriage. Everything had to be perfect. But after almost two solid years of planning, managing permits, vendors, and landscapers, as well as textile designers, custom craftsman, and contractors, when the home was finished and ready for move-in, Andrew's attention had waned, Rebecca's excitement had cooled, and it was just another hollow accomplishment. They retreated to their separate corners of the estate and the marriage. Andrew had tried a time or two to rally and bring a fresh sense of passion into their marriage, but neither he nor Rebecca was able to see it through. Their affections constantly wilted under the weight of the knowledge that Andrew had one great love and that Rebecca was not it.

Andrew turned the temperature knob further towards the red indicator and pressed the button for steam, wondering if he could just stay in the shower forever. Here, in this shower, no one could reach him, and life could not touch him. In this shower, he did not have a dead son or a wife that he couldn't love properly. In this shower, people were not pressing him for answers about the leaked coroner's report or possible suspects. As the steam filled the shower and began to blanket him, he had the overwhelming sensation of being invisible and laughed out loud at the sudden memory that surrounded him, along with the tendrils of steam. He dropped to the long bench, covered his face, and lost himself in the memory as the water ran in rivulets down his body.

Many years before they had built this glass mansion, the live oaks on Andrews's father's ranch were so large, wide, and low that no particular climbing skill was needed to climb them. A person could simply walk up the lowest branches and then transfer from branch to branch on foot until they found the most suitable curving nook where the branch met the tree to have a seat. It was into one of these perfect seats designed by nature where Andrew would settle, his back curled against the trunk, legs dangling on either side of the giant branch, with Monica's back curled into his chest and her arms pressed into his thighs like she was at home in a recliner. They were completely obscured from view by the leaves of the oak, and Monica had begun calling these frequent tree meetings "the invisible." She would stride by him in the hallways at school, her long, powerfully lean legs and confident stride distracting both students and teachers, her braided hair sweeping the small of her back. Without even turning to face him, she would call out in a low voice, "the invisible," and his heart would race. He'd learned to maintain composure and not acknowledge her words, but for the rest of the day, his body would move through the school on autopilot as his mind and heart yearned in rapt anticipation of a chance to steal more of those quiet, invisible moments in the oak trees after football practice.

As he lay under the steam in the shower, the memory of one particular night in the *invisible* played in his mind, causing his heart to ache in his chest as the steam settled on his face in droplets, camouflaging his tears. That day, they had curled into the oak, imagining a future for themselves. They would both be in college the following year, a freedom that would release them from all of the sneaking and pretending not to be anything more than classmates.

They were both headed to California, and although their campuses were over five hours apart, it wouldn't matter because they would be AWAY. Away from Jolivette and the Tucker family reach, which held the entire city by the throat and would never allow a tall, fearless Black girl to strut in and interrupt the marriage records, no matter how smart she was or how fast she was on a track. They'd already worked out how to alternate their school breaks between the two campuses, and when they graduated with their degrees, they would just stay in California and start a life. He'd pressed his mouth to her neck and whispered into the warm smell of cocoa butter and amber, "I love you," and she had let her head fall back into the hollow between his neck and his shoulder, presenting her mouth upwards for him to kiss.

"You promise?" she'd whispered as he felt her heart beating a warm staccato under the weight of his hands.

She tilted her body to meet his gaze, and the angle threw her slightly off balance. Her eyes widened as her hands shot out, grasping for something to stop her fall.

Andrew quickly wrapped his broad arms around her entire torso, holding her steady, and laughed into her hair.

"Easy, my angel," he'd whispered. "You don't have your wings yet, so you can't fly."

Monica had laughed that intoxicating laugh that sent him spinning further into her orbit and shot back, "you'd better not let me fall!"

Andrew held her tighter and swore it.

"I promise. I'll never let you fall, I'll never let you go."

But he had. That's exactly what he had done. He'd driven down to her campus to see her after his father made the ultimatum clear. And after spending the entire weekend in her sparsely decorated dorm room, cocooned by love, he told her that he couldn't see her anymore. His father's reach had stretched further than he had anticipated, and he had to focus on his future, he'd said. It was for the best, he'd insisted as she pleaded for him to reconsider and not to let his father win. But he couldn't take it and threw out the last bit of information he'd been holding. "I'm marrying Rebecca Abbot this summer. It's already set."

He'd watched in horror as her face crumpled into a broken mask of sorrow and then reforged itself into hot, angry steel. The look in her eyes that day haunted him still. She was almost unrecognizable. Gone was the little twinkle always playing at the uplifted corners of her almond eyes.

The tears dried quickly as well. In their place was a hollowness that made him feel that she was no longer looking at him but instead looking through him to something else that he could not see.

Over the years, he'd blamed his father. He'd blamed his bigoted family. He'd even blamed racism in America writ large when he was particularly drunk and waxing philosophical, grabbing at anyone else to blame but himself. But in the end, there was no one else to blame. To preserve his own comfort—his own legacy—he had let her go. And nothing had ever been the same. He'd wondered where she was. What she'd been up to. Why she had never come home. He'd hunted her across social media for a few years, once stooping low enough to hire a private investigator, but he had nothing for the PI to go on. He didn't even know where she lived, if she'd gotten married, or if she'd left the country. A few years ago, he'd heard her father had died. A giant of a man with a penchant for making peace and helping others, a great deal of the who's who of Jolivette and several major pastors from around the State turned out to Pop Walker's funeral, Black, white, Hispanic, and everything in between. It was a homegoing worthy of a man who had always walked with principle and conviction. Andrew had stood in the back of the packed church, peering at the first three rows where the family was seated, hoping to catch a glimpse of her. But, nothing. He'd finally slipped out just before the recessional, crestfallen and resolved to stop waiting and hoping for an impossibility. If she had not come back for her father's funeral, he'd realized she was never coming back.

Chapter 16

May 20 Angel - The Prodigal Returns

While Angel was not known for being overly chatty, she was known for being a good listener and giving solid advice. In the L.A. circles she moved in, most women—and men—had aspirations of landing a whale. The elusive L.A. whale is a suitor of extreme wealth that leads an off-screen life (no actors, no athletes) and has enough gas in the tank to try their hand at marriage just one more time. Ideally, these whales would be so successful and established in their careers that they could dedicate considerable time—and money, of course—to helping their new, gorgeous trophy wife/husband achieve their own dreams. They'd pull a few strings, get their new adoring lover a talking role in a feature film, or bankroll studio time to help them put out an album. It was the dream that fueled the youngest, tightest, prettiest new transplants to keep racking up credit debt at salons and designer boutiques, and the dream that the more seasoned hopefuls clung to, knowing their opportunity window would soon close.

One evening, as she was leaving a lounge with her friends, Angel had heard a young waitress bubbling effervescently to her friend about an older, married man she'd met that was buying her gifts. She was gesticulating wildly, as if she just knew he was the ONE. Angel stopped behind her and placed a hand on her shoulder softly.

When the girl turned to her, Angel said, matter-of-factly, "The man of your dreams is never going to be someone else's husband while you are dating."

The girl's eyes registered a mixture of shame and annoyance. Before she could even stammer out a response, Angel added a soft landing.

"I'm not saying to return the gifts. I'm just saying that while you are spending his money, you should keep looking."

The girl's friend chimed in then with an "I know that's right!" and the awkwardness dissipated as they went back to worrying about what bikini she should get for her covert side-chick trip to St. Barts.

Angel had shaken her head and wondered if she'd ever been that young and silly. Thinking about it now as the road rumbled beneath her, she realized that she had been exactly that silly, and maybe she still was.

The miles of highway continued to stretch out before her, and she turned up the radio to drown out her thoughts. She had booked a flight to Texas as soon as she'd seen the news story. It was as if all of the dreams and ever more urgent pull she'd felt from her tormented memories were warning her that it was past time to go home. She'd landed at Bush Intercontinental Airport in Houston and tried to rent a simple Toyota sedan for the long drive to Jolivette, but her last-minute booking forced her to accept a bright red Jeep. She'd hoped to keep a low profile, and this was not a great start, but her options were limited to the candy red Jeep or an Escalade, and she was definitely not going to be able to roll into Jolivette undetected in an Escalade, looking like a part of a presidential motorcade. At least in the Jeep, she thought, she could "off-road" it a bit before she got there, so it would be dusty and the wheels mud-caked, taking it down a notch or two on the "look at me" scale.

There was so much open, flat road to cover that her thoughts began to wander and dip back into the memories she had been using the speed of Los Angeles to suppress.

Overwhelmed by the anxiety of what she may be walking into, she finally broke down and selected a playlist to connect to the jeep's bluetooth - drowning her own guilt and shame in a Neo Soul playlist dominated by D'Angelo, Erykah, and Jill. The speed limit signs said 75mph, so Angel held her pace steady at 90 until she recognized the speed traps that were a clear indicator that she was nearing her destination.

Angel eased off the gas altogether as she turned into her old neighborhood and slowed to a roll when she saw the house come into view. Her heart had already started racing when she bumped over the railroad tracks, and now she was approaching the long row of old but neatly kept houses, raised off the dirt with brick and cinderblock piers covered in white lattice and flanked on the sides with orderly rows of flowers and bushes. A small part of her heart swelled with reluctant pride as she acknowledged the unwavering care that this community had always taken in manicuring their lawns and adding touches of southern beauty at every turn. Empty rockers sat solemnly on porches like sentinels keeping guard. She lowered the windows and slowed even more. Wind chimes and a few yips of a dog detecting a visitor on the block were the only sounds that greeted her. As she made the final turn, her childhood home came into view. Situated directly in the deepest hook of the culdesac, its yawning porch wrapped around one side of the house, ending in a rear deck just off the kitchen. The porch swing was shifting ever so slightly with the breeze. The meticulous curving lawn and plant beds sloped inward to match the curve of the blacktopped street. New cracks had emerged, crisscrossing the long driveway that led to the garage behind the house. But those spidering cracks were the only tell-tale sign of just how old the house really was. Everything else about this house spoke to its story of great care and loving upkeep. Fresh paint glistened from the blue shutters and gables.

Angel had a flashback to summer Saturdays, her dad seeding and weeding that perfect lawn, then drinking frosted lemonade on the porch while he looked out at his handiwork. But the warm memories quickly turned cold, a shiver of regret causing tears to well up as she remembered that she would never see her father alive again and recalled how she had left this place without so much as a goodbye hug for the man who had raised her. The hard memories rolled in fast after that. Giving birth to her daughter in the bathtub. Sneaking out of the window. She fought back the tears pressing behind her eyes and thickening in her throat.

She looked up and down the street again, trying to make sense of the fact that there was not a single child, man, or woman, working, walking, running, or playing, before realizing that there wouldn't be anyone here for a while. It was Sunday morning, 10 a.m. Every soul within miles would be crowded into one of Jolivette's two black churches. Greater Sanai AME, where the service was short and succinct, allowing all of the husbands to return to their recliners in plenty of time for the football game, or Bible Way Pentecostal, where her mother would be seated on the front row, silently directing every aspect of the service with subtle nods of her wide-brimmed hat.

Angel had a choice to make. She could either crank up the air and sit in the driveway for hours or drive the three miles to Bible Way. She rubbed the heels of her hands against her eyes and then laid her forehead against the wheel. There had to be another alternative. Maybe she could check into a hotel and return later or grab a bite to eat. But the thought that someone would recognize her and get word to her mother that she was back before she had a chance to tell her herself was unthinkable. She just couldn't take the chance. Angel slapped the wheel in self-loathing for this poorly planned pop up, then turned the Jeep around in the culdesac, and headed back out to the main road…towards her late father's church.

Angel heard the church before she saw it. Her grandfather and father had always left the front doors wide open so that the clapping and singing could float out and down the road to passersby, an added benefit to the primary purpose of facilitating the cross breeze that cooled the congregants for many years before the central air that was added during the 1982 renovations. Although the windows could no longer be opened, and the inner doors remained closed and guarded militantly by ushers, the exterior doors leading into the vestibule still stood open wide, tracking with tradition. After the church shooting in Charleston that killed Reverend Pinkney and the White Settlement shooting a few years later, the board had secured the services of two full-time security guards, one that manned the doors and another who circled the lot. Angel hadn't been here for any of those changes. Seeing the armed guards slowed her pace a little.

For a moment, she had the fleeting thought that the added security was a bit much for a small town church, but then she could almost hear her father's voice echoing in her mind, "Can never be too careful in a town full of Tuckers."

Angel grabbed a long maxi skirt from her luggage and slipped it on over her yoga tights before exiting the Jeep while quietly congratulating herself for packing with her mother's relentless judgment in mind. The t-shirt probably wouldn't go over well for a Sunday service attire choice, but it was modest, and that was enough to skate by on. She wouldn't have made it past the ushers in the yoga pants though. As she walked into the vestibule, she instinctively turned left to head up the short flight of stairs that led up to the balcony, her best bet at remaining undetected as a late arrival; but the stairs were cordoned off. She started to reach for the golden rope, but the burly man at the door called out brusquely, "The balcony is full."

Angel was turning in a slow circle, trying to decide if she should just head back to the car or hide in the bathrooms just opposite the stairs, when the guard, staring quizzically, said, "There are always a few seats on the second row reserved for special visitors."

Angel closed her eyes in defeat and let out a low sigh. The prospect of walking all the way to the front of the church felt like a waking nightmare. When she re-opened her eyes, the guard met her gaze, smirking a bit.

"Long time since you've been to church, hunh?" he asked with humor in his tone.

Adjusting her sunglasses and straightening her back, Angel replied curtly, "Long time since I've been to THIS church."

She didn't know why she was bristling at him. Her defensiveness was misplaced and phony. She actually hadn't set foot in a church since she left Jolivette, but being read so easily triggered her in a way that she hadn't expected.

The guard raised a sardonic brow and then turned back to the door to help a man with a walker navigate the lip of the entryway. Angel steeled her nerves, pivoted on her heel, and headed towards the side entrance to the sanctuary.

The distance between the back of the church and the second row was probably no more than 30 feet, but it may as well have been an airstrip. Fortunately, the choir was singing an upbeat gospel song with driving bass and belting their hearts out at full volume. Most of the church was on their feet, clapping, stomping, and rocking. She adopted a brisk pace using the praise as cover, glued her eyes to her feet, and marched forward until she slid into the side aisle seat in the second row. With her eyes still trained on her feet, she removed her shades and slid them into the pocket of her maxi skirt. Her fingers lingered on the phone in her pocket as she thought about whether she should shoot a text to

Yami in L.A. to let her know that she had arrived, but she thought the better of it. There would be questions if she reached out to Yami, and she was not ready to answer anyone's questions, much less the rapid-fire Panamanian spice versions Yami would probably be pelting her with. She left the phone in her pocket and crossed her hands in her lap instead.

The choir ended the song with gusto, and the presiding pastor walked onstage still humming the last refrains of the song. The congregation instinctively took their seats. Angel scanned the row in front of her and caught her mother's profile on the far end of the pew, close to the center aisle. It was unmistakable. Jean Walker had the precision posture of a marine, ramrod straight. Her neat red pillbox hat sat slightly askew, just enough to allow its cage veil to swoop effortlessly over one side of her face. Her long silver hair spilled out in shimmering waves that swept around her shoulders.

Angel had a sudden memory of sitting up at night, helping her mother pin those curls tightly against her scalp as they watched the evening news. An unexpected heat prickled behind her eyes, and she fought against the tears trying again to form. She averted her gaze from her mother and noticed the figure sitting beside her. She studied this new profile. She could only see the young woman's jawline and full lips. The rest of her face was shrouded in gorgeous, coiled heaps of brown and caramel hair. Angel felt the heat return, this time creeping up her neck, and an immovable lump lodged itself in her throat. She knew who it was, but was caught in the disbelief that her little girl could be a young woman now.   Despite her best efforts at keeping her breathing steady, Angel's heart pounded, and her chest tightened like a giant had wrapped her in its fist and was slowly squeezing. She wanted to see the girl's entire face; compare it to the face she saw every night in her dreams. Without thinking, Angel jerked forward, her hand gripping the pew in front of her, to catch a better view, and as she did, her mother glanced back over her shoulder, and their eyes met. Angel hesitated only a moment before standing and heading back toward the exit.

***

Angel paced back and forth in the parking lot of the church. *What is wrong with you?* She chided herself. *You are not a child anymore. You are a grown woman, running out of church because you are afraid of your own mother. Get it together! You are already here,* she told herself over and over again. *You have come too far to run away again now.*

Angel had made it to within ten feet of her mother and daughter in that pew, but when she saw the recognition and emotion register on her mother's face, she felt panic rise and wash over her body like ice water. Now here she was, pacing the parking lot like a caged tiger, trying to figure out if coming back to Jolivette was a mistake. Why would her daughter even want to see her after all these years?

In her mind, she had convinced herself that leaving Freedom behind was the best thing for her. A baby in the steady hands of Mama Jean meant that the girl would be cared for, not dragged across the country with a penniless college student for a mother. But Angel wasn't a college student anymore, and she wasn't penniless. And the truth was always standing there like a hulking shadow casting its knowing judgment over her excuses and justifications. She'd run away because she wanted to be someone else. She didn't want to be a single-Black-mother story trapped in Jolivette. She didn't want to watch someone else have the life that should have been hers while she clocked in every day at Mama Jean's cleaners and cried herself to sleep. She wanted to be the woman that she had told everyone, including herself, she would become—the successful Hollywood starlet with the world at her feet. But all of these years later, that hadn't happened either, and she couldn't help thinking that nothing really great would ever happen to her because she had destroyed her own Karma. The night she left Jolivette without her baby, she had sown the seeds of regret, loneliness, and emptiness that she had been harvesting ever since.

This is a mistake, she thought. *I have no business coming back here like I can help. Why would anyone want my help now?*

Angel was abruptly snapped out of her spiral of self-loathing when the doors of the church flew open, and the people began to spill out with the high buzzing hum of greetings, lunch plans, laughter, and "ain't God goods floating amongst them." Angel watched the exiting crowd swell and then thin as the church emptied and cars began maneuvering out of their parking spaces. She turned her body to avoid being recognized by anyone in the lingering groups still chatting about who was hosting mid-week bible study and how many pies they'd need for the bake sale. A few folks threw her sidelong glances as they walked by, and she adjusted her oversized sunglasses, wondering how long she could stay incognito in this gossipy crowd. She didn't like her chances. She shifted from one foot to the other, trying to decide whether she should have just stayed in

Mama Jean's driveway and waited for them to get home, but deep down, she already knew that she was counting on Mama Jean's aversion to causing a public scene as a layer of security to prevent this little reunion from becoming a catastrophe.

Angel had abandoned her daughter, no-showed at her father's funeral, and left Mama Jean with full responsibility for running the cleaners in her old age. She could not imagine the steel that she would be met with for showing up here unannounced and thought it was best to be in an environment where everyone would have to hold their tongue just a bit. Still, it was now dawning on her that she didn't know much about how her daughter could be expected to handle this meeting and that she may have seriously miscalculated the wisdom of coming to the church.

She turned and reached for the Jeep's door handle, but stopped, frozen in place as she caught the reflection of her mother in the window's glass. At 60 years old, she was still lean and graceful. Her descent down the stairs looked more like floating than walking. And even from five yards away, with her eyes obscured by the mirrored sunglasses she wore, Angel knew that her mother was looking right at her. She turned around as Mama Jean left the last step of the church and began heading directly towards her. Angel scoured her own mind for the words she had prepared for this moment and came up empty. Words were her superpower. She could smooth-talk her way in or out of nearly any situation, sell water to a fish and ice to an Inuit, but words were failing her now, and she scrambled to put even the right sounds together in her mouth that would make sense when Mama Jean finally reached the car.

Like some trick of time, Mama Jean covered the ground between them in an instant, and just like that, they were there together, standing in the sweltering May heat that radiated both down from the sky and up from the asphalt of the parking lot. Still, Angel could not find a single word. Mama Jean pushed her sunglasses up onto her head, where they swooped her hair away from her face like a headband. Her dark skin was still smooth and even, but the skin around her eyes was crisscrossed with a maze of wrinkles that Angel had never seen. Her hair shone and glittered in the sun, glossy strands of silvery gray, pressed, as always, into bone straight obedience.

When Angel had last seen her mother, she could count the grays on her head, which she often did, and now there was no strand of any other color. As beautiful as she was to Angel, she looked tired. Angel could see the question etched across Mama Jean's face. *Why are you here. Why now?*

Without thinking, she blurted out, " I saw the news."

A different look appeared on her mother's face then. One she could not read. The silence stretched out between them, and Angel felt her earlier resolve begin to crumble. The years of regret coursed through her veins with a prickling heat, and she opened her mouth to say, "I'm sorry," but, instead, what came was a painful, gut-wrenching sob that shook her frame and crushed her chest.

Mama Jean closed the small distance left between them and folded her daughter in her arms. Angel squeezed her eyes shut, her face contorting with the tidal wave of emotion she had been suppressing for almost 18 years, and she felt her body giving out beneath her as it was met by the solid, unwavering steadiness of Mama Jean holding her up. *How had she come from a woman of iron resolve with unbreakable fortitude like this and still turned out to be a coward?* she thought. The realization of how she failed to stack up to her mother only intensified Angel's sobbing.

Mama Jean tightened her grip and spoke into Angel's ear, "Welcome home. We've been waiting for you."

Angel opened her eyes, her chin still pressed into Mama Jean's neck, and was startled to find a pair of golden flecked green eyes looking right back at her.

Chapter 17

May 20 Free - The Thin Line

Freedom silently rode home in the front seat of Mama Jean's Buick. She had not said a single word as she watched the woman who had haunted her dreams for all of these years materialize out of thin air in the parking lot after church and then cry and sputter onto Mama Jean's white linen blazer. When Mama Jean tried to meet her eyes, Freedom turned her back, walked away, and climbed into the passenger seat of Mama Jean's car, training her eyes on her own hands that were now twisting a flyer she'd been handed during church into a cylinder. The compulsive twisting had narrowed the sheet of paper to the size of a straw. She continued twisting the long tube tighter and tighter, her eyes occasionally darting to the side mirror where the red Jeep hovered, trailing them home.

Freedom was now dreading the confrontation that she had spent most of her life imagining with bitter mirth. She'd run through countless scenarios in which she confronted her long-lost mother. She had spent many, many nights planning what she would say when the day came that she found her mother or her mother found her. In her elaborate plans, she always planned to point out all of the great things that she had accomplished. But she had egregiously miscalculated, because in her imaginings, she was already successful, wealthy, critically acclaimed, not a high school student just weeks from graduation, unable to return to campus, and suspected of involvement in the death of a classmate. In fact, she could not think of a worse time to be confronted with the earth-tilting surprise of her mother's reappearance.

She was now fisting and unfisting her hands too tightly and had dug small crescent moons into her palms with her nails that were beginning to sting. What was she going to say to this woman? Lying to the police was one thing, but lying to her mother was an entirely different proposition, and she was being washed over by icy fear and hot flashes of anger in staggered waves. By the time they reached the house, anger was in the lead, dominating her emotions, and she was practically vibrating with outrage at the audacity of this woman. To disappear and stay gone for countless milestones, heartbreaks, Pop Pop's funeral...ALL OF THAT, and then show up right now, when no one asked for, expected, or needed her! Unbelievable! She threw open the door, leaped from the car before it had even come to a complete stop, and began stalking towards the red jeep her mother was maneuvering into the space behind them in the open driveway.

"Freedom!"

She could hear Mama Jean's voice calling sharply behind her, but ignored it. She had no intention of being deterred. She yanked forcefully on the driver's door of the jeep, but Monica had not unlocked it, and she sat stoically, her eyes cast down as though studying the steering wheel.

"Get out!" Freedom screamed, a bit shocked at her own forcefulness.

Angel turned to meet her daughter's fiery gaze. Those golden eyes, glowing first greenish then blue, always with the golden flecks were hauntingly beautiful. The girl looked mad enough to swing on her, and a part of Angel's heart was proud to see it. *This one has fight in her,* Angel thought. *This one wouldn't ever just settle for a life of finessing men to stay afloat. She would be more than that. She would be everything.*

Monica was reaching for the button to unlock the door, apparently ready to take whatever was coming, when Mama Jean finally reached Freedom's side.

"Free, baby," she said evenly while rubbing the girl's back. "Free, this is our family business, and we will handle it like family business. We don't need an audience."

Mama Jean used one long finger to gently tip Free's chin in the direction of the street. Free's eyes broke briefly from their deathlock on her mother, and she saw that a few neighbors had wandered out into intentionally unintentional stations on their porches to get a direct view and better listening vantage point to the commotion Free had started. Yelling that was coming from Mama Jean's house was virtually unheard of.

"I may be a lot of things, Mama Jean would say, but I'll never be a spectacle." Free's unbridled fury cooled just a degree or two, as she turned away from the looky looks to face Mama Jean.

"Why is she here?" she hissed, gesturing roughly over her shoulder to her mother, still in the jeep.

"We will find out, okay baby. Inside."

As Free huffed an exasperated breath and stalked back up the driveway towards the house, she heard Mama Jean ask Monica to pull into the detached garage and come in through the kitchen's side door. She could feel her bravery slipping and her shoulders dropping in defeat. That almost-confrontation was her moment to finally take all of her pain and throw it back into the hands that had caused it, and she'd missed her big, dramatic chance. The moment was gone.

Freedom stormed into her room, slamming the door behind her. Her entire body was ablaze with fury. She could not slow her mind down, and it raced with a million jumbled thoughts all competing for top billing. She was wrestling disbelief that this woman, the single largest disappointment coloring every thread of her life's fabric, had suddenly appeared from thin air. Everything Free had done, every choice she had made, every extra effort she had poured into trying to be the best had been driven by her unspoken need, for her mother to find out through the grapevine, or maybe even the world wide web that the daughter she hadn't wanted had turned out to be amazing and hadn't needed her at all. That was the song playing on repeat in the back of her mind. But that was not how things were playing out. Instead, she was staring down the reality of what may well become a total failure to launch that she wouldn't be able to explain to anyone without incriminating herself.

So many of her ambitions and sacrifices suddenly didn't make sense to her. She hadn't ever been able to make or accept close friendships; she'd never trusted the intention of any of the boys who had shown interest in her. She was turning 18 in less than a week, and she had never let herself love, or trust, or be close to anyone other than Mama Jean and Pop. All of this time, she'd convinced herself that this was for the best. That this was the only way to ensure that she didn't get herself tied down to Jolivette or any of the people in it and could make a clean break once she graduated. But now, facing the sudden reality of her mother looking healthy, beautiful, and perfectly fine, she knew that she had kept everyone out, not so that she could leave, but because she didn't want to give anyone else a chance to leave her for something better. Her mother had hurt her in a way that she now understood may never heal. And she was here now in the flesh, physical confirmation of the thing that Free had most feared - the thing the kids had said to her all of her life. Her mother just hadn't wanted her.

It had taken half of her young life to accept the hard truth that even your mother can decide that you aren't worth knowing. But once Free had accepted it, she began steeling herself against the stinging pain the thought unleashed in her body. She had never really entertained the idea that her mother would pop back up here. It was supposed to be a chance encounter after Free had found wealth and acclaim and was undeniably worth knowing. This moment represented the death of the only dream she'd clung to, and as the dream dissipated before her eyes, it took a piece of her soul with it.

Chapter 18

May 21 Andrew - A Shift in Loyalties

A ndrew entered the high school through the back doors and took an empty hallway to the administration office, which was a maze of doors, printers, and file cabinets. At this time of the morning, there weren't usually many people on campus other than janitors and the zero-period students trying to leverage additional hours as a way of pulling up less than impressive grades. Andrew was irritated to have been summoned to this place—a place where every single thing reminded him of the school year and football season his son was never going to get to finish. But his wife had asked him to meet her there, and for all of his emotional unavailability, he had never failed to show up for her when she asked him to be somewhere.

He rounded a corner and almost collided with a plump woman with bleach blond hair and a shocking amount of exposed cleavage.

"Oh, I'm so sorry," she drawled. Her eyes widened in recognition and surprise. "Oh Mr. Mayor, you poor thing! Are you doing ok? Bless your heart. We are all praying for you," she gushed, pulling him into the ample bosom threatening to escape her shiny blouse.

Andrew extracted himself awkwardly, and she blushed deeply, smoothing her hair, which could not have possibly moved under the hold of its webbed prison of hair spray.

"Uh, yes. Ah...thank you," Andrew stammered. "I'm here to see Skooner."

"Of course! Principle Skooner is right this way," she said, extending her arm like a Price is Right showcase model to direct him towards the correct office. "Do you want me to walk you down? Can I take your jacket? We have a coat rack at the front if you'd like me to hang it. It can get a little warm in Skooner's office. Can I get you anything? Anything at all?"

Andrew shook his head, a bit flustered by her combination of obsequious word spray and exposed breast. He ran his hand along the back of his neck and tightened his grip on his suit jacket that was draped over his left arm.

"I'm just fine," he said graciously. "Thank you, umm."

His eyes darted around for a placard or anything that would clue him in on her name, not daring to let his eyes drop to her actual name tag swinging dangerously on a lanyard just below her heaving breasts.

"Shelly!" The woman cheerfully piped up with her name.

Andrew offered her a tight smile, thanked her again, and moved swiftly toward the hall Shelly had pointed out as the path to Principal Skooner's office. The door was open, and Andrew stepped into the room with his hand extended to shake the principal's hand.

"Hey Skooner," he greeted the diminutive man dressed in wire frame glasses, an overstarched button-down, and a Jolivette High tie with tiny wildcats imprinted all over it.

"Mayor, " Skooner responded tightly while pumping the handshake one time too many for Andrew's liking.

Andrew was confused by the principal's formalness when he had always known the man to be jovial and easygoing. Andrew turned to look at his wife quizzically. Rebecca was there, already seated just in front of the desk in a chair covered in the hideous maroon fabric in accordance with the school colors. The school had really overdone the integration of their colors and mascots into everything, and Andrew imagined that Rebecca was probably counting the minutes until she could escape the tacky piece of furniture that she was managing to sit in, but still avoid touching. Andrew was about to ask Rebecca why he'd been summoned when a movement caught his eye, and he looked up to see his brother standing in the far corner of the office, a deep scowl painted on his face.

"What are YOU doing here, John?" Andrew growled, immediately annoyed.

"Rebecca ASKED me to come," John shot back, his tone filled with venom.

Now, Andrew was many things, but stupid was not one of them. He knew he was a flawed man, so he tended to extend a good bit of leeway for the flaws of others. Through the years, it was this tendency towards grace that had allowed him to refrain from commenting on the number of times he had seen his brother on their home security cameras, picking up and dropping off his wife when Andrew was out of town. It was also the reason he frequently ignored his brother's angry, tantrum-like outbursts over Drew's seemingly innocuous offenses like being late to a family dinner or beating him in a round of golf. John was obviously taken with his wife. He had harboured a crush on her for most of their teen years, and Andrew knew it. But Rebecca had chosen Andrew, and Andrew had resolved to do his best to take care of her until she stopped choosing him.

To his credit, John had run off and gotten married three months after Andrew and Rebecca's wedding. He married a fiery redheaded woman from several towns over that no one had met—a seemingly calculated move meant to put an end to his Rebecca crush. Unfortunately, the escape he'd built for himself had become more or less a prison of his own making. By the time the years had eroded Drew and Rebecca's facade enough for those close to them to realize that their marriage was more of a binding contract than an abiding love, John had already ruined his own marriage in the rough, uncouth way that only John could. John and his old lady had become a public spectacle more than once - storming out of restaurants, bars, and public luncheons and galas as their communication styles clashed, crashed, and flamed over every little thing. Once she was tired of the fighting, dramatic break ups, and reconciliations, she finally packed up and left.

Andrew wasn't sure if John's wife had ever figured out that she was always competing with John's idolization of Rebecca, but he suspected she hadn't because that woman had too much mouth and fire to have let something that big go unsaid. Andrew had actually seen her haul off and slap John into a spin for less egregious revelations. John had always liked attention, but Andrew doubted he was crazy enough to push the kind of buttons on his now ex-wife that could get him featured, post-mortem, on an episode of Snapped. But while he had managed to keep that information under his hat while he was married, he apparently did not have the good sense or common decency not to show up at this meeting looking for all the world like Rebecca's jealous boyfriend. Andrew considered pressing his brother on this lack of tact and respect, but decided that he neither had the energy nor the desire to wade into that mud in front of Principal Skooner. This wasn't the time. He would handle it privately later.

Andrew brushed off John's hostile tone and took the seat next to his wife's.

"What's all this about?" Andrew asked.

Principal Skooner cut his eyes at John, looking genuinely irritated by his presence, before addressing Drew.

"As you know, graduation is looming close, and the young lady that was involved in the um…accident that um…well, the incident with your son that led to his death–

I mean, well… she is supposed to speak at the ceremony because she is technically the valedictorian, having accumulated the highest core and total GPA…"

Skooner's neck had turned red, and the color was crawling towards his face. Andrew decided to cut in mercifully.

"The girl that Eric was helping with her car when he was hit?" Andrew asked. "She is the valedictorian?"

Skooner nodded and formed two little tents with his hands on the desk in front of him.

"Bullshit!" John rocked forward in his seat and cut into the conversation with his usual lack of tact - hands flailing. "What is this? Some kinda D-E-I horse shit? Ain't the valedictorian supposed to be the smartest kid in school? You tryna tell us that some little nig-"

"John!" Andrew's voice boomed in like thunder, cutting off his brother's words and most of the oxygen in the room. "I will drag your sorry hide out of here by the scruff of your own racist red neck if you don't sit your ignorant ass back in that seat and let the adults finish talking!"

The brothers held one another's gaze, fury crackling across the room. John surveyed the seriousness and severity in Andrew's face, along with the flush blooming on

Rebecca's cheeks, and made the decision to back down, settling back into his chair. The brothers had had this fight before. They'd undoubtedly get the chance to have it again. But not today. At John's retreat, Andrew turned back to the Principal, who now held a thick sheen of sweat across his brow and was sporting slowly widening circles of moisture where the chest of his shirt met the sleeves.

"Uh, yes. At this moment, she is," he said, bouncing his tented hands on the desk, "she has not been notified that we are reconsidering her standing, but I don't feel that it would be appropriate for her to address the school at graduation, given the swirling tension around the event, and it seems your wife…err…Mrs. Tucker tends to agree."

Andrew furrowed his brows in confusion.

"What tension are you talking about? Eric stopped to help the girl with her tire, and he was hit by an 18-wheeler." Andrew tried to fix John with a hard look, but John wouldn't meet his eyes.

Dammit, Andrew thought. *John must be telling everyone.* Sheriff Oltorf had denied the young reporter's on-air claims in a follow up statement to the media, but it seemed like the news was spreading like wildfire anyway, despite Andrew's PR team resources.

"Of course, yes," Principal Skooner sputtered, "but then, of course, there is the matter of the gunshot wounds."

Skooner let his voice trail off, and Andrew suddenly felt very tired. His brother was avoiding eye contact, so he directed his attention back to his wife, who was visibly shaking with anger. So John had told her anyway, and these two were set on telling everyone now. So much for keeping the family name out of drama. He knew she was hurting, but she hadn't been answering his calls.

"Rebecca…" Andrew reached toward his wife, but she recoiled, leaning out of the chair almost to the point of tipping it to avoid his touch. He quickly withdrew his hand and cleared his throat.

"Okay," he said, turning back to Skooner. "So what can we do about it? If she is the valedictorian, then she just is. Right?"

Principal Skooner pushed his fingers back together into a diamond. "Well, we could announce that someone else is the valedictorian in order to avoid a controversy, which will take some convincing because this girl… well, she has been leading her class, academically, since elementary school, and it's not close. Both she and most of her classmates know it. An even bigger issue is that your wife has requested that we suspend her from school altogether, pending the outcome of this whole debacle. She hasn't returned yet since the incident, but she will become an enormous distraction if she does. I'd prefer she complete these last few weeks from home. I'm going to make that recommendation to the district's general counsel when inquired about her Valedictorian position. You are well acquainted with general counsel–" he paused before adding, "–and can help persuade him to our cause."

Andrew finally started putting the pieces together. The principal, his brother, his wife—they weren't asking him what to do. They were letting him know what he needed to make happen and what type of cover they would need to keep this from blowing back on them. He needed to grease the wheels and mitigate any legal damages that might turn up. For the second time in less than ten minutes, he felt a wave of exhaustion wash over him and wished he had just stayed in the shower this morning - never stepping out into the real world. Andrew rubbed his forehead where a stress headache was beginning to bloom and nodded.

"I will make some calls," he acquiesced. From the corner of his eye, he saw John nod, and then his wife of 18 years stood up without a word or cursory glance at him and left the room with his brother. Andrew watched them go before gathering his jacket and attaché. Principal Skooner made a sniffling sound, a not so subtle nudge for Andrew to get going, then rose and extended his hand. Andrew averted his eyes from the soft, clammy, turned-up palm until Skooner let it fall awkwardly back by his side.

"The girl?" Andrew asked without making eye contact with sniveling Skooner.

"What about the girl, sir?"

"What's her name? Her information wasn't in the police report because she is a minor, but I want to know who she is since someone obviously felt it was okay to tell you."

Skooner had the decency to look chastised.

"Well, yes. I mean, the students talk so much. It wasn't hard to figure out, and she hasn't been back to campus since the, uh, incident, so I was able to piece things together."

"Yeah, okay, Skooner," Drew asked again, impatiently. "Who is she?"

"Her name is Walker. Freedom Walker."

All of the hair on the back of Andrew's neck stood on end. A Walker?

No! he thought. *You are reaching, hoping she is related to Monica because you are lonely, he chided himself. There are*

probably dozens of Walkers in this town. What is wrong with you?
He tried to rein his mind in as he blew air out and turned his
attention back to Principal Skooner.

"Any relation to the family that owns the Walker's
Dry Cleaning across town?" He tried to keep his expression
nonchalant as though it didn't much matter to him either
way.

"Uh maybe," Skooner said, knitting his brows
together. I'm not really sure."

"Thank you," Andrew said curtly and headed
towards the exit.

Andrew's mind was still swirling from the meeting
as he barrelled out of the back doors and collided with a
young black reporter smoking a cigarette. The cigarette went
flying, but not before some of the embers landed on
Andrew's shirt and burnt tiny holes into the expensive cotton
blend. The reporter recovered faster than Andrew, and he
had his microphone in Drew's face by the time he'd steadied
himself. The cameraman must have beamed in from another
planet because there was a giant lens now aimed directly at
Drew that had not been there just moments ago. Drew
groaned and swore under his breath as he brushed the ashes
from his jacket. *Not this guy again.*

Chapter 19

May 21 Carlos - A Not So Chance Encounter

Carlos felt his adrenaline spike when he realized that he had just been nearly trampled by Andrew Tucker. This was it! The boy's father! No one has been able to get him for an interview or get him to corroborate a single fact or rumor. He'd been inexplicably moving around the town undetected, but two appetizers and three glasses of white zinfandel from Applebee's was all it took to get Shelly to let it slip that Eric's mother had a meeting with the high school principal in the morning. Reporter's intuition had led him to the obscure rear entrance on the side of the gym, and pure luck had landed him directly in front of the door as Andrew Tucker came flying out like a man on fire.

"Mayor Tucker!" Carlos rushed into his questions as the camera rolled. "Carlos Jackson, HWK2 News."

Carlos shoved a dog-eared business card into Andrews's hand and charged ahead with his questions.

"The entire town is reeling from the tragic loss of your son. Why haven't you commented on the reports of foul play? There are theories floating around that Eric had quite a few enemies. Do you have a suspect in custody yet? Sources have confirmed that Eric's body was riddled with gunshot wounds. Shouldn't someone have to answer for his murder?"

"What do you mean riddled?" Andrew snapped incredulously before realizing his mistake.

But the reporter was already on it.

"So you acknowledge that he was shot. Did you have a chance to view his body?"

Andrew felt a warm flush crawling up his neck and face. He considered the young man for a moment. He was tall and fit, but Andrew had him by at least two inches and several pounds, with enough football left in his muscle memory to knock the kid out of his shoes. He contemplated doing exactly that for a moment, then thought better of it. This was the same kid he'd seen an officer tackle on television less than a week ago, and that had only added fuel to the fire. The kid knew what he was doing, but he wouldn't be getting any viral interview moments at Andrew's expense. Andrew thought about the absurdity of the moment. His son was reduced to ash in a metal container, his wife had left him and was walking around on his own brother's arm, and the entire city of Jolivette was waiting for him to say something—anything– that would give them permission to unleash their sadness and fury at Eric's death onto some little girl that, up until a week ago, was a high school valedictorian with no cares in the world beyond SAT scores and college admissions. The investigators had already explained that there was very little opportunity and no credible evidence that the girl had fired any sort of weapon, and the idea of trying to sift through the many enemies his son had amassed in his young life felt like an impossibility. He was tired.

Andrew straightened his back and looked into the camera shouldered by the stocky cameraman.

"My son is gone, and we are doing our best to put the pieces together and figure out why. Please allow law enforcement to do their jobs. We are trusting them to make sure that justice is served. In the meantime, we refuse to jump to conclusions just to alleviate our own pain. That won't bring Eric back."

With that, Andrew turned and stalked off, feeling the palpable disappointment from the young reporter. The kid probably hadn't gotten what he wanted, but Andrew knew that he would still be smugly satisfied at his prowess in cornering his target and forcing a statement. Andrew hoped that managing to deftly side-step the reporters' guerilla interview tactics would buy him some time—time that he desperately needed now.

Chapter 20

May 21 Angel - Full Circle

Angel stood at the side of the bed, pushing her perfectly pedicured toes back and forth along the worn surface of the rug between the four-poster bed and the antique dresser against the wall. The rug has been worn nearly smooth, but its swirling classic Turkish pattern was still visible despite the fading. She thought of all the times that she'd watched Andrew dive to the floor on this very rug and then roll under the bed before Mama Jean could reach the door. By then, Angel would be sitting at the small desk in the corner, pretending to study and look up as if surprised by Mama Jean's arrival.

"Hey, mama," she'd say. "How was work?" A small half smile reached her face at the memory.

Now the walls were covered in posters of periodic tables, anatomy diagrams, one-name musicians she'd never heard of, like Samoht, Yebba, Bilal, Mali, and some that she had, like Miles Davis, John Coltrane, Beyonce, Prince, and

Rihanna. She had to give it to the girl; she had her mother's eclectic taste in music.

She looked around the room, then turned to look at her daughter, spent and sleeping, curled in the fetal position. Her little girl was all grown up and more than ready to let her know just how worthless she'd been as a mother. The minute they stepped in from the front porch, Free had rounded on her with a barrage of how-dare-you's, I-don't-need-you's, and I wish-you-were-deads. Angel had taken every verbal blow without shield or deflection. She didn't want to soften the blows. It almost felt cathartic. A flagellation she deserved.

"You don't have anything to say?" her daughter screeched when she finally stopped for breath, and Angel crossed the room to her and wrapped her in a hug.

The petite girl went stiff as a soldier, then thrashed trying to break her hold before finally dissolving into shuddering, heaving sobs. Angel continued to hold her until she had quieted, whispering "I'm so sorry" every few moments into her hair. That was nearly an hour ago.

Now Free lay sleeping, a few soggy tissues still strewn about, on the same bed Angel had last slept in eighteen years ago. Angel leaned over to smooth her hair, then walked out and closed the door softly behind her.

Mama Jean had let that entire scene play out without intervening and was now sitting at the table, two cups of tea set out, eyes shining with tears. Angel knew she owed her mother something greater than an apology, but the moments with Free had left her spent and wordless. She took a seat at the table.

"Mama…" she started, then stopped.

"I know, baby," Mama Jean said, covering Angel's hands with her own. "Your dad always said you'd be back, and I'm glad you are here. We need you."

Angel thought she had cried out, but the mention of her father sprung fresh tears to her eyes.

"I was there," she said, moving her hands to cover her mother's.

"You were where?" Mama Jean's face creased with confusion.

"At dad's funeral."

Mama Jean sucked in air, her eyes narrowing.

"What? Why didn't you come to the graveside? Why didn't we see you?"

"I-I couldn't… the guilt. And there was…well, there were too many people there. I wasn't ready to face them or Freedom either. Not then, when we were both losing the only father we'd ever known. I just...I couldn't face it all."

Mama Jean sighed, seemingly uninterested in challenging Angel's version of the events and strange rationale.

"Well, then" she asked, folding her hands into her lap. "Why are you back now?" she asked.

"I saw the boy," Angel said, looking down at her hands. "That story about Eric Tucker. It's everywhere. I saw it on the news. And they showed his picture. He looks so much like...just like..."

"His father," Mama Jean finished for her.

"Yeah." Angel said, lifting her teacup to her lips and letting the scalding liquid rush down her throat - a painful and welcomed distraction.

Mama Jean shook her head and laughed.

"You always thought that the two of you were so slick. Sneaking in and out of any window in the house that you could get open." Angel's eyes widened in surprise at her mother's words.

"Oh what? You think I didn't know, child? A wry smile spread across Mama Jean's face. We did our best to keep you in the house and him out, but we couldn't watch you all day and night. The boy wasn't as sneaky as he thought he was because he left a trail of expensive cologne behind him everywhere he went. Your dad always said that he'd lose interest eventually or else his family would help him lose interest, and that it was better to let y'all fall out of love than to try to force you out of love and lose you in the process. I didn't believe him, but I went along with it." She paused here and gave a mirthless laugh. "We lost you anyway though. When you showed up after only one year of college, big and pregnant, and not whispering a single word about the baby's father, I thought, 'that boy done been to see her at school.' And when baby Free slipped into the world with those green-gold eyes and all of those big wavy curls, I was sure I was right. By then, I guess you were already set on leaving here. But then the Tucker boy finally came back in town, years older, serious, and married too, and I figured that maybe I had jumped to conclusions too fast. I wasn't so sure anymore, because for whatever else he was, young Mr. Andrew was a pretty decent kid and so smitten with you. I couldn't imagine he wouldn't have come to see the baby. So then I figured, well, maybe you ran into some other white boy out there in California and got yourself knocked up." At this last statement, Mama Jean threw up her hands and rolled her eyes.

"No, you were right," Angel responded, feeling the sadness fill her heart again. "Freedom is his daughter, but I never told him I was pregnant. I already knew he was planning on marrying Rebecca by then."

Mama Jean nodded solemnly. "Well, we did the best we could by her, Monica, but you should have told Freedom who her father was. You would have saved her a whole heap of heartache."

Angel shook her head in disbelief. "Are you kidding?" she sputtered. "That family would have eaten her up and spit her out. You know how the Tuckers are. They would have never made her feel like she belonged, and they probably would have run our whole family out of town on the next thing smoking."

"Child, please!" Mama Jean shot back, her voice growing irritated. "Do you know how many brown-skinned Tuckers are running around Jolivette? For all of that family's hatred of colored folk, they do NOT mind laying with them. In fact, let me tell it, they prefer it. Something exciting and forbidden."

Angel recoiled at the implication. It stung most because it was true. She had thought she was special. But Andrew has used and discarded her just as easily as any other Tucker would have. She lashed out defensively at the sting of the truth.

"It wasn't always like that!" she sputtered. "We were...he really...we were in..." her voice trailed off, now unconvinced of what she was asserting.

"I know, girl," Mama Jean huffed as she stood to take her teacup to the sink. "You were in love. And maybe he really did love you. Lord knows they always say they do. But not more than they love their name, their legacy, and their facades. Your daughter grew up with two huge holes in her heart, and you could have stayed and filled one of them or told her about her father and let her fill the other the best she could. Instead, you left her here, an orphan, and even now, she is still paying for your mistakes. That boy that's dead? That's her brother isn't it? And you are going to be the one to tell her because I'm done carrying that load." Mama Jean moved to the sink with the empty tea cups.

"What happened out there, Mama? Did she tell you?" Angel pleaded, needing to know how involved her daughter was with what had happened to Andrew's kid. Mama Jean kept her back to her, but answered. "You're going to have to ask your daughter about that." And with

that, Mama Jean flicked the light off and left Angel sitting at
the table in the dark.

Chapter 21

May 21 Andrew - A Reckoning

A ndrew went over his plan again. It seemed even more stupid this time, but he was mentally committed. His plan was to walk up to the door of the Walker's house while holding a package like an Amazon delivery person. He would then ring the bell, and when whoever opened it, he'd ask if Freedom was there to sign for it. But he kept finding holes in the plan that didn't make sense, and had to start over. What if the girl, Freedom was the one who answered and said, "yeah, that's me"? Then what? What did that even prove? Was she going to just look guilty when she answered the door? What if the girl screamed for help? He couldn't get into a back and forth with a kid. If that got out, he'd be all over the news tomorrow. And what if Mama Jean answered? He shivered at the thought. That woman still struck fear into his heart, and he doubted that she would be happy to see the white boy who had spent at least five years sneaking in and out of her house while she and her husband tried to raise a respectable daughter. Mama Jean had never let on that she knew, but the way her eyes narrowed when she'd see Drew at the grocery store and her clipped tone with him whenever his father sent him to pick up his suits from her dry cleaning business—he just felt like she knew, and that if she could ever get him alone, she'd make him pay for it.

Drew shook off his crawling fear of the indomitable Jean Walker and tried to focus. *She probably wouldn't even remember all that stuff from back then,* he reasoned... but he really didn't want to find out. *Ugh!* Andrew slapped at the wheel a few more times. *Stop being a coward!* He coached himself. He was parked close to the address that the school provided for Freedom Walker, and it was the exact house he thought it would be. *I'm just a bereaved father trying to get answers. I deserve answers,* he chanted in his head. He felt a lump forming in his throat. The truth was that he *used* to be a father. He wasn't so sure he still fit in that category. The back of his eyes burned as he allowed himself to wonder, for a moment, if a father whose only child was dead could still be considered a father. What was the parallel word for widow when it came to a parent losing a child?

He quickly rubbed his eyes with his fist to remove himself from that thought spiral and focused back on the mission at hand. He'd brought his old pickup truck to avoid attracting attention with the flashy Mercedes AMG that he took back and forth to work. He'd also parked about six houses down to avoid suspicion, but regretted that decision immediately when he exited the truck and a sudden summer shower began before he could walk 10 steps. He quickened his pace, but the rain matched his energy. What had moments before been the beautiful colors of a setting sun was now a mass of gray clouds, releasing rain so heavy it looked to be coming down sideways. He shouldn't have been surprised. The Texas sky out here just loved to open up and drown the earth without warning in April and May. He turned back quickly and grabbed his WeatherTech hunting jacket from the passenger seat, then returned to his march towards the house nestled in the cul-de-sac. Nostalgia flooded over him as he drew closer.

There had always been something about the humble beauty of the small, well-kept homes in this neighborhood that made him feel like more of himself when he was there. In the sprawling square footage of his own glass house or his father's overdone ranch, he felt accomplished, important even. But here, when he'd been nestled in the tiny bedroom or sat in the tidy living room, cocooned with Monica, he'd felt grounded and peaceful. This neighborhood was a portal to a place where he could exist without having to contort himself into who other people thought he should be. He remembered laughing in awe as girls in the street jumped two ropes at a time and boys ran shirtless football routes in the street, pausing their game only occasionally when a car pulled slowly into the dead end street. He'd played games of 21 and make-it-take-it on a sand-anchored basketball hoop with the neighborhood kids right in this cul-de-sac more summer nights than he could count.

If Drew had been paying closer attention as he walked, instead of losing himself in the haze of memories, he would have noticed the van he walked past, parked on the street with the engine idling, just a few houses before the Walkers. But he was too busy playing and replaying his half-cocked plan and wishing he was 17 again to do a proper sweep of his surroundings. When he reached the house, he abandoned his stupid delivery boy plan, realizing he'd forgotten to bring a fake package.

After a moment of indecision, his body defaulted to muscle memory. He walked around to the back and climbed the short set of steps to the back section of the wraparound porch, grateful that there was no dog to bribe with bacon strips like he'd had to do with Rex, the shockingly ineffective guard dog the Walkers had when he and Monica were in high school. Sliding his hands along the familiar railing, he walked slowly, avoiding what he remembered to be the creakiest bits of the porch until he reached the window outside of Monica's old room. The shades were drawn, and he couldn't see any movement, so he walked several more feet until he was outside the oversized kitchen windows. He kept most of his body concealed by pressing himself into the wooden siding and then craned his neck to peep into the breakfast nook. The kitchen was dark, save the moonlight, but he could make out a figure at the table. It was clearly a woman's profile, and the woman turned slightly towards the window as though she detected Drew's presence. That small turn was just enough for the moonlight to catch her sleek profile. He knew instantly that it was her.

"Jesus!" he yelled aloud, his hand flying to his mouth - too late to stop the word from escaping, and he saw her jump up, her chair shoving backward from the table. He dropped his hand and stepped out of the shadows and into full view from the windows. Monica quickly crossed the distance of the room to the back door. He saw her snatch up a baseball bat from its place against the door jam as her other hand flicked on the porch light. Then she threw the door open. Drew stood illuminated, bathed in the yellow porch light, water dripping from his weather tech, and he saw the recognition slowly register on her face. Then he heard, rather than saw, the bat clatter to the floor with a thud.

Chapter 22

May 21 Angel & Andrew – Revelations

Angel looked like she'd seen a ghost, and in many ways, she may as well have. She could not make any sense of what she was seeing. Was it possible that she was hallucinating? What was the other explanation? What exactly had Mama Jean put in that tea? Her mind was making nonsensical leaps to explain what she was looking at. With the door open and nothing but two feet of air standing between her and Andrew Tucker, she felt as though she was outside of her body.

Andrew stepped in first, closing the distance until they were breathing the same few inches of air. Angel could feel every nerve-ending in her body straining towards him and balled her hands into fists at her side to keep herself rooted to the worn linoleum where she stood. Andrew, experiencing the same struggle, felt his hand raise, an old, buried habit, propelling it to cup her face, but he caught himself and stopped it in midair, his arm and extended hand hovering between the two of them awkwardly. Something in her that she'd thought had died moved her against her will so that she rested her face against the palm of his outstretched hand. A strong current shot from the soles of her feet up through the core of her and connected with the section of her face cradled in the warmth of his hand. She closed her eyes for just a moment, her senses overwhelmed by the warmth and smell of him. But the reality of where they were and why she was back in the town suddenly descended on her conscience like a sheet of ice, and she stepped back, her eyes snapping open. The air was still crackling, surging with electricity around them, but Angel shook her head forcefully to rid herself of the spell he's always been able to cast on her.

"What are you doing here?" she whispered, still in disbelief.

Andrew searched her eyes with his own before he answered.

"My son..." he started and stopped, then began again. "A girl that lives here - she knows what happened to my son. I have to talk to her. Is she your...I mean, are you her..."

Again, his words trailed off like he couldn't complete a sentence, but Angel knew that he was putting the pieces together already.

Angel pulled the door closed behind her and stepped out further onto the porch.

"Not here!" she hissed.

Andrew, in no rush for a run-in with Mama Jean, understood immediately and pulled the keys from his pocket to signal that he could take them somewhere else to talk. Angel nodded and then hesitated, looking down at her feet. She was barefoot. Turning back towards the house, their eyes both landed on a tall set of rubber boots by the back door, and Angel's hand flew to her mouth, stifling a giggle. Andrew's face broke into a wide grin. Those were Pop's old boots, and this wouldn't be the first time she'd had to use them to slip out into the night with Andrew. Her laugh faded, and his smile faltered as they both slipped into their own memories of Pop Walker.

Pop was a good man who had given his all for his family and his community. He had built the cleaning business, their home, and modernized his father's church from the ground up. He'd carved out the space for a good life in hostile territory, but it had never been enough for his daughter. He couldn't shield her from the reality that there were hard limits here that her skin would not allow her to cross. Couldn't hide the fact that all of the school administrators, the elected officials, and the wealthy and powerful folk of Jolivette were white men or their wives. He couldn't make it okay that although she'd been sewing and studying acting all of her life, every application she put in for summer jobs or audition for local plays went unanswered by the small local theater or the boutiques that lined Main Street.

Although he did his best to make sure that she was always loved and supported, he couldn't give her what she so desperately wanted—a place where she felt like she was enough, equal, powerful, and seen. She had caught glimpses of it as the crowd cheered her across the finish line at her out-of-town track meets. But then reality would slap her in the face again on the bus ride home. Her own teammates barely acknowledged her. Pop Walker couldn't make Jolivette feel like home for his daughter; her dreams were too big. Her need to be free of the microaggressions and blatant disregard by her white peers at the newly integrated school system eclipsed any semblance of power he had created for them on their side of the tracks. He knew she wouldn't stay in Jolivette after she graduated. So he was as surprised as anyone would be when he first noticed a young Andrew Tucker cutting his engine and coasting up to the house in the middle of the night to see his daughter.

At first, the two kids would just sit and talk on the back porch for hours, sometimes walking down to the wooded treeline. He kept an ear peeled for any sign that the boy was aggressive or pressuring his daughter. But for the most part, the two of them simply dreamed aloud of futures unencumbered by the stifling fist of small-town living and Tucker influence. But one night, as it was getting cool, he'd watched Monica hop the porch rail and run out to join the boy in his car. He had been a young man once and knew that a car was as bad as a hotel when you were a teenager. So the next time Andrew pulled up, it was Pop that met him in the driveway and climbed into his car. Andrew still went pale and clammy at the memory of that night. Pop had made it clear that as a father, he would die for his little girl—then he had offered Andrew the same fate. Andrew had never been threatened by anyone other than his father, and the feeling was disconcerting. But as he looked into the older man's face, creased with wisdom and fearless resolve, there was no room for doubt. He'd never pulled up to the house at night again after that.

Angel slid her bare feet into the too-big wading boots, and they walked down the stairs in a heavy silence. Andrew pulled off his jacket and held it over her head as they made a run for his truck through the pelting rain, Angel high-stepping to accommodate the awkward length of the boots.

All the while, Carlos snapped as many photos as he could from the row of rhododendrons he'd tucked himself behind and then made a beeline back to the van to figure out where the mayor was headed with the long-legged woman he'd just emerged from Freedom Walker's home with.

***

The plan had been to ride around for a bit so they could talk, but despite Drew's chivalrous attempt at shielding Monica from the rain, they'd both been soaked to the bone by the slanting rain and were steaming up the interior of the extended cab truck with their damp heat. Drew's jeans clung to him, heavy and itchy, and he tried to keep his eyes averted from the way that the wet cotton of Monica's summer shift dress now lay plastered to her skin, outlining every dip and curve. He had turned on the defroster and was still thinking through a few places they could go to dry off when Monica broke the silence.

"You have a tail," she said, her eyes trained on the side mirror.

"What?" Andrew's eyes darted to the rearview mirror "How do you know?"

"I'm saying that you are being followed," she clarified. "And I know what it's like to be followed."

"I know what a tail is," Andrew said, irritated by the realization and the fact that he hadn't noticed before she did.

Angel rolled her eyes.

"Well, good. I'm glad you do because that van has matched every turn and lane change you've made at that exact same distance for the last three miles, as though they learned how to tail a car from a YouTube video."

Andrew tightened his grip on the wheel.

"It's got to be that reporter," he mumbled.

"Which reporter?" Angel asked, turning slightly in her seat to get a better look at the van. "Isn't the whole town crawling with them these days?"

"Yeah," Andrew grunted. "But this one is relentless. He's been popping up everywhere! He's got something to prove, and he doesn't care how he does it."

Angel thought about the footage she'd seen on the news.

"Is it the young black guy? With the dimples and nice teeth? He does seem to be enjoying himself."

"Yeah, TOO much!" Andrew shot back.

He felt an unexpected pang of jealousy that she had commented on the man's looks. He shook his head, surprised at himself. He really needed to get control of his emotions.

"If I didn't think that they'd get carried away and kill him, I'd get my family to run him out of town," he said, still scowling. Angel turned to look at Andrew with something dark and disapproving in her eyes.

"Oh, yes. Of course. Sic the Tuckers on him. If anyone can make a n*gga disappear, it's them."

Andrew jerked as though the slur and her words had physically landed like a punch. He jammed his foot on the brakes, swerving onto the shoulder and cutting the engine. Angel was taken off guard and grabbed the dashboard to steady herself. When he cut the engine and turned to face her, Angel's face had settled into a stony mask. The impact of her words was still stinging behind his eyes as if she had slapped him, and he blinked back the sensation. Neither of them even noticed the white van fly past them.

"I looked for you," Andrew finally said, breaking the silence as he glanced at her. Her face, even now, was so perfect to him, flawless and beautiful.

"Oh, yeah? When?" Angel's tone was more of an accusation than a question.

"After things settled down I...I wanted to find you. I mean, I knew I owed you an apology."

"An apology," Angel repeated, still not meeting his gaze, her voice still hard.

"Yes I...I was young, foolish, and selfish. I didn't know how to stand up to my father then. I didn't trust myself enough to make my own choices."

"How long did you look for me, Andrew?" Angel finally turned to face him. Her face still gave nothing but stony resolve. "Where? Where did you look for me?

"I--I..." Andrew stammered. "After I graduated and came home, I started searching. I never stopped. I even looked to see if the university had a forwarding address for you in the campus records. There was no record of you graduating. I mean, it's like you disappeared. No Monica Walker anywhere. I didn't want to draw too much attention, but I... I even hired someone..." Andrew's voice trailed off as he realized he may have been saying too much.

"Now was this before or after you married the blue-eyed blonde with the rich daddy that your father picked out for you?" Angel's clipped tone interrupted Andrew's pity party.

To Drew, she sounded tired and uninterested in his alleged efforts.

"You weren't trying to find me, Andrew. I changed my name, but I was findable…"

"You changed your name," he cut in. "Why?"

I dated a local guy from L.A. after you and I—broke up." She hesitated before "broke up," considering that it was less of a mutual break up and more of her being unceremoniously dumped, then she continued. "The guy—he was quirky, I thought. Different. But he was so into me, so willing to take me everywhere. Show me off everywhere like I was the greatest thing on earth. He wasn't hiding me from his daddy or his friends."

At this obvious dig, Drew's hands tightened around the wheel until his knuckles whitened, but he said nothing.

"Well, the attention went from great to scary. He got a little…obsessed. He never wanted me to go anywhere or do anything without him. He started stalking me, following me. Showing up outside my dorm, my classroom, and my job. It went on for a long time. It was terrifying, honestly. The police wouldn't help me. Then he finally went far enough to get law enforcement involved. He was arrested one night breaking into our girls' dorm building with zip ties, chloroform, and a concealed handgun. I was able to press charges on the stalking and attempted assault. He was convicted, but I knew he would get out eventually, so I had the court change my name. Changing my name felt like a chance to start over. Something I had been waiting on for a long time. I needed it. But it came at a cost. While I was avoiding that lunatic, I lost my track scholarship. Lost everything really. That's why you won't see the name Monica Walker as a graduate. I didn't."

"Oh," Andrew said, unsure of how to respond to this new information.

"But I know you," Angel continued, "and I know how far your reach is. If you really wanted to find me, you would have."

Andrew considered the weight of that accusation. He had dreamed of her, yearned for her, conjured her when he was alone. But had he really tried to find her?

"Well...if it's not Monica, then what's your name?" he asked. "Now, I mean. What's your name now?"

Angel dropped her eyes for a moment and then met Andrew's again.

"It's Angel."

Andrew let the word slice into him. Angel. His nickname for her.

It had started out as a little joke. But as they grew closer, inseparable really, he'd taken to whispering it in her ear and scribbling it on notes he'd shove through the slats in her locker. Andrew sat looking at her, her face lit only by the slivers of moonlight cutting across the truck. His heart was slamming, and his emotions were all over the place as what she said started to make sense. She went through all of that trouble to change her name, only to choose a name that meant as much to him as it did to her. A name he would have recognized if, as she said, he had really looked. She may have been running from Jolivette and a stalker, but she was not running from him. Andrew could not shake the thought that perhaps he really was a coward, and he'd probably never deserved her.

"Andrew," Angel placed a hand on the dashboard.

"Yeah?" he whispered, expecting her to say, " Take me home."

"The van is back. We've got to get out of here." The white van was approaching slowly from the opposite lane.

Andrew confirmed the letters on the van as those of the young reporter who'd ambushed him behind the school.

"I can't believe this guy," Andrew muttered. "Is your seatbelt on?" he asked, starting the ignition back up and checking his mirrors.

"Yup," Angel answered.

"Well, then hold on!"

Angel grabbed onto the handle in the ceiling over the door, knowing exactly what Andrew was about to do. They'd torn through many open fields in high school, mudding and testing the limits of whatever new toy his father had added to their ranch vehicle fleet.

"I bet this asshole won't take that clunky van off-road," Andrew said, yanking the wheel of his truck hard right and sending them careening off the farm-to-market road and into the muddy fields, still slick from the recent rain. With only the headlights to illuminate the path, the ground appeared to stretch out forever into the pitch black night. Angel looked back over her shoulder and saw that the van had remained on the road, its own bright lights casting an odd glow behind them.

"You haven't changed much at all, huh?" Angel said as the truck porpoised left and right through the muddy field. "Where are we going?"

"Home, if that's okay?" Andrew answered.

***

Andrew stood in the hallway outside the guest bath, waiting for the door to open. Angel finally cracked the door just enough to toss her damp clothes to him and grab the towel from his other hand.

"What do I put on when I get out?" she asked through the door.

"Oh, we keep a few sets of guest nightgowns and slippers in the basket under the sink," he called back to her. They both paused for a moment as that "we" landed between them like a ton of bricks.

"Where is your wife anyway?" Angel asked.

"Oh, she's staying with her family...or maybe my family. Honestly, I don't know," he said, rubbing the stress lines that had formed over his brow. "She left me."

Andrew sounded more resolved than sad, and Angel wanted to poke her head out to see his face, but she didn't want him to think she cared.

"Oh, sorry to hear that," she said, closing the door with a soft click.

Andrew stood at the bar, dropping large spheres of ice into the two glasses he'd poured when Angel finally rounded the corner into the den to join him. He let out a small chuckle when he realized how high the sleeves of the gown were above her wrist and that she was tugging at the hem of the gown which, despite its length, still revealed her immaculate athletic legs almost to mid-thigh. Angel rolled her eyes.

"Are most of your guests children?" she asked.

"No," he laughed, "but we don't get many Amazons either."

He held out the drink to her, and she only hesitated a brief moment before accepting it and taking a slow sip.

"Rum?" she asked, eyebrows shooting up. "I thought you Tucker boys were all scotch and bourbon."

"Yeah, well, I've tried to avoid anything that reminds me too much of my dad, so rum it is."

"Rum it is," Angel repeated, taking another sip, then setting the glass down and finding a seat on the oversized sectional. "Well, what now?" she asked.

Andrew thought of all the things that he wanted to say. He thought of the half-life that he had been living since he left her in that dorm room. Andrew wondered who he would have been if he had never let Angel go. The man he was when he was with her all of those years ago was the best version of himself that he had ever been. He wanted to go back. Would he have been a better man—a better father? It had taken him almost no time to turn into his own father and start using money to smooth over and remove consequences for Eric, himself, and his family name. And for what? He had failed as a father anyway. Instead of setting a higher example, he had become the exact thing that he had run to California to escape, a privilege-peddler who set his son up for success at any cost and without consequence.

Andrew met Angel's eyes with his own, trying mightily to hold back any tears. He wanted to tell her his regrets, to beg her to forgive him. But when he opened his mouth to begin, his voice caught in his throat. Memories of their last night together began to flood his senses. The tender way that she had opened herself to him, unaware that a few hours later, he would walk out on her. The guilt felt like an anvil crushing his chest, and at that moment, something in Andrew broke loose. The tears that he hadn't cried at his father's or his son's funeral spilled out, hot and stinging, and before he could register what he was doing, he reached for her. His arms were around her waist before he could stop to think it through, and much to his surprise, Angel reached back, her own arms circling his neck, her hands fisting in his hair. At that moment, time fell away, and he felt himself drowning in her love the way he had so many years ago.

His warm mouth covered hers, and he tasted her salty tears mixed with his own. Andrew moved his hands over her with desperation, needing to feel all of her at once, needing to be as close to her as possible. He wanted to melt into her skin. He registered that Angel had disengaged his belt buckle and was now pulling at his shirt. He took his hands briefly from her velvet skin to help her lift the shirt up and over his head, but even that moment felt like too long of an interruption. His fingers fumbled at the buttons on the ill-fitting nightgown that was now clinging to her like a film, but he couldn't slow his need enough to concentrate and instead ripped the gown open in frustration, sending the rest of the buttons flying this way and that. He heard Angel's sharp intake of breath, surprised at his brutish actions, but she rewarded his efforts immediately with the contact of her warm skin and curving breasts pressed against his own chest that was barely containing the frantic tempo of his racing heart. Andrew pulled her into his lap with one arm and wrapped his other around her smooth back, burying his face in her neck and hair.

"Wait," Angel said, panting. She pulled away slightly, her hands moving to either side of his face. "Slow down."

Her voice was husky and thick with emotion. Andrew didn't move. His arms still circled her, but he remained perfectly still to focus on regaining control of the electrical currents racing through his body. He closed his eyes and focused on the pace of his breathing, inhaling and exhaling as she ran her fingers through his hair and then up and down his back. His mind began to slow and process as well, and he shook his head at the way life had come full circle. It felt like a dream to have Angel in his arms at this moment. How could she be exactly the same after so much time? Her scent, the magical quality of her touch, the soothing effect of her voice? He moved his hands up her back to the nape of her neck, and she was like silk beneath his fingers. They remained like that for a few more moments, bodies stilled, silently contemplating the gravity and potential repercussions of this moment.

"I...I never really got over you." Angel whispered, her mouth so close to Drew's ear that he could feel the warmth of her voice.

"I'm sorry," Drew whispered back, knowing the quick apology was still inadequate. "But what about now? Do you have someone, a husband, a...anything?"

Angel didn't respond immediately, and Drew felt his heart begin racing with a fear he had no right to possess. He had moved on and gotten married; what right did he have to hope that she had not?

She finally responded. "No, I just...could never really figure out how to trust someone enough to love them after...everything. And I guess a part of me never stopped thinking that maybe...maybe you would..."

"Come back for you," Drew said, finishing her sentence.

Drew's heartbeat was still thundering but had slowed significantly. The silence and regret lapped over them, both buried in their own swirl of thoughts. And then Angel brought her lips to his again. He felt his body respond immediately, and when he pushed his tongue gently against her lips, she opened her mouth and let him taste her. His hands slid back down to her waist when he felt her hips begin to move in slow circular waves; his own body responded immediately, pressing up towards her warmth. Angel let a soft moan escape into his mouth, and he felt himself unraveling.

He wanted to lose himself in her. He wanted to strip away all of the pressure and pain of being himself and become a part of her instead. He pushed the tattered remains of the gown up over her hips so that the fabric simply circled her waist. There was nothing between them now. Another wave of deep need crashed over him, and an involuntary groan escaped him. He lifted her, positioning their bodies for what they both knew was coming, and then he hesitated, guilt shoving its way back into his consciousness. This is what he had always done. All through high school, and even that first year of college, this is what he had done with his pain, anger, confusion, love, and joy—escaped into Angel with it. She was the soft place to cry, to vent, to admit weakness, and she had always been ready to open herself to him - to comfort him and reassure him of his strength and intelligence. But when it was time for him to reciprocate in real life, to show up for her the way she had shown up for him, he had abandoned her.

How was this any different? He was right back to getting what he wanted at her expense. He couldn't do this. What if he hurt her again? He pushed her hips back and away from the center of him, trying to extract himself from the heady rush that held him in a trance.

"Angel," his voice rasped out hoarsely. "I'm sorry. I shouldn't do this. I don't deserve…"

The rest of his words were lost as Angel leaned her face down and sucked first his lips and then his tongue into her warm mouth. She raised her hips just enough to position herself over him again and then descended slowly, joining them together. Andrew's head rolled back, a tidal wave of feeling crashing over him, his guilt temporarily forgotten. He was home. She was the home he had been missing all of these years. His hands gripped her full bottom, and some guttural sound he hadn't made in decades slipped from his throat. He felt himself transforming, his mounting failures melting away. In this moment, he wasn't a failed husband with a dead son trying to pretend to care about being a mayor. Instead, he existed only inside of this woman's world, his personal angel, all of his senses attuned to the music of her panting breaths, her movements, and her moans, concerned only with conducting that song to its crescendo.

She moved her body as though she, too, was trying to shed herself and become that magical thing they only ever were when they were together. They were meant to be like this, always. The rhythm of their bodies took on a hypnotic cadence, and he knew that he wouldn't be able to hold on to himself much longer. As good as he felt, the reality that it was going to end soon pushed fresh tears from his eyes despite the magnificent pleasure rising through his body. He felt unhinged, wild, and desperate to hold onto this feeling as long as he could. His hand instinctively fisted in her hair, pulling her head back until her long, graceful neck was exposed, its deep melanin shade reflecting the moonlight filtering through the high windows and skylights. His other arm tightened around the small of her back, making it impossible for her to move or pull away as he sank into her until he did not know where his body stopped and hers began.

Angel cried out, and they crested and exploded together—again, and again, and again—her pulsing explosion initiating his, and his creating another for her, on and on until their bodies, spent and slick with sweat and euphoria, stilled. The crashing tide of their desire reduced to gentle waves lapping against the shore of a dulled reality that neither of them was ready to see go.

***

It was nearly 1:00 am when Andrew finally walked Angel up to his big master shower. He laid her on the oversized bench and turned the steam up to full blast. He watched as her hair waved and then coiled, becoming a thick, frizzy mane that swept about her face and clung to her shoulder blades. He sat on the adjacent bench and wondered again how this was happening. How could it be that they were them again? If he was being honest, he could now admit that he had never felt safer and more like himself than when he was with Angel. Experiencing that peace again almost didn't feel real, and maybe it wasn't. Outside of this shower, there was still a nightmare of a to-do list awaiting him, and even though he didn't want to, he had to find the answers to what had happened to his son. He had to file for divorce to make it official if his marriage was really over. He had to figure out how to disappoint what was now obviously Angel's daughter by taking away her valedictorian class ranking. He closed his eyes, a feeble attempt to thwart the curtain of reality that was descending. Sensing the shift in his mood, Angel sat up, swinging her legs to the shower floor.

"Okay," she said, as though reading his mind. "What now?

Andrew realized that with the two of them sitting here in nothing but their skin, there wasn't much use trying to be evasive, so he opted to be blunt.

"Monica(?)...I mean, Angel, my son is dead." The statement sucked all of the air out of the sauna, but he pushed through. "Not only is he dead, but there is only one person on this earth that might know what happened to him, and she lives in *your* old house with *your* mother. So I need to know for sure. Who is Freedom Walker to you, and what does she know?"

Angel weighed her words carefully, unsure of how exposed she really wanted to be, and then instantly realized the irony of that based on her current state.

"I am very, very sorry about your son, Andrew. And I want to help you. But there is something you need to know."

"About the girl?" he asked, ignoring her condolences and pressing for an answer.

"Yes, about the girl. She's not just a girl. She's my daughter."

Andrew rocked back. He had already put the pieces together, but hearing it outright was still jarring. He rubbed his palms up and down his thighs, a motion that Angel knew he only did when he was nervous.

"Your daughter. I thought that might be the case. She is a senior in high school, so that makes her what - maybe seventeen or eighteen?" His questions felt stilted, like he knew where he was going but didn't want to get there.

Angel nodded a simple yes. She wouldn't rush him.

"Okay," Andrew said again. "Okay. So you had her while you were in college." He pushed down the absurd jealousy that was rising in his chest again. Even though he was the one who ended things, the idea that someone else had laid claim so quickly to what was once his was throwing him into a weird head space. "And her dad?" he asked. "Where is he?"

"Here," Angel answered softly.

"In Jolivette?!" Andrew boomed, standing to his feet, incredulous. He hadn't meant to raise his voice, and he knew he must look absurd getting upset while standing naked in the shower, but he really felt that he would be sick if she'd had a kid by one of these Jolivette locals and he'd never known.

Everyone in Jolivette knew that Monica belonged to Drew. As archaic as it may sound, he believed then and irrationally now that her heart quickened only for him, and his for her. Drew wondered, with irritation, whom she could have moved on to so quickly.

"No," Angel grabbed his hand and pulled down until he acquiesced and returned to his seat on the shower bench. "No," she said again, still gripping his hand. "I don't just mean here in Jolivette." She slid closer to him on the bench and placed her other hand on his chest. "I mean *right* here. I mean you."

Drew felt something sharp and hot zip through his body as the realization closed in around him - blurring his vision and arresting his heart.

Chapter 23

May 22 Free - Nowhere to Run

*S*he's gone, Free realized, her heart beginning to race. *She's GONE!*

Freedom retraced her steps, living room, dining room, bathroom, spare bedroom, porch, and kitchen. She felt herself unraveling and steadied herself against the wall to take deep breaths. *No,* she told herself. *That's not right. She can't be gone. Breathe,* she told herself. *Just breathe.*

She heard Mama Jean's door creak open and moved to the pantry to give the impression that she was just digging around for breakfast and conceal the tears in her eyes.

"Good morning," Mama Jean said, entering the kitchen. She shuffled her worn slippers further onto her feet and clicked the coffee machine on.

Freedom didn't respond, not trusting that her voice wouldn't betray her panic. She could feel Mama Jean's eyes on her, but did not turn.

"Her Jeep is still in the garage," Mama Jean said, returning to filling the coffee machine with grinds. "She probably went for a run." Freedom loosened her grip on the pantry door and pulled a box of cereal.

"Oh," she responded, almost ashamed at the relief that washed over her.

Her relief quickly turned to anger. *Why should I care?* she scolded herself internally as she plunked down a bowl and moved to the refrigerator for the oat milk. *Why am I even expecting her to stay?* She lifted the milk to pour it, then set it back down when she realized her hands were shaking.

Mama Jean continued reading her mind. "It's okay to care, want a relationship with her, and feel connected to her. She is still your mother."

Mama Jean's wisdom was interrupted by aggressive knocking on the back door. They both turned to see Angel in the window, wearing an oversized hooded sweatshirt pulled tightly around her face and dark glasses. Freedom hustled to open the door, shocked by her mother's harried appearance, which looked even stranger as she stepped in from the porch, revealing rolled-up striped pajama bottoms covered in grass stains and oversized wading boots.

"What in God's name!" Mama Jean rushed over, closing the door behind Angel and taking in her appearance with a cluck of her tongue. "Are those your daddy's old wading boots? What the devil are you wearing? What happened to your hair?" She asked, noticing Angel's unwieldy afro. "Where have you been?"

Angel ignored them both and rushed to the front of the house to secure the few partially open blinds and snatch the shades closed over them.

"Have y'all not looked out front?" she huffed, breathless from her harried efforts. "It's crawling with reporters! I had to come in through the park and climb the fence!" she said, referring to the wooded area and small creek behind the house that was dry more than half the year. Angel plucked a dry leaf from her hair and strode swiftly toward the living room. "Turn on the television!"

"What?" Mama Jean shuffled briskly to the small window over the kitchen sink and lifted a small corner of the shade as Free hustled to find the remote control and turn to the local news channel. Mama Jean sucked in a breath as she took in the scene in front of her house. The entire culdesac was brimming with vans, cameras, and reporters. A few of the reporters were on their phones, and some were just milling about, bored. One woman was styling her hair with a curling wand, using the van's side mirror as a vanity. Mama Jean quickly dropped the shade and stepped away from the window.

"Why are they here?" She asked, turning to Angel with anger etched across her face.

"You KNOW why they are here," Angel's strained tone was just as fiery as Mama Jean's as she rushed to the other side of the house, checking all the windows. "Has no one texted or called you two?" she yelled over her shoulder, still in a flurry of motion. "Freedom, you are a teenager! Aren't teenagers permanently attached to their phones? None of your friends has said anything to you?"

Free flushed with embarrassment. She didn't want her mother to know she didn't have real friends. Even the few people she considered "sort of friends" wouldn't call or text her unless it was about schoolwork. Mama Jean always quoted the scripture, "To have friends, one must first show themselves friendly," as she attempted to prod and guilt Free into attending more of the youth bible studies or joining the youth choir. But she wasn't interested in having friends. From all she'd come to know, people were not to be trusted with closeness. Mama Jean found Free's antisocial behavior intolerable and would grumble that "for a child who had never lain eyes on her own mother, she sure did act like her clone." Free would shrug the comments off, but she heard the accusation and felt its sting. She didn't want to be anything like a mother that could turn off her vulnerability and emotions enough to abandon a child; but she didn't believe that forming a bunch of shallow friendships would help her escape Jolivette. So she absorbed the darts Mama Jean threw about her mother and stayed to herself despite Mama Jean's incessant prodding.

"Seriously? It's seven o'clock in the morning on a Saturday," Free snapped back flippantly. "What teenager do you think is up watching the news and texting about it?"

She crossed her arms protectively over her chest and flipped the channels to see if the news was on any other station. She'd sounded convincing enough to herself. Her mother didn't need to know she was a social failure.

Angel ignored Free's tone and instead grabbed the remote from her hand.

"Do you mind if I change the channel?" she asked as if it mattered when she had already taken the device.

Free lowered her eyes to slits at the inconsiderate action and contemplated whether she could generate enough force to shove her mother to the ground despite the height difference. She wasn't sure, but she decided it was worth the risk.

"You know what," Free started as she stepped towards Angel.

"Wait! Ssshhh!"

Angel said absentmindedly, reaching out and grabbing Free's hand, her eyes glued to the TV screen.

"Here it is."

Free snatched her hand back from Angel's grip and turned to see what was on the television. What she saw on the screen was a birdseye view of her street and her house, with a scrolling banner running below the image stating, "Person of Interest Identified in Slaying of Jolivette Football Star, Eric Tucker."

A strangled cry escaped Free's throat. "Oh no! How do they know who I am? I thought you said that they don't release the names of minors?" she whirled to face Mama Jean, but Mama Jean was still staring intently at the television, her hand slowly rising to her chest. The sound was on, but Free couldn't make out a word with the sound of her own heart thudding in her ears. The image changed; the screen suddenly filled with footage of Monica, well, Angel now, running through the rain, with Andrew Tucker, running alongside her, his coat held aloft to shield her from the downpour. The image was not clear at all. The rain and the shadows from the tree-lined street made their features hard to make out, and the coat held over Angel's head was obstructing most of her face. Maybe other folk would be confused, but there was no confusion for Mama Jean, Free, or Angel about who and what they were seeing.

Angel dropped to the couch.

"Oh my God," she said. "Oh, my God."

Mama Jean whipped around the couch, snatching the remote from Angel and turning the volume up.

"What is this!?" she yelled, hurling the words up into the air as if they would come back down with answers.

The image of Angel and Mayor Tucker remained on one half of the screen. Free felt her knees go out from under her as she collapsed onto the couch - never taking her eyes from the screen. Then the young, handsome, copper-skinned news reporter filled the screen. His peek-a-boo dimples and muscular build were unmistakable. Free immediately recognized him from the newscast at the police station and her high school. Carlos Jackson. She was overwhelmed by the thought that he seemed to be everywhere and knew too much of everything. How had he found her home?

"Late last night, an unidentified woman was seen exiting this address, currently believed to be the home of the teen who was present during the recent slaying of Jolivette high school senior and football star Eric Tucker." The reporter gestured towards the house they were all sitting in, and a surreal chill fell over the Walker women. "The man she is shown leaving with appears to be the Mayor of Jolivette, Andrew Tucker, who is the slain boy's father. This senseless killing has rocked this small town to its core, with speculation running wild about what happened on that fateful night and why Eric's life was taken. The only person with those answers lives here, in this home, and it would seem that Eric's father has taken it into his own hands to come looking for those answers himself."

The screen then flipped to an image of two news anchors at a desk.

"Wow, Carlos, who could have known that what was turning out to be an amazing run at a state championship for a sleepy football town would spin into this type of tragic mystery?"

Carlos appeared back on screen, shaking his head, his eyebrows knitted into a look of deep concern.

"Truly, Jim. This story has caught everyone off guard and captured the attention of the entire country. Even the Texas Governor has taken notice now, tweeting yesterday afternoon that his thoughts and prayers are with the Tucker family and that he is praying for swift justice. This is Carlos Jackson, Houston KVH2 News."

The reporter signed off, and the screen flitted back to the anchors who were sudddenly cooing over a story about puppies helping pediatric cancer patients. Mama Jean muted the tv then and turned to face off with Angel. Free, despite her best efforts, was unraveling. Her chest was heaving with hard-to-draw breaths, and she leaned over to drop her head into her hands. Angel rubbed her hands compulsively up and down the fabric of her borrowed pants, avoiding eye contact with Mama Jean, who was standing so eerily still that you could almost see the waves of anger rolling off her skin.

"What did you do?" Mama Jean hissed at Angel through gritted teeth. "What did you do?

Chapter 24

May 23 Andrew - Chickens Come Home to Roost

Andrew's phone shimmied across the coffee table, vibrating angrily like a swarm of killer bees, but he didn't move. He couldn't move. His head was throbbing to the beat of his heart, and his mouth felt full of sand. He'd had plenty of hangovers in his life, but this moment was something worse than that. He hadn't even realized that there were any remaining pieces of his heart that hadn't been broken the night he identified Eric's body, but Angel had managed to find the last few and obliterate them. He felt like he'd been kicked in the chest by a Clydesdale. After Angel dropped her truth bomb in the shower, things had not gone well. Incredulous at her big reveal, he'd said quite a few things he knew he'd live to regret and sent her to sleep in the guest room, but was certain that neither of them had slept much. Once the sun was up, he'd driven her home in total silence. He felt off-kilter, as though the entire world had shifted on its axis, and he was

in danger of sliding off into the insane void. He'd pulled into the wooded area behind the house and watched Angel's flawless, athletic form run through the underbrush and disappear into the darkness like she used to when he would sneak her home in high school. The drive home alone was even worse, and his body must have been on autopilot because he had no memory of navigating the trip. He wasn't even sure what time he got home. He had collapsed into the oversized sectional in the game room, choosing to avoid his bedroom and the living room. He didn't want to see anything that made him think of the life he had ruined with Rebecca or the night he had just spent with Angel. The thought occurred to him that he would have to move out now that the memories of both women haunted the entire house.

Eventually, as he drifted towards sleep from sheer exhaustion, his eyes passed over the row of Eric's Pop Warner football trophies lining the bookshelf, and he squeezed his eyes shut against the memories and pain. Drew had fallen into a fitful, sweaty sleep haunted by the nightmare reel of Eric's body on the cold autopsy table, mangled, discolored, and distorted that played on a loop in his dreams.

He couldn't have slept more than three hours before the buzzing phone awoke him. He peered at the screen, quickly tapped ignore, then shuffled carefully to the kitchen for water and ibuprofen. He wondered if this were the rock bottom he'd often heard referred to as a prerequisite for a new life. For decades, his brother had accused him of living a charmed, struggle-free life. It seems those accusations would finally come to an end because his life was nothing more than jagged, broken shards of dreams he had single-handedly destroyed in pursuit of his father's approval.

Drew chugged down the water and thought about that long drive he had made back to Stanford almost 19 years ago from Angel's UCLA dorm with tears streaming down his face. He had told her that his father demanded he make a choice. He had been adamant that his family was important to him, and that continuing to be with her was tearing it apart. He thought he had just been sad to end one of his first real relationships then, but now, with this relentless pain compressing his chest and his head a throbbing nightmare, Drew realized that he had been too young and immature to realize what a broken heart really was.

At 20 years old, he naively believed that love was everywhere and that, with time, he would find another great love just as strong as he'd had with Angel. He had been wrong, and life had not delivered anything close to that love again. So many times, he had wondered how things would have been if he had chosen his heart over his father. Maybe he would have less stuff, a smaller house, but he would have been in love—really in love. Happy, even. But never in his wildest imagination had he considered that Angel was pregnant and gave birth to his child. To discover that he had a daughter just a few miles from where he slept every night was more than he could process. Last night, in a matter of moments, he had gone from believing that life had finally brought Angel back into his life to learning that Angel had hidden an entire child from him for 18 years. How could that be true? And how is it that she had hated him enough never to say a single word about it? Worst of all, how could the child have existed in his city, and he had never crossed paths with her?

Drew dropped his head into his hands, pulling at his hair. Just how horrible did Angel think he was? Did she think he wouldn't have taken care of his daughter? Drew hesitated for a moment, imagining what his father would have said. *Hell, maybe she was right,* he thought. *I didn't stand up to my father about her; how do I know I would have gone to battle with him over the baby? No, of course, I would have*, he thought, shaking off some of the self-loathing, but then he faltered again, straining to see himself clearly in his mind. Drew really wanted to think of himself as a good guy. He tried so hard to be the good guy for so many people, but what was unfolding was not the story of a good guy. This is hell, he thought. *I am in hell*. He took a handful of ibuprofen and Ambien and then collapsed back into the sofa.

When Andrew woke again, all of the pain was still there waiting for him, as well as nearly 50 missed calls on his phone. He scrolled through the call log—his brother, his mother, Rebecca, the city manager, and his lawyer. Call after call. Whatever it was, it was bad. He toggled over to his text messages to see if he could figure out what was going on without having to call any of those people back. The message from Grant was short and to the point: "What the f**k?"

The next message was more informative. His lawyer had texted him the link to a video on a Houston news site. He clicked it and immediately saw an image of himself and Angel from the night before.

"Shit."

He dialed his lawyer.

***

By mid-afternoon, Andrew's shock and despair were transforming into something darker and more brooding. To call it anger would have been a gross understatement. His thoughts had spiraled quickly after speaking with his attorney. When Angel had dropped the bomb of a confession on him, he was fatigued. His mind and body were gripped by regret and remorse. But now, in the glaring light of day, he was beginning to see how Angel's choice placed him in an impossible position. His lawyer claimed that the district attorney was livid that Andrew appeared to be interfering in an ongoing criminal investigation despite the fact that no charges were filed in connection with Eric's death. He hopped onto a conference call where they threw around terms like "obstruction," "appearance of impropriety," and "optics" until Andrew abruptly ended the call. Now he was stewing in anger, contemplating the jagged, unpolished truth of Angel and how her choices had changed his options.

She'd called him a coward, but intentionally hid his child from him because of what? Because he had broken things off? Because his family didn't like her? That wasn't Angel's choice to make. And she had not even raised their child, instead leaving the girl with her grandparents. Maybe

Angel was the real monster. Drew was not naive. He knew his family could be mean and bigoted and probably never would have accepted Angel, but he also knew himself. He could have kept his daughter safe and protected. He was a man of his own agency now. He wasn't the stupid, sheltered college boy needing his family's money to feel safe in the world. He'd made a selfish choice, trading Angel for the security of his family's reach and influence, but she had taken his mistake and made someone else pay for it. She made their child pay for it. Their child. He still could not get used to the two words together.

His left temple felt like it was being slammed by a sledgehammer, and the veins in his arm were puffing up from how tightly he'd clenched his fists during the call, but he couldn't calm down. All of this time, he had been privately tormenting himself for tossing aside the best thing that had ever happened to him, but she was just as bad as he was—worse even. Drew was up and pacing now. His family and this city wanted answers about what had happened to his son, and now he had to decide how far to push what was apparently his own daughter to get those answers.

Chapter 25

May 22 Free - Nowhere to Hide

Free shoved the desk chair beneath the doorknob of her bedroom at an angle so that pushing the door would only make it less likely to open. She wasn't even sure why she was barricading herself in her room, except that she wanted to keep Angel out. She threw a glance at the suitcases she had returned to packing, still sitting open on the floor of her bedroom. She had always said she wanted to leave Jolivette, but not like this. She could hear the muffled angry voices of both her mother and Mama Jean filtering down the hallway and knew that they would be checking on her soon.

"Mama, let me explain," Monica was pleading. Free heard Mama Jean's voice rise to an uncharacteristic volume such that her next words floated clearly down the hall.

"Listen, Monica; you ain't saying nothing slick to a can of oil. I was born at night, but not LAST night, and I KNEW you came back here for more than just Free! After all these years, I cannot believe you will still put anything and anyone in harm's way just to be with that Tucker boy...."

As the argument rounded the hallway and headed towards Mama Jean's room, their voices faded, and Free strained to hear more of the fight. She pressed her ear to the wall, but she heard Mama Jean's door slamming shut, and their angry words were once again muffled. It didn't matter, though. She had heard enough to know that her mother had not come back for her. Of course, there was someone else. There was always someone else. It was never Free, that her mother made decisions for,

Free threw herself across the bed, her head swimming, trying to make sense of the past 24 hours. First, her long-lost mother shows up with a new name.

"Angel! Ha! Some kind of Angel," Free scoffed.

Then this so-called Angel somehow managed to get chummy with the one family Free had spent the last eight years trying to avoid. How did Angel contact Eric's dad so quickly, and why would she secretly meet with him?

Free's mind was whirring, grasping at clues. She felt her skin prickling with anger as she seethed over the betrayal. After all she had been through with Eric and the way he had terrorized her for years on end, her mother's bright idea was to do what? To try to seduce his father? Pay him off? Strike some clandestine deal? What was Angel doing? Eric's father was the mayor, for God's sake! And his family had the entire city in a vice. How could her mother have possibly thought contacting Eric's father would fix anything? She hadn't even bothered to so much as run the idea by Free first. Nope, her selfish mother had just come blowing in like a tornado, and made a bad situation worse.

In less than 24 hours, she had brought Eric's father and the media to their door, and now Free was being forced to pack up and leave the only home she'd ever lived in like some sort of fugitive. Mama Jean had protested the idea of leaving the house, but Angel made it very clear that anyone with a television or a smartphone now had enough information to pop up at their home, and plenty of people would do exactly that. Free tried to think of a time that she had seen Mama Jean get as angry as she did when Angel explained that they had to move out of the house for a while. She'd called on Jesus and prayed aloud, but not to help their family, only to keep her from wringing her own daughter's neck.

As far as Free could tell, her mother had tried to punch way above her weight class with the illicit meeting with the mayor, and now the Tucker wrath was going to rain down on them all. Anyone who didn't know that Free was the last person to see Eric alive would know now. And they could pull her house up on Google earth, show up, and let her know exactly what they thought of her. Free looked at the half-packed suitcase and felt the tears clog behind her eyes. She wanted to howl and cry until she was empty, but Free was so much in the habit of keeping her emotions damned up, she fought the increasing pressure and tried to breathe through the sensation instead. Her heart was racing a mile a minute, and she felt her hands shaking. Unsure of what else to do, she grabbed a pillow, pressed it tightly over her face, and screamed into it until her lungs were on fire.

When her breath was spent, the tears finally escaped, running past her ears in hot trails and soaking into the quilt where she lay. She thought about all that she had sacrificed over the years—friendships, fun, everything, and for what? While her classmates were running around, falling in and out of crushes and relationships, making out in cars, and drinking cheap beer at parties, she had been locked into an invariable routine of studying, learning to play instruments, and doing service projects; a strategy that she had deduced to be the ivy league acceptance formula for kids without wealth. She knew that she wouldn't have the references or the big money of well-connected applicants, but what she did have was a dramatically sad origin story and an unblemished academic record. Free was counting on the horrible truth of her abandonment at birth being the ONE thing her useless mother would contribute to the success that Free was propelling herself towards. She had staked everything on her plan. Foregoing friendships and any chance at fitting in or belonging. And for what?

If she were being honest, her self-inflicted solitude hadn't actually started out as a choice. Mama Jean had been fiercely protective, wanting Free to always be in her sights. Wherever she had gone wrong with Free's mama, she seemed determined that the way to correct that mistake was to keep Free tucked under her wing and away from external influences for as long as possible.

Free didn't attend daycare and was home-schooled until sixth grade. When she was finally permitted to attend public school, she was immediately treated like a carnival side show—the girl with no parents—so she knew that school wouldn't be the place she found her people. But she had assumed that by going to a predominantly black church, where everyone was supposed to play nice, she would find her tribe. That didn't happen either. Her grandfather pastored Jolivette's largest black congregation, but instead of that fact working for her, it made her a liability. The other kids at church and in her neighborhood were reluctant to include her in anything they were planning or plotting to do over the weekends. In their mind, even if Free didn't snitch them out to her grandparents, the chance of everyone getting caught because Free was around was just too big a risk.

Pop Walker and Mama Jean knew everyone, and if they heard about a kid who was up to no good, they always alerted the parents. Free had found this shunning by her peers ridiculous since it was fairly easy for anyone with two eyes and a nose to figure out which kids were smoking weed, which kids were having sex, and which kids were sneaking out to shoot at bottles in the old abandoned train house. None of their less-than-stealthy schemes were particularly well thought out or intelligently crafted. So just like she'd done at school, Free convinced herself that she was content with being left out of their childish activities. She would keep a book on her at all times, so she could pretend to be engrossed in it and oblivious to the way the girls would whisper together about her.

"Ah, don't worry, baby," her grandmother had clucked when Free had come home upset about it the first few times. "Those little girls are just jealous. There aren't many pretty little things in Jolivette with all of that soft curly hair and eyes like the ocean shallows where the water meets the sand."

This had provided zero solace to a pre-teen who desperately wanted to belong somewhere.

"So they are mean to me because they think I'm pretty?" Free asked, confusion etched across her little face.

"Yea, that's about the size of it," Mama Jean stated matter-of-factly. "But they would talk about you even worse if you were ugly, so be grateful you have a pretty problem and not an ugly one. You know, it wouldn't hurt if you'd be a little more social. They think you are stuck up because you never talk to anyone. " With that, Mama Jean had waved her off and gone back to flouring chicken.

Free waited for things to get better, but instead, they got worse. In response, Free steeled her heart against the idea that friends in Jolivette were in the cards for her and set her sights on getting the hell out of this town, one way or another. The official plan, as it was scrawled in her Journal, had been to be "smarter, better, and richer than everyone in this crappy town." That. Was. The. Plan. It was high level, but she filled in the details over time, and it was working. She'd received three full-ride scholarship offers and early decision admission to her top three schools. She was on her way to getting out before Eric Tucker had gone out of his way to ruin all of that. Now that she was on the news, how long would it be before the schools started calling and pulling their offers? She wondered. For as long as she could remember, Eric had gone out of his way to make her feel small and worthless. And even now, from the grave, he was still making her life miserable.

Free wanted to scream again. Her head was pounding, and she closed her eyes tight against the pain. As soon as her eyes shut, Eric's face flashed into her mind. She recalled the shock and fear that had registered when the shot hit him and spun him almost in a full circle. She shook her head to rid herself of the vision, but it didn't budge. She could still recall the way his mouth had contorted, and his eyes blazed with disbelief and anger when he realized what had happened. The way he had shifted those burning orbs of rage to meet hers just before the truck plowed into him and he disappeared from sight. It had all happened so quickly. The memory was too vivid. Her stomach rolled, her mouth watered up, and she felt a wave of nausea coming. She had to find something else to do with her hands; she had to clear her mind.

Free grabbed her laptop from her bedside table and opened it to a fresh Google Chrome page. She stared at the blinking cursor in the blank search box for a few moments, unsure if what she was about to do made sense. She'd watched enough true murder TV to know that, eventually, someone was going to come and confiscate her computer and check her search history. That's how everyone on the ID channel got busted. But curiosity gnawed at her until she blew past her better judgment, shoved her fears aside, and typed his name into the browser. ERIC TUCKER. She hesitated and then added "+ Jolivette" to the search terms so that she wouldn't get every Eric Tucker in the country. She looked at the blinking cursor and thought about how many times he had probably had an article written about him. *The results are still going to be off-base,* she thought. She took a deep breath, blew it out, and then added "+ DEATH" to the search terms and hit enter.

The results slammed into Freedom like a freight train. Page after page of responsive links, posts, videos, articles, mentions, TikToks, and clips stretched out before her. The headlines sent a chill through her body and raised goosebumps down her arms.

Last Person to See Eric Tucker Alive and She's Not Talking.

No Weapon, But Plenty Of Motive - High School Valedictorian Becomes Person of Interest in Grizzly Death of Classmate.

Wealthy Son of Mayor Gunned Down Trying to Help a Classmate: Was Eric Tucker Set Up?

Beyond the digital news articles, there were YouTube video links, and Free began clicking them instinctively. There were social media influencers, radio shows, and visual podcasts all weighing in on what had happened. The more technically advanced accounts had clips rolling on a green screen behind them as they gestured wildly with their hands, speculating about who Freedom Walker was and why she wasn't talking to anyone.

Free couldn't peel her eyes away. She watched bits of her life pop up on the green screens, mortified. Footage of her grandparents' church, the cleaners, her school, the stretch of highway where her entire life had gone off the rails, and the old, fading Suburban she had been driving, now sitting in a police impound lot. There was footage of Mayor Tucker, looking mad enough to fight, storming out of Jolivette High. But there was one clip, in particular, that Free could not stop replaying. It featured the police officer lunging at the reporter, who she now knew was Carlos

Jackson. The same reporter who had stood not ten feet from her front door today, destroying any shred of anonymity she'd had left to cling to, and released the images of her mother and Mayor Tucker to the world. The clip she kept replaying on a loop showed the reporter confronting the cop before the officer swatted for his microphone as more officers poured from the building. The camera swung wildly for a few moments, presumably as the cameraman ran from the oncoming officers, but it still managed to catch a shaky view of the reporter stumbling, recovering, and then running toward the news van.

The scene was shocking. It made the police look like brutes and goons, and it had been shared over a million times, according to YouTube. But the part that Free kept rewinding and pausing was the brief moment when the reporter is seen leaping into the relative safety of his van and then looking in the direction of the cameraman and, therefore, the camera. Free hit pause and play over and over again, just to make sure that she wasn't imagining things or going crazy, but she was sure now.

After almost being pummeled by armed officers and having to run for cover, the reporter leapt into the van with a smile on his face. It was not a wide enough smile to be overtly perceptible, but it registered enough for his dimples to deepen and his eyebrows raised in what Free was sure now was excitement. Free couldn't believe it! He was having fun! The social media powers-that-be were referring to him as the breakout investigative journalist who uncovered the truth of Eric's death and unearthed Free's identity. They were practically hailing him as a hero. This man was the reason that her face and location were splashed all over the news. He was the reason that she was fairly certain she would never be safe again. And he had the unchecked audacity to be having fun?!

It took a moment for Free to realize that she was hyperventilating, and she began gulping for air. The room started a slow spin, and her peripheral vision started going white. Free had the fleeting thought that she might be dying, but quickly recalled reading an article about how panic attacks felt like impending death. She shut her eyes tight, leaned her head down between her knees, and started forcing herself to take slow, deliberate breaths.

In through your nose, out through your mouth. She repeated this single directive in her mind over and over again until her body began to comply. She could not afford for her johnny-come-lately of a mother to walk in and discover her passed out from panic. She couldn't bear the thought of that woman seeing weakness in her. After several minutes, the feeling began to subside, so she sat up slowly and dragged the computer back onto her lap, cleared her search history, and slid the laptop into her luggage.

Chapter 26

May 22 Angel - Calling in Reinforcements

own the hall from Freedom's room, the phone rang, and the muffled sounds of Angel and Mama Jean arguing stopped.

The loud ringing continued as Mama Jean and Angel stared at the cordless phone in its cradle. Mama Jean's eyes narrowed in suspicion. She never gave out the number to the house phone, and it rarely ever rang. Angel, growing impatient, reached for it, but Mama Jean slapped her hand away.

"You don't live here!" she hissed, and Angel held her smarting hand to her chest incredulously.

Mama Jean picked up the phone, ignoring Angel's shock at the swat.

"This is Jean," she said into the receiver.

Angel craned her head toward the phone, hoping to overhear something as she watched Mama Jean's brows knit together in confusion.

"Oh, I don't think so," Mama Jean said sharply, irritation was apparent in her voice. "What do these wild, unbased accusations have to do with her grades? Her academic performance is flawless, and you can't penalize her..." Mama Jean's voice trailed off as the caller interrupted her, and a dark look passed over her otherwise unflappable countenance. "Freedom has been a model student, never been in trouble, and has far and away the best academic record in your school's history!" she barked into the phone. "She has earned the right to that valedictorian title. Now, if you don't want her to give the speech, that's one thing, but you can't strip her of her accomplishment! She has gotten acceptances and scholarship offers to the best schools in the country based on her academic record, and you will not change it!"

Mama Jean went silent for a moment as the muffled voice continued on the other end of the call.

"You'll be hearing from our lawyer!" she announced, abruptly slamming down the receiver.

Angel, having promptly forgotten about her slapped hand, wounded ego and publicly being outed by the media for her evening with Drew, searched her mother's concerned face for answers. She wanted to ask Mama Jean who was on the phone, but she had heard enough to know the gist of it.

Instead, she asked, "What lawyer, Mama? Do you already have an attorney?"

"No, but we need one." Mama Jean grumbled.

At that moment, finally, Angel knew how she could help fix the mess she had made the day she left her baby in Jolivette.

Chapter 27

We've Got Action

Carlos let out an excited whoop! He was trending. Well, his story was trending, with a good number of references back to his original reporting, and he knew his career stock was rising. He had broken this story alone! He had leaked the homicide angle on live television, hunted down the players, found the girl, gotten the only real statement from the victim's father, and managed to sniff out the beginning of some shady business last night that he hadn't deciphered yet. He wasn't sure what he had, but he knew that catching the victim's father visiting the home of the person of interest was a thread that would turn to gold when he finished pulling it. And he had gotten the pics in the middle of a thunderstorm, no less. He wanted to pat his own back. Hell, he wanted to throw himself a ticker tape parade. He wondered what they were saying about him back at the station now that he was clearly making a name for himself. He was willing to bet that he wouldn't be doing any more small-change stories after this.

But he had to admit that things could still be a little better. If his boss had any sense, they would capitalize on this with a full nightly news segment. The case was garnering too much national attention to let cool. He hadn't seen this many podcasters and influencers developing theories of the crime since the Casey Anthony and Scott Peterson stories in turn. He had asked for three or four researchers on this, fulltime, to help him build out the details of the town, but they said it wasn't in the budget and said they'd put the intern on it.

Cheapskates til the very end, he thought. He wasn't a machine. He knew he couldn't do everything on his own, fueled by gas station freezer food and working out of a motel where the patio furniture was chained to the cement. Still, the station wanted more before they would carve out time for a primetime feature. He's warned them that they would regret it soon if someone else got the interview. Big names were starting to retweet the story, and national news stations had already reached out to him. Gayle King's team had made an exploratory call, and they had a lot more muscle than he did. He was not willing to watch someone else sit down and interview the dead kid's family or the girl he had finally chased down. It had to be him.

Carlos was sitting, flipping the channels on the television (which was also chained to the floor) between CNBC, CNN, and FOX NEWS as they regurgitated the family history of Eric Tucker that he had laid out for them like a treasure map with his local coverage. His microwaved burrito was turning waxy and cold, so he pushed it aside and kept watching. Some of the stations were really throwing on the sauce, painting it as a murder mystery for the ages. Others weren't willing to push the envelope quite so far. But they all made time to show the yearbook photo of the eighteen-year-old Freedom Walker. The girl was stunning, even in a run-of-the-mill school photo, and that, alone, made people want to talk about her. People always want salacious stories about beautiful people. He studied her image on the screen. The set of her jawline, the bright translucent green gold eyes, the big bold curls framing her face, and cascading around her shoulders. Her features were delicate and regal, symmetrical and clear. There was nothing hulking or brooding in the captured photo. And yet somehow she seemed inaccessible, aloof, shrouded. There was something there. A distrust or a pain. He couldn't figure it out. But he shook his head clear and reminded himself that she was just a puzzle piece in his story, and he could not afford to hyper focus on whatever was behind the haunting eyes in that photo. He had to find an angle to move the story coverage to the next level.

Carlos had already pitched a morning segment to keep the momentum going about the racist history of Jolivette, but his producer had stated, in no uncertain terms, that racism was not breaking news in Texas.

"Racism isn't a story in a red county in a red state. It's a foregone conclusion. If that sleepy city wasn't clinging to a confederate flag, that would be a bigger story," had been his station manager's exact words. "If we report it, it may incense our Houston viewers for a few minutes, but it won't stick. Find me something more."

Despite his station's reticence, the rest of America obviously still had an appetite for righteous indignation, and the spin had already started there. Conservative news outlets were reporting that Jolivette had been transformed into a southern jewel under the Tuckers' competent hands, rising from a barren shantytown to a bustling, picturesque, safe haven. The American ideal. They heaped posthumous praise on Eric, for his incredible courage, stopping on a dark night along a dangerous road to help a stranger—a poor kid from the wrong side of the tracks claiming to have car trouble.

The lead anchor looked right into the camera and said, "Eric Tucker was a team player. The kind that anyone could depend on, so he stopped to help the girl. That act of kindness would wind up costing him his life."

By the time they were done spinning the little bit of information that was available, it seemed probable, or even likely, that the girl had faked the car trouble to lure Eric to the scene with plans of robbing or killing him. The conjecture required gargantuan leaps from available facts to imaginative conclusions, but that's what the machinations of viewers were best known for, and the conservative stations were greasing the wheels without shame.

To good old Doc Fletcher's credit, the single page from the autopsy report that contained red circles drawn around the areas where the shot had entered Eric's body had never leaked out of the coroner's office. But Carlos' reference to it and citation that a credible source had obtained it had worked its way into coverage in the legal pundit circles. And because lawyers crave exhibits, he knew it would be online soon.

Surprisingly, *Good Day America* even managed to book some of the Jolivette High football team—young, sympathetic men with red-rimmed eyes, saddened at the loss of a teammate and a forever sullied senior year and season.

It was all masterfully done, and the co-host seemed genuinely choked up a time or two.

The progressive stations, on the other hand, had declined the warm, apple pie version of events and, instead, documented the city's history the way Carlos had wanted— as an uninterrupted Tucker political dynasty whose problematic prince had been snuffed out unexpectedly. They highlighted the appearance of Jolivette from 1936 to 1960 in the *Green Book* for Negro Motorists and other national archives as a sundown town to be avoided; a town where blacks and Hispanics were lynched if they were caught out after dark. They had unearthed reports of the city's very public resistance to integration all the way up through the Carter administration, complete with footage of the outspoken then-mayor Tucker declaring that they would close the schools before they forced their sons and daughters to eat and drink and change into their gym clothes in front of "animals."

Some brilliant staffer had even managed to unearth an Obama-era photo of a truck parked outside of city hall with three flags flying from the cab and bed: the Confederate battle flag, Come and Take It, and a flag with a camouflage background that read "Jolivette Militia."

"In this town," the anchor said in a cadence slow enough to build deliberate suspense, "a stranded Black girl being approached by a Tucker in the dark would certainly be cause for alarm. We may never know if he was there to help her or hurt her, but whatever the reason, that stop would become his last."

That take on the story was an absolute fire starter and had been the biggest catalyst for the influx of newsvans that now roamed the streets of Jolivette seeking out testimonials about life under the Tucker dynasty.

The public broadcast stations had predictably taken a more cerebral approach and proffered the current population maps of Jolivette along with population maps from the 1940s, 1950s, and 1960s, showing, in irrefutable bright red relief, that despite the increasing diversity in the schools, excellent academic standings, and apparent international makeup of their population, Jolivette was still invariably redlined into racial camps with no outliers. All of the communities of color were on one side of the railroad tracks that cut through the heart of the city.

The Asian population, which were predominantly Vietnamese, Cambodian, and Filipino, were clustered around waterways and the bit of bayou wetland and engaged largely in crawfish and textile industries. The Hispanics in the city hailed from any number of Latin origins but appeared to be hyper-concentrated in frontline agricultural or construction work. The Black neighborhoods were intentionally configured around three large churches and dotted by auto shops, small convenient stores, and local restaurants. The report, while presented without much color commentary, effectively painted Jolivette as a segregated relic, a stronghold remnant of the bitter confederate south.

They never spoke poorly of the victim or the girl, but they didn't paint anyone as a hero either. Primarily, they made it clear that Eric Tucker was heir to the throne in a long line of self-proclaimed ruling class family, and Freedom Walker was the only grandchild of a deceased spiritual giant in the Jolivette Black community, Reverend "Pop" Walker. The public broadcast stations held themselves out as the last bastions of journalistic integrity and therefore stopped short of casting doubt as to whether Eric's death was, in fact, a tragedy at all, but they certainly planted the thought that this incident represented frustrations finally reaching a boiling point. It was unflattering, but it threaded the needle well enough to keep those stations out of the slander suit filings that were always just one broadcast away for everyone.

Carlos understood the newsfeed continuum better than most, so he knew that this national ripple was the widest, most visible ripple in a cycle that he had to continue to feed, or it would disappear as quickly as it had popped up. He knew that none of these stations had enough information to make anything about Eric's death directly race-related at all. But he also knew, like them, that the polarizing color line was one that always caught attention and paid off in ratings—ratings that he needed to continue to generate for his network if he was ever going to get to an anchor desk. He could not afford for the story to die out. Not yet. Not while he was still fielding calls that could change his life. He needed time to consider their offers, and he needed more exclusive content to sweeten the deals. He was going to have to drop another rock and start a new ripple. He was holding the pocket ace breadcrumbs about a girl named Tracy dropped by the high school kids on their social media accounts. But he needed details, and he had hit a dead end.

Chapter 28

Eric Tucker- The Taker

E ric Tucker was a taker, albeit a beautiful one; he was a taker nonetheless. His chiseled jaw, generous mouth, and well-defined athletic physique had already marked him for a charmed life. His piercing blue-green eyes, a direct inheritance of his father, could make a blush crawl up the neck of women twice his age, teachers included. But what really marked Eric Tucker as one-of-one was that he was the worst kind of smart. He was the poster child for what higher-than-average intellect looked like when paired with below-average empathy and a borderline personality disorder. It could probably be said that he lacked empathy altogether. It didn't take long at all for those close to him to recognize that the treacherous Tucker gene that had run rampant in their history but had managed to skip his father had certainly not skipped him, and Eric learned to flex those villainous skills very early.

For one thing, Eric's grades were impeccable, but not because he studied hard or even studied at all. They were impeccable because he had secured the services of several of the best students in his class to complete all of his assignments and provide him with the answers to all of his exams. This arrangement was not made because Eric was not smart enough to do the work. He was. But he arranged these cheat codes because he realized that he could have someone else do the work for him and saw no reason to do more when he could do less. Sometimes he compensated his stable of homework horses, but more often, they did what he demanded to avoid being terrorized at school and because they were too timid to call Eric's bluff to have their parents evicted from properties that his family owned.

As he got older, Eric developed an interest in girls, and his strong-arming spirit pivoted naturally to getting what he wanted from them as well. His mother bought him a truck at fourteen and let him drive it against his father's lackluster protests. By fifteen, Eric was both surprised and then annoyed at how little effort and calculating it took to convince girls to climb into the bed of his truck under the stars on a Saturday night—well, most girls anyway. There were a few over the years that played hard to get or put up a half-committed fight, but Eric never took no for an answer. He simply didn't have to. Over the next year, he quickly grew bored of passing around sloppy, drunk girls in basement parties and talking uptight do-gooders out of their virginity in the Sunday school room at church. He needed a real challenge. By his sophomore year of high school, he had turned his full attention to the one girl that seemed completely immune to his charms and everyone else's too: Freedom Walker.

Eric was actually drawn to Free the first moment he set eyes on her. It was the sixth grade, and she sat at lunch alone, her table just across from his. She was one of only a handful of Black kids who had chosen to bus to Hillside Middle School, one of two white-flight elementary schools that had been nestled neatly in the affluent Northside of Jolivette in the late '80s when the town finally realized that they could no longer fight the tide of desegregation at the elementary schools located closer to the Black side of town. Despite the best efforts of the town's elite, by the early 2000s, even the white-flight schools like Hillside started to become dotted with color. Freedom was just such a dot. She was also the only Black girl who had tested into the gifted and talented classes, which irritated the G/T parents, who, in turn, made sure that their children shared in their disgust. Jolivette was big on traditions, and racism was one of its most hallowed. As a result, Freedom sat alone in all of her classes, and not a single one of the other kids would speak to her for years. And that is how, on the first day of sixth grade, Eric discovered Freedom. Quiet and alone. It struck him that even as a fish out of water, without a friend in sight, she had something special. He was too young to understand her confident beauty. He didn't have the language then to put it in terms, but to him, she seemed to be lit from the inside. Her skin was so smooth and buttery, an unblemished toasted caramel that he imagined it must feel like velvet. And when she looked up and made eye contact with him, her eyes seemed to glow, golden brown ringed by greens and blues. Her hair was usually wrangled into thick braids wrapped around her head like a crown at the start of class. But as the school day wore on, tendrils began to escape, springing every which way in dramatic coils. He would stare for long, torturous minutes at the golden hue of her soft brown skin and watch her full, pouty mouth twitch this way and that as she chewed her lip while figuring out an answer on an assignment.

Eric felt drawn to her as if she possessed some sort of magnetic force, and he always had to know where she was in the room, on the playground, or whatever space he was occupying. He could register her presence without even seeing her walk into the room and was always checking to see what she was wearing, what mood she seemed to be in, and whether she had noticed him.

Freedom, to her credit, wore her solitude like a badge of honor. It was obvious that someone had prepared her for what she would face at HIllside because she was calm even when the other children went out of their way to take verbal and sometimes physical jabs at her. She'd be hit with allegedly off-course kickballs when there was no game in progress. She would arrive at class to find that all of her pencils and crayons had been snapped in half and placed back in her desk. She knew that she wasn't like the other girls; she knew that they did not like her, and she didn't try to gain their respect or act more like them to lessen the distance.

This intrigued Eric more than anything else. He had watched plenty of poor kids try to act rich and observed as nearly every bused-in Black, Hispanic, and Asian kid took on the style, manner of speaking, and habits of the rich white kids. It's like they all slipped into a sort of ineffective camouflage as a coping mechanism. While this attempt to blend in was rarely successful, it was still an expectation—a demand, really. Kids learned very quickly not to bring ethnic dishes in their lunch boxes or wear their hair in ways that made them stand out. The athletic minorities seemed to fare best. They still found themselves the butt of mean-spirited jokes and subjected to every racial epithet under the sun when they underperformed. But when they were winning, the athletes were permitted to fly above the relentless emotional terrorism for the sake of the team or the school's athletic reputation. Freedom probably could have stayed off of Eric's radar a lot longer, also, if she had tried, like the others, to blend in. But either she couldn't or she wouldn't, and it sparked something uncomfortable in him that he could not snuff out.

Eric had not known Freedom's backstory when he enrolled at Hillside, but the other kids filled him in soon enough. They told him that she was motherless and fatherless, which made her even more of an enigma. Eric imagined that a girl with such a rough start to life would look downtrodden and plain, but Freedom looked amazing every day. Her clothes were always clean and pressed and interesting mixes of colors and patterns—flattering and neat. Eric also thought that an orphaned girl should look sad, but she never did. Instead, she carried herself, even then, like she was too good to be in this silly school with these childish kids. She never said it, but you could feel it crackling in the air around her. She acted as though she was just better.

The other kids, and sometimes the teachers, tried to break her down and make sure she knew and stayed in her place. They chose her last, if at all, for group projects and games. They made fun of her weird name. They turned their backs to box her out of conversations. They lowered their voices or stopped talking about birthday parties and weekend sleepovers whenever she was near. They hoped they could make her uncomfortable enough to leave their honors class, and every year, Eric thought, maybe she would. She was just a kid; how much of this could she take, he thought. But she never dropped the classes or left the school. In fact, Eric never saw her cry or lower her head. She just floated about in a world of her own, ethereal, impenetrable, and whip-smart.

To Eric, she was like a creature from another planet. At first, he just enjoyed watching her, marveling at her quiet defiance. But as they got older and she took on another level of breathtaking bloom, he realized that he wanted to have her, to possess her, to add her to the list of very cool things that other kids could only dream about having, but he actually had. Everything he'd ever wanted, he had been able to get with his name, his family's money, or the assistance of his resourceful mother. Freedom would not be an exception. He was sure of it.

In parallel to Freedom, Eric's arrival in Hillside Elementary's gifted and talented sixth-grade class had been a tumultuous one as well. He had been homeschooled by his mother since he was five years old, and she wanted to continue, but his dad had made it clear that Eric needed to be socializing beyond just his own small, affluent circle and insisted she enroll him in public school. There was a small private Christian school in Jolivette, but his dad didn't think that would have been much better for him than homeschool. Eric's only extended exposure to children outside of the plentiful Tucker clan had been a brief, two-year stint in Pop Warner football. He'd gotten in two fights in each of the first two games and broken one kid's nose and another's arm. His father had been asked to withdraw him for the sake of the league. A sizable campaign donation had accompanied the request. After that, his father began the persuasion offensive against his mother in earnest to enroll him in public school, where he could learn better how to cope with social situations and his own anger.

Eric had stayed up late and eavesdropped for months as his parents fought over the benefits and consequences of throwing Eric into the public school system.

Eric was torn because he very much wanted to attend a real school with lots of other kids and organized sports. At the same time, his father's argument for it often involved harsh whispers about Eric's character. He'd heard his father refer to him as spoiled, entitled, impulsive, manipulative, and aggressive. His father had really spared no violent adjective in warning his mother about the dangers of letting Eric continue to exist in a world where he could have whatever he wanted whenever he wanted.

Eric idolized his dad, and hearing those scathing critiques stung and burned in Eric's mind as he lay in bed, long after the tense conversations drifting from his parents' room had ended. But in the end, his dad had the last word, and Eric was able to go to public school. Eric took the placement assessment and, to his mother's credit, tested at a 6th-grade level in all subjects, even though he was more than a year younger than most of his classmates. What he lacked in age and maturity, he quickly made up for with his calculating wit.

At first, Eric's placement seemed like a great success to everyone. Eric was the best at nearly every sport he played; he instantly attracted friends and charmed his teachers. But in the end, his dad's theory that throwing Eric into a bigger pool would temper Eric's worst proclivities turned out to be misguided at best. What Eric got from the move, instead, was a larger source of victims. His prowess at covering his tracks and manipulating grew ever more powerful in the fertile ground of eager-to-please classmates. A fast learner, he bored quickly with easy conquests—the girls that giggled effusively when he stood close to them or the boys who challenged him to tests of strength or dominance. He was a natural athlete and a world-class talker. What he needed to keep him going was a worthy opponent, and by his sophomore year, Freedom had become one of the few left standing. But the challenge proved more than he anticipated.

Freedom rebuffed his every advance and seemed to look through him rather than at him when he poured on his patented charm and fixed her with his oceanic eyes. He'd taken to placing himself strategically on her route to and from classes. But she picked up on it soon enough, and he was infuriated to discover that she was adding circuitous routes and several additional minutes to her path just to avoid him between classes. He'd cursed her under his breath for her audacity, and his pursuit escalated immediately.

Every day, his frustration grew until his interest morphed into an ominous obsession fueled by a desperate fixation that he couldn't even explain anymore. A few times, he tried to distract himself with other girls, but each night, when the darkness and quiet descended, it was Freedom that occupied his dreams and nightmares. He knew where she worked and made sure to pick up his sports uniforms from the cleaners when she was there, even though they had a housekeeper whose job was to retrieve the wash. He would saunter into the small storefront under the chime of the bell and instantly register her discomfort, the way she angled herself away from him and kept her words to one or two syllables, trying to quickly complete their transactions. He would lean onto the counter and close the distance between them. When she turned to retrieve his garment, he would reach out and grab one of her curls before she stepped away. When he could catch her in the library, he would silently stalk her through the shelves until he could corner her and pin her against the stacks with the weight of his body, inhaling the mixture of cocoa, vanilla, and amber that seemed to envelop her like a cloud.

He knew his persistence terrified her and made her miserable, but she never gave him even a whimper or shudder for his satisfaction. Her body would get stiff as a board, and her breathing would slow until it was almost imperceptible. The slamming of her pulse beating just under the skin of her throat was the only tell-tale sign of her fear. He hated that she was refusing him a reaction and had taken to saying the most offensive and foul things he could think of any time he could get her isolated, hoping to get a rise out of her; to taunt her into hurling an insult back towards him. He'd repeated every rumor he remembered from grade school about her mother and added ruthless twists to them. He'd tell her that he knew her mom was a prostitute who had run off in the night after birthing her in a barn like an animal. Her eyes would glass over, but still no reaction.

Once, when he'd cornered her in the school stairwell, he'd grabbed a fist full of her hair and accused her of thinking she was better than other girls because she had light eyes, and she must have thought that made her something other than the n***r bi**h she was. He'd surprised even himself with the violence of his words that time, but he was already locked in and could not back off without showing weakness. She met the vitriol of his words with total silence, and his own heart pounded in his chest, incensed at her refusal to bend or break. Rage creeped up the back of his neck and into his skull like the fingers of the devil himself, spurring him on and pushing him to best her. He'd pulled her hair harder, forcing her head down and backwards until her neck was craned at an impossible angle, and he knew she should have been screaming out in pain, but instead, her eyes remained vacant and focused somewhere beyond the moment as though she had left her body entirely. He was livid and had the urge to either break her neck or kiss her until she kissed him back. He hovered in that moment of indecision a second too long and was interrupted by the sound of footsteps coming up the stairs. The intrusion forced him to release her hair and step back quickly. He watched her bend slowly to collect the books she'd dropped when he grabbed her.

A herd of students changing classes passed by them with barely a glance, and in the rush of the crowd, she stood, straightening herself to her full height, never once glancing his way, and continued on down the stairs as though nothing had ever happened. For weeks after these unhinged attacks, Eric would feel sick and afraid. He knew that he was going too far. What did she think of him now? Did he haunt her dreams like she haunted his? What if she told someone, or what if someone had caught him? Why couldn't he let this go? Why wouldn't she just do what he wanted? His family was powerful, which offered some safety, but even they had warned him that he needed to stay out of trouble these days.

He always wound up blaming the girl in his mind. All she had to do was acknowledge him, and he would stop. *Really*, he told himself, *he would*. But she had to be humbled. She had to see that he was in charge.

Over the years, his parents had spent hundreds of thousands of dollars making his legal problems and the angry parents of other kids go away in the wake of Eric's violent impulsiveness with their daughters and sometimes sons. He had tried to work through his endless compulsion for conflict through football. "Leave it all on the field," his uncle had warned him over and over. But every time he saw Freedom, he nearly came out of his skin. He'd begun to convince himself that she was the sole reason for every unpleasant feeling in his life. Whenever he underperformed in a game, had a bad day at school, had a heated misunderstanding with friends, or found himself in trouble at home, he invariably traced it back to Free and her refusal to acknowledge him or return his affections.

She was a nobody, and he was a Tucker. His family name was on every building in town. Being associated with him would have catapulted her into popularity, and he could have protected her from being a social pariah. But instead, she rebuffed his every advance and looked through him like he was no more than a nuisance in her way. He'd had a friend pull her number from the school files and called her no less than 100 times a week, sometimes from blocked numbers. She'd never picked up. Not even once. He would listen to her voicemail recording, and once he'd heard the beep, he would just listen for a few minutes more, imagining that she was on the other end of the line, and then he would hang up.

He never texted her, though. He knew better than that. Saved texts and screenshots had nearly landed him in serious trouble more than once, and he had learned his lesson. Because she never answered calls or went anywhere other than school, work, and church, she was hard to corner. She never showed up to school parties, football games, or weekend kickbacks. It was becoming more difficult to get to her without risking being caught at school. His frustration continued to grow.

When he learned through the school announcements that she had accepted a scholarship to Cornell University, half a world away, he realized that he was in his final window. Soon, she would be completely out of his orbit, and he had no intention of letting her leave his town or his world without giving him what he wanted. He began to fashion a plan. Eric Tucker was a taker. And he had decided that her pride was what he wanted.

Chapter 29

May 22 Angel - The Lawyer

Angel took a deep breath before dialing the number. She knew that she was about to cross a line where her two lives collided, and she wouldn't be able to undo it. She had spent her entire life running from this moment, where the people who thought that she was a dreamy, untouchable sophisticate would learn that she was just a country, insecure girl from Nowhere, Texas, who got knocked up before she even had a year of college under her belt. She wanted more than anything to just jump into that God-awful Jeep that she was paying too much money to rent by the week and high tail it back to L.A. But she knew her family needed her, and she finally had a chance to do what she had never done—show up for her daughter. She dialed the phone, and Yami picked up on the very first ring.

"Jesus, Angel! I thought you were dead! Where are you? Why haven't you called or answered my calls? I was about to file a missing person report! I mean, I was literally just seconds from calling Michael!" Yami screeched, referencing the professional basketball player Angel had been stringing along as of late. "I thought maybe he had gone all Scott Peterson on you!"

Angel cringed.

"There is a code, you know!" Yami bellowed on. "Even if you want to be all mysterious and private, you can't just fall off the face of the earth and not send a text, or an email, a messenger pigeon, a raven! Something!!" Yami's voice was climbing the octaves, and Angel knew she would have to reel her in soon.

She waited for Yami to pause her rant before she started to speak.

"I'm sorry, Yami. I really am. You have been an incredible friend, and you deserve better than this. There has been a lot...well...there is a lot going on, and I'm not even sure how secure this phone call is."

"What?!" Yami gasped and then went quiet.

Angel could imagine Yami turning the phone in her hand, inspecting it as if it was in the 1930s and there was a bug planted in it instead of realizing the effortless wiretap ability that was the hallmark of the post-9/11 world.

"Yami?" Angel said, making sure she was still on the line.

"Yes?" Yami whispered, making Angel roll her eyes and almost chuckle, as though whispering would help if the phone line was tapped.

"Yami, listen to me carefully. I need you to call Gayle."

"GAYLE Gayle?" Yami asked in shock.

"Yes, GAYLE Gayle," Angel repeated. "Call her, and tell her that the Jolivette girl, the one from the news...that's my kid, and we need her here now."

The line was silent for another second. This time, Angel thought Yami, who was not prone to long, thoughtful silences, had hung up. But then Yami's voice came through clear and sober.

"You mean the girl they are talking about in connection with that rich boy's murder?"

"Yeah," Angel's voice betrayed her and cracked just a little. "That's my daughter."

"Okay, got it," Yami said. "Oh, and Angel?" she asked.

"Yes?" Angel asked cautiously

"Text me the address, and tell me which clothes or things you want me to ship to you from the condo."

Gratitude welled up in Angel's chest and throat, and hot tears stung behind her eyes. She didn't trust herself to try to say another word, but she didn't have to. Yami had ended the call. Yami was the kind of friend that Angel had never really allowed herself to believe existed. Now that she was watching out and rallying for Angel without hesitation, Angel realized that she had never allowed herself to enjoy or experience the fullness of Yami's friendship. Always so focused on protecting herself from feeling too much or trusting too much, she'd really never seen Yami for all that she was until just now: an unconditional friend. She hoped that she could count on an equally eager response from Gayle.

Gayle Lovett was a notorious Hollywood attorney. After 15 years buried in corporate cases at a big law giant, she sued the firm and her practice manager for sexual harassment and the creation and proliferation of a hostile work environment. She won and used the money to start her own practice. It didn't take long for her to hit the big time. She had cut her teeth on the earliest #MeToo" and #TimesUp cases, toppling several industry giants for their lascivious abuse of young Hollywood hopefuls, primed with the false hope of catching their big break. She was feared and revered and seemed to enjoy both reactions equally. She was also a sight to behold. Gayle had the stature of a Grecian goddess, standing six feet tall with legs that went on forever and a short platinum swing bob that was blunt cut and angled severely, starting at the nape of her neck and slanting hard toward her chin. Her complexion resisted the standard tan of the LA lifestyle and remained nearly Geisha pale. Paired with the platinum bob, her look read as sharp and a little scary. What she lacked in softness, she made up for in fashion. She wore signature, custom double-lapel pantsuits that were cut and tailored as razor-sharp as her bob and high heels that made her stature even more intimidating. When Gayle walked into a room, she was the only person worth watching in the room.

Angel had met Gayle when Gayle was still toiling away under the boot of her law firm. She'd roll into Venti y Dos, the posh lounge frequented by the A-listers, and spread out her files and laptop in a back corner booth at around 8 pm. This time was known as the dead zone. It was well after the gen x happy hour set had a few shots of remembered youth, paid their tabs, and jumped on the 405 to resume duties as responsible, domesticated adults, but it was the time before the late-night, pill-popping set could come sweeping in at midnight.

The food at Venti y Dos was great, but the regular crowds, always on-the-go, only stayed long enough for a few drinks and light appetizers. Angel had worked her way up from hostess to the manager of the dead shift and made sure that everyone on her roster was dressed magnificently. The uniform requirements at the lounge were that the waitstaff needed to wear all black, but the girls working Angel's shift were taught not just to wear it, but to be striking in black. They wore spike-heeled booties, elegant shorts, or trendy miniskirts, and sheer black blouses or turtlenecks. She drilled them on etiquette and subtle seduction until the dead zone became hugely popular with young single men looking for a really nice dinner experience with beautiful waitstaff to flirt with. As anticipated, young and old single women who were hunting for young single men began pouring in as well.

As the dead zone grew in popularity and began attracting up-and-coming chefs, Angel's reputation in the food services and hospitality circles spread like wildfire, far outpacing her paltry reputation as an actress. Gayle had a front-row seat to this transformation from the corner booth, which Angel never gave away. No matter how crowded the restaurant or how long the waitlist was, Angel insisted that the back corner booth remain permanently reserved for Gayle and that only Angel would wait on her table. She saw them as two scrappy women who deserved someone to hold space for them in the world. Gayle's tips for Angel grew increasingly more generous as she realized that her table was always prepared and ready for her at 8 pm, even while the once-quiet space boomed and swelled into a bustling restaurant slam. The friendship happened quietly in the silence of their arrangement, though neither of them formally acknowledged it. The sight of young, attractive Gayle officing from the back booth in the most sought-after reservation in town drew the attention of the patrons, who would whisper and speculate as to who she was

Is she one of the owners? Do you think she is someone big?
Soon, they began stopping by the table to introduce themselves and find out who she was. Gayle began to build her book of business from those intrigued patrons, and when she left the firm, she had more clients lined up than she could handle. She never forgot that Angel did that for her, and the two stayed in touch.

It was nearly one o'clock in the morning when Gayle got the call from Yami. She squinted at the alarm clock, incredulous, before sliding in one earbud and tapping it once to answer the incoming call.

"Someone had better be dead," she snapped, pulling the covers back up around her head.

"Oh, they are," said Yami. "And that's only half the problem."

Gayle sat up, her interest now piqued, legal antennae extending.

"Who is this?" Gayle growled into the receiver, wishing that she had checked the Caller ID before answering.

"It's Yami—Angel's friend Yami."

"Oh...okay..." Gayle said slowly.

She closed her eyes, her well-developed sense of worst-case scenarios making her wonder if Yami was about to tell her that Angel was dead.

"Right, well, let me just get straight to it," Yami pushed on. "I'm calling to tell you that Angel is in Texas right now because her daughter is being investigated as a person of interest in a murder investigation."

"Wait." Gayle shook her head to clear out some of the confusion. "Her what?"

"Right," said Yami. "It was a surprise to me too, but, yes, she has a daughter. An almost 18-year-old daughter who is in a world of trouble at the moment. She asked me to call you. She needs a lawyer."

Gayle blew out the breath that she had been holding. "Are you talking about the case that's been splattered all over the news?"

Yami cringed before answering.

"Um, yea, that's the one."

Holy Crap! Gayle's thoughts turned immediately to the PR nightmare that had been swirling around the incident, and she mentally started a to-do list of damage control efforts she would need to start assembling before she even swung her feet over the side of the bed.

"Okay, send me the details," Gayle ordered, her voice steady and projecting all business and poise. "I'll be on the first flight out."

Chapter 30

Carlos - An Unexpected Gift

When Carlos went to bed on Tuesday night, he knew that he was in danger of hitting a dead end with the Eric Tucker story. Despite the coverage that had rolled in earlier in the week, the internet, ever fickle, had moved on from endlessly hashtagging and conspiracy theorizing about whether Freedom or anyone else knew who killed Eric. He had known it would be difficult to compete with the constant cycle of fresh celebrity gossip and political scandal unless he could continue to drip new details. Unfortunately, he was staring down an endless well of nothingness. He discovered that the girl had lawyered up somehow, the Tucker family had gone eerily quiet, and teenagers, being teenagers, were now more concerned with graduation and summer plans than theorizing about who killed their classmate. In the local adult community, large pockets of Jolivette were still buzzing about it because the idea that a Tucker could be touched in this way upset the established order of their social system; but the rest of the country was already cooling a bit, and the calls for story sound bites had slowed to barely a trickle.

Carlos tried to get clearance to run with a story about the Twitter allegations he'd unearthed, alleging that a girl had withdrawn from Jolivette High and moved away after Eric assaulted her at a house party, but someone from the Tucker camp had gotten wind of it, and the lawyers were at the station threatening libel actions before Carlos even had a chance to submit his final copy. The Tucker machine was more nimble with a wider reach than he'd anticipated. Who did they know in the Houston office, he wondered?

Carlos debated back and forth over whether it was time to abandon ship and call time of death on the story. He'd already garnered some acclaim for breaking the story and the exclusive information he'd secured. In all honesty, he could probably pack it in, go back to Houston, and coast to the next level on what he had done here for months. But the story felt unfinished. For one, the Tuckers had been running roughshod over the city for decades, and if one of them had finally gotten his comeuppance, he wanted to prove that's what had happened. Plus, the girl's mother had gotten under his skin, accusing him of being a shallow fame-seeker when, in truth, he knew there was more to the story than anyone was telling, and the girl had more info than what she was sharing. Proving that cocky woman wrong felt like a vindication he had to have, or he would be chasing it like a ghost for the rest of his career. And there was something else that he was having trouble admitting, except in the quietest hours of the night, when he had run out of ways to distract himself. He couldn't stop thinking about the girl and the way a single current started at the top of his skull and ran down the entire length of his body whenever her image came on screen. He could not shake the feeling that she held the keys to more than just what happened that night. He felt, inexplicably, that he was supposed to know her. That their lives were destined to collide, and he needed to understand why.

Carlos nearly jumped out of his skin when his cell phone rang, interrupting his thoughts. He didn't recognize the number but picked it up anyway.

"Mr. Jackson," a cool woman's voice stated his name matter of factly.

"Uh yes, this is Carlos Jackson," he responded.

"Great. This is Gayle Lovett. I'm the Walker family attorney and represent the interests of Freedom Walker."

"Okay..." Carlos responded, awaiting the threat or cease and desist demand that was bound to be coming.

"She'd like to do an interview. With you."

Carlos pulled the phone away from his face and stared at the screen. Was it possible for his luck to be this good...or was this a prank? He had not gotten so much as a glimpse of the girl since the story broke, and now she was offering an exclusive interview. There had to be a catch.

Chapter 31

Free - Prime Time

The lightbulbs surrounding the small, portable makeup vanity were deceptively bright. Freedom squinted her eyes, allowing her lashes to filter some of the glare away. She still had a thin piece of paper jutting from the rounded collar of a black sheath dress with a pleated gold lamé belt. The outfit felt expensive. The materials had glided on over her skin and zipped up effortlessly. Nothing like her thrift store revamped fashion pieces Free had come to love. Free knew that she could never have afforded the dress on her own.

The lawyer, whom her mother kept insisting, unsuccessfully, that Freedom should call Aunt Gayle, had given her the dress in a black garment bag along with the Jimmy Choo sling-back pumps that had slid onto her feet like Cinderella's glass slippers. Her hair had been tamed into a slicked-back low bun that was giving her a headache from how tightly the elastic was gripping her curls to keep them straight. The team assigned to her had spared no detail. Her nails were shellacked in a neutral taupe, her eyebrows conservatively arched, demure pearl studs adorned her ears, and her lips were lightly lined and glossed.

Gayle had come blowing into her life like the winds that her name reflected. First, she'd relocated them to a hotel outside town under assumed names. Then she'd brought a veritable army of staff with her that had assessed Free like a remodeling project and begun coaching, shining, and buffing her from her speaking voice to her toenails. She tried to remember all of the directions from the coaching sessions she'd had, but trying to keep it all straight was increasing her anxiety.

Look directly at the host when answering questions, but look soft and feminine. Don't stare angrily. Answer quickly, so it doesn't seem like you are rehearsed, but also not too quickly. Cross your legs at the ankle only, never the knee (that one was from Mama Jean). They had gone over question after question with her for days, drilling her on the answers.

"Isn't this the kind of thing you do to prepare for a trial?" Freedom had complained as the prep sessions dragged on. " I haven't been charged with anything."

"Oh, this is definitely a trial, honey," Gayle had said matter-of-factly. "You have been on trial for weeks in the court of public opinion, and you have to win here first to get anywhere close to having a fair one in the courts. In fact," she went on, "if you do well enough in the court of social media, you'll never have to wind up in the real one."

"I think that only works for white people," Freedom mumbled under her breath.

"What's that, hon?" Gayle asked.

Freedom shook her head. Gayle was obviously smart and capable, but she was also not from her world. Still, Free knew that this was probably not the best time to offend the woman who was her best hope of getting her life back, so she swallowed her bit of social commentary and looked down at her new phone instead, also courtesy of Gayle. Hashtags about her were still popping up as trending tweets and comments. Freedom read over a few of the ones from the last few minutes and felt her stomach flip. Everyone from TMZ to Trevor Noah had begun to weigh in on the mystery of what had happened to Eric Tucker. People she actually watched and respected were opining on what they expected to come from her interview tonight, and the sharks were circling the impending airtime like chum.

When Gayle first discussed the plan, Free and Mama Jean had flat out refused. But Angel had insisted that this made sense because Freedom could not afford to remain quiet as though she had something to hide.

"She's 18 now Mama," Angel had stated matter-of-factly.

No one lingered on the realization that Free's birthday had come and gone without so much as a candle during the whole ordeal.

"The media, the courts, everyone is going to treat her and speak about her like an adult. So we have to make sure that they see with their own eyes how young and innocent she really is before they adultify her into a place beyond the reach of empathy."

"Yes, and she is READY," Gayle chimed in. "She is not the average 18 year old. She is smart and composed, and we have prepared her."

Freedom disagreed, but eventually Mama Jean acquiesced, and so the interview began to take shape. Gayle's team has clear goals and outcomes. They ran like a military unit of precision, running her through questions and scenarios she may encounter. And now the time had come. Free was overwhelmed by the moment and tormented with a million "what ifs" niggling at the corners of her mind. She thought of all the PR interviews that she had seen go very wrong and become memes even in her short lifetime. The infamous Whitney Houston "crack is wack," R Kelly crying and screaming that he couldn't have hog tied his victims because he didn't even know what a hog tie was.   Justin Bieber, Chris Brown, Diddy...ugh! Had interviews actually ever actually helped anyone? According to Gayle, they did more times than they didn't, and this was Free's only chance at humanizing herself and creating her own narrative.

"Two minutes to set!" someone barked loudly.

Free blew out the nerves that were crawling up her back. *This could go really badly,* she thought again. She wasn't a people person. And even if she did everything right, her words could still be spun as something else. If she knew anything about people, it was that they were NOT to be trusted, and they believed what they wanted to believe more often than they believed what you told them. But she's gotten a call from Cornell this week, and they had concerns about the distraction her presence may cause on campus in the fall. They gave her some time to work things through, but they sounded ready to pull the plus. She had to sway the public sentiment, and she knew it. She had nothing left to lose.

The activity swarmed around her went to fever pitch. Angel and Gayle spoke in quick, terse whispers with a man wearing a headset, and a woman dressed in all black appeared from thin air, removing Free's paper bi and said, "Live in one minute. Ready?"

Free nodded, and Angel came over and stood directly in front of her. She took both of Freedom's hands in her own and leveled her eyes until they were locked in a stare that felt more like a conversation.

"Freedom," she started. "I didn't do the right thing by you. I was selfish and could not think about anything other than my own pain." Freedom started to pull her hands away, but Angel held on tightly. "Please, just let me say this," Angel pleaded. "I hurt you and changed the entire course of your life. I left you in a town that had already chewed me up and spit me out. Left you to face all of the same demons that had haunted me. I will never forgive myself for that, and I will spend the rest of my natural life trying to earn your trust and love, trying to make this right. I took a lot from you, but what you have inside you is more than what I took. Your strength, your intelligence, your spirit. Baby girl, all of that is you. You are incredible. You are indomitable. You can handle this. You can do anything."

Freedom knew that she should have been warmed by her mother's confession-laden pep talk, but instead, she was annoyed. She met her mother's teary eyes with a steely look and a terse nod. Yes, she had been all of those things. But now she was just fighting for her life. *Too little, too late,* she thought before she stood and followed the woman dressed in black out under the hot, glaring lights of the stage in her own high school auditorium.

The stage looked more like a living room. There were deep, comfortable chairs and an expensive-looking oriental rug stretched out beneath them. The wall behind the chair had been covered in soft seafoam chevron-patterned wallpaper, staged with curtains and abutted sofa tables and tchotchkes in a beautiful palette of blues, greens, and natural wood. The whole setup was beautiful and created the illusion of a comfortable, homey living room. But taking in the bigger picture, it was oddly juxtaposed against the cable chords, light rigs, and floating wired cameras being worked and pivoted by the small swarm of technical staff.

Free settled herself as best she could onto the love seat she was directed to perch on and swept her eyes across the far side of the stage to make sure that her grandmother was in her line of sight. Mama Jean, as if expecting Free's hesitation, stood stoic and calm, her eyes ready to meet

Free's. Flanked by Angel and the statuesque lawyer, Mama Jean looked small but powerful, and Freedom felt her nerves calm by a mile just knowing that she was in the room and they were breathing the same air. She crossed her legs at the ankle and waited.

Free had watched more than a few poorly acted high school productions play out on this exact stage. She would slip in after the show had already begun and sit on the very last row, wishing she was on the stage, and then quickly dash the longing away as she remembered that her goal was to escape this place, not become a part of it. But now here she was, on the very stage she had daydreamed of floating across, waiting for her cue to give the performance of her life.

Chapter 32

Carlos - Lights, Camera, Action

Carlos ran his eyes nervously over his note cards for the hundredth time as anticipation and exhilaration mixed in his chest and threatened to overtake him. This was it. He was primetime. His small-town football story had ballooned into a nationally televised interview that was going to be watched by more than half the nation if the advanced buzz was any indication. The stakes were high. Just like politics, sports, and opinions about who should win "The Bachelor," the Eric Tucker murder mystery had turned out to be extremely polarizing, with talking heads and pundits across the news echelon throwing in their personal opinions passed off as facts.

For Carlos, landing the first and only televised interview with the single most enigmatic player in the whole sordid affair was more than luck; it was life-changing. He had worked for it, but there was no accounting for the sudden offer, and he hoped he wasn't walking into some sort of trap. He turned once more to the mirror and performed his high-pressure-situation calming ritual, which was just to get his face within three inches of the mirror, lock eyes with himself, and recite powerful lyrics. Sometimes they were rap lyrics, other times portions of the famous poem Invictus or something from James Baldwin. Today, he decided on the chorus of "My Shot" from Lin Manuel Miranda's *Hamilton*. It was cheesy and childish, but it worked.

"A yo, I'm just like my country. I'm young, scrappy, and hungry, and I am not throwing away my shot!" he whispered harshly to his reflection in the mirror, then turning on his heel, he strode out onto the Jolivette High School Stage that his news station had transformed into the spitting image of a Four Seasons sitting room. He was finally seeing what the long TV station money could do if they felt you deserved the budget and made a mental note to ask for a significant pay and title bump the moment he touched back down in Houston. Carlos could feel his star rising like Don Lemon in 2015, and he had every intention of capitalizing on this moment.

As he strode out onto the stage, Carlos was momentarily caught off guard by the sight of the girl perched delicately on the loveseat. Up until this point, he had been limited to the yearbook photocopies that he had managed to get, but they hadn't prepared him for her actual diminutive stature.

She seemed...small. Petite. Her hands were folded neatly in her lap, and her hair was drawn back into a neat bun with a few tendrils escaping in a way that seemed too perfect not to be intentional. Her eyes were cast down as though studying her own ankles, but as he took his seat, she looked up through her heavy lashes, and he felt his own eyebrows shoot up in surprise. Her face was breathtaking—regal cheekbones and a nose flaring gently at the base, a full mouth cupid's bowed in the middle, and expertly arched brows. She looked like the reimaginings of Nefertiri that adorned the living room walls of every pro-black dining room in the early 70s. And her eyes! They seemed to be lit from within, and their golden glow made him feel stuck. Taken aback by the reality of her, he held her gaze for a beat too long before he managed to clear his throat and introduce himself.

"Good evening, Freedom," he recovered neatly, extending his hand that quickly swallowed hers as he gave her his patented two-pump handshake and then settled back into his seat across from her.

"Good evening," she replied, her eyes still unwavering.

Almost reflexively, he averted his eyes from her intense gaze, looking down at his blazer, adjusting his collar and lapels to recenter his thoughts as the set producer began the countdown. He wasn't sure what he had been expecting, but it certainly wasn't this. He felt a bit off-center. The voice coming through his earpiece brought him swiftly back to the urgency of the moment.

"We are live in 5...4...3..2..."

Carlos stretched his thousand-watt smile onto his face, pushed away the tiny seed of discomfort that had suddenly begun roiling in his stomach, and remembered that this night could make or break his career.

Freedom's portion of the interview was scheduled to be approximately twenty minutes. That was all her attorney would agree to in negotiations, and the legal team had insisted on approving the questions and topics in advance. With commercials inserted, that was easily a 30 minute segment. When Carlos noticed the lawyer walking into the theater earlier, he immediately knew that she wasn't there for moral support. He'd Googled her and was well aware that her presence was meant as both intimidation and enforcement. Although he hadn't yet put together how the Jackson family had managed to secure her level of legal talent, he had enough sense to agree to her demands. Nonetheless, Carlos was intent on spending the next twenty minutes extracting from Freedom the type of explosive content that could rocket his reputation into the next echelon. The fact that he had even landed this interview was beyond his wildest expectations, so he planned to make the most of every minute. He knew the girl had been coached by a professional team, but he was not going to be bested by an 18 year old from Nowhere, USA. His game plan to get around the stiff rules on what he could ask was to avoid too many direct questions and, instead, tell the same stories that the various internet theorists were telling to see if Freedom bristled at the accusations defensively or otherwise gave any signs that would paint one or the other of the theories as more or less true. He was also pinning some hopes on the idea that teenage girls like to ramble on incessantly. He was sure something would slip. He had been at this story for what was now stretching into three weeks, and everything he had gleaned so far had convinced him that Freedom knew a lot more than what she had said in the sparse and dissatisfying police report. He was going to have to get her to talk.

After his welcome intro, he dialed down his signature smile and took on a more serious affect, one that he hoped was oozing national nightly news gravitas.

"Freedom, America has been following this story very closely since news of Eric Tucker's untimely death broke. As you may have seen or read, the theories of what could have happened are all over the place, but more importantly, they all center around you." He paused here to let the cameras zoom in on her reaction, but she didn't really seem to be displaying one. Instead, she was holding his eye contact and listening intently. Carlos furrowed his brow and threw out a few more bits of information to increase the pressure in the room. "From social media to school cafeterias, people have taken an almost fanatic interest in this story—, the State Governor, nationally elected leaders, movie stars, and influencers. In fact, I understand that you weren't able to return to complete your final weeks of high school or give your valedictorian speech at commencement."

Freedom raised her brows slightly, acknowledging the information but still not bothering to verbally confirm.

Oh, you are really going to make me work for it, huh? Okay, Carlos thought. He turned up the heat.

"Now that the initial shock of the loss has worn off, people are demanding answers. As the sole witness to Eric's death, you are the only one who truly holds those answers, but you're not talking. Why?"

He paused there to see if she would rush in to fill the tense silence he let fill the space at the end of his sentence. Freedom nodded slowly, her face not giving away much of anything.

"I told law enforcement everything," she stated calmly, returning the ball to his court.

Realizing that his opening remarks were not going to be enough to get her to start rambling, he decided to call up Eric's ghost and see how she responded to that.

"For those watching that are new to the story, Eric Tucker, a star athlete, straight-A student, and hometown hero, was killed on a remote stretch of highway in the town he grew up in. He was thought to have been hit by a truck, but autopsy results revealed that he was also shot, and no one seems to know who shot him." Here he paused, knowing that graphics were probably showing a montage of photographs of the handsome victim, then he dropped the hammer. "Well, no one except for you, that is."

Freedom nodded softly, her eyes shining lightly as though she were holding back tears. Sensing the vulnerability, Carlos pushed ahead. "Are you ready to tell us what you know?"

Freedom's eyes flitted quickly, almost imperceptibly, to the space over Carlos's left shoulder and then settled back on Carlos. Carlos knew that her support system was probably standing there, and he angled his body just enough to cut off her line of sight.

She began slowly.

"All of this has been really hard. I don't know who shot Eric. But people want me to know. My name and address have been put out on the news, so I can't live at home anymore."

At this, he felt a little steel creep into her eyes and felt immediately certain that she not only knew he was the one who had found her and brought the attention and hordes of news vans to her grandmother's home, but resented it. She was taking a shot at him that was imperceptible to the viewers, but he realized it was too late to react.

"And what you said is true," she continued. "I wasn't allowed back on my high school campus. I don't know if you know this, but I worked so hard to graduate with honors and become valedictorian for that, but because no one knows what happened to Eric, I was banned from graduation."

"That must be upsetting." Carlos was ready to return fire, "But at least you are alive and able to graduate. Eric Tucker can't say as much." Carlos looked intently for any sign that this heavy retort had hit its mark, but the girl took it in stride with an earnest nod.

"His death is terrible. Everything is terrible right now. Nothing is okay," she said. "And I know that people want answers. I do too! But you already know everything that I know about what happened to Eric." Her voice was soft but steady and assured. "That night was one of the most traumatic things I have ever experienced." Her voice trembled just a bit, and she clasped her hands to her stomach. "I was driving home from the library. It was late, and my car started swerving to one side. Nothing like that had happened to me before, and I... I was scared. I pulled onto the shoulder the best that I could, grabbed the flashlight from the glove box, and got out to see what was wrong with the car. There really aren't any lights on that stretch of road, and it was getting dark. It was a dangerous place to stop, but I didn't have a choice. My tires were blown."

Carlos set his note cards on the small table and leaned forward, thrilled that she was going into detail without his prodding. No matter what happened later, he knew that this first public retelling would be the one against which every other thing she said was measured and weighed against.

Freedom absentmindedly brushed a tendril of curls out of her face. It was a small movement, but somehow it made her seem younger, like a kid telling their mom about a tough day at school. He wondered if it was calculated.

"When I realized that I had not one but two flat tires, I knew there was no way for me to drive home. My pop pop taught me how to change a tire, but I'd never been told what to do when there are two flat tires. The suburban only has one spare in the trunk. I was planning to call my grandmother to see if she could send someone to help, but then Eric pulled up behind me."

"So you knew it was Eric pulling up?" Carlos interrupted.

"Yes," Freedom replied matter-of-factly.

"Well, I ask again because one theory of what happened to Eric," Carlos cut back in to explain his questions, "is that he startled you that night on the road, and you shot him thinking he was a threat."

Freedom's eyes widened in surprise, one hand flying up to her heart.

"What? No!" she exclaimed. " I knew who Eric was. I mean, everyone kind of knew Eric. He is a big deal here in Jolivette, and plus he did something to the exhaust pipes on his truck so that they make so much loud noise. You can always hear him coming. But I don't know why anyone would think I could have shot him. I've never fired a gun in my life. I don't even own a gun." Freedom furrowed her brows and shook her head in disbelief, another tear escaping. "The police did some kind of test that night to confirm that I had not fired any kind of weapon." She shrugged, her face still looking incredulous and sad.

Carlos folded his arms across his body and leaned his head to the side, a question forming behind his eyes.

"Let's go back to the moment Eric pulled up. How did you feel? Were you happy to see Eric?"

Freedom cocked her head at the same exact angle that Carlos had. He couldn't tell if she was mocking him or genuinely confused at the question.

"What do you mean?" she asked. "I was alone, at night, on a dark stretch of highway. I was glad to see a familiar face."

Carlos lowered his eyes to cynical slits.

"There have been some reports that Eric and his family were not always kind to other kids and families, especially families of...color."

Carlos searched Freedom's eyes for agreement, but she kept her head at the same angle as though waiting for more explanation. She was either smarter than he'd thought she was or had been prepared for this interview like a CIA spy. He couldn't believe her. Everyone in this God awful town knew that the Tucker family had an uninterrupted history of overt racism, and this girl was sitting there looking like a doe-eyed confused Bambi. He fought the urge to roll his eyes and, instead, returned to the timeline that she had begun laying out.

"Okay, so Eric pulled up behind you, and what happened next?"

"Well," Freedom continued, her eyes taking on a far-away look. "Eric came around to the driver's side of the car to look at the first flat tire. It was the side of the car close to traffic, but there really weren't any other cars out on the road. I was still sitting in the front driver's seat when I heard a shot ring out. I didn't know it was a shot at first. It sounded like an explosion."

"Where did the sound come from?" Carlos quizzed her.

"I don't know." Freedom's face was strained, her eyes registering confusion and fear as though she were back in the moment. "I ducked down and hid. When I finally peeked out of the window, Eric was out in the lane of the highway, walking backward really slowly. His hands were covering his chest, and he was just walking backward and looking into the treeline on the side of the road like he'd seen a ghost. I yelled out to warn him that he was walking too far into the highway lane, but then… then…" Freedom shut her eyes tightly, her entire body trembling as two tears escaped and slid down her face.

Carlos wanted to reach for the tissues on the side table, wanted to say something weighty and memorable, but he was riveted by the chilling energy radiating from Free as she recounted the story in real-time. This wasn't an act. It couldn't be.

"Take your time," he finally managed to say.

As his words landed in the silently charged air, Freedom's eyes opened. Tears continued to cascade down her cheeks. Her nose, now red-tipped from the emotional retelling, flared with every labored breath she took, and she whispered harshly in a tone so low that Carlos felt himself leaning towards her to catch every word.

"The truck came out of nowhere. One moment he was there, and then—" Freedom's body jerked suddenly like she was watching the impact again. "Then he was gone."

It seemed impossible, but the girl could have orchestrated this retelling as an act. Her eyes shone with the tears still escaping, her mouth trembled with the emotion, and her cheeks had flushed into a rosy color that she could not have possibly faked.

Carlos sat back hard in his seat and let the moment hang in the air. He was snapped back into action as he heard his producer through his earpiece practically yelling, "Ask the OTHER questions!"

Carlos quickly grabbed his note cards from the table and flipped to the card of unapproved questions. It was time to create his own viral moment. He felt a pang of hesitancy. Could he do this to her? *You don't know her. You don't owe her anything,* he coached himself.

"Freedom, I know this must be tough," he began his pivot. "But there are so many unanswered questions still hanging out there. In fact, over the last couple of weeks, we have learned a lot about Eric Tucker, but we haven't learned much about you at all. Were you friends? Why did he stop to help that night?"

Freedom did not respond immediately. Carlos tried to make eye contact with the girl, but she was still dabbing at her eyes with the Kleenex. It felt like a stall tactic. He decided to push the issue.

"You have no social media pages that we could find, no web footprint other than some academic and musical accolades. For a teenage girl, that level of anonymity is almost unheard of! Is there a reason you aren't on social media like so many of your peers?"

He forced a smile here to make his question appear light-hearted. She rewarded his smile with a small, sad smile of her own and shrugged.

Damnit, Carlos thought to himself. *She wasn't even going to attempt to explain.* He decided to go for the silver bullet.

"You know," he started somberly, "people want to know who you are. I even tried to figure out who you are. We know that you were raised by your grandmother, but we don't know why. Why weren't your parents around growing up?" Free looked up sharply, something other than sadness now brewing behind her eyes. Carlos felt the shift and pushed forward.

"In fact, I received a copy of your birth certificate. Your father's name was listed as unknown, and your mother never signed it. I searched for her everywhere, and there isn't even a record of a Monica Walker in existence in public records the year after you were born. It seems like she just, poof! Disappeared. On some of the message boards that have popped up, they are calling you the child that nobody wanted. How do you respond to that?"

At Carlos's last statement, Freedom had raised her head and pulled her shoulders back. The tears and soft, delicate demeanor from a moment before were gone, and in their place, something emptier had taken root. Free appeared to be looking intently at Carlos, but he could tell that she had gone somewhere else. Somewhere safer than this stage, where he had just asked her the most hurtful, insidious question he could have drummed up. Something twisted in his, and he wanted desperately to look away but could not drag his eyes from hers. He knew what dissociated survival mode looked like, and he had pushed her into it. He had gone too far.

"I know who I am, so I don't care if anyone else does," Free surprised him by answering the question. "I was raised by Pop and Jean Walker," she said, her voice even and strong. "Two incredible people who built a life for me when others cast me aside. I am the first Black valedictorian in the history of Jolivette High, even though they won't let me walk or give my speech. I have worked hard all of my life to make my grandparents proud and earn my way. And I have been called worse things than unwanted by better people than you."

Carlos' heart sank, but she continued. " I can't tell you who did this to Eric, but I can tell you that in trying to hurt him, they have hurt me too. My life has been totally hijacked, and all I did was stop to check my tires. Now my family is receiving death threats. I cannot go home to the only place I have ever lived or sleep through the night without worrying that someone is trying to make me pay for something I didn't do. I did nothing to deserve this. But my life has been torn apart by the media—by people like you because YOU want a story to tell that can get you likes, clicks, and followers and subscribers, and they don't care if it's real or right, or accurate. You are chasing fame, and all I have ever wanted is a life. Eric is gone now, and since they can't bring him back, they want a life for a life; mine for Eric's. But destroying me won't bring him back. And I won't be the sacrificial lamb to help people feel better about what happened to him. I want the same thing Eric wanted: a chance to grow up and do something great with my life."

It felt like time had stopped. There was a single tear rolling down Freedom's cheek, but Carlos had not missed the way that she'd answered the questions she'd wanted to answer instead of the one he had asked. She had effortlessly repositioned herself as the victim and recast him as a villain in the story he was covering. And in many ways, she was right. Her PR team had trained her like a navy SEAL, and he was losing this war on air and in his own conscience. If he was being honest, for a beat or two, he felt a small wave of embarrassment knowing that she had gotten the best of him just then, which annoyed him, and he threw his chin up, preparing to end on a question that would take some of the sting out of her well done soliloquy when he heard the biting voice of her lawyer echo across the stage.

"CUT!" Gayle called out. "This interview is over!" The sound of her clicking heels followed the boom of her voice and spurred Carlos into action.

"Wait a second!" Carlos yelled, standing to his feet. "You can't just end my interview!"

"I can, and I did!" Gayle sniped back.

"Throw a commercial!" his producer barked into his ears. Carlos pivoted towards the camera and quickly delivered his regrets.

"Sorry, folks. We need to take a quick break. More, when we return, on the story that started in small-town America and has now gripped the nation. What happened to Eric Tucker?"

The cameraman signaled all clear, and Carlos turned quickly to convince Free not to get up, but he was too late. The long-legged attorney had crossed the full expanse of the stage in the blink of an eye and was helping the girl to her feet.

"Wait! Wait!" Carlos held his palms out in front of him as a mea culpa and a silent plea to allow the interview to go on, but the attorney whirled on him and neatly stated,

" Expect to be served with a lawsuit in the morning, Mr. Jackson."

Freedom was hustled backstage under the arm of the lawyer, and Carlos followed behind them with the desperate, loping trot of a wounded animal. In his heart, he knew that he had gone too far, but this was the story people wanted—her backstory. They wanted to know if she had the origin story of that could have led her to kill or orchestrate the killing of a classmate. The public was clamoring for every new bit of information he could dig out about this story, and, thus far, the most difficult to mine bits of information were about Freedom herself.

The lawyer had put some distance between them, so he picked up his pace a bit to try to reach their dressing area, hoping to make one final plea to continue the interview before they locked him out. As he pushed the heavy stage curtain aside, he slammed forcefully into a tall, lithe woman whom he recognized immediately as the woman who had left Freedom's home with the mayor just a few nights ago. The impact knocked the wind out of him.

"Eh-excuse me," he stammered, wondering why she wasn't even a bit off balance and why he was the only one disheveled by the collision. A few days ago, he wouldn't have known who she was, but now, standing this close to her and having seen the similarities in Free's face, he placed her. It was the mother. Freedom's mother.

"Oh my God," he said.

He was quickly piecing together that Freedom's mother and Eric's father had a secret meet-up not long after the death of his son, and he was rapidly trying to figure out what that meant. This woman was supposed to be in the wind, having abandoned her daughter and never looked back, but here she was, in the flesh, and she was breathtaking up close. An older, much taller version of her petite daughter, but with warm copper eyes and deep mahogany skin. The similarity between her features and her daughter's was unmistakable.

"Watch your step." Angel interrupted Carlos's obvious staring. Her tone was cold and dripping with sarcasm. It dawned on Carlos then that their collision might not have been an accident after all, and he rubbed the part of his chest that was still smarting from the impact and was guaranteed to be bruised soon.

Sheesh! Did she lower her shoulder NFL style? He thought to himself.

Angel watched him, and a slow smile spread across her face that felt menacing.

"There is always one," she began slowly. "One Black man that can look around and see a monstrous system of unbridled white supremacy, rage, and discrimination, and STILL decide to target the victims. Drag the ones that are already fighting for their lives, barely keeping their heads above water. I guess that one is you tonight, huh **brotha**?" She emphasized "brotha" so that it would be clear that she was using the term ironically.

She stepped into him, then, closing what little gap was left between them.

"Would you be working this hard to discredit her if Free was the one in the morgue and that rich white boy was still running up and down a football field? Nah. You look like one of those fake woke brothers that ran around campus saying 'protect Black women, believe Black women' with your fist in the air and then went back to your dorm and shared nudes of the Black girls you slept with to the group chat so you could seem cool."

Carlos recoiled, surprised at the vitriol in the words she launched at him like missiles. The accusation was oddly specific and actually stung a bit because he knew that even though he'd never done that, he had been in the kind of group chats she was talking about, though he'd never admit it to this woman.

Angel stepped forward, once again closing the distance between the two of them uncomfortably.

"Free has been through enough. If you think that you are going to sacrifice her to launch your tired little career and run up the ratings for a network that will fire you the moment you stop picking their cotton, you are in for a rude awakening. I will sing at your funeral before I let that happen."

At this last comment, Carlos felt his own hackles rising. Maybe he hadn't always been the most respectful guy, but he was not about to let this woman paint him as some Stepin Fetchit Sambo. He was good at his job, and he had earned his way into this position. He curled his face into a sarcastic smile.

"Are you threatening me?" he growled. "Because I still have my mic on, and we can play this back on tomorrow's news, Monica, is it?" He'd hoped to startle her by making it clear that he knew exactly who she was, but Angel remained in his face, unflinching. She held his gaze and raised an amused eyebrow, looking for all the world like a cross between a cold-blooded killer and a pageant queen.

"Do I look afraid to you, little boy?" she challenged, her voice as smooth as buttercream now.

Carlos considered checking her for calling him a little boy, but decided against it. Freedom had just annihilated his attempts to knock her off her game, so the chance of winning a verbal spar with this leviathan of a woman was probably not in the cards, and he still had a show to do. He backed away a step. He would find a way to use this little run-in to his benefit. He'd been hunting for

Freedom's disappearing mother, and now here she was. He would have another chance to get at her. It didn't have to be today.

"Okay. I hear you loud and clear," he said, his hands raised in mock surrender. "But just to be clear, should I consider that threat off the record or on?" he asked rhetorically, pivoting on his heel and heading back out to the stage before she had a chance to respond.

Carlos had always known that his interview with Freedom was going to be fragile and could implode at any time, so he had scheduled another explosive guest with the assistance of the network. In order to ensure continuity, they decided that the second interview would not be live. They had agreed to a delayed airing, so the studio cut to the B-roll timeline they had worked up while Carlos sat down with his second guest, Rebecca Tucker, Eric's mother.

He'd watched the B-roll timeline treatment more than ten times the night before and was fully aware that while he was conducting his interview with Rebecca Tucker, the deep baritone of their best voiceover artist would be filling homes across America with the ominous opening monologue:

Murder, money, and mystery in Jolivette,
Texas.

In the piece, they'd chronicled the meteoric rise to power of the Jolivette Tuckers and sprinkled in a significant dose of the undeniably convenient string of unsolved deaths, disappearances, and property damage that seemed to have paved the way for that rise. Then the timeline would jump to the present-day parallels between the old Tucker regime of brute force and the new era of payoffs and blackmail tied to complaints they'd unearthed that had been filed against young Eric and then conveniently buried by Jolivette PD and the school's administration.

While Rebecca was telling the story of her poor, wonderful son, the news network would be simultaneously lighting that entire narrative on fire so that when her interview aired, it wouldn't be all that believable. But Rebecca wouldn't know that. Not until her interview was done. Carlos found himself hoping that Freedom's hellcat mother would see the replay. She'd hurled some nasty allegations, but he hoped, despite himself, that she would see that he was an equal opportunity journalist who would offer up anyone to the wolves that the story suggested should be sacrificed. Yeah, maybe he was painting Freedom as the culprit, but he was also making it clear that the victim wasn't all that much of a victim.

Rebbeca's interview went exactly to plan. Carlos started out asking Rebeca to describe the enormity of the loss their family was navigating. She braved her way through the details, clutching her Kleenex tightly in her fist. She was a wisp of a woman, and grief had clearly taken a lot out of her. The makeup artists, despite their best efforts, hadn't been able to fully conceal the dark circles and translucent pallor that gave her eyes a haunted look. As she talked about Eric as a child and what she would miss most, Carlos saw that she was slowly warming to him, letting her guard down, and lost in memory. When she seemed fully disarmed, he asked the question that he already knew the answer to.

"Rebecca, why would anyone want to hurt Eric?"

He was careful to keep his voice soft and reassuring. When she demurred by shrugging her shoulders, he rephrased the question.

"We all know about the incredible athletic feats and stellar academics of Eric Tucker, and, as a mother, we know you loved him deeply. But was anyone upset with him? Can you think of anyone who would have been angry enough to want to end his life?" He gave the question a light, airy tone, matching her incredulity with his own as though he expected her to be able to say no, but he did not miss the shift in her body language.

Her back stiffened, and her tears evaporated swiftly as a red flush crept up her neck and bloomed onto her face. He pushed her harder.

"There have been rumors that Eric wasn't always a hero. That he sometimes, and maybe often, took on the role of the villain."

Rebecca cut him off abruptly.

"Don't you dare! Don't you dare speak of my son that way!" she spat.

Carlos extended his hand to her as if trying to calm her, but she was already off to the races.

"My son did not deserve to die. Jolivette used to be a safe place!" she said, "A place where everyone knew their neighbors and looked out for one another. As a community, we fought hard to keep it that way. But over the years, all kinds of riff-raff have moved here. Strangers. We don't know their people or where they are from. They have no respect for the law or the families that built this city with their own blood, sweat, and tears. Hell, half of them don't even speak English! It's ridiculous, and now it's just not safe."

She paused here to catch her breath.

"If someone like Eric can't go to the library and come home without being murdered, well then…" Her voice trailed off a bit before she completed her sentence. "…then this is not the Jolivette I grew up in."

Carlos's brow shot up as he mentally logged the dog whistles and xenophobia in her statement, but he did not address it, instead opting to ask another question.

"So far, no arrests have been made in Eric's killing. Do you know if there are any leads?"

Rebecca turned her red-rimmed eyes directly to the camera.

"I know that GIRL knows more than what she is saying." She choked out the word "girl" like it hurt her to say it. "They are saying that there isn't any evidence that the girl had a weapon, or caused his death, but I know that it is not possible that my son was shot and then killed right in front of her, and she saw nothing. Nothing?!" she shrilled. "They should charge her with something! Anything! I bet after a couple of nights in jail, she will start talking."

Rebecca was shaking with anger, and Carlos was again exhilarated by the sheer possibility of the number of sound bites that would be extracted from tonight's interviews. Still, he maintained the serious, thoughtful look he'd adopted as his persona for the evening.

"But why would the girl hide the information if she knows something?" he quipped. "Wouldn't life be easier for her already if she gave the police someone else to look into?"

At this, Rebecca waved her hand dismissively.

"I wouldn't be surprised if she staged the whole car trouble thing just so she could get Eric out there alone at night. Everyone knows we have money. Maybe she and someone else were trying to rob him. I want whatever animal did this to pay!" Her voice was shaking again, and Carlos knew that they were out of time, so he turned to the camera to close.

"Well, the sheriff and police have been working in conjunction on this case for weeks now, with no additional information. There seems to be a real chance that we might never know what happened to Eric Tucker."

Hours after the show had wrapped, Carlos twisted the cap from a miniature bottle of Jack Daniel's and sat down heavily on the captain's chair in his hotel room. He looked around at the paintings and well-appointed furniture. All vastly different from the roach motel he'd been slumming in when he first arrived in Jolivette. It seemed like a lifetime ago, though it was mere weeks. He wanted to revel in his success. He wanted to be ecstatic. He thought about calling his mom and asking her if she had seen the interview, but something was gnawing at him. Or perhaps it was someone.

Despite his best efforts, he had been unable to stop replaying his exchange with Freedom's mother in his mind on a loop. He was absolutely sure, now, that the woman had seen him practically running after Freedom and decided to clothesline him. But what hurt more than his body was his pride. She had accused him of selling out his own culture just to get ahead. She may as well have called him an Uncle Tom, no matter how historically inaccurate that reference was. Sambo was the dancing sell out, not Uncle Tom, a distinction no one bothered to make anymore. Never in his life had Carlos been accused of being a sell-out, and the worst part of it all was that the more he drank, the more he wasn't convinced that she was wrong. He knew the Tucker story. He knew they had cut their teeth and fueled their fortune with blatant and violent racism. He also knew that the dead hero that the town was mourning was actually a nasty piece of work. But he'd still done what the network wanted and trotted out the information about Freedom being raised without a mother or father. It made her a little more of a stereotype and a little less human. And he had leaked her location information, without the studio's prompting on that part. He'd forced her into hiding and then made her seem like an unwanted orphan with shiftless parents, and he was starting to regret it, which was pissing him off.

He experienced another pang of guilt at how relentlessly he had pursued this story that had now morphed into a chaotic circus swirling around her character. In his mind, he had built her up to be something else. Something more sinister—a calculating, brooding genius that was somehow getting away with murder. But there, on the stage, she was just a girl. A quiet, bright girl buckling under the weight of speculation in a town that had probably never done her any favors.

Chapter 33

Andrew - A Family Meeting

Drew pulled around behind the big house and cut his engine. He knew a trap when he smelled one, and everything about this urgent invitation to his family's ranch smelled and felt like a trap. When he'd gotten the text that his mother had fallen and was refusing to go to the hospital, he'd felt his stomach drop. He knew the family was fraying at the seams and couldn't withstand another blow right now. But the next message felt forced and calculated, reminding him that he couldn't trust his own family, who had made an artform of passive aggression and subterfuge. He looked at the message from his sister again before he climbed out of his truck.

"We are really worried about her, and you know that you are the only one she will listen to."

He shook his head with irritation. When he was young, he'd been what they call a knee baby. Anytime you saw his mother, you saw him, right at her knee. He'd spent years soaking her in. The smell of freshly baked bread seemed to cling to her. He'd stare in awe at the unexpected strength of her arms and hands that flew through their kitchen, turning endless fresh ingredients into masterful meals that exploded with flavor in your mouth and stuck to your ribs. He'd listen to her hum old folk songs and hymns and shadow her in the kitchen, stirring this and kneading that as she cooked big meals for the family. She'd even started teaching him to sew a bit. He'd darned a few things and was helping her with a quilt when his father decided that he'd never become a man shuffling around behind his mama. Drew had protested, but his father wouldn't budge, and his mother seemed to agree, so he traded his time with blossoming domestic skills for whatever sport his father fancied each season and traded his quiet time with his mom for cold, miserable nights in the deer blind with his dad and brothers, hunting for things they could skin, jerky, and mount. By then, his mother was pregnant with his little sister, so he knew she would have someone else to teach all of the things she loved.

Over the years, there would be plenty more times when his father asserted his narrow and oppressive view of what was good for Drew onto him like a brand. In the beginning, he had assumed that his mom would take up for him and side against his father. But he quickly learned that his mother was devoted to her ideals of what a good wife should be, and chief amongst them was submission. In fact, she rarely stood up to his father about anything, choosing instead to "keep the peace," as she called it.

Gradually, Drew began to resent her. He didn't want to lump her in with his dismal opinion of his father, but she went along so quietly, so easily, and so often with his father's tyrannical nature that he decided one day that she wasn't any different from the old man at all. The final tear in their relationship was when Drew hurt his ankle in the championship game his senior year. He was in tears, excruciating pain vibrating up his leg, and his father had descended from the stands, red-faced, screaming for him to play through the pain like a real Tucker.

"Mom, please!" Drew had pleaded with his mother, just two rows up, to get his dad to back off.

She'd lowered her eyes and shrugged her shoulders. Drew finished the game, but they lost anyway, and by Monday, the doctor had confirmed that the ankle was broken. Compound fractures and torn ligaments. His father had nearly ended his football career and cost him college scholarships over a high school football game. He spent the entire summer in intensive therapy and constantly reinjured his ankle during his college playing years.

"You let him do this to me!" he'd practically hurled the words at his mother when she tried to placate him with a scratch apple pie after he had come home from the hospital with the news of the injury's extent.

"Your father just wants you to do your best," she'd replied weakly.

When Drew's father retold the story for years afterward, he would reframe it as though the game was lost because Drew was favoring a twisted ankle, afraid to get hit. His father always left out the part about the fractures, the grueling rehab, and the doctor pointing out that playing on it had been a grave error.

Once, Drew had been just drunk enough to call his dad out on the revised version he loved to tell in front of the company he was telling it to. They were hosting some banking bigwigs down from Dallas. His father had told him to quit exaggerating.

"It was just a sprain," he'd laughed, clapping the chuckling banker nearest him on the back. "My son, the drama queen."

The room had erupted in laughter. It was just that easy for his father, Drew realized. He could rewrite history in his mind in whatever way best suited him, and that version became his reality. He knew his father was gaslighting himself as much as he gaslit everyone around him. But his mother? Drew knew that she knew better, and she still never tried to save him. Drew's close relationship with his mother hadn't survived the broken ankle incident. He'd pulled as far away from her as he could, and he knew she felt the gulf between them. So the text from his sister rang hollow and was the most pathetic of the many attempts his siblings had pulled, to date, to bait him back to the ranch so they could pounce on him.

Still, even with total awareness that it was a trap, Drew walked into it willingly. It was a reckoning that had been brewing for a long time, and he was too exhausted to keep up the game of cat and mouse. He knew it was time to pay the piper. He'd watched the interview of Free and his wife in abject horror as he realized that he was standing between two worlds, both of them broken. More importantly, he had seen the direction the coverage of his family's reputation was taking, and it was time to lay it all out.

When he rounded the side of the house, the huge picture windows that framed the kitchen came into view, and he could see his sister, Anna, his brother, John, and his brother-in-law, Grant, their backs to him, colluding under the warm yellow light of the rustic deer antler chandelier. His mother was nowhere in sight, which was not a surprise. He was, however, surprised to see Becca sitting across from Anna, her face drawn and tight. Drew knew immediately that this would be a long night. He paused for a moment, his hand on the door, considering a swift retreat. But then he thought how much worse could his life really get than what it was. He had nothing left to lose. And with that thought, he blew out a breath, opened the door, and walked into his ambush.

When he stepped through the door, they were all seated on stools at the oversized island that stretched almost the entire length of the kitchen. Grant, John, and Anna all looked up as Drew's body filled the doorway, but not Rebecca. He gave Rebecca a long look, hoping that she would offer even a moment of eye contact, but she kept her gaze trained on her hands, clutched firmly in her lap. Anna was at the far end of the island and was the only one who bothered to greet him.

"Hey, big brother," she said, her voice hoarse and husky like she had been crying or yelling or both.

Drew met her greeting with a small smile. He knew she had greeted him the way she had when they were kids as an olive branch because whatever was coming next was going to be rough. Drew considered perching on one of the empty stools, then thought better of it. Sitting was a tactical disadvantage when it was one versus four. Instead, he crossed his arms over his chest and leaned against the edge of the cool granite counter closest to Grant. Grant raised an eyebrow, silently recognizing Drew's strategic body language. Drew ran his eyes over his little brother, who looked like he had been drinking. His skin was mottled, and the whites of his eyes were shot through with tiny red streaks. John bristled at the inspection and shot a glare over at Anna, making sure that she knew he wasn't pleased with the little verbal olive branch she had offered; then he set his attention back on Drew.

"What you're doing ain't right, Drew." He started right in. No warm-up. No soft opening.

"How do you mean?" Drew asked, placing his palms down on the island to help him remain calm.

"I mean, you know someone shot Eric. You know it. We all know it. And you ain't doing shit about it," his brother slurred back. Yes, he had definitely been drinking.

Drew's eyes darted to Rebecca again, but her eyes still had not left her own lap.

"What is it that you think I should do?" Drew asked his gin-soaked brother, still calm despite the storm he knew was brewing. "We don't have any evidence. No one has found the truck company or the trucker that dragged Eric. Hundreds of eighteen wheelers pass through this corridor every hour. Some through to Mexico, some North clear to Canada. They hit deer, coyote, javelina, and keep rolling. What do we have? We have one girl. A tiny little slip of a girl who tested negative for gunpowder residue according to the cops, right Grant?" he said, looking pointedly at his brother-in-law, who grunted in reluctant agreement.

"There was no weapon and no evidence of anyone else on the scene. And don't forget, thanks to all of your document leaks and impatient maneuvering, we now have a town crawling with reporters who are just as interested in exposing our family as a bunch of redneck racists as they are finding whoever killed Eric. So what do you propose we do? Add fuel to the fire or let this whole shit show die down some?"

He paused to let the truth sink in.

"All of this attention from the media is threatening everything we've built here."

That last statement lit a fire under John, who jumped to his feet and nearly stumbled doing so.

"Everything WE'VE built? WE? He slurred. What the f**k have you built, Drew?" John spat incredulously. "You haven't built a goddamn thing! All you have ever done is kiss daddy's boots and take all the credit for an empire built on all of the things you pretend to hate. That's what you've always done. Let the rest of us do the hard work— the ugly work, the man's work—and then show up with your pretty face and tailored suit to shake hands and accept the praise."

Anna cut in, her voice shaky, interrupting John's tirade.

"This isn't the time to rehash the unresolved brother feuds you two have been squabbling about forever. This is about Eric. He deserves justice. We have to find out what happened to him."

"Listen, Anna," Drew's voice was firm, but he could feel the fight going out of him. He really didn't have the energy to have this battle. His heart wasn't in it. He heaved a heavy sigh. "We all know that this is how it was always going to end for Eric. Yes, I loved him. We all loved him, but he was making enemies faster than we could pay them off! We just buried a rape case for him last year, for God's sake! Half of this f****ed up town is relieved that he is not here anymore!"

At this last statement, he heard a small sob escape Rebecca's mouth and immediately regretted his choice of words. When he turned to face her, her eyes were red and furious.

"How dare you!" her hoarse whisper stabbed at him. "He was my son! He was just a kid. No, he wasn't perfect, but he would have grown out of that impulsive behavior."

Drew shook his head. He was truly sorry for what Rebecca was going through, but he was done holding his tongue and letting women tell him who he was and what he knew. He had let Angel change the course of his life once already with her opinion of him. He had let Rebecca convince him to cover and coddle Eric even as the kid's behavior spiraled out of control. He was done with ceding his power to pushy women.

"Rebecca, impulsive behavior is cheating on a test or cutting class to go to the beach. Maybe even spray painting a building or stealing a car. But Eric had five classmates report allegations of violent assault and harassment—in just the last two years alone— that WE made disappear."

He pointed around the room to make sure that everyone remembered the part they played in covering Eric's sins.

"All of us. Have you forgotten that he broke a kid's arm for not helping him cheat on a calculus exam? That he choked a girl unconscious at a house party?"

Drew threw up his hands in frustration.

"Eric wasn't impulsive. He was dangerous, and you know it!" Drew slapped the table, and Anna jumped at the loud sound. Another sob escaped from Becca, and Drew turned to watch as his wife of 17 years crumpled into grief again, her shoulders heaving as sobs wracked her body. He wondered, then, if he had ever loved her. If he had ever really known her, or if she had known him. He knew she hated him now, but maybe, in a way, she always had.

"Where are you staying, Rebecca?" he asked softly. "You can come home. I'll leave if you want. You can have the house."

At this, John scraped back his chair and stepped in front of Drew, his anger having now grown into a full rage.

"She will never step foot back in that place, you piece of sh*t!" he spat, flecks of saliva dotting Drew's face. "I know you've had that Black b**ch in there. We saw her on the house cameras, coming in and leaving the next day in your clothes."

At this revelation, Anna gasped and covered her mouth. Drew was caught off guard. It hadn't even crossed his mind that his wife would be watching him on their security cameras. He had been careless, but there wasn't much that could be done about it now. He rubbed the bridge of his nose as the stress began to settle between his eyes like a dull ache.

"Isn't that the same little piece of tail you were chasing around in high school?" John's tone had gone from pissed to sinister, and an eerie smile stretched across his face. "Yeah, I'd recognize her anywhere. You've been running around, pretending to be the golden boy, Drew. Mr. Mayor. Playing like you're something better than the rest of us 'cause you went off and got a fancy degree and did everything Daddy told you to. But you ain't better than nobody. You shoulda kept your n*gger-loving pansy ass in California. We don't need you here."

"John!" Anna yelled out. "That is enough! For Christ's sake!" Her whole body was shaking, and she seemed close to fainting from the stress of the confrontation.

Drew knew deep down that Anna hated the blatant racism that so much of their family comfortably operated in. She had always been the sensitive one. Her empathy knew no limits, and she had a really hard time at 13 when their dad told her that she couldn't have her Black, Hispanic, or Asian friends over for sleepovers or go to their homes. She had come to Drew's room clutching her worn, stuffed rabbit with the missing button eye and cried herself to sleep. Anna was born for something better, higher. A family that would raise its next generation on love, not division and destruction. Maybe they had all deserved better. But Drew knew that there was no choosing the kind of family you were born into, there were only two options for him: becoming it or surviving it.

Unlike Anna, Drew was not rattled by John's vitriolic language. He realized that his brother was finally giving him the out he had been waiting for, for most of his life. If everyone was going to lay their cards on the table, Drew decided he was going to be the one to call. Drew stepped within inches of his brother, so close that he could smell the liquor and tobacco on his breath. But Drew did not raise his voice. Instead, he lowered it so low that only John could hear him. He knew the others were straining to hear, but he didn't care.

"I'm sorry about your son. I really am," his low voice rumbled close to John's ear. He felt his brother's body go stiff. "But if you say another word about Monica between this moment and the day you die, I will make sure to close the gap between the two." Drew stepped back then, returning his voice to full volume as John stood frozen and mute.

"John, I know you love Becca. I think I always knew it, but you are right. I was a coward who did everything Daddy told me to do. He told me to marry her, and I did it, despite knowing it would hurt you. I'm sorry that I took that from you. I thought when you married Jenny that maybe, I don't know, maybe you could forgive me for marrying Becca. But now I know that it was foolish of me to expect that from you. Love doesn't let go like that. It doesn't matter who else you try to plug in or how many years creep by. You love who you love."

Drew realized that he was talking about John and Becca but thinking about himself and Angel.

"We've all made our choices, John, and now we have to live with them. When were you planning to tell the family about you and Becca?" Drew waited to see if his brother would acknowledge the truth of all he'd just laid bare.

Instead, John took a step backward, his now red and watery eyes averted from Drew's.

"Is that true?" Anna asked, wide-eyed. Drew knew that they had been keeping their little sister in the dark about everything that mattered for far too long. Well, tonight she was getting all of the truth he had to offer. Anna looked to Becca for confirmation, but Becca just closed her eyes tightly, tears still escaping.

"Grant?" Anna shifted her question to her husband. "Did you know about all of this?" Grant shifted the taser and holster on his utility belt, then shoved his hand deep into his pockets. Anna's face contorted with incredulity and the offense of realizing that she was, in fact, the last to know. She wheeled on John. "Are you and Rebecca....I...I mean, were the two of you.." Anna's voice trailed off, and her husband placed an arm around her to calm her down. John ignored Anna and moved toward Becca to console her, but she lifted a hand, stopping him in his tracks. Becca finally turned to face Drew, square on.

"How long have you known?" she croaked through her tears.

"I know my brother," Drew sighed. "I remember how he used to talk about you when we were all in school."

"No," Becca interrupted Drew as though he was not addressing the question she had asked. "I want to know how long have you known that Eric was John's son and not yours?"

Anna, who was still reeling from the last bit of information, snapped her head back in Becca's direction.

"Oh, that." Drew felt drained, but he knew he had to follow this conversation through to its natural conclusion.

In truth, Drew had always known on some level that John was Eric's father. When Rebecca got pregnant, Drew and Becca were doing okay, but they were still newlyweds looking for commonalities. They hadn't had much of a courtship since Drew's father had chosen Rebecca for his son and arranged the whole thing. Drew was young and wearing condoms religiously, terrified of being stuck in a marriage that felt forced and sanitized to him. He was still longing for the type of connection he'd had with Angel, and deep down, only halfheartedly in his marriage with Becca.

He'd heard the fear in Becca's voice when she told him the news about the pregnancy and knew she had been back to visit Jolivette months before. There was so much sadness between them already, and he knew that she was terrified of him figuring it out, so he played along, tried to convince himself that condoms weren't 100% effective, and maybe it could be his. Eventually, he just shoved it all down. But he knew.

Becca and John had been sweet on each other since they were little kids, inseparable really. She was always around, hanging out at the Tucker ranch and even tagging along on a few family vacations. But she'd been there for John, not Drew. Nevertheless, her looks, lineage, and family were suitable to continue the Tucker line, and Drew's father wanted his firstborn to marry her.

As always, what daddy wanted, daddy got. A few times over the years, Drew thought that Rebecca knew he knew about Eric's real paternity, but he never called it out, and neither did she. After a while, he had pretty much forgotten that he was pretending to be Eric's father, but he knew Rebecca thought about it. So when she pushed on parenting issues, he had always let her have her way.

Drew knew she deserved the truth too, so he answered his wife. He smiled a sad, rueful smile and told her that he had always known. In his peripheral vision, he saw John's face glowing red with the avalanche of emotions he was holding back.

"Come on, guys," Drew said, addressing the whole room again. "This family has far too many secrets to risk these news cameras and social media types staying around digging for much longer. They are going to figure a lot of this stuff out, and then WE are going to be the story, not Eric, and not whoever the shooter was. Us. And the Tucker reputation that we've wasted so many years of our life curating, faking, and managing will crumble on a national stage through op eds, tell alls, and hit pieces. Once our image is gone, what will we have left? We have to put this whole thing to bed. We can't push it any further. Can we agree please, to let it go?"

John rubbed the back of his neck, his expression now a mixture of anger, frustration, and agreement. Rebecca sat quietly, wrung out, and spent from the events of the evening. Anna buried her face in her own hands, Grant slowly rubbing her back. In that moment, Andrew could suddenly feel the full weight of how deeply he had disappointed everyone in his life, including himself.

Chapter 34

Free - No Bill

Free stood in the doorway to the conference room for what must have been a moment too long because she felt Mama Jean nudging her to keep moving forward. The space was overwhelming. In the center, a massive, gleaming wood conference table stretched out like the lido deck of a cruise ship, flanked by 20 plush office chairs on each side with two 70-inch television screens, one at each end, standing in testament to just how much money law firms really make. Small microphones hung down intermittently from the ceiling to capture voices for meetings held by video or phone, and little flying saucer-like command centers with plugs, buttons, and Caller ID screens sat glowing every few feet along the table. If the room was meant to be intimidating, it was. Just outside of the floor-to-ceiling mirrored windows that ran down one side of the room, dozens of massive oak and mesquite trees, filled with birds flitting back and forth between the branches and the running bayou below, created a jarring contrast of nature to the stark high-tech reality of the space they were in.

Free could not help wishing that she was out there, among the trees and bubbling water, instead of in here, feeling out of place and uncomfortable. Once again, her hair had been pulled and tugged and gelled into a sleek low bun. Once again, her typical uniform of cotton tops and joggers had been forcefully wrested from her and replaced by a stiff pencil skirt and satin blouse. She took particular offense, this time, to the pantyhose that her grandmother had insisted on. It was full-blown summer outside, and they had driven nearly an hour from the hotel where they were staying under false names in what felt like the 100% humidity of Houston, Texas, yet her grandmother had forced her into nylon pantyhose as though they would affect the outcome of this meeting.

To Free's left, her mother sat clad in what was supposed to be a serious summer tweed suit. But the magenta hue and shortened skirt were giving more Elle Woods than Monica Obama, and Mama Jean had tried to talk her into changing to something less Jezebel coded. But when has Angel ever listened to anyone? Mama Jean was seated on the other side of Angel and had already shot a few sharp and disapproving glances at Angel's hemline and cleared her throat forcefully when Angel mindlessly crossed her legs and began bouncing the top leg nervously, inadvertently baring several more inches of thigh. Angel had quickly uncrossed her legs, but not before rolling her eyes. Free realized that she probably should have sat between them, but the increased distance from Mama Jean lessened the chance that the old lady would lick her finger and wipe imaginary smudges from Free's face, so she was grateful for it.

She had also wanted to sit as close as she could to Gayle. This was Gayle's meeting. A power move. And Free wanted to be as close as possible to that power. Directly to Free's right, Gayle sat clad in her signature white pantsuit. She looked more intimidating than usual, if that were possible, with her arms crossed lightly over her chest, her eyes casually perusing the notes in front of her. At exactly half past 10 am, the lawyers started filing in. Free couldn't tell one from another, and she wasn't even sure that it mattered. Black suits, navy blue suits, and gray suits, the drab and lifeless uniform of people who made their living demanding deference for purporting to be smarter than everyone else in the room. They all addressed Gayle directly and began settling in with their briefcases and accordion folders. Gayle had explained that this meeting was called to discuss the likelihood of an indictment being sought by the district attorney or a civil suit being filed by the Tucker family. Gayle had explained in mind-numbing detail that even if this meeting went well, that would not indefinitely remove the cloud of a civil trial brought by one or more family members from the realm of possibility; but getting everyone to put their cards on the table was the task of the hour.

Free had been told, in no uncertain terms, that speaking was not a part of her duties for the day, so she kept her eyes trained on her cell phone in her lap, where she had begun her daily habit of stalking the dimpled reporter's social media pages. He had tried to embarrass her, and just remembering the interview started a slow burn in her chest that made her want to punch something. She had never considered herself a vindictive person, but since the events that had unfolded over the past few weeks, she had begun a running mental list that Arya Stark would be proud of, composed of people she wanted to see wiped off the earth. Carlos Jackson was currently at the top of the list for his lead role in ruining her life. He was followed closely by Principal Scruggs for pulling her from the graduation ceremony despite her valedictorian status, even though Gayle had managed to convince the school to keep Free's GPA and valedictorian designation intact, Free had spent a lot of sleepless nights mentally writing and revising the go-to-hell speech she would give at her graduation, and now she would never get the chance, thanks to sorry Scruggs.

Holding down the number three most-hated spot on her list was her lifelong nemesis, her mother. Mama Jean had spent the night before trying to convince Free to forgive Angel. She had tried out every possible justification, from the fact that Angel had been very young to the fact that her return was the gift that brought Gayle into their lives to sort out the mess. But in Free's mind, there would have been no mess if her mother hadn't abandoned her in this trash town for Eric Tucker to terrorize in the first place, so forgiveness was not on her to-do list.

Free finally looked up when she saw the two detectives walk in that had been in her living room just weeks before, asking questions and digging for clues. They nodded towards her end of the table with tight-lipped smiles that did not reach their eyes. Free turned to Gayle to see if things were going to begin now that everyone seemed to be present and accounted for, but Gayle placed her hand over

Free's and whispered, "We are waiting for a couple more people."

They didn't have to wait long. The conference room doors swung open again, and this time Rebecca and Andrew Tucker, Eric's parents, walked in. Free's eyes widened in fear, and she felt her mother stiffen beside her. Gayle rose to shake their hands, greeting them warmly, or at least in a way that seemed warm for Gayle.

"Mayor Tucker. Mrs. Tucker," she said before sitting back down.

Free turned towards Angel and was surprised to see what looked like anger clouding her mother's face. Mama Jean placed a hand on Angel's back and began rubbing it as she whispered something in her ear. Free turned back towards the Tuckers, who were now seated directly across from them, and saw a fury that matched her own mother's on the face of Eric's mom. Mayor Tucker, however, had no anger on his face. To Free, he looked sad and exhausted. He was trying to get his wife's attention, but his wife had her sights locked on Angel. Free angled her head to see why Mrs. Tucker was looking at her mom and realized that the two of them were looking at each other. Really, they were locked in a tense staring contest of some sort. Free knew that something important, something she should be aware of, was being communicated between the two of them, but she couldn't figure out what.

"Rebecca, please!" The mayor broke the stare-off between the women by turning his wife's face towards his own.

Free looked to her mother to see her reaction and was surprised to note that her mother's posture and expression had shifted away from anger to something else. Gone was the stiff set of her jaw, haughtily arched brow, and squared shoulders. Free was fairly certain that she could see sadness clouding her mother's expression, and this sudden shift in countenance was shocking. From the moment her mother had arrived, she had been moving with confidence. Even her apologies to Free had seemed wrapped in the forgone conclusion that she would inevitably be forgiven. It was this entitlement that had irritated Free the most. The idea that her mother felt entitled to step back into her life and assume her place on the throne as the queen mother, strong and capable after disappearing for years, was mind-blowing to Free. As though by sheer virtue of her insistence and biological contributions, she could repair all that she had broken. Free thought that she may have eventually warmed to Angel, but then the woman had inexplicably decided to consort with the enemy, running off into the night to meet with Eric's dad, a choice that she hadn't made any effort at all to explain to Free.

Free was very much over Angel and her self-indulgent antics, but this new, more vulnerable look on her mother's face piqued her attention. Something about Eric's mom was under Angel's skin, and Free wanted to see where this was going.

"Don't 'Please Rebecca Me,' Andrew," Mrs. Tucker shot back. "There is nothing more that you can ask of me. You've taken enough."

Mr. Tucker scrambled to get his wife to lower her tone with hushed whispers.

"Not here," he whispered. He looked like he was panicking. For such a slight woman, Rebecca gave off a surprisingly powerful energy.

Gayle's voice cut through the impending chaos, firm and crisp.

"Mayor Tucker, As you know, the district attorney's office will not be pursuing charges against my client."

All heads in the room snapped to attention. Several of the suits lifted their pens expectantly, ready to scribble down...what?

Free thought to herself, *What on earth can they hope to jot down on the garishly yellow pads of lined paper?* But if she was being honest, she was sort of wishing that she had brought along something to take notes on too. As the thought occurred to her, she toggled to the voice notes app on her phone, which was still nestled in her lap beneath the table, and quietly pressed record.

Gayle had already launched into her prepared statement.

"As we have stated unequivocally from the start, my client holds no responsibility for the tragic loss of your son. The evidence recovered at the scene bears that out. Moreover, she is not in possession of any information beyond what she has already provided, and she has been incredibly cooperative. Nevertheless, my client has remained a person of interest in the court of public opinion, and she has suffered a great deal for that."

At this last assertion, Rebecca Tucker scoffed, folding her arms across her chest and dabbing at her red-rimmed eyes with a crumpled tissue. Gayle ignored the interruption and continued addressing the room.

"Are there any statements to the contrary from the state?"

One of the lawyers spoke up, simply saying "none."

"Good. Having now put to bed the threat of criminal charges, the outstanding issues to be resolved here today are of a more delicate nature and related to the wishes of Mr. and Mrs. Tucker as the parents of the deceased." Gayle paused here, expecting another interruption from Rebecca, but Rebecca's face had returned to a stony mask of anger that once again seemed to be directed at Angel. No one said a word or asked a question, so Gayle picked right back up, looking at Mayor Tucker.

"There have been a number of nasty rumors swirling about my client, and a great deal of your family, including your wife and brother, have gone on record with disparaging statements about her family, her personal character, and quite frankly, devaluing Black lives in general. In addition, there have been threats to burn down or otherwise destroy her childhood home, her grandfather's church, and her grandmother's small business, the dry cleaners."

"Now, wait just a minute! How can you say that it is my family making these threats?" Drew interrupted. "My media team has briefed me, and I understand these crazed threats are all over social media. It could be anyone!"

Gayle held up a hand to indicate that she was getting to the information he wanted if he would return to silence. Andrew caught the hint and quieted.

"My firm hired several very sophisticated and very expensive investigative cyber security firms the moment we were retained. At that point, we were already aware that this young woman had been publicly doxxed, and her school file with all of her identifying information was released to the media. Since that time, we have tracked almost every social media page and threat. As it turns out, a large percentage of threatening phone calls, emails, anonymous leaks, and public comments were easily traced back to your immediate family, primarily your wife and brother. Rebecca, you have been very busy," Gayle said, turning to look directly at Rebecca, who didn't even flinch.

"There are a number of charges that we can file against them for their slander, defamation, cyberbullying, harassment, and terroristic threats that would prevail in court, but, instead, we would like to discuss a better way forward."

Free was pissed by this revelation. She thought Gayle's job was to sue them. Why was she going to give them an out?

F**k a way forward, she thought, although she would never have said those words aloud for fear of Mama Jean slapping her lips off her face. But she was fuming. No one told her that today was about letting these racist jerks off the hook. She had been scrolling through devastating article after article, Twitter threads, and memes about her for weeks, despite Gayle's clear advice to stay off the internet. She had been convinced that she was America's most hated. But of course, it was the Tuckers creating all of that, she thought. Who else would have spent this much time making her life more miserable than it was when Eric was alive? The monster hadn't fallen far from the tree at all. This whole family was straight from hell.

Gayle slid one hand over Free's as though she could sense her rapidly rising anger as she slid a document with her other hand towards Andrew and Rebecca.

"This is a cease and desist. It is basically a demand that you immediately stop all communications, written and verbal, online or otherwise, that cast aspersions on my client and her family based on patent falsehoods and gross speculations. Moreover, we are requesting that you issue a public statement clearing her from suspicion in Eric's death."

Mayor Tucker pushed the papers toward his attorney without even glancing at them. He cleared his throat.

"And if we agree to these terms, what is your assurance to us?"

Gayle opened her mouth to explain that she would refrain from filing the charges that would surely bankrupt his family and tie them up in court for the next two to three years, but she had barely gotten two words out before

Rebecca slapped the table and hurtled from her seat, knocking the chair back until it banged against the massive windows.

"If we AGREE?!" she screeched at her husband. "What do you mean, agree?"

She was looking at Andrew, and he reached for her arm as their attorney went to grab the upturned chair, but Rebecca quickly turned her attention from her husband to Angel.

"This is your doing!" she fumed as she pointed a thin finger across the table. "I know it is. You have had some kind of hold on him all of his life, you calculating b*tch!"

Free was frozen in disbelief. Things were happening too quickly for her to process, but she knew what a fight looked like just before it broke out, so she braced herself for whatever was coming next. Angel, not frozen at all, was already on her feet.

"Me? I'm the b*tch? I didn't take anything from you. You took everything from me! But of course, you wouldn't realize that because you are used to getting everything you want when you want it. Poor little Becky, drowning in money and privilege, but that wasn't enough. You had to have Andrew too. You knew we were in love, and you didn't care. If you aren't happy, that's on you. Don't blame me for your sh*tty Karma."

"Are you kidding me?" Rebecca yelled back. "When? When did I have everything I wanted? When did I even really have Andrew? I've never had a single thing except what the men in my life said I could have. You want to talk about love? I had real love too. And I wasn't allowed to hold onto it any more than you were. My daddy said I was going to marry Andrew, so I married Andrew, and I made the best of it that I could. I figured it would work out eventually. He was good, and he was kind, and maybe we could have been happy, but you were always there in the background, like some ghost haunting him with memories and regrets and making sure that we could never really have peace; never really be happy. And you know what, Monica?

You aren't as special as you think you are. I heard you changed your name to Angel, which makes perfect sense since you always thought you were God's gift. Running around playing the victim like you were the only one that had to give up something; the only one that life wasn't fair to. Well, guess what! We all lost something to make sure the Tuckers got what they wanted. So if you dragged your sorry ass back here after all of these years for Andrew, then congratulations! You can have him. I'm done being some pawn in the games of powerful men. But I will be damned if I let this little b*tch get away with killing my son!!" Her finger jabbed the air in Free's direction, who leaned away in horror.

The words left Rebecca's mouth with such force that spit flew across the table, and something in her finally snapped because, in the blink of an eye, she lunged forward across the table, reaching with both hands for Free. But Rebecca wasn't faster than Angel, who snatched her by the hair mid-air, and slid her up the table as Free scrambled out of the way. Rebecca's dramatic leap also sent Gayle, the lawyers, and Andrew into motion simultaneously, and the room became a chaotic shuffle of papers, chairs, and suits as the people on the Tucker side of the table tried to restrain

Rebecca while Gayle and the district attorneys tried to extract Angel's fists from Rebecca's hair.

Free pressed her back against the conference room wall, her eyes darting wildly about as she tried to make sense of what was happening. Rebecca, finally freed from Angel's grip, was being shuffled from the room by her attorney when she turned back to see Drew, who had pinned both of Angel's hands behind her back with one hand and held her immobile, her back pressed tightly into his chest and his other arm wrapped around her entire torso. He was speaking directly into her ear at such a low rumble that his words couldn't be deciphered. At this sight, Rebecca's body went slack, and the lawyers, sensing her surrender, released their grips on her arms.

"I was your wife, Andrew," Rebecca said, her voice breaking. "I gave you almost 20 years of my life. And you would choose her and her daughter over me? Over Eric?"

The pain in Rebecca's eyes was visceral, and Free, who held no love for the Tuckers, suddenly felt a strange sensation of empathy for this woman.

Andrew looked at his wife.

"She's not just her daughter, Rebecca. She's my daughter too," he said. He looked tired and defeated, but he did not loosen his grip on Angel, who stood with her eyes closed, chest still heaving from the effort of the altercation.

Free could've sworn that she saw the light in Rebecca's eyes fade, but she couldn't think about Rebecca anymore. She was thinking about what Mayor Tucker had just said. Who was his daughter? The random events of the past few weeks started clicking into place. The ugly words yelled back and forth across the table just moments ago were no longer confusing and disjointed ramblings of two angry women. Eric's dad was her father. Her mother had loved him. And from Rebecca's angry assertions, he had loved her mother too.

But the thought that drowned out all of the other revelations falling into place was that Eric, the boy who had hated and tormented her, the boy she had hated with every fiber of her being, the boy who she had wanted dead, and who was finally and actually dead, was her brother.

Suddenly, the room felt like it was underwater and spinning. Free's ears were ringing painfully, and she felt her legs starting to go out from under her. She reached out to stop her fall, but there was nothing to grab at but air.

When Free had come to from her little blackout at the law firm, someone was waving smelling salts beneath her nose, which burned up into her brain like the satan had lit a match in her sinuses. When she looked around, the Tuckers were gone, and so were all of the lawyers. It was just Mama Jean, Angel, a medic, and an office manager who was skittering around nervously, making sure that they all had water and no intentions of suing the firm. The revelations from the meeting flooded quickly back into her mind, and she turned to Mama Jean for verification that she had not just dreamed it all.

"I'm sorry, baby," Mama Jean said, clasping her hand. "This is not how we wanted you to find out."

Free couldn't believe her ears.

"Mama Jean, you knew?!" she croaked out in astonishment.

This was a new level of hurt; one she hadn't been prepared for. Mama Jean might have been strict and stubborn sometimes and even a little pushy, but she had always shown up for Free. She was her biggest cheerleader, and she had only ever traded in the truth, no matter what. Free was frozen in grief at the idea that Mama Jean could have kept a secret like that from her for 18 years.

"No, baby. It's not what you think," Mama Jean said, reading Free's crestfallen face. "I didn't know about your father until a few weeks ago when your mama came home. I'd had my suspicions, but when your mama got pregnant, she was away at school and wouldn't tell me a thing about who, where, when, or why. I didn't have any real reason to believe that the father was Andrew. I didn't even know they were still seeing one another. The boy's family had announced his engagement. I thought he'd finally broken her heart. When I figured it out, I wanted to tell you right then sugar, but…well, it wasn't my story to tell, and your mama thought you were already going through enough. She asked me to give her some time."

"She was waiting for the right time to tell me?" Free gave a short, harsh laugh, then repeated the thought. "She was waiting for the right time to tell me…who my father was." Free could feel Angel's eyes on her then, willing her to look over at her, but she wouldn't give her the satisfaction. She kept her eyes and her ire aimed at Mama Jean. "Now, who does that help? Not me. But when has she ever really cared about me? Nope, she just let me spend my entire life in the dark, living in the cold shadow of my own father's power and his…his son." Free felt a cold chill at the resurrection of Eric's memory.

"Baby, your father didn't know either," Angel rushed to explain. "I never told him. He just found out a few days ago, too. I mean, it's so complicated. He was getting married to someone else and..I - I loved him, but I didn't think that he would or that he could love you. His family is so.. And his father was just.." Angel was flailing about looking for the right words and finding none. They would never have let me keep you. She tried to steady her voice and walked around to look her daughter in the eyes. "I know, now, that I was wrong. I shouldn't have kept you a secret from him. He could and would have loved you. I'm sure of that now."

Free could hear her racing heart pulsing in her ears. It sounded like the ocean coming to swallow her. She wanted to spin on her mother and scratch her lying tongue out. She wanted to scream so loud and long that the walls would crumble and bury them all alive. She wanted to run until her lungs were about to explode. All of the feelings she was having were too big. Too much. But she didn't do any of those things. Instead, she centered herself as she used to do after an unsteadying confrontation with Eric. She focused on a single spot on the hotel carpet and felt the cold steel walls of indifference she had learned to erect like a shield slowly locking into place around the big feelings, muffling them and steadying her heart rate. She was done being hurt, and she had to get back to the survival skills that she knew best. Angel wasn't going to keep her spiraling for one more second.

Ever since Angel had blown into town like trash through a Walmart parking lot, Free had been raw and vulnerable. The sudden return of a mother that had been the subject of her imagination for so long had caught her off guard and awakened a longing she thought she had abandoned long ago. Free realized that she had no one to blame but herself for being blindsided over and over again these past few weeks. She'd set all of her survival instincts aside to follow the media coaching of Gayle and Angel. Be likable. Be soft. Appear young and feminine, and trusting. All of the crap they had been drilling her on, day after day, about managing public perception so that the media wouldn't eat her alive had obviously preempted the instincts that Free had honed through years of surviving Eric and everyone else in Jolivette who treated her like some sort of circus side show. But she was back now. She heard her old mantras playing in her head.

Trust no one, believe no one, care about no one. Never let them see you sweat. Never let them see you cry. In the end, success is revenge.

As she'd felt the ice returning to her veins and her emotions shutter, she'd spotted her phone beneath the conference table, retrieved it, then walked out of the conference room, never stopping to look at her mother. She was ready to go on the offense. There was to be no more running and hiding for Free. She had spent her entire life as a dirty secret. And all this time, she had just thought of herself as her mother's shame—an unwed young girl who could not afford to start out in life dragging a baby alongside her. But now, she could add cast-off, and bastard of a family dynasty to her resume.

She thought about Eric and all of the things she knew he had done to other kids at the school without consequence, thanks to his rich, Mayor Daddy. She shuddered at the memory of the times he had pressed himself against her, licked her neck and face, and shoved his hands up her shirt or pulled at her pants. He was the main reason that she never once wore a skirt despite Mama Jean's incessant chiding about how a woman should dress. Free knew it would have left her too vulnerable to the groping, violent hands of that sociopath. She could hardly believe that all this time, he was her actual brother. The thought made her sick. She was again struck by how deeply her relief ran at the fact that he was dead. Now she was ready to make the rest of them pay. All of them.

Chapter 35

Free - To Be InFamous

Free lay still, her body sprawled out over the rumpled hotel comforter like she was half way through making a snow angel, arms stretched wide. Her eyes were open, staring up at the boring beige ceiling of the extended stay hotel where they had been secreted away miserably for weeks. Though she was looking up toward the ceiling, she couldn't see it at all. Instead, her mind was projecting a cobbled film of her life as it had played out.

Wow. I really wasted all of these years for nothing, she thought. She tried to take stock of what had been the greatest cost of her tireless efforts to hold herself above and apart from the town she lived in. She'd never been kissed, never been asked to a dance or a movie. She had no close girlfriends to talk about life with. She'd escaped almost entirely into books and movies and music, forging friendships that existed entirely in her imagination with the characters who disappeared the moment she closed the cover or watched the credits roll. She imagined a life of luxury, walking promenades with the ladies of Bridgerton. Her blood had warmed imagining herself as Santiago's girl in the Coldest Winter. She daydreamed of planning a revenge to end all vendettas alongside Dantes in the Count of Monte Cristo. She curled her body around the notes and dripping warm tones of Jill Scott, Erykah Badu, Lianne la Havas, and Yebba crooning of love won, betrayed, and lost, while never having so much as held the hands with a boy.

If she were being honest, she did want to be desired, to be perceived as someone who could not be lived without. But in her mind, the risk was greater than the reward. How could she let herself care for someone who may try to alter her plans of escape, knowing that at any moment, they could change their mind and walk away? Her own mother had been able to do it. She'd been sure that she couldn't survive letting someone else have the chance to break her the same way. But now, staring into the wreckage of her plans, she realized she'd never had any control over her destiny. In holding herself so completely apart from everyone and everything, she had limited her experience, her fleeting chance at present contentment in favor of her imagined future. What was worse, she realized, was that in choosing to remain unknown and unclaimed by any clique of high school friends, she had also guaranteed that there was no one to watch her back or protect her from the almost daily torment of Eric Tucker. She could see now that she had contributed to her own misery in a million tiny ways, just as Mama Jean had warned her. And now that this rapid-fire series of revelations had landed at her feet, she wasn't sure what she had been running from or running to was real.

Was it too late to want something different? Her entire life plan had unraveled pitifully in a single encounter on a county road - and her mother, who had left her like Lot left Sodom... without so much as a glance back, was now being regaled as the conquering hero for showing up and bringing a lawyer, so what did she have left to lose or prove? Despite everything she'd done, she was still being cast as the bad guy in her own story.

If nothing is going to work out for me, Free thought, *then maybe it's time I make sure that nothing works out for anyone else either.*

The young reporter's face, who had revealed her home address, floated into her thoughts again for the millionth time. Carlos Jackson. She felt a strange mix of emotion whenever she replayed the timeline of his sudden presence in Jolivette and everything that had unfolded since.

She recalled the way he had stood on the street outside of her home, gesturing at the very windows she was standing beyond and had painted a target on her back. Initially, she had just thought of him as one part of the untamed many-tentacled beast that is the media. They can find out anything, locate anyone - and the reporter in that moment was just the messenger. She'd watched mesmerized day after day as he gave updates on what he kept calling "the Eric Tucker story." Each time it felt like an out of body experience, knowing that the characters and events he was sensationalizing were her actual life. Each time he stood against the backdrop of a location like the school, city hall, or the road where Eric died, like they were a Hollywood set, she reeled at the knowledge that for the reporter it was just staging, but for her, these were places that she had passed, entered, or visited every day for the entirety of her life.

Mama Jean had suggested that she stop watching the news altogether, but she was drawn back to the reporter over and over. On the one hand, she hated his guts. On the other hand, his chiseled jaw and colgate smile lit up the screen like Larenz Tate in Love Jones. He was really good. The consummate storyteller. She couldn't stop watching him. When she was in her hotel room alone, she had taken to pulling up older broadcasts of his on YouTube. While it was evident that this was his first major news story, even on the most mundane of topics, he was compelling to watch.

She thought back to the interview. The way he'd openly stared at her when he first came on stage. The way he'd leaned in to comfort her when she'd cried. It had all felt real and electric, right up until he'd called her the child nobody wanted. But Gayle had already prepped her for that question, and Free had done well. Being in the same room with him, feeling his energy and reading his body language, things had finally clicked for her. No one was feeding him information or written copy and sending him out to repeat the script like a parrot. He was personally digging up the information, and chasing down the secrets that were upending her life. He was enjoying the story not just because it was boosting his visibility and reputation.

Carlos Jackson was enjoying reporting the story because he was the one creating it. He really believed that the story somehow belonged to him. She'd really seen him then. Who he was apart from the general job of being in the media. The way he had tried to bait her into an emotional confession. The smug look he had every time he delivered a new update about her life on the air for the world to dissect and judge like she was some kind of Kardashian. His eyes would go all bright and excited, his mouth twitching up into a half smile just before he dropped another bomb of a revelation about the case. But it wasn't just some case. And she wasn't a celebrity. And this wasn't his story. This was her life, her real life, and he was destroying it. In the last 24 hours, she'd had the entire world pulled out from under her. Suddenly, she had been handed a father from the most powerful family in the city. A father that her mother had intentionally left her in the same city with, but without a single clue that they were related.

With that little grenade came the realization that she had been tormented and assaulted for the last 5 years by her own brother. A brother who knew nothing about her and was now a four pound bag of ash. Nope, all the reporter cared about was getting famous, and he would sacrifice anyone to get there. In fact, the steeper the consequences, the more likely he was to repeat what he heard. It was time for her to use him to her advantage for a change.

Chapter 36

Carlos - House Call

Carlos got the call at 2:00 am. He was groggy and out of it, but the hotel phone rang loud as an air siren, yanking him out of sleep.

"Hello?" he croaked. His voice not yet fully awake.

"Yeah, hi. Mr. Jackson?" The voice sounded familiar, but he couldn't place it.

"Yeah, this is Carlos Jackson." He felt his brain starting to fire up with the effort of placing the voice.

"Uh... yes, this is Freedom Walker."

Carlos was fully awake then.

"Ms. Walker!" he said louder than he had intended. "To what do I owe the pleasure of this call?" Carlos cringed as soon as the words left his mouth, but it was too late to think of something less cheesy to say.

There was a pause on the other end of the line that Carlos instinctively knew she was rolling her eyes at his cringey approach. He held his breath, hoping that she wouldn't hang up. She didn't.

"Uh, yea. I'm calling because I'd like to meet with you to discuss something."

"When," he asked, thinking about his schedule tomorrow. The phone remained silent. "Now?" Carlos asked, confused, glancing at the time on his cellphone glowing from the nightstand.

"Yeah, now."

There was no hesitation in Free's voice, and Carlos's suspicions kicked in strong.

Why would she be trying to meet with him at two o'clock in the morning? What could she possibly want to talk about? Oh, shoot! Was this a setup?

He knew that the Walker family viewed him as an enemy and a glory-chasing weasel, a fact that her mother had made abundantly clear the night of the interview. They had a high-powered attorney, and who knows what other connections and ties. They could be trying to shut him up for good. Scenes of being cornered in a dark alley and a bag thrown over his face as he is shoved into a blacked-out van flashed in his mind.

"Miss Walker," he began. "I'm not sure that meeting with a young woman at two o'clock in the morning is appropriate."

There was another pause on the line, and Carlos really wished he could see her face so he could read her.

"I'm sure you aren't worried about me, Mr. Jackson, but I didn't take you for someone who spent a lot of time being paranoid," Free remarked.

That shot immediately hit its target, and Carlos felt himself flushing with embarrassment that she had read his abduction thoughts, but he remained silent.

"Look, you can pick the place. Somewhere where you feel safe. But if you want to know what happened to Eric Tucker, it's now or never."

Carlos felt his heartbeat pick up. Was she ready to reveal the killer? He tried to weigh the risk of being kidnapped and killed against the chance to finally bust this story wide open with exclusive information that no one else could scoop. He must have hesitated too long because Free repeated herself.

"Now or Never."

"Okay, where are you?" he asked.

Free explained that she was in a small city between Houston and Jolivette. Carlos calculated that it would probably take him a little over 45 minutes to get to her. He also calculated the risks of getting stopped by police in one of these rural towns at this hour of the morning. That was the thing about Texas. Anyone could feel relatively safe and almost invisible in some of the big cities, like Houston and San Antonio, but if you drove more than forty minutes in any direction out of town, it was like leaping into a time machine to Emmit Till's Mississippi. But he couldn't think about that now.

He took down the address of the hotel, and he insisted that she meet him in the lobby in plain sight of the front desk personnel so someone could testify that they saw him with her last if he came up missing. She laughed at this but agreed. For some reason, her laugh actually made him feel reassured that he wasn't walking directly into his own death. He threw his things into the same tired bag that he had been using for remote assignments since he started at the station and set off into the night.

Chapter 37

Carlos - No Risk, No Reward

When Carlos arrived at the extended stay hotel, he was surprised to see Free sitting outside on an oversized planter. She had on a hoodie pulled up over her hair and baggy sweatpants, but he still recognized her face and wild curls escaping from the pullover from across the lot. Even with a bare face and dressed like a street urchin, she was flawless. He thought momentarily of the ancient siren tales - beautiful creatures, sent to lure men to their deaths. He shook the thought from his mind as quickly as it came. He couldn't afford to seem nervous, even though….he could be about to have an off-the-books meeting in the middle of nowhere with an unapologetic killer who had left her own classmate in the street. His eyes wandered over her face, now illuminated by the hotel's parking lot lights, looking for any sign that she was scheming. This had not been the agreement. He'd said they needed to meet inside where there were people and probably cameras, and here she was. already changing up the meet details. His spidey senses were tingling, but he gritted his teeth and kept his head on a swivel, sweeping the lot for parked cars with engines running or people inside; movements behind the bushes, or anything else suspicious. He'd watched enough seasons of the Blacklist to be paranoid at any meet up. Free remained still, eyeing him with open amusement.

He stepped closer to her cautiously, relieved that she had at least chosen a spot that was brightly lit. As he reached her side, he realized that she was laughing under her breath.

"Boo!" she said, throwing her hands out towards Carlos. He nearly jumped out of his skin and then bristled at her for getting the better of him.

"What the hell, Free. This was not our agreement. We were supposed to meet in the lobby. Why are you floating around the parking lot like some kind of haint!"

"Haint?" She repeated, her eyebrows shooting up. "Spoken like a real southern grandma." When she realized that he was not amused by her continued ribbing, she addressed his statement. "Don't worry, I'm not a duppy. Yes, I know. I said we could meet in the lobby, but while I was waiting for you, I realized that sitting in the lobby where every late check-in who has seen me on the news can easily identify me is probably not a great plan for me. I've been stuck here hiding for weeks. If I get spotted, who knows how much worse the next place they find to put us in will be. And honestly, I know you picked the meet spot for your safety, but I care about me more than I care about you. So this will have to do."

"Fair enough." Carlos acknowledged.

He couldn't really argue with that logic. She was more exposed and in more danger from the general public than he was. No one had threatened to kill him recently, but he understood that there were a growing number of folk across the country who had offered to help her take her last breath.

"Alright, let's go," she said, hopping up and walking towards the side of the building that was far less lit. It was actually almost pitch black with the clouds covering much of the moon's glow.

Carlos didn't move. This was definitely a trap. He fisted and unfisted his hands and then shoved them in his pockets, but not before she noticed the anxious movement. Free rolled her eyes again.

"Oh, for Pete's sake," she said, throwing up her hands. "What do you think I'm going to do? You must really think I killed Eric, don't you?"

Carlos hadn't expected her to say that, and couldn't tell if her exasperation was all part of an act. He met her eyes and experienced that same tingling rush he'd felt during the interview. He wasn't sure if it was from an appreciation of her undeniable beauty, or the sort of tingle people feel when they meet a killer in real life. He averted his eyes and shrugged. The shrug caught her off-guard, and when he looked back at her face, he saw the frustration she'd had just moments before had turned to a genuine sadness. She walked back towards him.

"There is a side entrance around that corner that opens right into the elevators to my floor. No one knows I'm meeting with you, including my grandmother and…my…mom, so I'd like to try to avoid bumping into either of them."

Carlos noticed her reluctance to mention her mother. He wondered how that relationship was faring. He knew Monica was here and by her daughter's side like some sort of menacing sentry. Or actually, more like a runway model moonlighting as a body guard. But what Carlos couldn't figure out was if Monica had always been around, hanging in the wings of Free's life, or if she had just shown back up. And either way, why was there no record of her home address, phone number, or employment on the face of the earth? How does a woman disappear from public record and then resurface with no discernable history? It didn't really matter at the moment, but if he got the chance, he was definitely going to poke at that spot in hopes of adding some interesting depth to this story. He was still trying to find out who shot Eric without getting killed himself, and walking around the dark side of a hotel in the middle of nowhere wasn't a solid "stay alive" plan.

Free lifted the small plastic key card from her hoodie's pocket and waggled it in the air.

"This will get us in through the side entrance. I can't risk them finding out that I am out of my room and down here with you."

Still nursing hopes of being the reporter that pulls out the confession in a huge case, Carlos silenced his spidey senses and nodded his agreement to follow her around the building. Screw it, he thought as they rounded the dark side of the building. True to her word, Free swiped them in through the side, and they rode the elevators up to the fifth floor without seeing a single person. She peeked around the corner briefly before walking him down to her room, which was at the end of the hall. Carlos watched her stealthy little movement and wondered, all over again, if he was about to be killed. He also couldn't help but wonder whether he had always been this dumb or if it was a new development brought about by his need to prove himself unafraid to this odd young woman. This girl and this case had him so far out of his comfort zone that he didn't recognize himself.

Free quickly opened the door with the key card and flicked on a desk lamp. Much to Carlos's relief, no one popped out with an assault rifle, so he let the door close softly behind him. The room was much larger than he had expected. It was obviously a suite. There was a full kitchenette with a stove, dishwasher, and microwave. A sleek modern desk with a gooseneck lamp and a wheeled captain's chair stood just inside the door next to an oversized love seat that faced an impressive flat screen TV and modern coffee table. Discarded to-go food bags and containers littered the table and desk, and Free made a half-hearted apology when she saw Carlos looking at the mess.

"I haven't been able to leave this room for weeks, other than when I am escorted by the security detail to legal meetings. And they won't let housekeeping service the room, on the off chance that they figure out who we are and let someone in who can hurt us."

Carlos simply nodded, understanding cabin fever when he saw it. He'd almost forgotten that she was here because he had outed her in the first place. He thought back to the day he'd stood on the small street outside of her home, gesturing grandly to the shuttered windows and yawning porch as he removed her from anonymity and opened her life to such incredible disruption that she was now living out of a bag in a hotel room, half buried in take-out trash. The parallels of their situations were not lost on him. An unexpected pang of guilt zipped through him, and he gritted his teeth until it passed. He was a journalist. This was his job. He'd been living his own version of this cooped-up existence in Jolivette hotels for almost the same amount of time she'd been stuck in this room. And maybe he wasn't getting death threats as she was, but he wasn't the cause of that. He wasn't here to make her life easier. He was here to expose a killer. At least that's what he told himself to force the guilt down and refocus on the moment.

Beyond the living room, there was a small door that led into what must have been the main bedroom. Carlos could see one half of a king-sized bed pushed against the far wall and another large screen tv.

"Mind if I use the restroom? It was a long drive," he added by way of explanation as Free tossed the hotel key card onto the table and took a seat on the couch.

Free shrugged her response and flung an arm toward the entryway to the bedroom so he would know where to go.

Carlos headed through the bedroom towards the bathroom, stopping to take a peek in the closet. He didn't actually need to use the bathroom, but he did want to make sure that they were the only two in the hotel room, still not ready to let go of his ambush kidnap/murder theory and still hoping to end this night alive. He went ahead and used the restroom in case she was listening from the other room and washed his hands. Then he scanned the bedroom and closet one more time on his way back through the bedroom. Finally satisfied that there was no one lying in wait for him, he returned to the love seat.

"Nice room," he said, looking around.

"Mmm hmmm," Free smirked. Her raised eyebrow and sardonic half smile made it fairly evident that she was aware his restroom trip was really just a reconnaissance mission. He was instantly embarrassed…again.

A look of amusement was dancing across her face as she asked, "you good?"

Carlos was starting to resent the fact that every move he made was so transparent to a girl who had just barely graduated high school. How was she reading him? What did she know of subterfuge and cynicism? And what did it say about him that she was in his head without even trying? He ignored her question and tried to press down his irritation.

"So," he said, clearing his throat again. Where do you want to begin?"

Free cocked her head to one side and said, "Empty your pockets."

Carlos' eyebrows shot up in disbelief.

"Excuse me?"

"You heard me," she said, her voice deadpan. "I want to see the phone AND the tape recorder."

Carlos held her unflinching gaze for a moment, contemplating his next move, but then he chuckled despite himself. This girl was unbelievable. He pulled his phone and the tape recorder, both of which were already running, from his pockets. Underestimated would be an understatement. She was consistently a few steps ahead of him, which meant that she hadn't called him on an impulse. His presence here was a real plan that she'd orchestrated. Or someone had. His irritation was slowly morphing into budding admiration.

Once Free was sure the recording had been stopped on both devices, she removed the tiny battery from the handheld recorder and powered his phone off.

"Are we good now?" Carlos asked, still gobsmacked at how naive he had expected her to be and how wrong he was.

"Almost," she said. "Lift your shirt.

Carlos' face instantly heated. "Now hold up! You want me to take my shirt off? Why? So I can get busted on some hidden camera half disrobed in a hotel room with the barely legal suspect in a high profile murder..no. Absolutely not." He was incredulous at the audacity of her demand and physically flushed despite himself at the idea of showing her his body for reasons that he couldn't quite name.

Her emotive eyes flashed from their cool green gold to a darker and angrier hue, and Carlos felt his skin goosebump again as it had during her interview.

"I am not now nor have I ever been a murder suspect," she seethed. " I was named as a person of interest and a potential witness. YOU, made me a suspect. She jabbed a slender finger in the air towards him. You unilaterally decided that there must be something I had done to Eric." She rose from the couch and stepped towards him, still jabbing one accusatory finger. "You decided that I deserved a public dragging and then threw my family and my home to the wolves. But you are wrong." She was only inches away from him now, and Carlos flinched as he felt guilt wash over him again from head to toe.

He dropped his gaze to his hands. He was tired of mentally defending himself in his own internal struggle with what he had done. If he was being honest, he had been justifying a lot of his actions since landing in Jolivette by prioritizing the potential career benefits. In fact, his phone had buzzed the entire ride over here with texts from the buxom over-painted Shelly wanting to know when their next "date" would be. It was going to take him months to unravel that emotional mess he had made in the name of chasing fresh leads. He sighed.

"You are right. I'm sorry. And I should never have gone to your house with the cameras. I–I...I didn't know what I had or what would happen next. I just knew that I was onto something. I felt like I was finally first to know something big, and in my business, you have to jump on moments like that and drag them to the ground like a lion on a wildebeest. In journalism, you don't get a second shot at being first.

Free heaved a weary sigh of her own, her eyes cooling again like a mood ring. "Yea but isn't being right more important than being first? Isn't being accurate, or hell, being a human being more important than being first? You really think people care about which news outlet broke news of Kobe Bryant's death first? You think they kept that little random factoid in their memory? More so than the death of an international sports hero. She sighed again. No one cares. But the family cared that the public knew before them, and they will never forget that pain. You care about being first because the people who pay you care about viewership, and your whole world is probably a little news media echo chamber of people clamouring to be first at knowing something. But if you touched grass for a second, you'd realize that not everyone lives in that world. And if you start up a story in people's minds, however false it may be, it cannot be easily snuffed out by the truth. As they say, a lie travels twice as fast as the truth, and if there is more than one, the first lie wins."

Free's voice faded, and the fight in her eyes seemed to be waning. Seeing the sadness slowly spread across her features made Carlos suddenly miss the anger that was there only seconds earlier. His chest felt tight. He knew that this could all be an act. A ploy to get him to stop digging into the story. Yet, something in her felt like it kept hardwiring into his emotions, hijacking his feelings, and he was spinning, trying to remain objective and calculated. He shoved his hands into his now empty pockets to resist the sudden compulsion to reach out and comfort the girl.

"It doesn't matter," she said, blowing out another breath. "You didn't owe me anything. You don't even know me. It's the people you expect to have your back that really have the power to hurt you."

Carlos registered the loaded statement and knew he should prod to get her to say more. But having just barely averted the crisis from his last unmeasured comment, he remained quiet for another beat, and Free spoke again.

"I need you to lift your shirt to see if you are wearing a wire," she said into the silence.

Carlos stared openly with his mouth agape. She was not going to let this go. A nervous laugh escaped as he removed his light windbreaker and reached for the hem of his shirt. This girl really was something else.

"A wire?" He scoffed. "What is this 1987?"

"Whatever!" Free gestured flippantly. "Just do it."

Carlos shrugged and lifted the front of his shirt, to show that he was not wearing a wire, although he was pretty sure that the 1980's technology had come and gone, replaced by better and more subtle listening devices. He felt her eyes flick over his chest, a bit of appreciation registering on her face before she looked away and cleared her throat.

"Okay fine," she said. "You can p-put it away, I mean put me down. Put your muscles down, I mean put your shirt down."

Her discomfort made him feel like he was back on even footing. This reaction, he knew and understood how to leverage.

Now it was Carlos' turn to be amused. He wasn't an excessively vain man, but he knew he had an effect on women and that his commitment to the gym rarely went unnoticed. He registered the fact that she was not immune.

"Are You Good?" he asked, watching a flush creep into her cheeks, unable to resist tossing her earlier barb back at her. "And are you ready to tell me what you called me over here to say?"

"Yeah, we are good," she shot back quickly. "I just want to ask you a few questions first, if that's cool?"

"Of course."

Carlos could not wait to hear what these questions were going to be. This was supposed to be his chance to get answers, but he found himself unsurprised that she wanted to take the lead. He was starting to respect her subtle gangster and knew that whatever she had to say would be unexpected at the least and entertaining at best.

"May I sit?" he asked, gesturing at the sofa beside them.

Free nodded her agreement, and Carlos settled in, taking out his notepad and sharpening his mental focus since she had made sure that he would no longer have a taped recording to refer back to later.

Free sat also, crossing her legs on the couch to get comfortable. She removed the big hoodie to reveal a thin Jimmy Hendrix cotton t-shirt that fit snugly enough against her curves for Carlos to tell that she was not wearing a bra. He quickly averted his eyes, focusing instead on the ugly hotel art on the wall just over her shoulder.

Picking up on his discomfort, she crossed her arms over her chest but did not put the hoodie back on. Grateful for the obstruction to her physique, he turned his attention back to her then.

"He's a little before your time, wouldn't you say?" Carlos tried to ease the awkward tension from the previous moments by gesturing towards the now partially obscured t-shirt, and Free shrugged again.

"You mean OUR time, don't you? Free quipped. "And good music is good music. Jimmy was a genius." She looked him up and down then. "How old are you anyway?" She seemed annoyed at his comment that painted her as a child. Subconsciously, maybe he had meant it to remind her that he was the grown-up in the room, but he hadn't meant to offend her.

"I'm twenty-two," he said.

She nodded as if he had proven her point.

"Wow! A whole four years older than me. You're ancient. Practically a mummy." She rolled her eyes, and he ignored her sarcastic statement.

"Don't you mean five years?" he corrected her. "You're only seventeen."

"Actually," she shot back, unphased by his condescending tone, "my birthday was last week. Happy birthday to me," she muttered without enthusiasm.

Carlos felt a pang of guilt at the realization that she spent her birthday hidden in a hotel room, riding out a PR nightmare instead of the usual fete of 18 year old celebrations. He really should not have doxed her by shooting at her home. She had been a minor. A full body wave of regret hit him again.

"Anyway, I'm asking the questions now," she said, brushing off the birthday revelation altogether. "So what are you?" she asked. "Dominican? Cuban? Haitian?" she lobbed a few wild ethnicity guesses at Carlos.

His amusement returned. Talking to Free was turning out to be an emotional rollercoaster.

"Oh what? Because my name is Carlos?" he retorted, rolling the R in his name to make it more dramatic. "That means I have to be something Latino or Spanish?"

"Well, yes," she replied matter-of-factly. "I'm sure I'm not the first person to ask. Plus, you've got all of...this... going on," she said, swirling her hand in a circle in front of his face, indicating the wave of his hair, his complexion, and what he could only assume was the general way his features sat on his face.

Carlos nodded.

"Okay, point taken. To be honest, I just consider myself Black since the rest of the world isn't going to distinguish anyway. But, if you need greater detail, my father is a good ol' American Negro, history untraceable beyond plantation records, and my mother is Jamaican, which, as far as I know, can be any hodgepodge of British,

Spanish, Asian, and African. You know how it is. Our names aren't our names. They are name branded by whoever colonized whatever piece of land your family worked on. So I am named after my mother's grandfather. And until I give my DNA to 23 and Me, which I won't, I'll just assume I'm a bit of everything, but mostly and undeniably, I am Black." He paused for a moment, then continued. "I have to say, I'm surprised you asked. You look like you've been on the receiving end of more than your fair share of what-are-you inquiries. You don't think it's rude to ask?"

"Yup," she agreed. He wasn't sure if she was agreeing that she was asked a lot or agreeing that it was rude. She didn't bother to clarify. "You know, I'd never really known what I was either. Growing up in a small town that actively categorizes people's importance by their race, I was constantly reminded that people needed an answer to the question, but I didn't have one. I knew my momma was Black. But I also knew that something else was mixed in."

"Everywhere I go, people ask if I have any Hispanic or Creole in my family. I didn't know what to think at the time, but living this close to Mexico and Lousianna, both of those were plausible options. I couldn't figure it out because there was no way for me to really know. Mama Jean just told me that my mom came home from college pregnant and didn't want to tell her who the father was. So I would lay in bed at night and imagine what he looked like, how he talked, where he was from." Free laughed softly, lost in the memory. "I convinced myself that he was some famous movie star from California who had sworn my mom to secrecy because he was married. As a matter of fact, for two solid years, I was absolutely positive that my dad was Michael Ealy, the guy from *What Men Want*. And then, a year later, I stumbled onto a channel showing repeats of *Grey's Anatomy* and was even more certain that my dad was Jessie Williams."

At that, she threw her head back and laughed. Her laugh was loud and real and surprisingly beautiful. Carlos couldn't help but laugh a little himself. He could actually see how she drew those conclusions. Both actors were fair-skinned Black men with eye colors that most folk had never seen on people with their complexions before. He recognized that to be the way Free must see herself. She'd just assumed that since she had come out several shades lighter than her mother with arresting eyes, then those were the exact traits her father would have. Free's laughter faded, and she looked down at her hands where she was joining and unjoining her fingers repetitively. At that moment, Carlos finally saw a glimmer of something that looked like vulnerability on her, a gap in her impenetrable wall of bravado, sarcasm, and infuriating composure.

"I thought he was a whole world away," she said barely above a whisper. "But the entire time, he was right here."

"Here, where?" Carlos pressed, realizing that she was on the verge of clearing up at least one mystery for him. This was the information that he pushed her to answer during the live interview, but it had backfired on him then. Now here she was dangling the answer like bait.

"Here in Texas?" he asked again, trying to prod her forward.

She looked up from her hands and locked eyes with Carlos, and he felt a ripple of something run up his back. Fear? Attraction? God, she was confusing to be around. He couldn't even identify the sensation, but she had done the same thing to him during the interview. It was like she was reaching into him and touching something he didn't want her to see or touch. It was unnerving.

He felt wildly uncomfortable for a moment, a hot flush crawling up his neck, and then she broke the silence and the eye contact.

"I didn't kill Eric," she said.

"I believe you," Carlos said softly, surprising himself. And he really did believe her. He could finally admit that to himself. "But, I think you know who did kill him, Free. Will you tell me? Was it your father? You just said that your father was here. Did he kill Eric to protect you?"

At this, Free's eyes widened, and she erupted in laughter. This time, the laughter wasn't big and joyful. It was sarcastic with a sharp edge to it.

"Aww, man!" she said when she finally caught her breath, wiping stray tears from her eyes. "That's your guess? A top-notch investigative journalist from the big city, and THAT is the working theory you just came up with? That is wonderful. Out of the blue, my absentee father swept back into my life and rescued me from Eric Tucker by gunning him down on the highway?"

Carlos, taken aback by Free once again laughing at him, felt his hackles rising. He'd had enough of her games and enough of playing the minstrel for her entertainment. She had him on a string, and she was toying with him. He hadn't driven through the night for her to mock his competence.

Look, you're the one who invited me here," Carlos said, standing to his feet. "I didn't ask to come here, and I'm not interested in this bullshit guessing game. I have real work to do."

Free's face registered genuine shock at the expletive he'd thrown out. Immediately, Carlos remembered that she had grown up in a very religious household. He started to apologize and then decided against it. She wasn't some sheltered, helpless kid. They were only a few years apart, as she had just pointed out. Plus, she'd had half the country glued to a tragic story for weeks that she could have solved a month ago by just telling the truth about what she had seen that night. And she was clearly dragging this out, enjoying his attention, but she wasn't going to get another minute of it.

He reached for his phone and recorder on the table. "I'm going..."

"Wait!" Free blurted out, standing to her feet as well. "Sit down. I'm sorry. I'm sorry! I wasn't laughing at you. It's just. It's way more complicated than that. I...I didn't mean to lash out."

She rested her hands on his chest to show she was sincere.

"Please sit back down," she asked again, seemingly contrite.

Carlos hesitated a moment. He wanted to leave, and he wanted to stay. The spot on his chest where her hands rested was sending currents of warm electricity through his skin down to the pit of his stomach, and now he wasn't sure that he trusted himself to be alone in a hotel room with this girl. He wasn't sure if she was doing it on purpose or not, but she was definitely doing something to him. He'd had too many big feelings since he'd been in her presence, and it made him feel off kilter. His eyes dropped to the place where her hand lay across his pecs, burning a hole through his shirt. She must have felt the energy shift because she pulled her hands back quickly, like she'd been burned, and let them fall by her side.

Carlos felt his eyes roam back over her tight t-shirt, where he noticed that there were now two hardened points pressing against the fabric. He held in a groan. Dear God! He had to get off this rollercoaster immediately. This was all getting to be too much.

"Ummm, you know what? This was a bad idea," he blurted out. "Let's pick this back up tomorrow. I'll go book

a room to check into tonight, and we can meet for breakfast
in a few hours, okay?"

"No, please." Free's voice was taking on a hoarse
quality like she was trying not to get choked up. "I need to
get this out. I won't laugh at you again."

At that point, laughter was the least of Carlos's
concerns. He was now fully worried about himself and his
growing physiological response to being this close to her
more than he was concerned with whatever story she was
gearing up to tell him. But stubbornly and stupidly, he still
wanted to know why she had called him here. His curiosity,
he knew, could either pay off with a big break in the story or
blow up in his face. He really couldn't afford to tank all of
his success thus far by falling prey to whatever game she was
playing though. He turned and strode toward the door, then
stopped himself. He was already here. He could hear her out
for a few more minutes. He turned back towards her and
plunked down in the single desk chair furthest away from
her.

This is safer, he thought to himself. *I'm off the couch.
She can't touch me. She can't manipulate me.*

Free was visibly relieved to see that he was going to
stay and sat back down on the loveseat.

"No more games, Freedom," Carlos warned.

"I promise I am not playing games," her voice sounded genuine. "I just didn't expect you to say that about my dad being a possible suspect. It sort of hit a raw spot that I don't know what to do with."

Carlos leaned back in the chair, prepared to listen.

"Carlos, I want you to drop this whole story about Eric being shot before the truck hit him, and in return, I will give you another story. A story that is even better than the who dunnit- piece that you are working into the ground."

"What?" Carlos asked, suspicion creeping into his tone. "So are you NOT going to tell me who shot Eric?"

"I can't. I really can't, If I could, I would, but I can give you a better story. A story that people will obsess over even more than this one. I mean, think about it. What do people love more than a murder?" she asked. Carlos waited, assuming that she was asking rhetorically, and planned to answer her own question. He was right.

"A love triangle!" she said emphatically.

Carlos stared at her blankly, trying to decide whether he should storm out or curse her out. He took a beat to temper his irritation before he spoke.

"So let me get this straight. You are telling me that I should stop covering a murder that you've been implicated in—that has already made national news—to instead cover some menage e trois esque story? You must really think I'm slow on the uptake."

"Not a threesome!" she practically yelled, her face flushing deeply. "A love triangle. One that, if it leaks—no, WHEN it leaks—is going to eclipse the story that you are still beating like a steel drum. I'm telling you, once news gets out about the information I have, no one is going to be talking about anything else. And I have it on good authority that Mayor Tucker is going to be releasing a public statement soon that completely clears me from suspicion in the death of his son. So your whodunit story is about to flame out anyway."

"Is that right?" Carlos asked. He looked her over carefully, trying to figure out whether she was bluffing. "Who all is involved in this love triangle, and how many people know about it?" He was annoyed at himself for taking this flimsy bait, but still willing as always to follow a lead that meant he would beat the other stations to a good scoop.

"For one, Mayor Tucker," she replied.

Carlos narrowed his eyes.

"Oh, so you are trying to send me off to do a smutty smear campaign on the father of a dead teenager. You are trying to end my career, just like I thought."

"No, I swear I'm not. I've got skin in this game too."

"What skin?" he huffed at her dismissively.

"This skin!" she shot back, pulling her own phone from her pocket. She placed the phone on the arm of the couch, opened the voice notes app, and pressed play. The room filled with the sound of her attorney's no-nonsense voice.

"Mayor Tucker. Mrs. Tucker. Thank you for coming," she was saying.

"Did you record your legal negotiations?" Carlos started to ask, but Free shushed him and held up her hand so he would just listen to the recording.

Thirty minutes later, Carlos was leaving the fifth floor and headed to the front desk to see if he could get a room to catch a few hours of sleep. His feet barely touched the floor the whole way there. He was practically floating! Free had served up both of her parents like sacrificial lambs. A forbidden love triangle that ended with both of the mayor's kids, one legitimate and white, the other one unclaimed and

Black, involved in a mysterious incident on a dark road at night that only one of them would survive.

I'm going to win a freaking Pulitzer when I'm done with this, he thought to himself.

Chapter 38

Free - A Hasty Escape

Free awoke to the sounds of pounding knocks on her door. She glanced at the blinking clock on the hotel nightstand and saw that it was 9:00 am. She had only fallen asleep three hours ago, and her head was swimming. After Carlos left, she had been a ball of nerves, unable to fall asleep. Unable to stop thinking about how much information he had about her and her family now. Even worse, she was unable to stop thinking about the way her body had responded to him. As soon as he'd lifted his shirt, she knew the request had been a mistake.

A heat has spread low in her belly and parts further south, if she was being honest. Then, just when she thought she had recovered, she'd touched his chest. Something had passed between them. She knew it. Whatever she felt, he had felt it too, it had warped and bent the air in the room like that hallway scene in *The Matrix*, and it scared her. She had never dated anyone or been involved with any boy aside from the constant unwanted attention from Eric. But from that experience alone, she knew that the look she had seen in Carlos' eye for the fleeting moment when her hand was on his chest was at the very least a variation of the looks Eric would give her when he had cornered her enough to press himself against her. That kind of look could lead to nothing but trouble.

Mama Jean had told her over and over again, "Attention from a boy for your body might seem exciting, but it won't lead to anything but trouble." She could practically hear her voice in her mind. *Keep your head down and work on learning as much as you can until you come across a boy that is attracted to your mind, not your shiny coat. Remember, everybody wants a showpony, but not everyone wants to feed it.*

Free still wasn't even sure what that statement meant, but Pop had always laughed when Mama Jean said it, his eyes crinkling as he whispered to Free under his breath, "well, I feed mine real good," as he swatted at whatever leg, or thigh, or hip of Mama Jean's that was closest to him. Although Free had always cringed and acted like they were nauseating her, she secretly enjoyed that they had such a warm affection for each other after so many years. She was still holding out a sliver of hope that that type of enduring love was in her future. But until then, she took her grandmother's words seriously. Free was certain that she didn't want to be anyone's showhorse, so she pushed the thoughts about Carlos and the lightning he created when he was in the room away.

The continued pounding at the door snapped her out of her thoughts, and she yelled out, "I'm coming!" as she untangled herself from the sheets. She grabbed her phone on the way to the door and saw that she had 14 missed calls from Angel. That solved the mystery of who was pounding on the door before she even reached the peephole.

Just as she suspected, when she cracked open the door, Angel was standing on the other side in pajamas, gnawing nervously on her lip. As much as she did not want to see her, Free was done letting her mother see any emotion in her. She stepped back and opened the door, her face a disinterested mask.

"What do you want?" she asked. "It's very early."

Angel looked her up and down as if she was checking for cuts and bruises or something.

"I know you needed time to process what happened yesterday, so I tried to give you your space. But when I called you this morning, you didn't answer. Then I had the staff call your room, and you didn't answer that either. I was afraid that maybe you'd..."

"Maybe I had what, Angel? Left in the middle of the night with no note or explanation, leaving my family to pick up the pieces?" She saw the sharp words land, and Angel actually flinched. She waited for another half-apology to come in response, but it didn't.

"I deserve that," Angel said. Her voice was a little shaky, but her face was resolved. "Can I come in, please? The press conference is about to start."

"What press conference?" Free asked, suspicion clouding her face. "And where is Mama Jean?"

"She's not feeling well. I dropped some soup by her room before I came over here. And if you remember, Drew promised to do the press release to clear your name like we agreed, but I guess his team decided that a live conference was more befitting his station as mayor, and it's starting now."

Free heaved a heavy sigh, annoyed that her mother was calling the mayor by such a personal name. She knew that meant that they were close, that her mother still held affection for him, and thinking about that would send her over the edge, so she compartmentalized the thought and shoved it away. Then she stepped back so her mother could enter the room. Angel made a beeline for the remote and flipped through until she found the local news stations. They were all covering the live story. She stopped on a station with an older male anchor looking directly into the camera.

"We go now to Jolivette, Texas, a small town that has been hurtled into the limelight over the last month when the son of the sitting mayor was slain under suspicious circumstances. Once thought to be a hit and run, it was later revealed that the rising senior and all-star athlete was shot before he was struck by the vehicle. For weeks, rumors have swirled that the young woman who was present on the scene played a part in his murder. In a recently aired interview with Houston 2's own Carlos Jackson, the young woman denied any involvement in his death, yet still failed to provide any real information on what happened that night. We are hearing this morning that the slain boy's family is prepared to give an update on the case. Perhaps today, the mystery will finally be solved."

The image switched to a young female reporter standing at the edge of a swarm of other reporters crowded in front of Jolivette City Hall.

"That's right. The mayor is expected to be out at any moment, and this town is absolutely buzzing. Protestors were out earlier with a variety of strong views. Some were here to protest doxxing and racial inequality. A group of migrant workers was out, protesting the paltry wages and lack of basic humanity present in the Tucker-owned businesses, including their ranching and cattle business. Others were here in the now-infamous red hats and khakis, calling for law enforcement to make Jolivette Great Again by protecting its white sons. It has continued to shock me and the other correspondents here just how much racial and political animosity was running beneath the surface of this sleepy town that most Americans had never heard of. And how quickly this isolated event fanned that flame into a full-on fire. Jolivvette is truly a microcosm of the issues that we are coping with on a national scale. Watching it play out here has been both disheartening and revelatory."

The rustle and buzz around the young woman suddenly died down to silence, and the camera image switched to the top step of Jolivette City Hall.

Mayor Tucker stood at a sleek glass podium emblazoned with the Jolivette town shield. A number of staffers, his sister, and his brother-in-law, donning his sheriff's uniform, stood just off to his left. His mother, a sturdy-looking woman with a weather-worn face and hands, sat in a chair to his right. It was obvious that she had been a beautiful woman once, but the deep lines on her face alluded to hard living and not the pampered life one would have imagined for the sitting matriarch of a family dynasty. Noticeably missing from this Tucker family tableau was Andrew's wife. Free glanced over at her mother, who was still standing but had begun wringing her hands incessantly like some Shakespearean antagonist. Free pushed the desk chair over towards her mom and directed her to sit down.

"You are making my nerves bad with all of that hand wringing. What do you think he is going to say? He's not going to tell everyone that he just found out that he's my dad and is therefore letting me off the hook for killing my brother if that's what you are scared of," Free scoffed sarcastically. "I don't think either of us has to worry about him publicly admitting to being my dad."

Angel made a sour look with her face.

"Don't say things like that, Freedom, even as a joke. I know you didn't kill that boy, but that doesn't mean other people won't always think that you did. You can't even play around like that."

Freedom rolled her eyes and turned back to the TV before her mother could realize that her chastisement had actually landed and shaken Free a bit.

Andrew adjusted the thin microphone, and a high-pitched squeal emitted before silence returned, and he began addressing the crowd.

"Good morning. As many of you know, my family has been going through a very difficult time with the loss of our son, Eric. The grief has been unbearable at times, and we have done our best to contain it so that we can continue to live and serve the city of Jolivette. As you well know, the Tucker family is involved in so many aspects of daily life here that our influence and opinion can often become the only ones that are heard. With a platform of that size comes a great deal of responsibility. The responsibility is to be truthful, fair, and merciful. I am sorry to say that dealing with the sudden loss of our son, grandson, nephew, and cousin has affected our judgment and allowed us to lose sight of that responsibility. But I am here today to right that wrong."

"When news of Eric's death surfaced, we, much like you, wanted to know who was responsible. The need for some type of closure, some level of understanding about why this happened, was so great that we ran with the first name we came across, which happened to be a young classmate of Eric's. In recent weeks, a number of my family members wrote many hurtful and disparaging remarks about the young lady that Eric had pulled over to assist that night. After a thorough investigation, we now know that she was not responsible for the death of our son. There is not even a scintilla of evidence linking her to this tragedy, and I assure you that we have searched high and low for it."

"On behalf of myself and my family, I would like to publicly apologize to Ms. Walker and her family for any pain we have caused with our own misdirected pain. We hope that you can accept this apology and that you will go on to lead a long, fulfilling life, like the one we had always hoped and wished for Eric. As for my family, we will continue to search for answers in the hopes that we can, one day, have a greater understanding of why our son is no longer here with us."

The moment Andrew stopped speaking, the pit of reporters erupted into a cacophony of questions.

"Do you know who actually did it?"

"Has the investigation been officially closed?"

"Where is Eric's mother? We are hearing that she moved out of the family home."

"Is she in a mental facility?"

"Have you separated?"

"Was Eric's death too much for your marriage to survive?"

Andrew ignored the loaded questions and, instead, helped his mother to her feet and strode off stage with her, trailed by the rest of his family.

The Sheriff stepped to the microphone and stated, "There will be no questions taken today. Please disperse."

Angel turned off the television then, and the two of them sat in silence. They were in the same room but worlds apart.

Angel was thinking about the man that Andrew had become. How honorable and consistent he was. He'd called her last night and asked to meet again, but she wasn't ready yet. Mostly, she wasn't ready to face the fact that she made so many bad decisions out of the pain of losing Drew that she could never fix or make right. Yes, she had been young, but he hadn't been much older. She didn't know what it was like to come from a family like Andrew's that ruled everything with an iron fist and demanded staunch loyalty over all else. She hadn't even tried to put herself in his shoes. She just wrote him off. She'd given up on him and given up on her chance at being a real mother at the same time, and look how many people had wound up paying for it.

Free wasn't thinking about Andrew at all. Her mind instantly flipped to the realization that if her plan worked, Carlos would be going public with the truth about her parents soon. She'd had a small twinge of almost regret the night before for putting the plan in motion, but now, after listening to Mayor Tucker give that phony Captain America speech, knowing that he would never give her the kind of life he had given Eric, she was once again glad she had done it. Those two clowns that called themselves her parents had really strolled off into the sunset and lived their entire lives without lifting a finger to help her. They had turned out to be exactly who people had always said they were—two people who couldn't get away from her fast enough.

Now that she was publicly cleared from any wrongdoing in Eric's murder, thanks to Gayle's relentless work and Mayor Tucker's press conference, she felt a small seed of hope growing. Her plan would definitely work.

At this very moment, Carlos would be brokering with his station to secure a handsome payment for her in exchange for her providing him with a copy of the conference room brawl recording, which would air out the nasty business of how many lives were being manipulated by the Tucker machine. It was also going to drag her mother and Mayor Tucker into the light for the deadbeats that they were. She had thought about feeling bad for the mayor since her mother had kept him in the dark about her existence and paternity, but then she remembered that he was responsible for raising the monster Eric turned out to be. And for that alone, he deserved whatever was coming to him. Free was going to find a way to meet Carlos in Houston tomorrow to get the money and then head up north to start her new life, her real life, on her own.

Angel stood up and faced Free.

"I guess I'll head back down to check on Mama."

Free looked at her mother. She was still beautiful, but she looked like she had aged ten years in the weeks since she had been home. All of the cock sure bravado was gone. She was still standing there waiting for a response, so Free gave her a flat one.

"Yeah, okay. You do that."

Apparently, that wasn't enough to get Angel to leave her alone.

"She's worried about you, Free. We both are."

Free wanted to toss back another snide retort about Angel waiting an awfully long time to decide to worry about her, but Mama Jean was all she had, and she owed her life to her. Mama Jean was the one who had stepped up and raised her, loved her, and worked well past her retirement age to make sure she could provide a good life for her. Free might be running from Jolivette, but she knew she would not run from Mama Jean as Angel had done.

"Okay," Free said. "I'll go down and check on her. Make sure she's okay."

Angel nodded, satisfied with that response, and headed towards the door. When she reached for the door, her phone started buzzing, and she pulled it from her pocket to check the screen. She accepted the call quickly and held the phone close to her ear.

"I can't talk right now," she said, still reaching for the door, but then she stopped, her hand hovering in mid-air, her back to Free.

Free looked on, annoyed. She was entirely disinterested in her mother's social life and peeved that her mother was taking a personal call in her room. Free had packing to do. She needed to arrange her Uber and start making tracks away from everything that reminded her of Eric.

"How do you think they got it?" Angel said into the phone, fear creeping into her voice. "It had to be Rebecca! Who else would benefit from taking you down a peg or two? Unless you think John was behind it. I just don't understand how this could have gotten out so fast! Everyone signed non-disclosure agreements, and the receptionist collected their phones when they came in. Gayle insisted on it. I need to call Gayle. She will figure out how to kill the story."

Free could not believe what she was hearing. She wanted to scream. Carlos had one job! One single job! How had their plans to leak the conference tape made it full circle to her mother already? Was there anything the Tucker's *couldn't* kill? She pulled out her phone and sent a text to the number Carlos had given her.

WTF!?	
	???
Why is my mom on the phone talking with someone about killing the story that I just gave you? The story YOU were supposed to be carefully delivering?	

The typing bubbles started and stopped so many

times that Free could feel the panic begin gripping her. From the corner of her eye, she could see her mother dialing a number and then stepping out into the hallway to start the call. As soon as the door clicked closed, Free started throwing her few clothes into her duffle bag and backpack, checking her phone every few seconds for Carlos's reply. Finally, she heard the whoosh of a new message.

	I just spoke to the station manager. They had to corroborate the story before they could agree to the purchase. Someone vetted it with the ADA, who was in the room at the conference. The DA must have tipped the Tuckers off.
Why didn't you tell me that was a part of the process?!	
	I thought they would be more discreet. I guess they don't know

	how far the Tucker reach is. But the story is a go, so no need to worry.
Are you on crack? The Tuckers have enough money to bury this story AND ME!	
	They don't know you gave me the story.
Not YET, but how long do you think it will take them to figure it out. You don't know these people.	

	. . . .
	Where are you?
I'm still in my room.	
	Okay, meet me in the south stairwell on the third-floor landing in 5min. Bring whatever you can carry.
Do you have a plan?	
	Do you?

Free looked at the suitcase in the closet and decided it was too big to run with. She threw her backpack over one shoulder and her duffle over the other, then pulled on her running shoes and headed toward the door. She opened it slowly, checking the hall for signs that her mother was still floating around, but it was clear. She remembered seeing the stairwell across from the ice machines and sprinted in that direction, barely breathing until she heard the heavy stairwell door slam behind her. She trotted down the stairwell as fast as she could without dropping the bags and froze mid-stride when she saw the third-floor door swing open. Carlos flew out onto the landing, grabbing her hand and placing one finger of his other hand to his lips for her to be quiet. He gestured over his shoulder to indicate that someone had been behind him, and that's when Free heard Angel's voice booming down the hall in their direction.

"How did you find us here, you opportunistic slimy fake news reporting son of a…."

"How did you get spotted by my mom!? Can you do anything covertly?" Free quietly yelled in a harsh whisper. The footsteps were getting closer, and Free's eyes widened in horror as Carlos mouthed the word "RUN!"

They took off down the stairwell, skipping whole sets of steps at a time. When they reached the bottom, they exploded out into the lot and began making their way towards Carlos's car, weaving through the vehicles in case someone was looking out into the parking lot for them from the higher floors.

Free spotted Gayle's security team Escalade pull up in front of the hotel and pointed them out to Carlos just as they reached his car, which meant someone would be in her room looking for her in a matter of minutes. She was incredibly glad to see Carlos' wheels were not that big, clunky news van but a rented Dodge Charger.

"Nice wheels," she commented as he hit the keyfob and they slid in, keeping their heads lowered. They barely breathed until the motor had purred to life and they were headed towards the edge of the lot. They had just done a nerve-wracking runner, and she thought she should say something to cut the tension.

"Is it yours?" she tried again.

Carlos didn't respond. He just gave her a tight-lipped smile as he navigated the vehicle slowly out of the lot and onto the highway.

Chapter 39

Carlos: Point of No Return

C arlos knew that once he pulled off the lot of the extended stay hotel, there was no going back. He had committed the cardinal sin of an investigative reporter. Rule number one: never become a part of the story yourself. Now he was over-involved, and it would be his own fault when they pulled him off the coverage so that someone else could tell the increasingly sketchy tale unfolding of how their reporter had absconded with a critical eye-witness. He wasn't sure why he had decided to help Free, but it didn't matter. She had pushed all of his buttons and wedged into any weak spot she sussed out with her lightning quick quips and the unnerving way she managed to seem innocent while wielding truth like a hot blade separating him from his common sense. He was an adrenaline junky chasing the high of this story. She knew it, and she was feeding his habit whether it destroyed him or not.

Carlos knew that the hired security goons that had come with Free's high dollar legal team had clocked where he was staying in Jolivette and kept a pretty consistent eye on him. Up until now, they had primarily considered him a nuisance, not a threat. He hadn't been particularly worried about any of that when his only intentions were to come to the hotel last night to hear Free's side of the story and take it back to his team. But now that he had been spotted on the premises by Free's mother, who he was finally willing to admit terrified him, it was a foregone conclusion that the security team and her mother would all piece together Free's absence and his sudden presence in the hotel no one was supposed to know they were staying in. Regret crawled up his spine like a spider, and he smacked his palm against the wheel. "Shit." How had he gotten himself backed into this corner? She'd been so convincing last night about how her mother was just an actress and didn't care if Free lived or died, and how the Tuckers, never the kind of family to leave loose ends alive, were sure to come for her if they discovered her as the leak. From what Carlos had gathered researching the story, the Tuckers had done some pretty bad things for less compelling reasons, and she was right to be scared. He still wanted this story, but he didn't want Free to die for it.

So now she was in his care, which seemed like a gross miscalculation of judgment on both their parts.

He pulled onto the highway following the speed limit to the decimal in order to avoid attracting any attention and hoped that it would take the security team and the police a few hours, at least, to track down what vehicle he was driving. He had swapped out the Honda he'd first rented for the popular muscle car he had now just a couple of nights ago, a favor from a buddy of his that was running a group of luxury Rental locations. It had all been a little under the table, so Carlos wouldn't have to pay extra, and the station couldn't give him grief for an unapproved upgrade. He silently prayed that his buddy wouldn't give up any details too quickly if or when the calls started coming in.

The two rode in silence for nearly twenty minutes with Carlos' eyes darting to the rearview mirror every few seconds, long enough for Carlos to be fairly certain that he wasn't being tailed. He thought Free might have fallen asleep, but when he glanced over, her eyes were darting between the rear and side view mirrors, just like his had been.

"You okay?" he finally asked. Free nodded instead of answering out loud, and he picked up that she wasn't feeling very talkative. "Well, I can turn on some music, or we can try to talk through what happens next."

More silence from Free. Carlos sighed.

"What is it now?" he asked, having dealt with more than his fair share of women with mercurial changes in mood.

She turned to look at him, a curious expression on her face.

"I want to know if or how to trust you," she said. Her words caught Carlos off guard, and he wasn't sure how to respond, but he blurted out the first thought that came to his mind.

"I don't really think you have a choice now."

Free nodded, understanding exactly what he meant.

"Logically, I know that you are right. All of my eggs are in your basket right now, and I'm the one who put them there. But I don't know how to trust someone else to help me. I'm not used to it, and I don't like how it feels, especially when, not even a week ago, you were doing everything in your power to destroy my life. Your station already alerted the Tuckers of our plan, and somehow you ran into my mom in a hotel where you were supposed to be laying low. So, I don't know. I don't want to trust you anymore than I absolutely have to."

Carlos tried to mask the fact that her comments stung a bit. Maybe he had imagined it, but he was sure that they had connected last night; that she understood that he had just been working a story the way he had been trained to, and not personally attacking her. He'd watched the tears form in her eyes as she played the recording of Mayor Tucker's words, "She's my daughter too," into the silence of her hotel room. He had noticed her breathing change and knew she was fighting a wave of emotion - too stubborn to show it to him. And even though the tears had not fallen from her eyes, he'd seen them flicker and change in color - almost otherworldly as the pain stung behind them, and he covered her hand with his own, squeezing gently to let her know that she would be okay. It was impulsive, and he wasn't sure why he'd done it.

They had been at each other's throats, all sarcasm, claws, and teeth just moments before. But the genuine devastation playing out behind the carefully composed mask she tried to hold together moved something in him, and he wanted to ease her pain. So he reached for her hand and held it. Much to his surprise, she hadn't pulled her hand away. They had sat like that as the seconds passed, feeling like hours - waves of energy coursing between them. He couldn't process what he was feeling, why he suddenly wanted to be her knight in shining armour, or why his heart leapt when she had chosen not to pull her hand away. But she was definitely pulling away now. The words she shot across at him from her balustrade in the passenger's seat of the car were measured, cold, and defensive. She was retreating back into her cocoon, and for reasons he couldn't quite explain, this upset him. He felt a flush of angry heat rush up his neck.

"Oh wow. What has suddenly changed hunh, princess?" he asked, his voice icy. "Last night, you were willing to tell me your whole life story. In fact, not an hour ago, you were begging me to rescue you - to whisk you away from your extended stay jail cell with the free wifi and stocked kitchen. And now here you are in my car, headed wherever I decide to take you without a single plan for your survival other than depending on me to come through for you on this story. And yet, you have decided that I, me, your only hope, is not trustworthy. I guess all of that handholding and chest rubbing you were laying on me in your hotel room was just an act. You are your mother's daughter afterall, hunh?"

Free was taken aback. Her facade faltered, and for a moment she couldn't even mask the shock. Her mouth fell open in disbelief. She hadn't meant to offend him by saying she wasn't ready to trust him. She was just being honest. *Why do people ask questions that they don't want the real answers to?* She thought incredulously. But inadvertent offense aside, how dare he? Hand holding and chest rubbing? What the hell? He couldn't possibly be serious. She had touched him, but it was only to stop him leaving before she could play the tape, she told herself. She wasn't even sure she had meant to do that. It was a reflex. Maybe she had left her hand there too long. Maybe something unspoken had passed between them then, but she never rubbed anything. And **he** was the one who had reached for **her** hand with all the subtlety of a straight to streaming Hallmark film. That had been his unsolicited 90s heartthrob move, not hers.

Now, this condescending, ambulance-chasing reporter was painting her as a calculating jezebel, who has somehow seduced him into saving her. She knew it wasn't true, but the fact that he had even inferred it sent a column of fire from her sternum to her stomach like the time she had snuck and tasted Pop Walkers sipping whiskey from the place he hid it in the pantry. For a moment, she felt her fists begin to curl, and her lips press into a threatening line as she prepared to tell him exactly where he could get off, and let her out on the way. But, she was nothing if not practical, and she did need him to help her. What he had said was partially true. She didn't have the liberty to **not** trust him. He was holding all of the cards. Reality, shut her up before a single word escaped. Carlos was clearly committed to misunderstanding her. And trying to change his mind could have dire consequences for her. So she kept her eyes on the road and kept her mouth shut, silently fuming and remembering, again, that the list of people she could trust on this earth had still not changed: Mama Jean and herself. No more. No less.

Chapter 40

Angel - Gone

Angel was unhinged. She was flying around the room in a tizzy, throwing clothes into bags and yelling nonsensical threats at no one and everyone. Her tirade paused only long enough to allow her to check her phone for any possible updates. She knew the moment she had seen that feckless reporter in the hall that something bad was going to happen. She had rushed back to Free's room to warn her that the reporter was on the premises, but there was no answer to her knocking. The front desk sent someone up to open the door, and Angel quickly discovered that the girl and half of her things were gone.

Everything after that was starting to blur together. She'd called Gayle and her security team, who explained that at 18 years old, Free could legally pack her things and go anywhere she wanted, but they would send someone to check the security footage to make sure she hadn't been taken against her will. Next, she'd gone to Mama Jean's room to fill her in, and Mama Jean had barely reacted.

"She has to build her own life, Monica. I don't understand why you can't see what is happening. She is so much like you, it feels like déjà vu. Andrew cleared her name today. She has her life back; her future back. And her future is not here. You girls...I tried so hard to keep you close, to hold you near my heart, but the tighter I held on, the more you wanted to go. I thought I'd done better with Free, but in the end, things were even worse for her than you."

At this, Mama Jean heaved a heavy sigh and turned back to reading the small bible she kept with her at all times.

Angel wanted to tell her mother that none of this was her fault; that she knew, now, that her love had always been pure and unwavering. She wanted to tell her that she understood now that a mother's love should eclipse everything and that Mama Jean had given her all she could. Angel knew that Mama Jean could not have protected her from the thing that haunted her the most—her own beautiful, dark skin in a world that refused to respect it.

She wanted to say so many things to her mother, but she didn't have time now. Mama Jean had made it clear that Angel was on her own to find Free, and Angel was petrified that she didn't have any time to waste. She had just gotten back into her daughter's life after all of these years, and she wouldn't accept that she was gone already. Angel's intuition was telling her that the flashy reporter and his Cheshire grin had something to do with Free going missing, and she was going to figure out what that cocky little showboater had done.

With no idea of who else to call, her body frantic with anxious energy, she called Andrew.

Chapter 41

Free - A Work of Art

Free walked through Carlos's small apartment, touching the smooth, clean surfaces. It was not what she had expected. In her mind, a young single man lives in a mess of video games, Dorito bags, and cheap furniture. Instead, his apartment, although small, was breathtaking. The kitchen, living, and dining area were all in one large open space and done in black and white with raw wood accents. The kitchen featured black cabinets and a moody, black glass backsplash contrasted by blonde woodblock counters that matched the blonde hardwood floors stretching wall to wall and ending at the picturesque floor-to-ceiling windows that revealed a view of Houston's downtown she had only ever seen on television—tall, imposing buildings interrupted by intentional green spaces where parks and trails hid beneath their canopy. All of his furniture was low, modern, and sleek. His live edged wood coffee table looked like something from a luxury home magazine. She viewed his art pieces with shy intrigue as she

saw where his tastes matched her own. Gordon Parks,
Kehinde Wiley, and Dawoud Bey reprints were featured
along the walls, each with their own small curved sconce to
cast them in the perfect light.

Carlos stood still, watching her explore his
sanctuary, a place he brought no one into other than his
inner circle. They hadn't talked much for most of the ride
after his little dig about her manipulating him. His regret for
saying it grew with every silent mile, but he had no idea how
to fix it now. He watched Free as she wandered down the
short hallway to his room, then stood gazing at the
enormous piece of artwork that served as his headboard. The
piece stretched from the ceiling to the bedframe and was as
wide as his king-sized bed. It featured a young black man in
the middle who was leaping into the sky, fully outstretched,
clouds beneath his feet. His skin was a deep midnight black,
and the sky behind him was soft blue. But what was arresting
to Free was the incredible display of color in different print
patterns, stripes, checks, and complex textures exploding
and rippling out from the boy's form towards the edge of the
piece. Some of the colorful pieces were flat; others were
three-dimensional, lifting off the canvas and projecting out
into the room. The hues were electric hot pinks, neon
yellows, purples, vibrant greens, electric blues—every high-

pigment color you could think of. The rest of the room yielded itself to the art pieces' explosion of color. The bed and all of its bedding were black, as were the small writing desk, leather chair, and yoga mat in the corner. Everything in the room was muted in deference, content to let the art hold her full attention.

Free felt some unidentified emotion welling up in her. The art was nudging her toward something - reminding her of a forgotten piece of herself; some possibility that she was right on the cusp of that had slipped her grasp entirely over the last month. She had fought so hard for so many years to build a future that could feel like this painting, bursting with bold, technicolor relief. An escape from the drab two-dimensional thought prison that was Jolivette society. And in one evening, all of that had been doused in impossibility and then swallowed by the protracted struggle to survive the aftermath of Eric's death. Her face and her name were splattered everywhere. People who had not known she existed suddenly hated her and wished her dead. What little semblance of control she had been clinging to was ripped from under her by her mother's sudden resurfacing and the nightmarish string of family skeletons she had danced in with. In the end, what had been a decade-long tunnel of unwavering focus leading her to freedom had turned into a carnival hall of mirrors.

She had been pressing it down, compartmentalizing, icing the emotions for weeks, but the art piece was stirring something back up in her that she had lost sight of. The feelings were too big - and they were coming too quickly. Her breath caught in her throat, and then she suddenly felt like the air she was taking in wasn't actually making it to her lungs. She inhaled harder, faster, hearing her blood rushing in her ears. "Help," she gasped out. The thought on repeat in her head was *do not pass out again. Don't be weak. Hold it together*. She wanted to double over to catch her breath, but she was aware of Carlos' eyes on her and reluctant to tear her eyes away from the painting to meet his. She knew she was sliding into a full blown panic attack, but felt powerless to stop it. Free wondered, not for the first time, if a person could actually die from a panic attack as she began to lean forward.

Carlos' voice was suddenly close to her ear. "Ssshhhhh he whispered," sounding every bit like a white noise machine. His strong arms snaked around her shoulders, and she pulled into his body like a vice, pinning her own arms across her chest, casket style. Under other circumstances, someone - anyone applying force to her body in a way that immobilized her would have sent her spinning into fight or flight mode. Plenty of times, the simple act of someone grabbing her arm had caused her to spin on a student or teacher like a bat out of hell - a practiced reaction to surviving a life in Eric Tucker's crosshairs. But somehow, the pressure that Carlos was applying now felt more like the comfort of a weighted blanket than an unwanted aggression. She felt herself relax slowly into the security of it. Carlos was taking big, exaggerated slow breaths, and without thinking, she began matching her own breathing to his until her own heart slowed and the panic began to recede. Within moments, she was out of the danger zone, but she didn't attempt to break his hold. She had never been held this way, and she wasn't sure she was ready to walk out of the embrace yet. She let her head fall back, resting on his chest as she continued to pull air into her lungs.

"Wow, you must really like this painting?" Carlos laughed once he realized her breathing was even. The low baritone of his voice sounded different now. Huskier. She nodded silently, not trusting her own voice yet. She couldn't be sure, but to Free, it felt like he was smiling. "It's an original Temi Coker piece. Have you heard of him?" he nodded towards the small metal rectangle affixed to the wall just beside the painting. Free knew he was distracting her from the panic, but she hadn't recovered her voice yet, so she just shook her head, not sure whether to be impressed or embarrassed that he had recognized her crisis and so easily reeled her in. Carlos bent his head down at an angle to get a look at her face. "Are you icing me out like you did for the first half of my interview?"

Free fought the urge to smile. She knew she had bested him then, and she was glad to know he's noted it. But he had also been mean, so he didn't get to make a joke about it already. She kept her eyes on the art, giving him nothing. He shook his head.

"Well, Temi is this young cat out of Dallas. We went to college together for a few years, and his stuff is next level. He did this piece right in our dorm room on campus before he blew up. I wouldn't be able to afford a reprint of it now, much less this original. Got lucky, I guess."

The silence settled between them again, both of them very conscious of how connected they were physically - still breathing in sync for several long moments before Free finally spoke.

"It feels practically alive. The colors and images. I wasn't ready for it. I guess it just reminded me of something I really wanted: a chance to feel like that. A chance to be all of the things I could never be in Jolivette; to reach as far and high as I can go and let every colorful talent and dream explode and take me wherever they lead. And then I remembered…that the dream was gone now. I'll be lucky if even after the Mayor's big speech I am ever known as anything other than the girl who saw Eric Tucker die." The melancholy rolled back over her at this confession, and she shrugged her shoulders up to break Carlos's hold and with it the illusion of a protective bubble. She was nothing if not a realist, and this had gone on long enough. They weren't real friends, and he couldn't really save her.

Carlos stood beside her, his hands deep in his pockets. He cleared his throat. "Free, I -uh..I wanted to apologize for what I said before…in the car."

She turned her body slightly. Just enough to see his face, but not enough to actually face him. She was going back into protective mode, and he knew it. He didn't want her to disappear back into the shell, so he continued his apology, now even more aware that he had taken a verbal swing at her in the car when she was already broken and hurting.

"I don't know why it upset me so much when you said that you couldn't trust me on the ride here. I overreacted. And I'm sorry," he admitted.

She didn't respond right away, so he waited to see if she would accept his apology or hang onto her irritation with him.

She sniffed and ran the back of her hand over her cheeks to make sure there were no traitorous tears left that may have escaped before she turned to him and responded, "I didn't say that I couldn't trust you, Carlos. I said that I didn't know how to trust you - as a personal preference. I was just answering you honestly. Believe it or not, trusting people has not generally panned out well for me. And you weren't completely off base. I did call you to get something I wanted. But I didn't try to…seduce you with my feminine wiles or whatever you implied."

Carlos gave a wry laugh, recognizing her dry brand of self-depricating humor. He understood her though. He kept a tight circle himself and was not a huge fan of pulling new people in. But he wanted to pull her in. Something about her kept him on his back foot, and he felt like he wouldn't find balance again until she was somehow a real part of his life. But he wasn't going to say that to her and scare her with this unexpected revelation. He was having a hard enough time processing it himself. He looked down at her again, and this time she had lifted her face to meet his eyes. He felt once again, like he had been struck by lightning under her unflinching gaze - the same way he had on stage at the prime time interview when she had finally raised her eyes to meet his.

Carlos was no newbie to beautiful women; they were everywhere. In fact, he had already developed a healthy mistrust of superficial beauty when not paired with deeper, more substantial character. But standing in this room, this close to this Free was confusing him beyond his ability to comprehend. She was inarguably externally beautiful. But there was something else in her that kept pulling at him, as if there was something in her he needed in order to continue to exist. He did not want to toss her onto his bed. He did not want to take her to extract pleasure from her. In fact, he did not want to take anything. He felt inexplicably compelled to give her anything and everything she needed.

The desire to make her feel safe, at peace, loved, cared for, and satisfied had been pounding in his chest like an African drum calling its warriors to battle since they left the hotel, and he had never experienced anything like it. The intensity frightened him, and he didn't trust himself to say much to her for fear of blurting it all out like a fool. *She is only eighteen anyway, fool*, he reminded himself. She had scoffed at their age difference the night before, like it was nothing. But he knew that almost everything he had really learned about himself he learned in the four years of college that stood as the differentiator between them. She hadn't set foot into that world yet, and couldn't possibly know enough about herself to partner with him in a meaningful way. How much could she really know about life and love? His hand itched to reach for her, but he wasn't sure that was appropriate. So instead, he shoved both hands deeper still into his pockets and turned his attention back to the painting, letting his eyes run over the vivid strokes of color. When he had first seen it, his reaction wasn't all that different from Free's.

He'd been struggling at the time, afraid to leave the relative safety of his family's dreams for him to launch out on his own in pursuit of a career in broadcasting. There were so many tense years where he barely spoke to either of his parents; unwilling to be subjected to hours of criticism and well-intentioned but hurtful advice meant to steer him to a more stable profession and a more lucrative future. His parents had done very well for themselves despite his mother being an immigrant from Jamaica and his father, the son of South Carolina sharecropper who grew up working in a factory running car parts.

Those two young parents had scraped and saved and built an amazing life for their family. They had sacrificed every frivolous luxury for years to make sure that Carlos and his siblings would have access to tremendous opportunities, and they could not see journalism or broadcasting as a legitimate pursuit when being a doctor, lawyer, and engineer were all better options. For many years, they were intent on killing his dreams as an act of love, saddling him with their fears as though they were nuggets of wisdom. But once they had seen how happy and fulfilled he was in broadcast and that he was able to support himself, they had come around...slowly. These days, they recorded every report that aired with him in it, even if it was only a few minutes long. He began laughing to himself, but a sudden realization caused the laugh to stop short, caught in his throat.

It was in that memory of how long it had taken him to mend fences with his parents that he realized what he was really doing with Free; even worse, what he was doing to her. By running to his station with the story she had fed him, he was helping Freedom destroy her family and, in doing so, destroy herself. Yes, her life had been tough, and both of her parents had a lot to answer for. No one would ever accuse those two of being perfect or hand them any awards for their decisions. But he could see clear as day, now, that the course they'd chosen as teenagers was not the one they were walking now.

Free's mother was fighting like a lioness, tooth and nail, to protect her daughter from the mess that she had made of things by abandoning her. And her father, even while mourning the loss of his only son, had gone out of his way to publicly clear her of any implication in the boy's murder, regardless of whether she was really clear or not. Free's father had lost one child and was choosing to save the one that was left. From what he had heard on the deposition recording, the Mayor stood to lose a great deal of his own family's support in his bid to make things right with his estranged daughter.

Contrary to what Free might want to believe, and how accelerating it would be for his reputation, Carlos knew that shifting the spotlight to Mayor Tucker's indiscretions was not going to bury the murder mystery from the headlines. If anything, it would add captivating depth to a story that was already intriguing. The stories would become intertwined and take off like a rocket, probably launching his national anchor career in its wake, and Free would be left to pick up the pieces. He couldn't let her go on believing this was going to help her just so he could keep milking the limelight to feed his own ego. The entire realization came down on him like a ton of bricks, and he recognized the horror of what he had to do next. He couldn't let Free sell this story about her parents to the media. It would haunt her for life. He had to kill the story himself. He knew killing the story meant the end of his magical run in the sunshine, but even worse, he knew Free would hate him for it.

Chapter 42

Carlos - Bait & Switch

Free ran her hands through her big curls and let them fall back into place, framing her face, brushing her neck, and then settling, finally, around her back and shoulders like a gorgeous jumble of curled ribbon. She had considered pulling and taming her curls into the neat, low bun that Gayle had coached her on for public appearances and interviews. But she didn't need to follow the "look more sympathetic and relatable, act more docile" script anymore. She was getting this deal on her terms. Carlos had arranged a meeting with some of the station executives to go over the terms of their agreement and finalize the compensation numbers for the story. Free had agonized over the tiny wardrobe that she had to choose from due to her harried packing. She ultimately decided on a beautiful, pink A-line dress with a pleated skirt and a thin golden chain at the waist. The wide scooped neckline and capped sleeves made her look mature and feminine. She assumed that the subtle sexiness is what got the dress cut as

an option for her other appearances and meetings led by
Gayle. But here, on the day that she was finally going to
advocate for herself and be the powerful woman at the helm
of the meeting instead of the quiet girl at the table, she
thought that a little vamp couldn't hurt. It was worth a shot
anyway. She was inventing the new Free today. No more of
the carefully curated little miss people pleaser act.

After she'd fastened on a pair of small diamond
earrings, also courtesy of the big law wardrobe people, she
emerged from Carlos' bathroom to get his thoughts on her
look. He looked up from the black writing desk where he had
been hunched over his phone, a look of concern etched into
his face. It took a moment for him to register what he was
seeing. The previous versions he had seen of Free were only
two. One was the structured business casual pieces and
librarian hair she showed up to the interview with. The other
was the worn t-shirt and baggy sweats from the hotel. Those
had seemed like opposite sides of a coin; but both had clearly
been costumes, or disguises. Because the way she looked
now, this had to be who she really was. She was exuding
both power and peace, and she seemed very comfortable
with both. For one thing, the way her hair expanded and
curled in every direction, shiny and wild like a lion's mane,

catching the light and throwing it back was entirely unexpected, a bold declaration of her willingness to fill the room with her truest self. As his eyes traveled beyond her hair, he realized exactly what the baggy sweats and tailored suits had been designed to downplay. She was drop-dead gorgeous from head to polished pink toenails. Her shape curved out and tucked in at all the right places. She looked unreal. Realizing that his jaw had dropped open, he snapped it shut, but not before she giggled and spun a few circles to let the pleated skirt rise and whirl around her legs.

"It's good, right?" she asked.

Carlos detected a tiny bit of uncertainty in her voice and knew that she really wanted his approval, but would never say so.

"You look amazing," he said in a hushed tone.

"I'm not overdressed, am I?" she inquired again. "I've never met with executives before."

Carlos smiled a sad, half smile.

"I promise you," he said. "You are not overdressed."

She nodded, taking him at his word and giving him a coy smile.

A lot had changed between them since the evening before, and Free was wearing all of it like a radiant aura.

This was not the coached girl he'd met in Jolivette. This was the real Free, whose simple existence intimidated her classmates and teachers.

***

Last night, they'd talked about everything from art to philosophy to politics. He was constantly surprised by her breadth of knowledge and well-formed perspectives. She'd shared her dreams of starting over in New York, and he'd surprised himself by showing her his written timeline to success that was scrawled in his terrible handwriting across four pages of his journal. When she told him that she was pleasantly surprised to meet someone more neurotic about success than she was, they had both laughed in that unbridled way that only comes from hearing an undeniable, unflattering truth about yourself. He had to admit to himself by the second hour that he was enjoying having her here with him.

Their conversation was easy, and he was mesmerized by every small mannerism that she had. The way she bit down on her thumbnail before posing a counterargument to one of his own. The way she could hold his eye contact for the longest moments while describing a piece of art or literature that she found revolutionary. She was not a shrinking violet who felt the need to look away, and if he was honest with himself, he didn't want her to look away. He felt himself expanding under her admiration every time she realized that their perspectives aligned or he shared his own insights with her on a subject she cared deeply about. It was breathtaking to watch her come out of her shell - slowly unfurling like a hot house rose. They laughed and talked until the wee hours of the morning descended, and he noticed that she was drifting off. He left her in his room, sprawled on his bed, and quietly grabbed a blanket and pillow to settle on his living room sofa. But the couch was impractical. Its minimal modern design had clearly prioritized looks over comfort, and he'd cursed his furniture selection as he tossed this way and that in search of a comfortable position.

Eventually, he gave up and slid to the floor in hopes of better luck on the carpet. He lay there, between the sofa and the coffee table wondering, ruefully how she was enjoying his Egyptian cotton sheets and memory foam pillows. At some point, his mind, unbidden, ventured to more dangerous territory, and he found himself wondering how it would feel to be laying beside her, his frame curled around hers. The idea was so vivid and raw that he couldn't shake the imagery. He couldn't know whether the intensity of thoughts created so much telekinetic energy that he woke her, or if it was pure coincidence - but he heard the soft padding of her bare feet coming down the hall before he saw her head peek around the corner. At the sight of her, a goofy smile spread across his entire face before he had a chance to check it into something more cool and befitting of the persona he was used to carrying. He sat up, tossing off the cable knit blanket, and she shook her head at him in mock annoyance.

"Come on," she said, laughing softly. " I know you will be on your best behavior. And anyway, that expensive couch looks about as comfortable as a prison cot."

She wasn't wrong, and he wasn't going to make her ask twice. In the end he drifted off to sleep exactly as he'd wished, with his own powerful frame cocooning hers, and he had never been more honored to hold the awesome responsibility of serving as the big spoon. He was so blissed out by the moment that he lost sight of the fact that in just a few hours, he was going to become her biggest disappointment and maybe her enemy...again.

***

In the light of day, reality descended swiftly onto Carlos' shoulders like a weighted vest. He'd told Free that he'd arranged to host a few station executives for an early dinner at the apartment to allow them to finalize her deal in relative privacy, and she had been absolutely glowing with anticipation ever since. But Carlos was carrying the truth, and he knew that there would be no executives, not now that he'd decided he couldn't allow her to torpedo what was left of her family by throwing it to the media. Watching her spin in excitement to show off her pink dress was creating a pit in his stomach, and he turned back to his computer to avoid her reading his mood in his eyes. All afternoon, her palpable excitement crushed his conscience, grinding it to a fine powder like mortar and pestle. He knew that he wasn't going to keep his word to her and that she would probably never forgive him. Worse, he knew that he was running the risk of never seeing her again. He couldn't look her in the eye, and by early evening, she was starting to respond to his shift in mood.

"Are you okay?" she asked suddenly, warily.

She stood directly in front of where he sat, frowning pensively at the papers on his desk. He could feel her eyes on him, but didn't look up. He knew that if he met her eyes with his own, she would be able to see through him, and his cover would be blown.

"Uh, yea, just tired. I'm going to have a glass of wine, do you want one?" he asked, getting quickly to his feet and heading for the kitchen area, carefully avoiding eye contact.

He realized with a start halfway to the wine rack that she wasn't old enough to drink and turned to apologize. "Oh, I'm sorry," he started to say, but as he turned, he bumped directly into Free, almost knocking her to the floor. He hadn't realized that she'd been following him so closely to the kitchen.

She grabbed his arms to steady herself as he reached to do the same, and the sudden physical contact unnerved him. He was not going to survive these constant jolts of electricity every time she so much as brushed his arm. He took a steadying breath and reminded himself that he was not some impulsive kid and had surely developed enough internal discipline to pack these feelings away.

Free smoothed her dress back down where it had been ruffled in the collision and smirked.

" Sheesh, you didn't have to push me down to apologize. I was actually going to say yes. I'd love a glass. Unless you are going to rescind the offer?" she smiled playfully, but he couldn't relax enough to return the smile.

She misread his mood for judgment and rolled her eyes. "Do you really expect me to believe that you made it through the first three years of college, from eighteen to twenty-one, without a drop of alcohol? I'm sure I can manage a glass of wine without getting either of us thrown into jail."

Carlos cleared his throat. "No, of course. I realize that you are not a child. I just hadn't wanted to offend you, with your upbringing and all."

At this, Free dropped her hands from his arms. "Carlos, I was raised as a Pentecostal, not a monk. I've seen alcohol before. I did attend a public high school, remember? And my Pop had a drink every now and then. It's cool. I'm not a narc." She rolled her eyes playfully, pleased with her outdated slang.

"Yes, I know. But a few weeks ago, you were literally still in high school," Carlos reminded her in a way that felt like a jab. Free tilted her head and narrowed her eyes as his sharp comment found its mark.

"Cheap shot, Jackson," she said with her eyebrows bunched, causing his face to flush.

He knew he was wrong for reminding her of the place that had chewed her up and spit her out, despite how hard she'd worked as a student. He was belittling her. He also knew that he was taking out his frayed nerves on her. Between his guilt, his attraction, and the looming blowback he could expect to get from the station when he reneged on the new story angle, he was having trouble regulating his emotions. He really needed that glass of wine he'd come to the kitchen for. *Screw it*, he thought, turning to grab the glasses and retrieve the bottle of wine. He kept his back turned to her to pour the wine and then spun back to her, extending a glass for her to take.

That was a cheap shot," he admitted. "Please accept this glass as an apology."

She took the glass but didn't change the expression of suspicion on her face.

"What's wrong, Los?" she asked.

Carlos wasn't sure where the new nickname had just come from, but he didn't hate it.

"Nothing's wrong, I just...I've really enjoyed this time with you, and I hate that it has to end."

Free took a small sip of the wine and rolled it around her mouth before swallowing.

"What do you mean? Are you not allowed to speak with me or see me anymore after we sign the deal with the station?"

Carlos sighed and tried to figure out how to answer her question without becoming any more of a liar than he already was.

"I don't know. Things are going to get complicated quickly. A reporter is never supposed to become a part of the story they are covering. Plus, you're planning to leave for school soon anyway. I just don't think we will ever be together like this, just the two of us, again."

Free nodded, her expression softening.

"That's the thing about life, Carlos. No one ever gets to repeat a moment. So when you have one that feels important or special, you have to make the most of it. Max it out, you know? That's the thing I didn't understand until everything started falling apart. I hadn't been living in any of my moments. I'd been spending all of my time waiting to escape to some other place at some future date to start living. I don't want to live like that anymore."

She stood looking at him as her words settled something in his mind. Carlos knew she was right. And even though he had told himself not to do it at least a dozen times since the night he'd met her at the hotel, he silenced the voice of reason in his brain, leaned in slowly, and when she didn't back away, he kissed her.

The kiss was soft at first. He just wanted to feel her lips under his. But when she didn't end the kiss or push him away, he set his glass down and wound the fingers of his right hand into the soft curls at the base of her neck, then wrapped his left hand gently around her throat, using the leverage to raise her face slightly toward him so that he could deepen the kiss. He was surprised when she responded by parting her lips and hooking her arms around his back, inviting him to stay locked in the embrace.

Carlos felt like he was having an out-of-body experience. He couldn't even think of a time when kissing felt like the desired destination rather than an inconvenient stop on the way to something more fun. But kissing Freedom, he felt another part of his soul clicked into place. Being with her made him feel like he was becoming more of himself. He didn't want to push her toward anything else and was careful to keep his hands respectful. He even tried—and failed—to maintain some distance between their bodies. But she stepped into him, removing what little space was left and setting his entire body on fire. When they finally pulled away, he looked down at her soft lips, now flushed and slightly swollen. Her eyes stayed closed, and her hands rested lightly on his shoulders. She let out a little hum, and he smiled at her determination to prolong the feeling even though the kiss had ended. After another moment, she looked up slowly at him, her eyes glistening brightly like ocean green Caribbean waters against a golden shoreline.

"That was really nice," she hummed.

He laughed then, thrilled by the irrefutable truth and innocence of her statement.

"Oh yea, how did I do? He said, his competitive nature bleeding through. Top five at least, huh?"

"That was actually my first kiss," she responded matter-of-factly. "But if I'd known they could be like that, I would have started sooner."

Carlos started to laugh, but then the impact of her words hit him, and the laughter turned into a short gasp.

"Wait, what?" You've never been KISSED before? Like never ever?"

She shook her head and shrugged. Carlos suddenly felt like a full-on villain. What was he doing? He could not afford to be this girl's first anything, not when he was on a direct trajectory to betraying her trust beyond repair within the hour.

"I'm sorry, Free. If I had known that, I wouldn't have… I didn't mean to. I don't want you to think I'm taking advantage of your situation."

"Oh, good grief!" Free tossed her hands in exasperation. "You haven't corrupted me with a glass of wine and a kiss. Calm down Los. I just said it was nice. I wanted you to kiss me, and you did. Everyone here was on one consenting accord."

Carlos nodded. He should have felt better, but he couldn't imagine that what he had just done would make the rest of the evening any less traitorous. *Maybe*, he thought, *he should just come out and tell her what was going on. Tell her that there was no meeting with the station execs.* Keeping her in the dark was beginning to feel cruel. He opened his mouth to say something else, but his thoughts were interrupted by the doorbell, and his heart sank. They were early.

"Oh, let me put my shoes on!" Free chirped, excited by the doorbell signaling the anticipated start to the evening. She scuttled off to retrieve her sandals, and Carlos headed to the door, dread filling his chest.

Chapter 43

Angel & Andrew - The End of Secrets

Angel and Andrew stood outside the high-rise unit marked 24B. Andrew was focused on calming his nerves and preparing for whatever was about to come. He hadn't had this much adrenaline coursing through his veins since his last college bowl game, and the intensity was staggering. He glanced over at Angel, who was clenching and unclenching her fists like she wanted to fight, and shook his head.

"Angel, please. Relax. The boy invited us here. I think he is trying to do the right thing."

"The right thing. Ha!" Angel snorted. "This kid has been hunting my family and yours for over a month to try to make a name for himself on our pain. If you don't think this is some kind of trick, you are crazy. I'll tell you one thing, though, my daughter had BETTER be in here, safe and sound. Because if he dragged us here just to stoke the fires of scandal for his report, I am going to wring his neck and pluck him like a chicken!"

Andrew could see the fear hovering just behind the anger on Angel's face. He reached out and held her hand. When she looked up at him, he smiled and said, "What a country thing to say, Ms. California. You can take the girl out of Jolivette, but you can't take the Jolivette out of the girl."

Angel smiled against her own will.

"Shut up, Drew," she smirked. "I really don't think we should trust him."

When the door swung open, they were greeted by the smells of roasted chicken and potatoes au gratin. Carlos stood in the door frame, his body blocking most of their view of the apartment. He looked hesitant, like he was considering closing the door in their faces. Before he could make good on such a thought, Andrew placed his full arm against the door and planted a smile on his face.

"Aren't you going to ask us in?" he said in his smooth politician's voice. " I mean, this dinner was your idea."

"Uh, yes, of course," Carlos conceded, removing himself from the entryway.

Angel stepped into the small foyer and immediately recognized the Miles Davis tune spinning on the record player in the small dining area just a few feet away. The smell of good food mingled in the air with the rich jazz notes of "Blue in Green," and Angel reluctantly felt herself relaxing. She chided herself silently, then glanced around the space for any signs of her daughter and saw none. The small kitchen just beyond the entrance held a large island that was set up with an incredible charcuterie board, spilling over with grapes, cheeses, delicately sliced meats folded like flowers, and crackers of a million varieties.

Beside the board stood a few bottles of uncorked wine and several glasses. Angel could look clear across the apartment and see the sun setting, casting blue, pink, purple, and golden hues over the city. She would have been overjoyed viewing that phenomenal sunset from those massive windows if her mind had not been whirring a mile a minute trying to determine whether this dinner was a journalist's ruse. Carlos had promised her that her daughter would be here, but the condo was a wide open space, and so far, she hadn't seen her. As though reading her mind, Free suddenly emerged from a small hallway that Angel hadn't noticed just off the kitchen in a gorgeous pink dress with strappy high heeled sandals on her feet and a glass of white wine in her hand. The bright smile she wore faded awkwardly as she recognized her mother. Angel tensed as

she watched Free's eye dart from herself to Andrew and then land on Carlos with confusion and panic. Angel opened her mouth to explain, but let the words die in her throat when she saw the looks that were passing between her daughter and the reporter. The anger was so palpable that she realized immediately that if anyone had been set up by this dinner, it was Free.

Angel and Andrew were aware that they had come here to talk Free out of going public with their disastrous love affair, but Free had clearly not been told that they were coming. From what she knew of her daughter, this was probably not going to end well for Carlos, and Angel actually felt a little pity for him growing in her heart. Surprisingly, Free never ended well for anyone. She could testify to this fact in the worst way. The girl could hold a grudge.

Carlos cleared his throat and looked like he was going to explain things, but Free held up a hand to silence him. Angel felt Andrew squeeze her own hand, which she had forgotten he was holding. He must have been piecing together the situation just as she was. As if she felt the squeeze also, Free looked towards them and then down at their joined fingers. Her face clouded with fury, then she turned on one heel and walked back out of the room. Carlos threw Angel and Andrew an apologetic look as he rushed from the room after a quickly retreating Free.

In the awkward silence that followed, Andrew and Angel looked around the small apartment with its high ceilings and breathtaking view, unsure of what to do next.

"Well, we could always eat," Andrew shrugged.

Angel rolled her eyes at his ability to think about his stomach at a time like this. She wanted to go see what was going on in the back room. She wanted to check on her daughter and assure her that this was all for her own good. But she knew that rushing into an issue that was not of her making would only make matters worse. She had enough of her own mistakes to make up for, no need to wade into someone else's. She cast one more anxious glance at the hall Free had escaped down, and then she walked over to the counter and poured herself a glass of the wine that had been set out to breathe while appraising the bottle, a South African Chenin Blanc.

"Wow!" she reluctantly exclaimed, acknowledging the excellent selection with raised brows. That was twice in the last two minutes that she had been impressed by the young reporter and his taste, although she knew she would never admit it to him. She turned to find that Andrew had taken a seat at the dining table and begun spooning potatoes onto his plate. She gaped at him.

"How can you even eat at a time like this?"

Andrew shrugged again.

"Being hungry won't help when she comes flying out of that room with whatever her weapon of choice is." He quipped, In fact, you should come eat too. Wine on an empty stomach is not your best look."

Angel rolled her eyes, knowing that he was teasing her over a night during her sophomore year when he had snuck a bottle of wine from his mother's wine cellar, and they drank the entire thing in the woods. She'd been so drunk that he was afraid to take her home, so he'd pumped her full of water and Gatorade and watched her sleep in the back of his truck until it was dangerously close to 5 a.m., when he knew Pop Walker would be up and walking their house. He drove her home but had to almost drag her up the back porch of the house and shove her through her own window.

Angel was slightly annoyed that he still saw her as the high school girl who couldn't hold her liquor, but felt a small thrill at finally being with someone who really knew her again after years of having to be unknowable. She only hesitated a brief moment before she acquiesced to his suggestion and began making a plate. For a few minutes, all that could be heard was the scrape and clink of the two of them adding chicken, potatoes, and bits of salad to their plate. But soon, the rising volume of angry voices began spilling over from the bedroom and floating out into the dining space. As though sharing a single brainwave, Angel and Andrew froze, their utensils suspended in the air, ears straining to try to make out the conversation.

***

"You invited them here? Why would you bring them here? What was the point of helping me get away from them and then leading them right to me?!" Free screeched incredulously. "Was there ever really a meeting with the executives? Or have you been lying to me, non-stop, for three solid days! Unbelievable!" she screeched, not even waiting for his answer. "This! This is why I never trust anyone!"

Carlos tried to jump in and correct her, hoping to make clear that there was initially going to be a meeting with the executives and that he had lost quite a bit of goodwill with the station by backing out, but Free steamrolled forward with no intention of letting him explain himself.

"I cannot believe you with your whole wanna-be Black Savior! Whisking me out of the hotel, playing the part of the perfect host, and oh my God! That kiss! You are wasting your talents in the news broadcast, Mr. Jackson. You should be on Broadway with the rest of the actors!"

Carlos stood silently, letting her expend her energy and fury. He marveled at the fact that even as her words crescendoed, filling the room with their heavy accusations and vitriol, all that he saw in her face was sadness, disappointment, and pain. He wanted to comfort her. He wanted to tell her that he had done this for her. But he knew that she would rebuff anything he said because she believed him to have betrayed her.

Unsure of how to proceed, he crossed the room in two steps and wrapped her in his arms. He felt her pull back half-heartedly, then go slack in his arms, emotionally spent. He used that moment to bend down and scoop her legs up with one arm, then carried her into the large master bathroom, hoping their voices would be further away from her parents in the small apartment, where sound tended to carry. He set her down on the long sink counter facing him, then wet a towel with cool water and began wiping the hot, angry tears from her face.

As he wiped her face, he began trying to explain.

"Free, parents are our first real test in life. We don't get to choose them. We aren't able to force them to change or improve. And for many years, everything that we are, experience, or have access to is based solely on the choices that they make. We have no say, and it can be infuriating, challenging, devastating, and demoralizing trying to live with their decisions."

"So now I guess you are supposed to be able to relate to my life, huh, Dr. Phil? Now you know exactly how I feel, right?" Free's voice was hoarse and steely.

"No, I'm not saying that at all," Carlos answered softly. "I know that I was fortunate to grow up with my family still intact. But the craziest part is that accepting the decisions and behaviors of parents that are present is not always easier than coping with parents who choose to be absent. I can't compare my situation to yours or pretend that I understand what you are going through, but there is one thing that I do know, and that is that when it comes to family, there are some things you cannot come back from. Your mother made a selfish choice, and she is here asking for forgiveness. Your father didn't have any choice at all when it comes to you, yet he is here today, too, asking for forgiveness all the same. And you? You have a choice to make as well. Do you want to build a new reality for yourself? One that can include a loving mother and father? Or do you want to blow the whole thing up, permanently, by airing out every choice your parents made when they were basically your age, for public consumption in the media? Because I'm telling you now, Free, it might feel good, at first, to hurt them the way you feel they hurt you, but once you put a piece of information out into the world, you cannot snatch it back from the wolves. You cannot control its trajectory, and you cannot stop the mob from manipulating it, reading into it, weaponizing it, or using it against you. I made that mistake when I used your name to build my story. I already caused that kind of damage. I don't want to do it again." Free was still silent, so Carlos forged ahead. "I can't stop you from going forward with the story. It's your story. I just wanted you to talk to the two people who you would be affecting with the story before you sign the deal."

"I am not a child, Carlos." Free croaked. I don't need someone shepherding my decisions."

Even though the words were combative, the fight had gone out of her voice, and Carlos knew that she would probably entertain the conversation with her parents, if he could just get her to the table. She was too exhausted to fight anymore.

"I know you don't need me to tell you what to do, and I respect that. But I care about you. I really do. And I owe it to you, to make sure you hear all of the truth there is, before you ring a bell that you can't unring."

He stood for a few moments, taking in the flush from crying that had painted her cheeks and her long, sweeping lashes with tiny bits of moisture still collecting at their tips from her tear-filled rant. Her hands lay in her lap, palms up, seemingly a subconscious sign of surrender. He moved closer to her, and she moved her legs apart so that he could step in as close as possible. He rested his chin on her head and felt her slip her arms around his back, sliding her thumbs into his belt loops. Shoes long ago discarded, she wrapped her legs around his, hooking her heels inside his calves. He couldn't believe it. She didn't hate him. He whispered a silent prayer of thanks to whatever divine providence had shown mercy on him.

Carlos hadn't realized that he was holding tremendous tension in his body, but when he felt her pull him into the warmth of her embrace, he felt every muscle relax and exhaled a sigh of relief. Even though he'd known the risks, he had not wanted to consider what would happen if she refused the meeting with her parents and walked out of his life. After spending only a few days with her, he was unable to fathom a world in which he could not see her first thing in the morning or listen to her hypnotic voice laying out her dreams and plans for the future as his jazz records spun softly in the background. He felt his body respond, unprovoked, to her closeness and his ardor for her and pulled back slightly. He could not afford to send the wrong signal now, and he obviously couldn't trust his body. He was barely back in her good graces. She raised one brow quizzically at his unexpected pulling away but said nothing.

"Free, I am sorry for surprising you like this. I really am," he whispered into her hair, his voice hitching slightly. "But I couldn't think of any other way to get you to hear them out or even get you all in the same room."

He heard her soft, resigned sigh; part frustration, part surrender.

"Alright then," she said, her voice stronger, more assured. She flicked away the last of her tears, unwound her legs from his, and pushed herself off the counter. "You know, I never used to cry this much," she said, turning to pat at her wet eyes in the mirror. "But ever since I've started, I can't seem to stop." He watched her, waiting for a cue that she was ready to go face her parents. She shrugged again. "May as well get this over with."

***

Truth be told, Carlos could have spent a while longer in the quiet bubble of the bathroom with her, the world held at bay. But he had already come too far to back out now. It was time to pay the piper.

As they emerged from the room, Carlos noticed Angel and Andrew take a sudden over-interest in the food on their plates and realized that they had probably been listening to him being loudly dressed down by their daughter just moments ago. He shook his head, realizing that there was no saving face now, if he even had any face left to save, so it wasn't worth being embarrassed about.

Carlos took the seat across from Angel, leaving Free to take the only other available seat, which was across from Andrew. He looked to Angel to see if she wanted to begin, but Angel was looking at Andrew and gnawing her bottom lip nervously, a tell that signified a chink in her otherwise impenetrable armor that Carlos hadn't expected to see. Andrew pushed his chair back a bit and turned his attention to Free, who was already leaning back in her chair, arms crossed protectively across her chest, attitude etched across her face and shoulders. As far as body language went, they weren't off to a great start.

"Hello, Free. I know that we have never truly met, if you don't count that circus of a legal conference, which I don't, so I would like to introduce myself to you."

Free met Andrew's gaze and raised her eyebrows, but said nothing.

"My name is Andrew Tucker. I have known your family all of my life and grew up with your mother. I loved...love your mother, very much, but I haven't always shown that love. In fact, I hurt her pretty badly. So much so that when she found out that she was pregnant with you, she decided it was better not to tell me. I can't say whether that was the right decision or not because I do not have a time machine, but I understand why she thought it was. My family is... well, some of my family can be very... uh hateful." He faltered on the word, unsure of whether it really captured the extent of his family's historical and enduring bigotry. "Your mother experienced that first hand, and she didn't want you to have to experience it too. She wanted to protect you from the pain she had lived."

The look on Free's face was something a little scary between a smile and a snarl, and Carlos started to reach for her to calm her down, but Angel placed a hand on his arm, fixing him in place. It was not his place to interrupt, and Angel's firm hand made that clear.

"She wanted to protect me," Free repeated, echoing Andrew's last words.

An odd little strangled laugh escaped her, and Andrew glanced over at Angel to make sure that he hadn't said the wrong thing. Angel dropped her eyes to the table, giving him nothing.

"What a strange way to protect me; by leaving me to fend for myself in the same pit, with the same lions that had almost devoured her." At this, she jerked a thumb towards Angel. "How very strange indeed." Free's voice was different than Carlos had ever heard it, and he wondered if Andrew was as stressed as he was about the tone the conversation was taking.

Andrew tried again.

"I'm not saying your life was easy or even easier than your mother's. Jolivette can be tough when you are not…" Andrew paused in search of the right turn of phrase

"What rich and white?" Free supplied.

"Well, yes actually," Drew knew that was right. "But what your mom was trying to save you from was more than that. It was us, specifically. The Tuckers. My family. And keeping you from me was her way of doing that."

At this, Free sprang to her feet and slapped her hand down so close to Andrew's plate that his fork went flying off the edge of the table, leaving flecks of potato on everything in its wake.

"She did NOT protect me from your family! No one is safe in a town full of Tuckers!"

Angel made an odd sound—something between a gasp and a whimper—as she recognized her father's words coming from Free's mouth.

"Who the hell was protecting me from Eric?!" Free yelled, her face only a few inches from Andrew's now.

Andrew looked confused.

"Eric? What does Eric have to do with…." his voice trailed off, and he felt a cold chill traveling up his back, forcing all of the hairs on his neck and arms to stand on end. "Did Eric, uh…did he hurt you?"

At this, Free suddenly snatched at the bodice of her dress, ripping it down and away so that a small portion of her breast not covered by her nude bra was exposed. Angel gasped, and Andrew tried to look away quickly, but Free moved back into his sightline, demanding he look at her.

"I want you to see what your son did, Mr. Mayor!" She was practically screaming now.

When Andrew turned back to look, he saw the raised and discolored oblong scar that she had uncovered. At first, he thought it was an oval of sorts, but soon realized, in horror, that it was the perfectly preserved reverse impression of a human bite mark. The bite looked as though it had not only broken the skin but taken some flesh with it. He felt his heartbeat begin to race.

" I...I didn't know," he stammered pathetically.

"You didn't know what, Mr. Mayor?" Free asked, her voice no longer a scream but twice as unsettling in its sudden calmness.

"You didn't know that the animal you were raising was a monster? Didn't know that he terrorized anyone he chose to, whenever he chose to? That he broke a kid's arm right in the hallway at school? You didn't know that he was suspected of raping classmates, both boys and girls? Huh? What is it that you didn't know, Mr. Mayor? Because with as much chaos and violence as he kept up, SOMEBODY had to be keeping him away from juvenile detention, court houses, cops, and any of the other natural consequences of his behavior that should have found him. Who do you want us to believe that somebody was, hunh, Mr. Mayor? I wonder who in Jolivette has enough power and political capital to keep their horror show of a son out of lock up?" Free sing-songed with a chilling undercurrent of rage while tapping at her chin in mock contemplation.

Carlos could not believe his eyes. His blood was boiling from seeing the scar, and he wanted to cross the table and land a left hook on the Mayor. He wanted to dig up Eric's cold, decomposed body and kill it again. He wanted to avenge Free, but he knew this was not his fight, and he could not insert himself at the moment. He forced himself to remain in his seat, but he could feel his back and palms sweating from the effort. To his right, Angel sat perfectly still, tears streaming down her stoic face. She was also clearly engaged in a herculean effort to remain on the sidelines of this conversation.

Andrew dragged his hands down the length of his face and then balled his hands into fists on his knees.

"I knew…some of that. I thought—we thought— that we could get him help. We sent him to therapy. We tried to make sure that the families of anyone he hurt were taken care of."

At this revelation, Angel started to lose her composure. Carlos saw that her mouth had opened in surprise, and she was visibly shaking. Andrew, with all of his attention still trained on Free, did not notice Angel unraveling.

"I knew about the broken arm, yes. And a girl at a party said... well, we thought he had gotten carried away. He was young and impulsive. I suggested that we send him away somewhere where he could get more one-on-one help, but in the end, his mother said she would take care of it, and I just sort of...checked out. It was all getting to be too much. I let her handle the school and the complaints. I just didn't know what to do anymore. But I swear to you, I didn't know about all the rest of what you just said. And I didn't know that he'd...h-hurt you."

"What difference would it have made, Mr. Mayor? You didn't know me then, and you barely know me now. You would have written my family a check like all the others, right?"

Andrew pressed his fist into his eyes. He knew Free was probably right. That's how they fixed everything in his family. Throw some money at it.

"What did he...I mean, how badly did he..." Andrew's voice trailed off again. He just couldn't even put words to the ineffable horror he was imagining.

"Oh, don't you worry your pretty little head, Mr. Mayor," Free snapped. "Your little monster never got the chance to deflower me, but it wasn't for lack of trying. He has ripped hair from my scalp, spit in my mouth, choked me until I almost blacked out, and had to wear a turtle neck for a week in the middle of summer, but he never got what he wanted. So you don't have to add incestuous, sister raping, lunatic to his list of crimes. Lucky you!"

The silence that stretched out behind Free's words was oppressively heavy. The room and its inhabitants were all suffocating in various depths of grief. Finally, Andrew cleared his throat.

"You aren't brother and sister," Andrew said flatly at a loss for anything more impactful to say. His face was uncharacteristically pale, his cheeks wet, and his hands fisted tightly, but the sentence came out again, clearly. "You aren't Eric's sister."

It was the only sentence he hadn't stumbled through all night.

"What?" Free and Carlos asked in unison.

Free whipped her head around, having forgotten that Carlos was even in the room until she heard his voice.

He threw his hands up immediately in apology for interrupting, and she turned her attention back to Andrew.

"Are you my father or not? Because I know that's what you said at the conference. Are you reneging on that now too?"

"No, I am. I am your father, Free. I mean, God, you look so much like me that it's scary. I can't believe no one ever... Well, anyway... I am your father. But I wasn't Eric's biological father. My brother John was actually his father. It's a long, rich-people, bullshit story, some of which you heard a little of at the conference. But the long and short of it is that we all let my father push us around like chess pieces on a board when we were younger, and now everyone in our lives is paying for it."

Free was stunned. The earth kept moving beneath her feet, and she wasn't sure what, if anything, was true anymore. Her tormenter, whom she had just days ago been told was her brother, was now not her brother at all.

Carlos's eyes could not have been buckled out any further. He was having serious second thoughts about whether he should be talking Free out of selling this story after all. It was a made-for-TV movie if he had ever heard one. He was deep in thought, trying to recall which of his friends knew a guy at Tyler Perry studios who could push a script through, when he realized that everyone was looking at him.

"Oh, I'm sorry! Did you ask me something?" he blurted.

"Yes," Andrew said impatiently. "I asked you how much the station already knows about all of this."

"Oh, um," Carlos cleared his throat. They know the general outline of the relationship with you and Angel now. I called in the storyline that could expose the girl that Eric had stopped to help was not so random, but was in fact his own disowned half-sister. They were reluctant to bite. The whole thing seemed really far-fetched to the producers, so I offered to deliver proof this week that Free was related to the dead– I mean, the deceased kid."

"The proof being a recording of me admitting that Free is my daughter at the closed conference?" Andrew asked.

"Yeah," Carlos admitted, feeling a little sleazy for having agreed to leak the story in the first place. But he met Andrew's eye when he said it. Because of the two of them, he certainly wasn't the biggest bad guy anymore. Not tonight. And he felt a sudden sense of kinship at the debt they both owed to Free for their decisions.

"Is this what you want to do, Free?" Andrew turned back to face his daughter, who still looked as though she were trying to mentally piece together the entire 18 years of her life. When she didn't answer, Angel asked the question again.

"Free, baby, is that what you want? I don't know how drawing more attention to a situation that is already this stressful for you is going to help matters."

"I wouldn't expect you to understand, Monica," Free said, making a point to use Angel's original government name. "You haven't lived your entire life as a dirty secret. You haven't had to carry around the weight of knowing that the woman who gave birth to you ran away from you as fast as her feet could carry her and never tried to set eyes on you again. You haven't laid awake all night, trying to imagine what your father might look like and whether he would like you if he met you. You have never felt the pain of waking up in a cold sweat because you dreamed that your parents had started a new family that they loved and adored, but had decided that you didn't fit into it because you were a mistake. You say that you left me here for a better life, but you may as well have ripped my heart out and fed it to dogs for all the good you did. I mean, look at me! I didn't even know *what* I was! Brown skin and green eyes. Blonde streaked kinky curly hair that isn't quite Black enough, certainly not white enough. I couldn't fit into any box or any group, so I was left out of them all. That's the 'better' life you gave me, Monica. A lifetime of my grandmother trying to teach me to walk a tightrope of perfect behavior so I wouldn't turn out like you, the daughter that broke her heart and shamed the family. That's the shadow that casts over every waking moment of my life. So excuse me if I want, for even just one moment, for people to know who I actually am and how I actually came to be here; for people to see and judge the two of you for once instead of me.

The station said it was going to offer me enough money to finally start a real life somewhere else, where I'm not just some discarded, half-breed anymore. Don't I deserve that? You two were supposed to love me. That was your only job. But instead, you took all of your pain and humiliation and handed it to me as my tragic inheritance! Well, guess what? I'm ready to give it back now. I don't want to carry your shit anymore!" Her voice broke over her last words, and both Angel and Carlos flinched.

The sharp expletive punctuating the harsh truth coming from Free, who never cursed, felt like a slap.

Andrew stood to his feet, and instinctively, Carlos did too. Carlos wasn't sure whether the man was going to storm out or throw a punch, but he wanted to be prepared for whichever. Fortunately, Andrew did neither. Instead, he reached his arms beneath Free's slumped shoulders, pulled her gently to her feet, and crushed her in a hug. Carlos exhaled and collapsed back into his seat. Angel's sniffles and Andrew's trembling baritone voice were the only sounds in the room as he spoke close to Free's ear.

"Freedom Walker, you are an incredible young woman, and I am not ashamed of you. I cannot wait to tell the world that you are my daughter, the best thing that I have ever done. Maybe the only good thing that will ever come from me. A blessing I was given, despite who I am, not because of who I am. Anything that you will ever need or want, I will move heaven and earth to make sure that you have it. I can't fix all the ways that I went wrong with Eric. But I can be a better father for you."

As he spoke, Andrew could feel Free's body quaking with the tears she was fighting against, willing not to fall. Drew knew that she was struggling to hold onto her armor; that she didn't want to love him back, but he loved her. He realized that, maybe, he had always loved her, even before he knew she existed. He knew that there was a better version of him somewhere that he couldn't quite get a grasp on. He had thought it was the Andrew he would have been if he had remained in California and built a life with Angel, but now he knew that the better version of him was Freedom, a young woman who had gotten the best bits of him and Angel. She was beautiful and smart; cultured and determined; indomitable and unwilling to let anyone else tell her who to be. She was better than the sum of all of his choices, and his heart swelled with the realization that he was looking at a chance to be a father again. A real one. An involved, invested father who would not leave his child's fate up to anyone else's judgment, not even her mother's. She hadn't pulled away, so he held her tighter.

"I can't fix what we have done to you, what my family and...Eric... did to you. But I promise you that I will spend the rest of my life protecting you. You will never be a secret again."

Free sobbed openly into her father's chest as he continued to assure her that there was nothing on earth that he wanted more than to be her dad.

Angel, unable to fight the swell in her heart, rose from her seat and cautiously approached their embrace, uncertain as to whether her presence would break the spell that Andrew had cast over the room. But she needn't have worried. When Andrew felt her approach, he extended his arm and pulled her into the hug. Free did not extract herself, so the three of them stood locked together, illuminated by the soft glow of the apartment's wall sconces and the moonlight now streaming in through the wall of windows. Carlos watched the scene in complete awe and made a note to himself to call his parents and tell them that he loved them.

Epilogue

Free loaded the last of her boxes and watched the automatic trunk slowly close and lock with a soft whir on her new BMW X5, admiring its custom army green matte finish. She ran through a mental checklist of items she could not afford to leave behind to be confident that everything had been packed, loaded, and secured. Feeling assured, she turned and trudged back up the steps of the porch and plopped down next to Mama Jean on the slowly shifting porch swing. Mama Jean frowned and swatted at her as she always did when Free set the swing's trajectory askew. Free laughed, and Mama Jean tsked her teeth in mock disapproval.

"Sorry, Mama Jean," she cooed, wrapping her arms around her grandmother and resting her head on the older woman's thin shoulder.

They rocked there for a moment, feeling the soft breeze whisper across the porch, providing a brief respite from the sweltering heat. Then Free turned to Mama Jean and asked the question that had been weighing her down all day.

"Are you sure that you'll be okay here by yourself?" Free asked, the concern lacing her voice and creasing her forehead.

Mama Jean waved her off dismissively with one hand and took a sip of lemonade from the frosted glass in the other.

"Chile, go on and get your education. Why are you worrying yourself about me? This is the next level you've been waiting for, isn't it?"

Free interrupted her.

"Yeah, but what if something happens? Who will…"

Mama Jean clucked her disapproval of Free's line of thought.

"Chile, I still have plenty enough to keep me busy, and I'm already overrun with a slew of folk from the church traipsing through here with half-seasoned chicken and nasty casseroles like I'm some charity case. I don't need you acting like that too. And anyway, even when I'm by myself, I am never alone. Long as I got King Jesus, I don't need nobody else!"

Mama Jean slapped her knee to add emphasis to that last statement, and Free chuckled, hearing her grandmother's favorite country gospel quote. Still, a pang of guilt pulled at her.

"Anyway," Mama Jean added. "I doubt I'll get even one day to myself the way your mama comes by here, checking on me every five minutes like I'm an invalid. That girl is liable to work my last nerve! That's who you need to be talking to. She's been shuffling around here all week, acting like she's okay but looking just as pitiful as a weeping willow."

As if on cue, Angel emerged from the house, letting the screen door slam behind her.

"Y'all out here talking about me?" she asked jovially.

"Chile, people got stuff to talk about more important than you!" Mama Jean snarked back. "But yes, yes, we are. I was just saying that you are over here more than you are at your own house, fussing over me like I'm the child and you're the mama! The whole time you lived here, I couldn't get you out from under that Tucker boy. Now you live with him, and I can't get you away from here! He must not be laying it down like he was doing back in the day!"

Free burst out laughing as Angel gasped and clutched at her imaginary pearls.

"Mama Jean! You have no chill!" Free shrieked, still laughing.

Mama Jean chuckled to herself, happy to see that she had made her daughter blush a little.

"Alright, go on now before you get stuck in traffic." Mama Jean pushed at Free's shoulder.

"Yes, ma'am," Free said as she pulled herself up from the porch swing.

She turned and leaned in to give Mama Jean a last hug, memorizing her narrow frame, the smell of gardenias in her perfume, and the softness of the wrinkled skin along her cheek.

"Thank you for everything. I love you, lady," she whispered into her soft roller-set hair.

"I love you too, baby," Mama Jean whispered back, taking Free's face into her thin, strong hands, just beginning to gnarl with age. "Oh, that reminds me, help your old gramma up," Mama Jean said, reaching for Free's hand.

Free clutched her grandmother's arms and helped leverage her up from the porch swing.

"I'll be back in two shakes of a lamb's tail," Mama Jean said, disappearing into the house.

As the door swung shut behind her, Carlos appeared around the curve of the porch, slapping dirt from his hands.

"Welp, all the cameras are installed now, and I've left the paper with the new alarm code on the kitchen table."

"Oh, thank God," Angel chirped. "I can barely sleep thinking of her over here by herself. At least now I can check on her and know that she is relatively safe."

Free rolled her eyes.

"Mama Jean has been taking care of herself and everyone else for a long time. I know she is getting older, but I'm pretty sure that the lady is invincible."

"Well, you never know with all these crazies out here," Carlos interjected, and Angel nodded her agreement.

"Okay. Well, you take good care of her then." Free said, touching Angel's shoulder. "I'll be back to visit as soon as I get settled.

Angel pulled Free into a hug that was too tight for comfort, but Free let her have it. Free knew Angel was sad, and honestly, she was a little sad herself. The woman was a force. She filled every atom with her presence when she entered a room and captivated so much admiration and respect. Free found herself admiring her mother despite her best efforts to still keep her at arm's length.

Cerebrally, she knew that her and her mother's struggles had been opposite sides of the same coin and identified with the type of armor her mother had erected for herself, having built a similar fortress around her own heart to survive her life in Jolivette. But the abandonment still bubbled up and stung her every now and then. She didn't know that she would fully recognize herself without her security blanket of anger for her mother. But she was working on it and was focused on better things now, and learning that there was strength in vulnerability since Carlos insisted on teaching it to her.

Angel finally released Free from her arms as Mama Jean stepped back onto the porch carrying a 12-gauge shotgun, its oak stock and grip shined to a gleaming high gloss. She turned the gun over in her hands, deftly sliding her weathered fingers along the barrel before handing the beautiful weapon to Free, who took it gingerly as Mama Jean removed its case from her shoulder.

"This little lady has been protecting the Walker women for generations. Pop always wanted you to have it, so now she is yours. You take care of her, you hear?" Mama Jean said, lightly touching the sight at the end of the shotgun barrel and fussing over some imaginary smudge that she polished out with the sleeve of her blouse.

"As a single woman out in the world, you never know when you might need it," she winked at Free. "Always keep the stock tucked tight against you, and if you aim it, shoot it."

This time she didn't wink, and the gravity and importance of her words hung in the air.

Free slipped the shotgun into its case and slung it over her shoulder as Angel slipped her arm around Mama Jean.

"Alright, Mama. I'm sure she will be fine. Pop made sure we all knew how to handle any piece of steel we got our hands on."

Mama Jean nodded her affirmation, and Free turned to head for the car, yelling over her shoulder to Carlos, "Alright! Are you ready to go? We have to beat this traffic."

When she turned back to see his progress, Carlos was still rooted to the porch, his jaw slack, one hand gripping the porch railing and the other, frozen mid-air, pointed towards the case slung over Free's shoulder.

"Is that…is that the gun from Eric's…" his voice cut out, and he started again. "Was Mama Jean, the uh…the…?"

He was struggling to get a sentence to come together. Mama Jean gave Carlos the once-over, in the way that only she could, so that it felt like she was deeply unimpressed with his loose grip on the realities of life.

"Listen young man," Mama Jean fixed Carlos with an unflinching stare. "If my granddaughter ever tells me she is in trouble, for any reason, I'd walk through hell, high water, or the woods along a rainy highway at night to get her out. Do you understand me?"

Carlos nodded slowly, his mouth still agape. "Good. And you'd do well to keep that in mind, young man." Mama Jean looked Carlos up and down as he registered the note of warning in her voice. Then turned and walked back into her house, shaking her head all the way.

Once Mama Jean had safely disappeared, Free looked at Angel, and they both burst out laughing.

"Go on, now, Carlos," Angel said as her laughter finally subsided. She pushed Carlos's shoulder softly. "You wanted a Walker woman, and you've got her. Ain't no need in being scared now! It's too late for all of that. Trust me, this little filly is going to be worth the trouble. She's a show pony if I've ever seen one."

Carlos frowned at Angel's confusing mixed metaphor, and when he looked back towards Free, she was leaning against the car, one hand on her hip and the other dangling the keys toward him.

"Are you in or are you out, Jackson?" she said, a smile playing across her lips.

Carlos let out an incredulous laugh. He had no idea what he was in for, but he knew he was in. He walked over and leaned down to kiss her as he snatched the dangling keys from her hand irreverently. She surprised him by nipping his lip between her teeth, then laughed up at him, when he jumped.

"Mama Jean?!" he mouthed silently, incredulous. His befuddled face made Free laugh even harder.

"Walker women are a lot of things, Los, but helpless isn't one of them."

He let her words sink in and then nodded his understanding, but by then, she was already walking around to the passenger side of the car.

"I guess I'm driving," he said. But he could feel the adrenaline rush he usually got at the start of a new assignment, and he knew that with Free in the car, he was about to take the ride of his life.